THE LAND

MILDRED D. TAYLOR

THE LAND

PREQUEL TO
NEWBERY MEDAL WINNER
Roll of Thunder, Hear My Cry

SCHOLASTIC INC.
New York Toronto London Auckland Sydney
Mexico City New Delhi Hong Kong Buenos Aires

ISBN 0-439-44241-9

12 11 10 9 8 7 6 5 4 3 2 1   2 3 4 5 6 7/0

Printed in the U.S.A.   23

First Scholastic printing, September 2002

Designed by Nancy R. Leo-Kelly

Text set in Janson

To my family, past, present, and future,
and
to the memory of my beloved father,
the storyteller,
for without his words, my words would not have been

Acknowledgements

Five years ago when I was in the early stages of writing *The Land*, my two uncles came to visit. As I cooked breakfast one morning, they and other family members gathered in the kitchen and soon, as always happens when my family gets together, the stories began. There were hilarious stories about my father, my uncles, and my aunts growing up on the family land in Mississippi. There were stories about my grandparents and great-uncles, and there were stories about my great-grandparents. Most of the stories I had heard many times before, but they were so freshly and wonderfully told that I pulled out my tape recorder and began to record them. As my uncles spoke, I knew I had all the rich material I would need to finish *The Land*.

Once again my uncles had come to my aid.

When I first started writing, I had always gone to my father concerning family history. Since his death in 1976 I have relied on my uncles, Mr. James E. Taylor and Mr. Eugene Taylor, for that history and they, like my father, have never failed to supply the information I have needed. I am deeply indebted to them and I thank them for helping to make so many of my books possible.

I am indebted to many others as well, including Mr. Jan Raynak, Ms. Linda Brown, and Mr. Keith Brown, for answering my many questions during my research for *The Land*, and I thank them for their time and interest. I am also indebted to all the family and friends who encouraged me throughout the many years of my writing *The Land* and who provided me on so many occasions with countless hours of child care so that I could write uninterrupted.

My last words of thanks are to Ms. Phyllis J. Fogelman, my editor and publisher for more than twenty-five years. As always, Phyllis's belief in my writing and in the stories I have to tell urged me forward. Even when the writing became so difficult, I was ready to stop working on the book, Phyllis's quiet insistence that *The Land* was a story I *had* to write, for no one else could, kept me writing. Finally, after three years I considered the story finished. Phyllis did not agree. It's a great beginning, she said, but it could be better. Now, four years later, I believe it is. Thank you, Phyllis.

Contents

PART I: CHILDHOOD

Mitchell   *3*

The Stallion   *18*

Family   *35*

Betrayal   *70*

East Texas   *94*

PART II: MANHOOD

The Land   *129*

Caroline   *163*

The Bargain   *220*

The Promise   *273*

Family   *308*

PART III: LEGACY

Epilogue   *365*

Author's Note   *371*

LOGAN FAMILY TREE

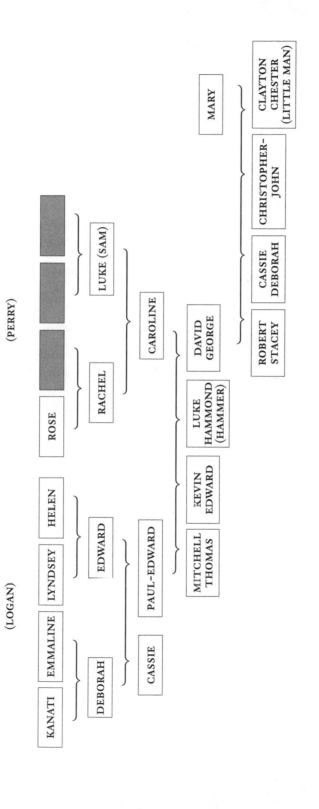

A Note to the Reader

All of my books are based on stories told by my family, and on the history of the United States. In my writing I have attempted to be true to those stories and the history. I have included characters, incidents, and language that present life as it was in many parts of the United States before the Civil Rights Movement. Although there are those who wish to ban my books because I have used language that is painful, I have chosen to use the language that was spoken during the period, for I refuse to whitewash history. The language was painful and life was painful for many African Americans, including my family.

I remember the pain.

Since writing my first book, *Song of the Trees*, it has been my wish to have readers walk in the shoes of the Logan family, who are based on my family, and to feel what they felt. It has been my wish that by understanding this family and what they endured, there would be a further understanding of what millions of families endured, and there would also be a further understanding of why there was a Civil Rights Movement, a movement that changed our nation.

Mildred D. Taylor

CHILDHOOD

Mitchell

I loved my daddy. I loved my brothers too. But in the end it was Mitchell Thomas and I who were most like brothers, with a bond that couldn't be broken. The two of us came into Mississippi together by way of East Texas, and that was when we were still boys, long after we had come to our understanding of each other. Seeing that we were a long way from our Georgia home and both of us being strangers here in Mississippi, the two of us depended on each other and became as family.

But it wasn't always that way.

In the beginning the two of us didn't get along at all. Fact to business, there was a time it seemed like to me Mitchell Thomas lived just to taunt me. There were other boys too who picked on me, but Mitchell was the worst. I recall one time in particular when I was about nine or so and I was reading beside a creek on my daddy's land, and Mitchell came up from behind me and just whopped me on the head. For no reason. Just whopped me on the head! Course I jumped up mad. "What ya do that for?" I cried.

"Felt like it," he said. That's all; he felt like it. "Ya wanna do somethin' 'bout it?"

But I said nothing. Sure, I wanted to do something about it, all right, but I was no fool. Besides the fact I was a small-built boy, Mitchell was a year and some months older than me, a big boy too, stronger than most boys his age, and he could've broken me in two if he'd had the mind. Mitchell stared at me and I stared at him, then he turned and walked away. He didn't laugh, he didn't gloat; he just walked away, but I knew he'd be back.

And he was. Time and time again.

At first I just tried to stay out of Mitchell's way, but that didn't solve the problem. So I went to my sister, Cassie, about Mitchell. Now, my sister was a beautiful girl and I knew even Mitchell had eyes for her. But Cassie was not only beautiful, she was tough, smart, and just a bit cocky. She was six years older than I was and pretty much like a mother hen when it came to me; I knew she'd take my part. "Cassie, you know 'bout Mitchell?" I asked her.

"Course I know about Mitchell," she answered. "Why're you letting him beat up on you?"

"I'm not letting him!" I exclaimed in outrage. "You thinking I'm liking him beating up on me?"

"Well, if you're not, you'd better make him stop."

"Well, I'm trying."

"Well, you'd better try harder."

"I've tried fighting back, but he's too strong. Thing is, I don't know how to stop him."

"You'd better figure a way," she said matter-of-factly, then looked me in the eyes. "You want me to talk to him?"

I didn't even need to think on that. "Naw, course not! You did, then they'd all be saying I had my sister fighting my battles!"

Cassie shrugged. "Then you'd better figure something out quick."

Well, I didn't figure anything out quick enough before Mitchell whalloped me again. And again. Finally things got so bad, I told my daddy about Mitchell and about how he and other boys too were always picking on me. Now, the thing was, Mitchell and his family and the other boys lived on my daddy's land, and I figured my daddy with one word could put a stop to Mitchell and the rest. But my daddy said, "What you expect me to do about it?"

"I don't know," I replied, even though I knew exactly what I wanted him to do about it.

"You expect me to stop this boy Mitchell and the others from messing with you?"

I didn't say anything.

"You want it stopped, Paul," he said, "then you stop it. This here is between you and Mitchell and whatever other boys. I'm not getting into it."

My daddy was true to his word too. More than one time he saw me with a busted lip or a bruised eye, but he showed me no sympathy. He just looked at me and said, "See you didn't stop it yet." After a while, though, he said, "Paul, you don't stop this soon, those boys are going to kill you."

"Well, they're bigger and stronger'n me!" I protested.

"Then you use what you strongest at, boy! You use your head. Now take care of it."

I took care of it, all right. I enlisted the aid of my brothers, Hammond, George, and Robert. I figured Hammond and George could sure enough stop Mitchell. Course, they already knew of my troubles. They'd seen my busted lip and bruises too, but they had been away at school during most of the time Mitchell had been beating on me, and I hadn't been able to turn to them for my rescue. Robert, of course, had wanted to help me out, but there hadn't been much he could do. He was as small as I was. Now Hammond and George were back home and I figured to settle this thing.

"So what do you want us to do?" Hammond asked.

I was looking for complete and absolute revenge, and I figured Hammond at eighteen and George at sixteen could provide that for me. "Put the fear of God into 'em!" I declared.

Hammond smiled; so did George. Robert, though, nodded solemnly. "We can do that." Robert was nine, same age as me. Of my brothers, I was closest with Robert. I suppose, in part, being the same year's children made us close, but there were other things too. We had been together practically since birth, and we always took care of each other. When I got into trouble, Robert was there to pull me out of it if he could, or at least to see me through it, and I did the same for him. More than one time when one of us would be getting a licking from either my mama or our daddy, the other would jump in to try to stop it and we'd both get whipped. We shared everything together. Back then, Robert was always on my side. "They got no business beating on you," Robert said, expressing my sentiments exactly.

"That's what I figure too," I said.

"We'll take care of 'em tomorrow," Robert promised.

"Now wait a minute," said Hammond. "I don't know if that's such a good idea."

"What's not good about it?" I asked. "Mitchell and those other boys been beating on me for the longest time, so y'all go beat on them awhile and they'll stop."

Hammond was quiet a moment, then said, "Well, I don't know if that's quite fair."

"Sounds fair to me."

"Me too," said Robert.

"But George and I are older than Mitchell and those other boys, and we'd have the advantage," said Hammond.

"Well, that's the point of the thing!" I said.

Hammond shook his head. "'Sides that, they live here on our place, and if we get into it with them, it'll look like we're bullying them—"

"Well, they've been bullying me!"

George looked at me dead center. "You tell our daddy about this?" One thing I liked about my brother George was that he laid things right on the line; he said exactly what was on his mind. On the surface he was an easygoing sort of boy with a body that seemed to hang in a lazy fashion, such as always having one leg dangling over the arm of a chair when our daddy wasn't around. But the truth was, he had himself a fierce kind of temper when baited and a steely right hand to match. He had never used either against me. I always told him the truth. "I told him, all right," I replied in answer to his question.

"Well, what'd he say?"

I didn't speak right up.

"Well? I know he said something."

"He told me he wasn't getting into it. He told me to stop it, so that's what I'm trying to do."

George laughed. "Yeah, you trying to stop it, all right. You trying to get us to stop it for you."

"Same thing," said Robert. Those were my thoughts exactly.

"Look, Paul," said Hammond. "I'll have a talk with Mitchell, but I'm not going to go beating up on him for you. Understood?"

I looked at Hammond and nodded solemnly, but I was figuring the only thing Mitchell Thomas would ever understand was a good whipping.

That very next morning Robert and I, sitting behind Hammond and George on their bays, went over to the patch of ground Mitchell's family tended. Now, the Thomases, like all the other families who lived on my daddy's land, were sharecroppers, and because of that fact, they were obliged to take heed of whatever my daddy or my brothers said. Miz Thomas was sure enough taking heed right now.

"Edna," said Hammond as Mitchell's mother stood in her

dark doorway, "where's Willie?" Willie Thomas was Mitchell's daddy. "He gone off already?'

"Yes, suh," answered Miz Thomas. "He in the fields."

"Well, doesn't matter. We come to see Mitchell. He with his daddy?"

"Mitchell?" questioned Miz Thomas. "Well, suh, he's out in them woods yonder choppin' wood for the fire."

Hammond nodded. "Whereabout?"

"North yonder . . . by the creek."

"All right," said Hammond. "We'll find him."

We turned to go, but then Miz Thomas said, "That Mitchell, he done somethin'? He in trouble?"

"We just want to talk to him, Edna," Hammond assured her. Still, though, as we rode away, I saw Miz Thomas frown, and young as I was, I knew she was worried. She was worried because my brothers had come. My brothers had come asking about Mitchell, and my brothers were white.

The Georgia sun was blazing by the time my brothers and I located Mitchell chopping wood on the north bank of the creek. Two of his younger brothers were with him, stacking the logs he split. As we dismounted, Mitchell struck his axe into a fallen log, then yanked it out again and held it across his chest. To tell the truth, I'd have preferred it if we had found him tending some other chore. I for one knew that Mitchell had a hot temper, and there was no telling what he might take a notion to do with that axe. Hammond, though, seemed to take no notice of the axe as he and George walked over to Mitchell. Robert and I stayed by the horses.

"See you got quite a woodpile there, Mitchell," said Hammond cordially.

Mitchell glanced over at me, then back at Hammond before he nodded. "Yeah," he said. His brothers were silent and still.

"Well, now, Mitchell," Hammond went on, "we rode over because we wanted to have a little talk with you."

"That's right," said George. "We understand that you been beating up on Paul there." I appreciated the fact that George was getting right to the heart of this matter. "Quite often, as a matter of fact."

Mitchell's grip tightened on the axe, but he said nothing.

"We'd like to know why," said Hammond.

I kept my eyes on the axe. I felt like I needed to warn Hammond and George. They didn't know how crazy Mitchell could be.

"We'd like to know why you have it in for Paul," Hammond went on. "Did he do something to you?'

Mitchell eyed his axe and didn't speak.

Hammond and George waited; then George grew impatient. "Well? Don't you have anything to say? Did Paul do something to you or not?" Mitchell kept on looking at that axe. "Speak up!"

Mitchell then shook his head. "Naw," he mumbled, but I could see his fingers tightening on the handle.

"Well, if Paul hasn't done anything to you," said Hammond, "then I see no reason for you to be continuously picking on him. You're older than him, bigger than him, and it's certainly not a fair kind of thing."

"We want it stopped," said George, as if that should put an end to the matter right there, and I thought, Good. Now we're getting to the point of this thing.

Hammond continued to be diplomatic. "We want you two to try to be friends, Mitchell. We're all living here on the same land, and we all have to work together, so I don't want to hear of any more fights between the two of you. Understood?"

Mitchell once again had nothing to say. George lost patience and grasped the handle of Mitchell's axe. "Boy, you better answer!" he demanded, but Mitchell in a dangerous move yanked on the axe. George too yanked on the axe in an attempt to twist it from Mitchell's grasp, but then Hammond intervened, stepping between George and Mitchell. George's hand slipped from the axe, but he still tried to get at Mitchell.

Hammond pushed him back. "Stop it, George!" he ordered. Then he turned to Mitchell. "Now, you, boy, you put that axe down." There was a moment when I didn't know if Mitchell would obey. Hammond didn't waver. "I said put it down! Now!" Mitchell looked at George, at Hammond, then slammed the axe into a log. Hammond stepped back calmly. "There's to be no more of that."

George shoved past Hammond and pointed his finger right in Mitchell's face. "You try that on me again and I'll have your head, boy! You hear me? You best be remembering I'm not Paul!"

I was afraid Mitchell was going to slap George's hand away and the two of them would get into it right there, but Mitchell only glared at George and kept his silence. Hammond eyed the both of them and said to Mitchell, "There's to be no more fighting with Paul."

Mitchell looked at the ground.

"Is that understood?"

Mitchell looked up, first at Hammond, then at me, and I felt my knees go weak. "Yeah," he mumbled, his eyes fixed on me, and at that moment I knew that my troubles with Mitchell were far from over.

And I was right.

The next time Mitchell Thomas caught up with me alone, he near to whipped the living daylights out of me. "Now, go tell your brothers 'bout this beatin', you white nigger!" he cried as he pummeled me. "For all I care, you can tell yo' white daddy 'bout it too!"

But after Mitchell got finished beating on me, I told no one. Instead, I made my way over to the creek and sat on its bank, looked out over my daddy's land, and pondered why Mitchell and the other boys hated me so. Now, what Mitchell said was true: I did have a white daddy. My daddy was Edward Logan, and Edward Logan was a much-respected man. He was a prosperous man too, or at least he had been before the war had come in 1861, and still now that the war was over by several years, he was doing better than most. He owned a lot of land, and until a few years back he had owned his share of slaves too.

My mama had been one of those slaves.

My mama was called by the name of Deborah, and she was equally of the African people and of the native people, the Indians, whom we called the Nation. She was a beautiful woman. My daddy took a liking to her soon after she came into her womanhood, and he took her for his colored woman, and that's how my older sister Cassie and I came to be. Cassie and I were our daddy's children, and both of us were born into slavery. Now, there were a lot of white men who fathered colored children in those days, even though the law said no white man could legally father a black child; that was in part so no child of color could inherit from his white daddy. Some white men took care of their colored children; most didn't. My daddy was one who did. Not only did he take care of Cassie and me, but he acknowledged that we were his, though it was quietly spoken, and he raised us as his, pretty much the same as his white children, and that's what made us different, what made me different.

I was a colored boy who looked almost white. Though I had a mixed look to me, upon first seeing me, most folks thought I was white, and for some folks, if they didn't know different, they kept thinking so. My hair was brown and straight and hung somewhat long most times, to my shoulders. Some called that the Indian look in me, and my mama liked that. My skin was what some folks call olive for some reason, and my features being what they were, people made their own judgments about who and what I was.

Because my daddy was who he was, I had some of the privileges of a white boy, privileges denied to Mitchell and other colored folks on the place. Cassie and I sat right alongside Hammond, George, and Robert at our daddy's table. We wore good clothes, and our daddy educated us. He'd taught us himself how to read and write and figure, even though when he taught Cassie, it was against the law at the time, and when he taught me, it was against what so many of his white neighbors held dear. He also made Hammond and George and Robert share their books and all their school learning with us. When he traveled on business around the community, he oftentimes took me with him, along with my brothers. Just by being with Edward Logan and a part of his world, I was receiving an education none of the other boys of color on the place were privy to. My daddy protected me, and I was treated almost as if I were white. Yes, I was different, all right, and that was a fact. I sat there by the creek thinking on that, and finally decided it was no wonder Mitchell Thomas couldn't stand the sight of me. I supposed if I'd been Mitchell, I wouldn't've liked me much either.

I remember Robert came along as I was sitting there dwelling on all this and wanted to know what had happened. "What you think?" I said.

"Mitchell?"

"Mitchell."

Robert heaved a sigh and sat down beside me. "Looks bad."

"Feels worse."

"Why'd he do it this time?"

I looked at Robert. Though I'd figured it out, I wasn't ready to talk about it. "Same as always," I said. "He just doesn't like me."

Robert nodded, and we said no more for a good long while. Robert threw rocks into the creek, letting me be, and if he figured I was holding something back, he didn't say so. Robert and I didn't need to talk; we were that close.

Some time passed; then Robert spoke again. "You want to fish awhile?"

I glanced over at the rock opening where we kept our poles and shook my head. "Don't feel like it."

"Wanna do anything?"

"Not really."

"You hurting?"

"What you think?"

"Want me to get Hammond and George?"

I shook my head.

"What you going to do?"

"Sit right here."

"Okay," said Robert. "I'll sit with you." He continued to throw his rocks. I continued to stare out at the creek, and we said no more.

After my realization about myself and how some folks saw me, I gave more serious thought on how to stop Mitchell from beating on me. Despite now having more understanding of Mitchell's dislike of me, I couldn't fully understand his hate. I didn't figure I'd ever done anything directly to Mitchell. My mama, though, figured different. She rubbed salve on my wounds and said, "You haven't done anything, huh? Well, how you think it make Mitchell feel for you to be sending Hammond and George to his house to speak to him and scaring his mama?"

"They didn't scare her!" I protested. "All they did was ask where Mitchell was!"

"That's all they had to do. They're white."

"They're my brothers," I reminded her.

"Uh-huh . . . white brothers, and you best remember that."

I was hardly about to forget it, what with my mama always re-minding me of the fact, though in those early days it didn't seem important to me. Hammond, George, and Robert were simply my brothers, and my daddy was my daddy, and I got tired of my mama always reminding me different; but still I had to admit that there was something to what she said about me asking Hammond and George to talk to Mitchell, something that wasn't right. Mitchell had been born a slave on my daddy's land, and so had I. We had that much in common. My mama was right. I shouldn't have sent Hammond and George. I needed to settle this thing with Mitchell myself.

Once I came to that conclusion, to handle things myself, even when Hammond and George offered to help again, I said no. They had taken one look at me after Mitchell's last beating, and George said, "Looks like that talk we had with Mitchell didn't do much good."

"You want us to go talk to him again?" Hammond asked.

"Better still," said Robert, "this time we'll beat him up good for ya!"

"No," I replied. "You talk to him again or you whip him, he'll still come after me. I'll handle it my own self."

"Then least we'd better teach you how to fight better," said George.

"No," I said. "I've got it figured now. I'll be all right."

George laughed. "Hope you're right. We don't want to have to bury you."

Well, I didn't want them to have to bury me either. I had a plan, and all I could do was pray that it worked. That same day I went looking for Mitchell. When I found him, he seemed sur-prised to see me. He looked around. "Well, where they at?" he said.

"Who?" I asked.

"Your brothers. Ain't 'spected you to be out walkin' round without 'em."

"Well, I am. I come looking for you."

"What for? To get yo'self another whippin'?"

"To ask you something."

"And what's that?"

"I wanna know exactly how come you don't like me. I mean, I got some of your reasons figured, but far as I can tell, I never done anything to you."

Mitchell shrugged. "Just don't like you."

"Just don't?" I questioned.

He looked at me square and said matter-of-factly, "I got no use for white niggers."

I thought on that for a moment. I hated that word *nigger*, but I wasn't about to lecture Mitchell concerning it right now. Instead, I said, "I wasn't so white-looking, would you like me?"

"No."

"Why not?"

"'Cause you think you way better'n everybody else."

"Now, what makes you think I think that? You inside my head?"

"You know how come," Mitchell retorted.

"Just 'cause my daddy's white and he owns this place?" I asked. "Well, I didn't have a say about who my daddy is, and I didn't have a say about my looking white. It's just who I am." I dismissed all that with a shrug and hoped Mitchell would do the same. "What else makes you think I feel like I'm better?"

"You so smart, you go on figure it out," said Mitchell, having now said more to me than ever before without having started to pound on me.

I thought on what he said before I spoke again. "You know, Mitchell, you way stronger'n me, and 'cause you are, there're a whole lotta things you can do I can't. But there're some things I can do and you can't, like read and write and figure. Maybe you think I feel better'n everybody else 'cause I can do those things and you can't, so I was thinking: What if I taught you to read and write and figure? Then you'd pretty much know what I know and there wouldn't be any reason for you to think I'm thinking I'm so smart."

Mitchell scowled. "What I want t' read and write and figure for?"

"'Cause it's something worth knowing," I reasoned, "and 'cause most white folks don't want us knowing how, 'cause once we do know, we can learn all sorts of things white folks know. You ever think why it is most white folks don't want us to know how to read and write and figure? My daddy says it's 'cause they need us as workers and so they don't want us knowing much as they do. Long as they figure they know something we don't, they can figure they're smarter than us."

Mitchell thought on that. "Ain't you afraid of them night riders comin' to get you, you go tryin' to teach me how to do them things?" he asked dryly.

Now, the night riders were white folks who dressed up in sheets and such and rode around threatening colored folks and white folks too who started up schools for colored folks and taught colored folks anything other than what they figured colored folks needed to know. The night riders were certainly to be feared, but I wasn't worried about them, and I knew Mitchell really wasn't either. Neither of us had ever seen them and after all, this teaching thing would be just between Mitchell and me. I shrugged. "No need for them to find out. I'm not opening any school, just teaching you."

"And what you 'spect me t' do for you?" he asked.

The truth was, all I expected from Mitchell Thomas was for him to stop beating up on me, but I was realizing now with those words that Mitchell was more than just a bully. There was a pride in him too, and there'd have to be an exchange of learning for this truce I was proposing to work. "You could teach me to fight," I said.

"Can't teach you to win," he returned.

"Well, that'd be up to me," I replied.

Mitchell took his time in making up his mind. "All right then," he finally agreed. "You teach me how t' read and write and figure, and I'll teach you how t' fight, but I wants ya t' know one thing."

"What's that?"

"I still don't like ya."

"Well, I don't like you either," I admitted quite truthfully.

He nodded, accepting my honesty, and the deal was struck. So that's how things began between Mitchell and me. After that, Mitchell and I held our truce. We didn't become friends, but at least he wasn't beating up on me anymore. I taught him and he taught me. He wasn't the best student, but then again I wasn't a great fighter either. I learned how to defend myself, and maybe just as important, once the other colored boys saw Mitchell and me together without Mitchell picking on me and bopping me upside the head, they pretty much backed off and left me alone. I don't know if at the time Mitchell was aware of it or not, but though he never declared himself as such, his presence alone made him my protector.

The Stallion

A couple of years after Mitchell and I had come to our understanding, my daddy took himself a real interest in a stallion by the name of Ghost Wind. Now, my daddy loved horses and in particular fast horses, and he'd recently heard about Ghost Wind, who some folks claimed was the fastest thing on four legs. Since my daddy didn't own Ghost Wind, the fastest thing on four legs, he soon took steps to rectify that fact. After corresponding with the owner of that stallion, a man by the name of Waverly who lived in the neighboring county, he announced that he was going to take a look at the horse for himself, and if that stallion was as fast as everybody said, he intended to buy him. He decided to take all of us boys with him.

The Waverly farm was several hours away, so on the day my daddy went to bargain for the stallion, we started early, long before dawn. The night before, my daddy had chosen five of our best horses for us to ride. He said he wanted Jim Waverly to know he already had the best, so a stallion named Ghost Wind, though he wanted him, was not the only horse out there. He had gotten the best before, and even if he couldn't settle on a fair price for the stallion, he'd get the best somewhere else.

The only problem with his decision about taking his best five horses was Robert. Now, the thing was, Robert had always been skittish around horses. He had once been thrown by a horse, and his leg and ribs were broken. That fall had put a great fear into him, and he had never gotten over it, so it was difficult even to get him near a horse, let alone on one unless he was riding double with someone else. Robert much preferred to walk to get to where he was going or, if the distance proved too much, to ride in a buggy. My daddy, though, being the horseman he was, wasn't about to let Robert ride in a buggy to another horseman's farm. He was particularly proud of these five horses, and he wasn't going to have one of them hitched to a buggy. The concession he finally made to Robert was to replace one of the five with a lesser horse, but still of fine quality. This horse was slower and less spirited, and he figured even Robert shouldn't have a problem with him.

"Just keep a tight hold on the reins, let him know who's in charge," said my daddy to Robert, "and you'll do fine."

Robert looked at me mounted beside him, and I could tell he was figuring the horse was in charge, not him. Still, he said, "Yes, sir," to our daddy and made the ride, though he looked uncomfortable all the way. Now, I was just the opposite of Robert. I was eleven by then and could sit a horse well. In fact, I was good with horses and could handle most of them. My daddy said it seemed like to him I'd been born on one. So, while my daddy, Hammond, and George rode on ahead, I stayed behind with Robert, talking most of the way to the Waverly farm, keeping Robert's mind off his fear and his horse in line with my own.

Once we got to the Waverly farm, we went right away to see the stallion my daddy had come to buy, the great Ghost Wind. He was pure white and he was a beauty. My daddy admired him openly. Mr. Waverly invited him to mount, and my daddy did so. He walked the horse around the pasture, then nudged him into a gallop. Ghost Wind seemed to be floating.

"Like to put him into some real paces," said my daddy, "and see just how fast he is."

"Fine," agreed Mr. Waverly. "I'll just get mounted and show you the course. I'm sure your boys there would like to see it too. We can all ride along, though I'll tell you right now we won't be able to keep up."

Hammond and George were all for that. I was too, but Robert held back. He'd had enough of horses for a while. He said he'd rather wait at the finish line to see the horses come in. Although I wanted to ride the course along with my daddy, George, and Hammond, I stayed behind with Robert.

Now, Mr. Waverly had three boys. Percy was eleven, same as Robert and me, Jack was a couple of years younger, and Christian was the eldest. All three stayed behind. They had seen Ghost Wind race before and seemed to have no interest in seeing him race again. Soon as their daddy was gone, they said there was another horse we should see. "Called an Appaloosa," said Christian Waverly. "Come from out west somewheres. He's ours. Our daddy gave him to us."

"Wanna see him?" asked Jack Waverly.

I certainly did, but they weren't talking to me, and Robert was hesitant, having no desire to see another horse, no matter how special. Unfortunately, those boys sensed Robert's fear, and they brought the Appaloosa out anyway. The Appaloosa was a beautiful thing with deep colored patches of brown against a background of cream, but he seemed frightened, and the Waverlys had a hard time handling him. Finally, when they got him calmed, they invited Robert to mount.

Robert's eyes widened at the prospect and he backed away. "But . . . but he's wild."

The Waverlys scoffed. "No wilder'n most. Go 'head. Get on."

"No, thank you," Robert politely declined.

"Aw, come on," said Percy Waverly. "Sure your daddy would want you to try him out, seeing what a horseman he is."

"I said no," Robert repeated.

The Appaloosa suddenly reared, and Robert's eyes showed his terror. Backing away, he stumbled.

"You ain't scairt of him, are you?" asked Christian. "Come on, we'll help you up." Then two of the Waverlys scooped Robert up, while the third held the Appaloosa, and plopped him on the horse's back. Robert was terrified.

I yelled for them to take Robert off that horse and pushed my way toward the Appaloosa. "Let him down!" I ordered.

One of the Waverlys caught me by the lapel of my coat. "And just who do you think you are to be telling anybody to do anything? Oh, yeah, we heard about you."

I glanced at Robert, who was mute with fear. He was trying to get off the animal, but I knew that filled him with terror too; the ground to him was a long way down. "He doesn't have a way with horses," I tried to tell those boys. "He'll get hurt."

"Well, why don't you help him out then?" said Christian, and he and his brother Percy picked me up and tossed me on behind Robert. One of them threw up the reins, then slapped the Appaloosa on the rump, and Robert and I went flying across the meadow. The Waverlys laughed.

I managed to grab the reins, but seeing I was behind Robert, I couldn't gain control of the Appaloosa. The horse was frightened, and I wasn't strong enough to stop him. Robert was yelling at the top of his lungs, while all the time I was trying to rein in the horse. From far across the meadow I could hear the Waverlys yelling at us, but whatever concern they had was coming too late. The Appaloosa bucked and hurled us both off, and we hit the ground hard.

"Y'all all right?" asked the Waverlys as they ran up. I could tell their concern was genuine. Their voices and their manner had changed. They helped Robert up, but I figured I didn't need their help and pulled away when they offered it.

"Y'all hurt?" asked Percy once we were standing. "Didn't mean you any harm, just funning."

"Some funning," I said, brushing myself off, but Robert seemed too dazed to speak. He just stood there, his right arm holding his left. "Is it broken?" I said.

Robert just looked at me and didn't answer.

"Look," said Christian, "don't mention this to our daddies. We didn't mean for this to happen. Didn't figure you'd get hurt. Like we said, we were joshing, that's all."

"Yeah, we're sure sorry," said Jack in sudden repentance as he glanced nervously back at the road, as if expecting my daddy and his at any moment. "It wasn't right of us to put y'all on that Appaloosa."

Robert suddenly found his tongue. "Paul here, he could ride that Appaloosa, he had a fair chance."

The Waverlys laughed. "Yeah, sure he can," mocked Christian. "Listen, nobody can ride that Appaloosa."

"Paul can," said Robert with assurance.

I cut Robert a sideways glance as the Waverlys again laughed.

Robert didn't laugh; neither did I, though I wondered where Robert was going with this kind of talk.

"Wanna bet?" challenged my brother. "Paul, he ride the Appaloosa around this meadow without getting thrown, then he's ours."

"You're crazy!" declared Percy.

"Paul gets thrown," Robert went on, "then you keep the Appaloosa and we don't tell our daddy or yours about what just happened. You don't let Paul ride, then I'll have to tell them everything . . . and about what happened to my arm."

The Waverlys stopped their laughing.

"Got to make up your minds," said Robert, still holding his wounded arm with his good one. "They'll be back pretty soon, I expect."

The Waverlys looked at one another and decided. "All right," said Christian. "It's a bet."

It was then I pulled Robert aside. "You crazy?" I said, trying to keep my voice low. "What makes you think I can ride that horse?"

"'Cause you can ride anything," Robert returned.

"I never been on a Appaloosa."

"Yes you have," said Robert. "Just now."

I frowned apprehensively. "Don't know wild horses."

"Paul . . . you can ride anything." His confidence in me was unwavering.

"Easy for you to say," I retorted angrily. "And you could've asked me first!"

"'Ey! This boy going to ride, he better go on and do it," called Percy. "Our daddies'll be back any minute now."

I looked again at Robert, then headed slowly toward the Appaloosa. I began talking softly to calm him, and when I reached him, I dug into my pocket and pulled out an apple wedge I had brought along for the horse I had ridden to the Waverly farm. The Appaloosa took it. I gave him a second piece and he let me pat his forehead. All the while, I was talking to him, telling him I would like to ride him and that nobody was going to slap him this time. I took the reins, then took the time to walk the Appaloosa around the meadow, talking softly to him and giving him apple wedges. Finally, when I knew there wasn't much time left, I slowly mounted. The Appaloosa didn't rear. I leaned low to his neck and laid my head against him. I stayed that way for a minute or two, then straightened. I kept on talking and pushed my knees gently inward, and the Appaloosa started across the meadow. Clearly, the horse had been ridden before, but not by the Waverlys. They were too clumsy to ride him.

Again I leaned forward along the Appaloosa's neck. "All right, let's really show them," I said, feeling akin to him now. Then I straightened, dug in my knees, and we raced across the meadow. I had no fear of the Appaloosa throwing me this time. I was as one with him. The Appaloosa ran wild and free, enjoying the run, and allowed me the pleasure of enjoying it with him. I was still on the Appaloosa when I saw my daddy coming on Ghost Wind. It was clear the course was finished, for Mr. Waverly was mounted beside him, and George and Hammond were walking their horses behind. I slowed the Appaloosa and went to meet them.

"Don't tell me you can ride that devil!" exclaimed Mr. Waverly as I jumped down.

"Paul can ride just about any horse alive," said Robert proudly, and looked pointedly at the Waverly boys. I noticed the arm he had been holding was now hanging normally at his side.

Christian Waverly reddened, then said to his daddy, "Fact is, we made Robert here a wager, seeing it's our horse and all. Said . . . said, um, if that boy there could ride him, the Appaloosa was his."

"Well, seems like to me he rode him all right," said Mr. Waverly, who then turned to my daddy. "Looks like your son Robert's got himself a horse. What about you?"

"I think it's time we talked terms," said my daddy, patting Ghost Wind's neck. "He's a fine horse. As for the Appaloosa, we can talk about that too."

"Good," said Mr. Waverly before turning to his sons. "Christian, you boys wipe down that stallion and give him some water. Don't want these folks thinking we don't tend to our horses." Then he and my daddy dismounted and went to the house to haggle price. George and Hammond dismounted too, and took a closer look at the Appaloosa, then pulled Robert and me over toward the barn while the Waverlys took care of the stallion. "Now, just how did you two manage to get those Waverly boys to wager their horse?" asked Hammond.

Robert and I looked at each other and laughed. Then we told them what the Waverlys had done. George laughed too. "So it backfired on them, huh? Quick thinking, Robert."

"Well, it was Paul who done it, got us that horse!" Robert exclaimed. "Besides, it serves them right for putting us on that Appaloosa in the first place." He rubbed his arm. "My arm got hurt."

"Is it really hurt?" I asked.

"Just sprained, I think."

It was then Christian Waverly came over to us and he said, "That white nigger of y'alls got y'all a hell of a horse."

George turned quickly. "You talking about Paul?"

"Sure. Who else?"

In one liquid movement George slammed Christian hard against the barn wall, then thrust up his arm and locked it under Christian's jaw. "You talk about Paul," George said, his voice calm, "you best remember one thing: You're talking about us."

The other Waverlys stood startled and silent, watching from a distance. Robert and I stood silent too, not knowing what George might do. Hammond, as always, took charge. "That's enough, George. Let him go."

George glanced over his shoulder at Hammond, then turned back to Christian and smiled before loosening his hold and backing away. Hammond then stepped up to Christian and said quite crisply, "You have to understand something, Christian. Paul's our blood, and we make no bones about it. You have something to say to that?"

Christian Waverly glanced at George and shook his head.

"All right," said Hammond pleasantly, then turned to Robert and me. "Paul, you and Robert take care of that Appaloosa now and let's see about getting him home."

Late that afternoon we left the Waverly farm, and we took both the Appaloosa and Ghost Wind with us. My daddy rode the stallion, and Robert and I, with the Appaloosa between us, took turns holding his reins. We rode that way all the way back to my daddy's house.

※

After we were home, my daddy summoned Mitchell's daddy to the stables. Now, Willie Thomas was mighty good with horses, and my daddy entrusted the most prized of his horses to his care. Willie Thomas knew their ailments and how to fix most of them. He saw to their feeding, their hooving, all their care, but he didn't train or ride them. My daddy did that himself. By the time Willie Thomas arrived along with Mitchell, only I was with my daddy. Hammond and George were getting ready to go courting, and Robert had gone off to nurse his sore arm. "So, this here's Ghost Wind!" Willie Thomas exclaimed when he saw the stallion. "He ride good's he look, Mister Edward?"

"He's a fine riding horse, all right," said my daddy, "but he needs training. I figure he gets that training, he could be the best around."

"Yes, suh," said Willie Thomas, stroking the stallion's forehead. "He sure got a good look to him, I know that!"

"Now, Willie," said my daddy, "I expect you to take mighty good care of this horse. I'm depending on Ghost Wind to win me more than a few races by the coming year, and I want him in the best condition possible. I'll do the training myself, and I don't want anybody sitting him besides myself and Paul here. Paul's got a definite hand with horses, and I figure him to ride for me someday with his light weight."

This was the first time I'd heard this. I was actually going to ride Ghost Wind! I couldn't help but grin, and I glanced over at Mitchell in my pride. But Mitchell cut me a sour look, then looked back at the stallion.

Willie Thomas nodded. "Don't ya worry none, Mister Edward. I take good care of this horse for ya."

"I know you will," said my daddy.

Beginning the next day, I worked with my daddy in training Ghost Wind. Sometimes George and Hammond helped with the training, but once they went away to school, it was just my daddy and me, and I learned a lot from him. At first my daddy did not let me sit Ghost Wind, because he didn't think I could handle him yet. But finally one day he did let me mount and take the reins, and I discovered riding on Ghost Wind was what I figured floating on a cloud must be like. After that my daddy let me ride him a bit each day, and riding that stallion was what I looked forward to every dawn when I opened my eyes.

Then there came the time when my daddy let me take Ghost Wind out alone. He was going into town, and he didn't want the stallion's training interrupted. He wanted me to put the stallion through his paces, both in the morning and the afternoon, but not to race him. I felt proud that my daddy trusted me to take charge of the stallion on my own, and I did exactly as my daddy said. In the morning I led Ghost Wind to the meadow, mounted him, and let him walk for some time around the meadow before I allowed him to break into a trot, then finally into a gallop. In the late afternoon I did the same, but all the time I was on the stallion, I was aware that Mitchell was watching me. He had appeared on the edge of the woods and had just stood there watching Ghost Wind and me as we went round and round the meadow. Finally, on one of our turns past him, he said: "S'pose you thinkin' you a real somebody 'cause you can ride that stallion."

I looked down at Mitchell and stopped, knowing that despite our understanding, he was itching for a fight with me. Now, I don't know what possessed me in that moment to say the next thing I did. Maybe I was feeling guilty that because I was my daddy's son, I could ride Ghost Wind. Maybe it was that, but it wasn't out of fear I said what I said. I no longer was afraid of Mitchell. "You want to ride him?" I asked.

Mitchell took a step backward. It was obvious he hadn't expected me to say that. "You know I can't ride him," he said. "Your white daddy'd kill me."

"You want to ride him?" I asked again.

Mitchell looked at the stallion, then at me. "So, what if I do?"

"You figure you can ride Ghost Wind, then get on. Just bring him back to the stable when you're finished so I can rub him down." I dismounted, leaving the stallion with Mitchell, and headed toward the barn. Now, I truly expected that Mitchell would come after me with Ghost Wind. After all, despite my invitation, I knew Mitchell couldn't ride Ghost Wind. As far as I knew, Mitchell had never ridden more than a mule and had no idea how to ride a thoroughbred tornado like Ghost Wind. But instead of Mitchell following me, the next thing I knew, I heard a triumphant cry, turned, and saw Mitchell atop the stallion dashing across the meadow. For a moment all I could do was stand and stare. But then, as the stallion bucked, left the meadow, and headed for the woods, I suddenly found my legs and my voice, and I began running and screaming after Mitchell and the stallion. "Pull back the reins!" I hollered as I ran. "Mitchell, the reins! Pull back hard!"

As fast as my legs would take me, I crossed the meadow, but there was no catching them. Ghost Wind and Mitchell were gone, hidden by the deep green of the forest. I chased them along a forest trail, then heard the cracking of branches, and a high shrieking curse, along with a loud snort, and my heart pumped faster. When I finally reached the two of them, I found Mitchell on his rear end, his hands against his head, and the stallion limping several feet away. My first thoughts were for the stallion; I wasn't thinking about Mitchell. It was good to see him on his backside for a change.

"Whoa there, Wind," I said softly as I tried to get near the stallion. "It's me, boy. It's Paul." I extended my hand slowly. "Let me take a look at you now. It's all right. It's all right." The stallion pulled back at first. I kept talking, and he finally allowed me to touch him. He whinnied just a bit, and I patted him gingerly, trying to make him know me; then, when he was still, I took a closer look at his leg. There was a bad tear along his right foreleg, and there were scratches from the branches that had ripped along his sleek white coat. The scratches I knew would heal, but I wasn't sure about the leg. The way Ghost Wind had pulled back, I feared a ligament might be torn or even his leg fractured.

"He all right?" asked Mitchell, on his feet now.

Without looking at him, I shook my head. "Don't know. We got to get him back to the barn."

"Your daddy's gonna kill me," he said solemnly, yet with no fear in his voice, just a voice of matter of fact. "Course now, my daddy get t' me first, he'll do it. Don't blame him this time if he do, though, 'cause he's gonna lose his job sure once your daddy see that horse."

I just looked at Mitchell and took the reins. "Come on. Let's get him back."

Mitchell nodded and, for the first time, followed my lead.

Willie Thomas was waiting for us when we got back to the barn. "Ah, Lord, what done happened?" he asked, rushing over to the limping stallion. Willie stooped and examined the stallion's fore-leg, then straightened and glared accusingly at Mitchell. "Boy, you got somethin' t' do wit' this?"

Mitchell looked at him sulkily. "You'd think I did even if I ain't."

"You tell me, boy! You been on this stallion?"

"And so what if I was?"

Willie Thomas hauled off and slapped Mitchell across the face with the back of his hand. "Don't ya get smart wit' me!" Mitchell turned his head at the impact, but he didn't fall back. It was as if he had already braced himself for the attack. "You done had somethin' t' do wit' this here stallion bein' cut up, I knows it!" Willie raved on. "You had somethin' t' do wit' it, I gets the blame, and I lose my good job! Tell me what ya done!"

Mitchell stared coldly at his daddy. He said nothing. I stared at them both, fearful of what was to come. Next thing, Willie Thomas pulled a whip from the barn wall. It was then that my daddy came riding up on one of his mares. He took one look at Willie Thomas holding the whip, another at Mitchell and me, then his eyes settled on Ghost Wind. He dismounted and walked over to the stallion. Unlike Willie, he didn't inspect the stallion's leg. He just glanced at it, then turned to face the three of us. "So, what's happened to my horse?"

None of us spoke right up. I knew that was because we all had the same fear. My daddy's voice was soft, but we knew his mind. That was his prized horse standing there bleeding, and we knew he wasn't about to take that lightly.

"I asked a question," said my daddy, and his voice was still low. "I expect an answer." He looked straight at Mitchell's daddy. "Willie?"

Willie Thomas eyed his son, then cleared his throat. "W-well, now, Mister Edward," he began, not looking at my daddy but at Ghost Wind instead, "th-these here two boys jus' done brought this here stallion from them woods yonder, and they done brung him back all torn up like this. Seem like t' me Mitchell, he done rode this horse knowin' he ain't s'pose t', and I done told him that time and time again—"

My daddy cut him off. "How bad is he hurt?"

Willie Thomas now looked at my daddy. "Muscle all torn up on this leg here," he said, moving toward the stallion's right foreleg. "Don't know if it'll heal or not. Now, I can tend t' it, but I can't go lyin' and sayin' it'll heal like it's s'pose t'."

"What else?" demanded my daddy, glancing at the scratches.

Willie Thomas followed his look. "Well, them there, they'll heal all right. It's jus' that leg I ain't so sure of." He turned to my daddy. "It's my boy Mitchell done this, Mister Edward, and I know there ain't no way t' make it up t' ya if this here horse don't heal right, but I jus' 'bout t' put a strap t' Mitchell my own self 'bout what he done. I'm gonna put a strap t' him right now, matter of fact!" With that said, he positioned his whip and turned toward Mitchell.

"But it wasn't Mitchell!" I blurted out, stopping him and surprising myself. After all Mitchell had put me through, I shouldn't have cared if he got whipped or not. "Wasn't Mitchell rode that horse! It was me!"

Willie Thomas's whip stopped in midair and my daddy's gaze turned from Willie to me. Mitchell, though, stood stock-still. He didn't look at his daddy, he didn't look at my daddy, and he didn't look at me. He was gazing off somewhere else.

"You?" questioned my daddy. "Paul, you did this?"

"Yes, sir," I said, looking straight at him. "I did."

My daddy took a breath deep, then walked around Ghost Wind, inspecting him long and hard this time, before he came back and stood right in front of me. "Paul," he said to me, "you're a good horseman, one of the best I've ever seen, and you know how to handle Ghost Wind. Now you going to stand here and tell me you rode this horse and let this happen to him?"

I looked straight up at my daddy and lied again. "Yes, sir."

"How?"

"Sir?"

"How'd it happened?"

I glanced at Willie Thomas, still holding the strap, and at Mitchell, still looking off to God knew where. Then my eyes turned again to my daddy. "He . . . well, he just got away from me, Mister Edward," I said. "Ghost Wind . . . he . . . he was just too much horse for me, I reckon."

After I said that, there was only silence. My daddy's look pierced me; then he moved back to the stallion and stooped to take another look at his leg. He motioned Willie Thomas over. "Looks like to me," he said, "the leg's not that torn up. It should heal in time."

Willie, too, again studied the leg. "Yes, suh, I believes so," he agreed. "But not time 'nough for them races you was plannin' on."

My daddy straightened and nodded. "You just do what you need to do to make him right."

"Yes, suh."

"And, Willie . . ."

"Yes, suh?"

"Put that whip away. Paul says he rode the stallion. That's all I need to know."

Willie Thomas bit his lip, looked at Mitchell, then back at my daddy and said quietly, "Yes, suh." My daddy nodded as if an understanding had just been struck, and watched as Willie Thomas hung the whip back on the wall.

Then my daddy turned to me. "Paul, you come with me," he said, and left the barn.

I glanced again at Willie Thomas, but he didn't look at me.

He turned his attention instead back to the stallion. I looked then at Mitchell, and for the first time he was looking at me, but I couldn't read his eyes.

"Paul!"

I hurried after my daddy. When I caught up with him, I walked alongside him in silence until we were almost at the house before I said, "I s'pose you real mad at me."

"Not real happy with you."

"Well . . . I'm sorry about riding Ghost Wind that way. I . . . I won't do it again."

"Yes, I know you won't."

"You going to whip me?"

My daddy stopped and looked at me. "No," he said. "I'm not going to whip you, Paul. No, your punishment is that you'll never get to ride Ghost Wind again. I figure you'll remember that a whole lot longer than a whipping. You won't ride any of the other horses either, including the Appaloosa, until I say so."

"But, Mister Edward—"

"You were responsible for that stallion, and you let this happen."

"But—"

"It's finished, boy. Don't you think I know it was Mitchell rode that horse? Now you've got to pay the price for it."

❧

It wasn't until the next day I saw Mitchell again. "You get a whippin' for ridin' that stallion?" he asked as I made my way through the woods toward the creek.

I shook my head. "No. Just can't ride Ghost Wind anymore."

Mitchell glanced sideways at me, almost as if he felt bad about my predicament. "That bad as a whippin'?"

"Worse."

He shrugged. "Maybe so. Whippin', I s'pose, you get it over and done wit'."

"That's how I see it," I said, and started away.

"'Ey, Paul!" Mitchell called after me. "Anyways, you still get t' ride your own horse, that Appaloosa. So not ridin' Ghost Wind, that ain't so bad."

I turned and looked back at him. "No . . . don't get to ride him either, or any other horse . . . not 'til my daddy says I can. He was plenty mad."

"Had a right t' be," Mitchell conceded, "way that stallion was all scratched up and bruised. You know, my daddy was 'fraid he was gonna lose his job 'cause-a what I done."

"I know."

"Wouldn't've had t' be," he said, eyeing me in his old belligerent way, "he ain't been so scairt of your white daddy."

I looked him straight. "I know."

Mitchell seemed to relent.

I nodded and turned again to go.

"Paul," Mitchell called after me one final time. "You know my daddy would've near t' killed me, he'd've known for sure I'd been ridin' that stallion. I'd've taken the whippin', mind ya, but he would've near t' killed me."

"Then good thing you weren't riding Ghost Wind, isn't it?" I said.

Mitchell nodded, and that was as close as Mitchell Thomas came to thanking me and as close as I came to accepting his thanks. But after that, things began to change between Mitchell and me. Now, we still weren't the best of friends, but there was a new respect building. I believe that both of us were realizing that our judgments of each other were not truly founded. Each of us had something to him the other hadn't seen before, and out of this realization came a real respect, not just a truce.

Family

I loved my daddy's land. In the beginning I always thought of it as my land too. I knew every bit of the place. I knew every bit of lowland, every rise and knoll, every cave and watering place, every kind of plant and tree. My favorite spots were the pond nestled in the woods and a hillside that overlooked the pasture and my daddy's house. The pond was surrounded by big old pines that allowed splinters of light to peek through, and its waters were filled with fish. The hillside boasted only a few trees, so it was sunny and open, and the pasture below was dotted with cows and horses grazing. On many days I would sit for hours alone at either place just gazing out over the land. Whenever my family was needing me and I couldn't be found near my daddy's or my mama's house, they knew where to look for me.

Now, one of my favorite things to do was read, and I was always reading anything I could get my hands on. I especially liked reading by that pond, and when I wasn't fishing there with Robert, I usually took a book with me. People began to expect that of me. Once, though, my reading got me into more trouble with some of the colored boys on the place, and it was Mitchell who got me out of it. Those boys came along and started picking on me. There were four of them, and since my brothers weren't around and, at the moment, neither was Mitchell, I suppose they figured they could get away with it.

"Jus' look at that little nigger white boy sittin' there on the bank got nothin' t' do," said a boy I recognized as R. T. Roberts. "Got nothin' t' do but sit there lookin' at some fool book."

"Well, if I had me a white daddy who own the place, 'spect I wouldn't have nothin' t' do neither," said another.

I glanced up at them, but I said nothing.

"Let's see jus' what ya got there, nigger white boy," said R.T. Then he grabbed the book right out of my hands. That's when I jumped up, but I still said nothing. "Now, let's see what this here is." R.T. flipped through the pages.

"Got no pictures," observed one of the boys.

"What's them words?" asked another, peering over.

"Don't know," said R.T. "Jus' know they white folks' words." Then he looked at me. "What ya doin' usin' white folks' words, boy?" he barked at me, imitating the way I'd heard white men speak to black folks. He and the other boys broke into laughter.

"It's called English," I said, breaking my silence. "Anybody wants to read it can learn to read it."

The boys scoffed at my words. "So, maybe you want t' teach us, same as you teachin' Mitchell, huh?"

I shrugged. "You want to learn, I will."

"Yeah . . ." sneered another. "We got our own schools now, and we wanted t' learn any of that stuff, we'd be goin' there. We'd hardly be takin' any teachin' from the likes of you. You with yo' white daddy."

By now I was tired of folks putting me down because of my daddy. My daddy was a white man and there was nothing I could do about it, so I figured I might as well make use of the fact. "That's right," I said. "I've got a white daddy, all right, and you're standing on his land. Maybe you'd like to get off it."

The boy who had made the remark about my daddy stepped toward me, but R.T. put up his hand and stopped him. "Now wait a minute, wait a minute," he said. "Maybe this here boy Paul gots a point 'bout readin'. Maybe he can teach us somethin'. Let's see now . . . maybe he can teach us how t' read this here—" He tore a page from the book and thrust it at me.

"Don't do that!" I cried.

"Or maybe this one here." Another boy ripped out a second page.

"Stop it!"

"Ya know somethin'?" said R.T. "I don't much like this book no ways, seein' it ain't got no pictures, and what I don't like, I don't tolerate!" Then he grabbed a handful of pages and tore them from the binding.

With that I threw myself at R.T., punching him with all my might. I had learned how to fight well enough to defend myself, but I certainly wasn't capable of fighting four boys at once, and they let me know that too. They laughed and all of them had a shot at me—that is, until Mitchell Thomas came along. There was a sudden silence before I even knew Mitchell was there. All I knew was that R.T., who was beating at my face, was suddenly jerked away, and laid out flat to the ground with a thunderous pop. Then I saw Mitchell through the slit of my swollen eye. He stood over R.T. and pointed to me. "Now, anybody want at this boy'll hafta fight me," he said calmly.

All the boys were silent at first, then one of them laughed nervously. "Ah, we was jus' joshin' wit' him, Mitchell."

"Yeah," said another. "But then he gone and lit into R.T. there for no reason. He the one started it! Got what was comin' t' him!"

"Yeah! Jus' 'cause he got a white daddy, he think he can do whatever he wanna!" put in R.T. "Well, we don't be 'lowin' no white niggers t' be beatin' up on us. He ain't no better'n us!"

"He done said he was?" asked Mitchell.

"Well . . . might ain't said it, but might well as've. Sittin' there readin' that book."

Mitchell looked at the ground and saw the torn pages and the book lying now facedown in the mud. "Yeah . . . yeah, I see what ya mean, how Paul done started it and all. See how he done torn pages outa his own book and riled y'all. Well, y'all wanna fight this boy, then fight him fair, one at a time, but don't y'all be jumpin' him like ya done or y'all gonna have me t' fight right 'long with him."

"Ah, Mitchell, what ya doin' takin' up for him?" retorted R.T., getting to his feet and wiping at the blood Mitchell had drawn. "You used t' couldn't stand him yo' own self! I recalls correctly, you used t' always be beatin' up on him!"

"Yeah, that's right, and I ain't never had no help t' do it neither. Like I said, y'all wanna fight him, that's fine with me, but y'all go jumpin' him like ya done, all of y'all knockin' him round at once, I'm gonna back Paul up. Now, y'all got a problem with that?"

R.T. glanced at the other boys, then back at Mitchell, and shook his head. "Naw, ain't got no problem."

Mitchell nodded at the understanding and dismissed any grievance he had with R.T. "Look, I got me a wagon stuck in the mud down a ways. Y'all wanna come help get me out?"

"Oh, yeah, sure," the boys said, seemingly happy to do whatever Mitchell asked.

"'Fore ya do, though," added Mitchell, "y'all best pick up all them pages outa Paul's book there. And next time don't let him rile ya so."

R.T. and the others did what Mitchell said; then all of them went with Mitchell to help him with his wagon. I suppose I could have gone to help too, seeing how Mitchell had helped me out, but Mitchell hadn't asked me to come and I figured the others wouldn't have wanted me along anyway. I had no need to go where I wasn't wanted.

After they were gone, I sat on the bank alone and tried to put my book together. Although some of the pages were crumpled and muddy, they were still readable. I wiped them off as best I could, then put them in order and laid them in the binding. Afterward I just sat there thinking on those boys jumping me, then a while later, I went back to my reading, even though my right eye was swollen. I wasn't about to let R.T. and those other boys and their ignorance chase me from what I wanted to do.

I was still sitting there reading with my one good eye when Mitchell came back. "Some reason thought you'd still be here," he said. "Don't you ever get tired of readin'?"

I looked up at him. "Not really."

Mitchell shook his head as if finding it hard to understand that and sat down. "Got the wagon unstuck."

"Good."

"You know R.T. and them others, they had plenty t' say 'bout ya."

"S'pose they did."

"They said you gone and threatened them."

"Threatened them?"

"Yeah. Said they was on your daddy's land and maybe they mess wit' you, they'd be off it."

I took a moment. "I suppose it did come out that way."

"Paul, you wanna get along with these boys, how come you bringin' up your white daddy all the time?"

"I didn't bring him up. They did."

"Don't matter," said Mitchell. "Your daddy's the boss man—the white boss man—and you got no right t' throw that in their face."

"And they've got no right to judge me 'cause of who my daddy is. I'm not ashamed of who I am, and I'm not ashamed of my daddy!"

Mitchell was silent.

I closed my book and stared at him. "You figuring maybe I need to be?"

Mitchell looked at me. "Not figurin' anythin'. Jus' can't understand how it feels t' have a white daddy, that's all. Can't figure out how you could love a white daddy who owned your mama and you. Can't figure how you can be so crazy 'bout them white brothers of yours neither, when once y'all all grown, they'll be the boss and you'll be jus' another nigger."

I got up from the bank. "They never use that word to me, and that's not how it's going to be."

"What make you think so?"

"Because they're my family."

Mitchell nodded and faced the pond. "Still can't figure it."

"I've got to go. I'm going hunting."

"Who wit'?"

"With my daddy."

Mitchell looked around at me. "Good huntin', then" was all he said.

❧

"Mitchell been beating up on you again?" asked my daddy as we set up camp that evening.

"No, sir. Some other boys."

"How do they look?"

I grinned up at my daddy. "'Bout the same. Mitchell helped me out."

My daddy nodded, and the two of us went about building a fire. We were planning to hunt coon later in the night, and in the morning hunt some wild turkeys. My daddy often took me hunting. Sometimes we all went, my daddy and my brothers and me, though Hammond and George often went hunting on their own. There were times too when my daddy took just Robert and me. But the times that were most special were when it was only my daddy and me on a hunt. At those times I had my daddy all to myself, and I cherished that. I learned many things from my daddy, and when I was a small boy, there seemed no one like him to me. I'm not ashamed to admit it. In those early days I adored my daddy.

Now, when my daddy would take me on a hunt, he often talked about when he was a boy, and it made me proud when he said I reminded him of himself. "You're much like me," he told me once. "When I was a boy, I loved to read and I loved horses. I loved this land too. My granddaddy had gotten it before I was born, back before the turn of the century, when there were plenty of Indians settled around here. There still were some here when I was a boy, and I got to know a few and they taught me a lot."

"Mister Edward," I said when he told me that, thinking of my own Indian blood, "you ever meet my mama's daddy?" Now, I always called my daddy "Mister Edward," just as Cassie and my mama did, though I had come on my mama and daddy in their quiet times and had heard her say his name out straight Edward and that was all. It seemed peculiar to me at first that I called my daddy by a formal name while Robert and Hammond and George called him "Daddy." But my mama had broken both Cassie and me when we were still little from ever calling Edward Logan "Daddy." She had broken that misspeaking with bottom-warming spankings whenever we did. When I asked my mama why Cassie and I couldn't call our daddy the same as Robert and George and Hammond, she said simply, "They're white and you're not, and their mama was his legal wife." I didn't ask her again about it after that, and I settled into addressing my daddy as if he were not, and after a while calling him "Mister Edward" was the same as calling him Daddy, or at least that was what was in my mind.

As for what my daddy called me, sometimes when we were alone, he called me Paul-Edward. That's because my mama had wanted to name me Edward after him, but my daddy had said it wouldn't be fitting, seeing that none of his boys with his white wife had his name. Out of respect for her, he said, he couldn't give it to me official-like, but he would think of me that way. So there were times when my daddy called me Paul-Edward, and my mama and sometimes Cassie did the same, but it was only between them and me.

"No, can't say that I did," my daddy said in answer to my question. "I heard of him, though. My own daddy told me about him. His name was Kanati; means the lucky hunter. My daddy said he left with some of his people headed west into Alabama or Mississippi before the soldiers made them go. From what my daddy told me, Kanati knew they'd be made to go because folks like my daddy and others wanted the Nation's land, and there was nothing to be done about that. The Army was set to drive Kanati's people out, and your granddaddy didn't want any part of any soldiers."

"Wish I could've known him."

"Well, I know your mama wishes that too. She always wanted to know him herself."

"You expect we'll ever meet up with him? I mean, you expect he'll ever come back?"

My daddy looked at me then and answered me truthfully, as he always did. "I don't expect that's likely, Paul."

"This land," I said, "it belonged to his people first."

"That's a fact," my daddy agreed. "Maybe that's where you get part of your love for the land. Now, of all my boys, you and Robert seem to have the most feel for the land. I know Hammond loves it as home, and so does George, but I figure

Hammond will end up in business somewhere, and George has always been cut out to be a soldier. So when I pass on, there'll be you and Robert to take care of the place. Robert loves the land and has a good head, but I don't know if he's up to the hardships of farming. Besides that, he doesn't have a feel for the animals, especially the horses. I don't mean he doesn't care about them, I mean he just doesn't have a kinship with them, and you do. Why, the way you can calm a horse and ride him is an amazement, even to me." My pride swelled up when my daddy said that. "I was a good rider as a boy, but you're much better. You tend to know animals. Robert doesn't, but he does love this land."

"Then we can take care of it together." I dreamed on that.

"Perhaps so," said my daddy thoughtfully. "Thing is, though, when you get grown, you maybe'll want to leave this place and go out on your own."

"Leave it?" I questioned. "Why would I ever want to leave it?"

"Maybe one day," he said, "you'll know the answer to that question."

In the many times we had hunted together since he had said that, I had not yet figured out the answer. There was, as I saw it then, no reason to leave. But on that night after the boys had torn my book and beaten me, my daddy said to me, "I've decided to send you away to school."

I stared at him across our campfire. "Sir?"

"I want you to have an education and a trade. I want you to have a means of supporting yourself."

"B-but," I stuttered, "I know plenty already. I've been studying here, and you and Hammond and George, you all taught me—"

"What we taught you is only a beginning. Now, there are some colored schools opening up in Georgia and elsewhere

where colored boys and girls are going for higher education, and there's a school in Macon you can go to, part-time, and later on, you want to take more schooling, you can do it. But what I want you to concentrate on learning now is a skill you can always use, something you can always depend on to earn some money."

"Like horse training?"

"No. Like carpentry. Not just knowing how to nail two pieces of wood together, but how to build something fine and of quality. There'll always be a need for that. The Lord Jesus Christ Himself was a carpenter, so you know you couldn't ask for a better trade. You can use your horse training too, but carpentry is something solid and dependable, and there'll always be a need for it. You're good with your hands, Paul-Edward, and there's no question in my mind that you've got a good head. You can learn whatever you set out to learn. That's why I'm sending you to study with a man I know in Macon. He builds the finest furniture around. You can learn a lot from him. You can go to school while you're there too."

"Robert'll go to school with me then? He'll study with this man too?"

"No. I'll be sending Robert to school, but not there. I'm thinking on sending him to a boys' school in Savannah."

I was bewildered. "But why can't we go together? We've always studied together. Why not now?"

My daddy took a moment before he answered. "Because you're growing up."

"But that's got nothing to do with it."

"Oh, but it does," said my daddy. "It's got everything to do with it. Robert needs an education, and so do you. But you can't be educated in the same way."

"But—"

"Robert's white and you're a boy of color. I can't educate you in the same school—you know that. I can't educate you in the same way either. I need to look out for what I think is best for each of you. Later, when you become of age and maybe want to do something different, that's up to you. Right now, though, we'll do things my way. Come the fall, Robert'll go to Savannah to school, and you'll go to Macon to study. That's just the way it's got to be. I figure that's what's best for both of you."

I didn't figure that was what was best for us though, and neither did Robert. The next night after that trip, I spent the night in my daddy's house, as I sometimes did. While Robert and I were waiting for sleep, Robert said to me, "Our daddy talk to you about sending us off to school?"

"Yeah," I replied, and we both were silent.

"Well," said Robert as the moonlight slipped over us, "I don't want to go. I don't want to go off to any Savannah school without you."

"Well, I'm not real happy about going to Macon myself," I said. "I'd rather stay right here."

"Me too," Robert agreed.

"But our daddy said I need a trade. Said you did too."

Robert sighed heavily. "Wish we could go together, same school."

"Our daddy said that can't be."

Even though it was dark except for the moonlight, I could see Robert's eyes on me. "You know, Paul, I hate it sometimes. Hate we're not full brothers."

Robert had told me this before. Once he had even wished my mama was his mama too, and when he was younger, he had thought she was, for his own mama had died soon after he was born, and my mama was pretty much the only mama he knew.

"I hate folks thinking of me as white and you colored," he went on. "Wish folks thought of us as the same."

"Which the same?" I questioned. "White or colored?"

"Don't matter to me," said Robert without hesitation, "long as we were the same."

"I figure it'd matter you had to live colored awhile."

Robert was silent to that, then reluctantly agreed. "Maybe so . . . but I'll tell you something, Paul. You don't feel no different to me than Hammond or George. I hate folks saying that word 'half' brother. How can you be 'half' of a brother? Either you're brothers or you're not!"

"Well," I decided, "that's just the way things are."

"I s'pose."

"It's true."

We let the silence settle once more.

"Well, anyway," Robert said, breaking it again, "I don't want us going off to separate schools, miles and miles from each other."

"Me neither, but it's a ways off yet. Least we got the summer." I was trying to look on the bright side of the thing; I resigned myself to what was to come. "'Sides, it's our daddy's decision. We've got no say in it."

"Yeah . . . I know. But maybe he'll change his mind."

We looked at each other then. We both knew there was little our daddy ever changed his mind about. We knew, too, our daddy figured sending us off to school was what was best; still I couldn't help but feel something was being wedged between Robert and me.

❧

It was during that summer before Robert and I were supposed to go off to school that I came to the true realization that I had two families. In part it was Mitchell who brought me to this realization, and the things he said to me; in part it was all the little things of my life and a matter of growing up. There were my daddy and my brothers on the one side of our family, and Cassie, my mama, and me on the other. Though from the beginning there had been some separateness between us, what with my mama having her own house and Cassie and me staying with her, that hadn't seemed strange to me, seeing that we were always up to our daddy's house anyway and my daddy and my brothers were always around. We were all connected, but the family line was muddled by color, and as I grew older, things began to take on different meanings for me. When I was younger, before Mitchell and the other boys started in on me, I had given little thought to any difference: to the fact that my mama, Cassie, and I were colored, and my daddy and my brothers were white.

Maybe that was partly because I had never experienced any real hardship from being colored. Although I was born into slavery shortly before the start of the war that would end slavery, I had never been treated as a slave. It was the early 1870's when I was growing up, and by then life on my daddy's land had settled down from the four years of war. The farm had suffered badly during the war years; there had been no cash crops, and what was grown, including the animals, was confiscated. Things now, though, were going well. That's because after my daddy had returned from the fighting, he had begun to rebuild his land. His own daddy, Lyndsey Logan, along with his mama, Helen, had died of influenza during the conflict, and his brother had been killed in action, so everything fell on my daddy's shoulders. To save his land, my daddy had let part of it go for taxes and had allowed logging on another. He had also traded for horses both at home and in Texas. My mama often talked about the hard times of those days during and right after the war, and how my daddy had struggled to keep his land. She talked about the hard times of slavery too, and she said the war hadn't changed things totally for anybody. White folks ruled the world before the war, she said, and they ruled it still.

I was, of course, too young to remember slavery or even that much of the war, but I could see certain aspects of what my mama meant. I could see what she meant in the way some white folks talked to colored folks, in the way some colored folks talked to white folks. I could see it in the shanties colored folks lived in on my daddy's land and in the clothes they wore and in the food they ate. I could see it in the towns when I went with my daddy: White folks were in charge. Still, when I was a small boy, that didn't bother me so much. My life being as it was, my family being as it was, in the beginning I accepted things the way they were. I worked in the fields alongside my daddy and my brothers, and when the fieldwork was done, I helped tend the horses and the cattle too, but of course anything to do with horses wasn't work to me; that was pure joy. When there wasn't work to be done, I was often with my daddy or my brothers about the place or with them somewhere on my daddy's business. When I was little, I figured to always be on my daddy's land. After all, I had no reason to want to leave.

My life was good.

But then as I grew older, I began to take note that Cassie and I weren't always included in my daddy's and my brothers' lives. When folks came over to supper, Cassie and I weren't allowed to sit at our daddy's table, while Robert, Hammond, and George still did. Whenever there was any socializing at the place, we weren't allowed the roam of the house, but had to stay put in the kitchen, where my mama and others served up preparations for my daddy's guests. That's not to say there was a whole lot of socializing going on. My daddy was a private kind of man and he pretty much kept to his family, but he was also a businessman, a well-to-do businessman, and knew most of the people in the community, so there were some social exchanges.

Now, when I say that my daddy was a well-to-do man, I don't mean he was rich. Very few Southern folks, white or black, were, following the war. But he was comfortable, and by the time I was about to turn twelve, I wasn't wanting for anything that I needed, and neither were Cassie nor my brothers. My daddy didn't have thousands of acres of plantation land, as some folks had, nor had he owned hundreds of slaves. But he did have a sizeable piece of property with the necessary number of people to work it, enough to make him acceptable among the most prominent in the local society. Even the knowledge of a slave woman's children in his house didn't mar that acceptance. Only his blatant disregard of all social rules would have done that. Allowing Cassie and me to sit at his table while his company visited would have broken those social rules.

When I was a little boy, being sent off to the kitchen to eat or outside to play didn't bother me, because Robert was always sent off with me. But then as we grew older, Robert was allowed to stay when the visitors came for their socializing, though at first he wouldn't stay without me. Even his grandmother couldn't make him stay. Robert's grandma on his mama's side always hated the fact that my daddy allowed Cassie and me to sit at his table and enjoy the life she felt was owed only to her daughter's children. When the daughter died, her mother was there in my daddy's house. Of course, I was only a baby at the time, but later I grew to know her hatred. She had stayed on in my daddy's house and took over running it. I remember she was always hard on my mama, and on Cassie and me. When my daddy was away during mealtime, she would send Cassie and me from the table. When that happened, Robert always went with me, and she couldn't make him come back. Worse than that, she would sometimes say cruel things to us. "They're like mites," she said once. "You get them in your bed, and you don't ever get rid of them."

She said that right in my daddy's presence. My daddy spoke her name, as if to quiet her, but Cassie had been sitting at the table and she jumped up and threw her plate right on the floor. "Don't you think I know what you mean?" she cried. "I know what you mean, you hateful old thing! Come on, Paul!"

I got up, not fully understanding. My daddy told me to sit back down and I did so, but Cassie had run out.

Later Robert said to our daddy, "Why don't you just make her go away?" I was standing right beside him.

My daddy glanced at me, then said to Robert, "She's your mother's mother and she's to be respected."

"Well, she don't respect Paul and Cassie!"

My daddy nodded. "I've spoken to her."

"Well, she ain't listened!"

"Maybe not," said our daddy, "but she stays just the same. She's your mother's mother, and she'll be here as long as she wants to be. Both of you, all of you, you'll just have to put up with her ways." I noticed that my daddy glanced past us and that his eyes settled on my mama standing in the doorway.

Robert's grandmother died a few years later, but there were always others who sat at our daddy's table who thought the same as she had about Cassie and me. I suppose my daddy could have been trying in part to protect Cassie and me from all those people, while saving his own social standing, but even thinking of that possibility didn't ease our pain. We'd been sent off just the same.

Eventually there came the time on a late summer afternoon just before my twelfth birthday when folks came to visit and it was my mama, not my daddy, who ordered me to the kitchen. Robert was now expected to stay at my daddy's table, and no amount of protest on his part changed that. My mama set a lone plate for me on the sideboard in the kitchen. That was truly the first time I felt unwanted in my daddy's family. My daddy hadn't even bothered to tell me himself not to sit at his table. He had left that to my mama, and I resented not only him for it, but her too.

"You sit down," my mama said, "and I'll fix your plate."

"You don't have to fix me anything," I said, pouting.

"It'll be the same food I've cooked for your daddy."

"I don't want it."

"Paul, you hafta eat."

"Not in this house," I said, and left.

"Paul-Edward!" she called after me. "Boy, don't you go no farther'n them steps! You hear me?"

I heard her, all right. I just didn't admit I did. I walked the back side of the veranda, out of my mama's view, and leaned against a post and looked out across the backyard to my daddy's forest. I stared at that forest, the forest that had always seemed to be a part of me, and felt alienated from it, from it and everything that was my daddy's.

It was then that George and Robert came along, exiting from the kitchen in their best suits. "So, what's this I hear from your mama about you not taking any supper?" asked George.

I slipped my hands into my pockets and looked stone-faced at George and Robert. "You worried about me eating?"

"Not worried about it," said George jovially. "But considering how much you do eat, just was wondering why you're not."

"You're smart enough to be going off to a military academy," I said with a smart mouth, "you figure it out."

George moved closer to me, and his smile faded as he gazed at me with his sky-blue eyes. "Oh, I got it figured, all right. You want to be the fool because of it and not eat, that's up to you. Just know that your not getting good food isn't doing anybody any detriment except maybe for yourself. I was in your place, I'd eat my daddy out of house and home. I'd figure he owed me that much. Course, what you do is up to you." George stared at me a moment or two, then walked away, up the veranda toward the front of the house.

Now, George, when he was angry, was always short with me; he never minced his words. At other times he was the most jovial of my brothers, the most patient too, taking the time to teach me his skills. But he was known for his impatience with fools or those who gave themselves no worth, and that's what I was seeing in him now as he chose to have nothing more to do with me. He had said his piece, and now he was finished with it. I watched him go. Robert stayed with me. "You want me to bring you something, Paul?" he asked.

"No," I said, going down the steps.

"Well, then come on back in the kitchen and get yourself something. There's a lot of good food in there—ham and fried chicken, dumplings, sweet-potato pie and—"

"Don't want any," I replied, and started across the yard.

"Where you going?" Robert called. "Your mama told George and me you were to stay on this porch!"

"Well, that's between my mama and me!"

"You leave, you gonna miss out on all this good food!"

I stopped long enough to turn and shout, "Last thing I want is my daddy's food from a table he doesn't even want me to sit at when his company comes calling!" As I finished my words, I saw that Hammond was standing at the corner of the house. I knew he saw me too, but I didn't care. I turned and ran toward the woods with Robert calling after me to come back.

I headed for the creek. Before I reached it, Hammond joined me. "Mind some company?" he asked.

"It's your woods," I retorted, feeling a sudden anger and resentment for all my brothers as well as my daddy.

"I thought we all lived here," said Hammond.

"I might live here," I returned, "but there's not a thing I see here's mine."

Hammond didn't say anything to that. He just walked along beside me in silence for some while as we made our way through the woods. After a while he said, "Tell me something, Paul. You mad at everybody today or just our daddy?"

I glanced up at Hammond. "Who said I was mad?"

Hammond laughed. "You think I don't know when you're mad? Ever since you were a bit of a boy, you'd always go off by yourself when you got mad. You wouldn't put up a holler like Robert or fight like Cassie and George; you'd just go off by yourself."

"I suppose you figure I got no reason to be mad."

"Now, I didn't say that. From what I been hearing, I know what you're mad about, and I don't blame you for it. Fact is, I know how you feel."

I turned on Hammond. "How could you know anything about how I feel? How could you know how it feels being caught between colored folks and white folks? How could you know how it feels to be sent off from our daddy's house when his white company comes calling? How could you know anything?"

Hammond scratched at his neck. "You think you're the only one ever felt this way? Well, Paul, I might not know exactly how it feels to be turned away from our daddy's table, but I sure know how it feels to hate and resent our daddy, and I sure enough know how it feels to be caught between colored folks and white folks. I know how it feels too to resent the hell out of your own blood, your own brother and sister."

I stopped, and Hammond did too. He looked straight into my eyes. "You know, when Cassie was born, I was only three. But when you were born, and Robert, I was nine and old enough to understand some things about our daddy, and old enough to understand some things about my mama and how she was feeling. My mama was a good woman, but you know she had to feel bad about our daddy going off being with a colored woman and having children with her. Your mama had four children with our daddy, two of them stillborn, and I remember my mama saying once it was the justice of the Lord that those babies died.

"Then when my mama was expecting Robert, she found out

you were born, and I can only imagine what that was like for her, her expecting a baby same time as your mama. She got sick with fever when she was carrying Robert, and she died soon after he was born. Now, you know I had to resent your mama, you, and Cassie too."

I nodded, never having thought of things that way. "I don't remember you acting that way, like you didn't want us."

"That's because you were too young to realize it. Ask your mama. For a while there nobody could do a thing with me, I was hating everybody so much. But over time I got to realizing some things. Most important was that your mama took real good care of George and me, and especially Robert. You know, Robert was born sickly, and your mama used to stay up all through the night with him when he was a baby, tending to him."

My mama had already told me that. She had told me too that though she had tended to Robert, she had never nursed him; she had me to nurse. Besides that, she refused to nurse another woman's child. She had always had strong feelings about being Edward Logan's "colored woman," for there were those who faulted her for being so, despite the fact she'd had no choice in the beginning. She had told Cassie and me, even though she was Edward Logan's property before the war, there were some things she refused to do for him. Being Robert's wet nurse was one of them. She said having to nurse another woman's child reminded her of a sow being forced to suckle another sow's pig, and no matter what people thought of her, she was no sow.

"Now, even though your mama took good care of all of us," Hammond went on, "I didn't want anything to do with her, and I let her know it. I remember one time I disrespected her and my daddy heard, and he near about tore me up because of it. But that still didn't change things for me. Wasn't until I was about fourteen or fifteen and your mama herself talked straight to me that I began to let go of some of my feelings."

"What she say?"

Hammond shook his head and smiled. "I don't know if you're old enough to hear. Let's just say she told me my daddy, when he was a young man, was at first same as any fox in a henhouse where the hens couldn't get out, and she asked me if I'd be any different than my daddy if the war hadn't come and all the young chicks were still in the henhouse with no say in their taking. You think on that, she told me, before you go making any judgments.

"Well, by this time I was beginning to feel my manly needs, and I thought on what your mama said. That's not to say she totally turned me around in my thinking. At first I had kind of resented the way my daddy treated you and Cassie, bringing you up to the house, seating you at the table. Resented too the time he took with both of you and the fact that he himself taught you how to read and write, then expected George and me, along with Robert, to share at the end of each day with you and Cassie whatever we learned in school. I resented a lot of things at first, and I hated him for fathering you and Cassie, then treating you the same as he did my mama's children, and making us watch out for the two of you. More than one time I got bloodied taking up for you and Cassie when our white friends found out the way our daddy treated you. I even once told him there were plenty of other white men had colored children, but you didn't see them seating their colored children at their table and seeing that they learned from books."

"So what our daddy say to that?"

"Said if he treated any of his children less than any other, then what kind of father could he be to any of us? 'I fathered all of you,' he said, and said he was responsible for each and every one of us, regardless of who the mother was."

We both took a moment before I said in a low voice, "You sorry he feel that way?"

"You asking if I still hate him? I got over that a long while back, Paul."

"What about Cassie and me?" I asked, lower still.

"What about you? I've had to wipe your bottom and wipe your nose, clean you both up when you threw up, clean you up when you messed up, so I've gotten used to you. You're my brother, same as George and Robert, and Cassie's my sister. We might not be able to sit at the same table always, but that shouldn't make a difference with us."

"Hammond, how I'm feeling, it's not just about sitting at the table. It's that I'm my daddy's colored son, and that's how everybody sees me. White folks don't think I'm as good as you are, and there're some colored folks think I think I'm better than they are. When I go places with our daddy, he doesn't say, 'This is my son Paul.' He doesn't own up to me outside of this place, even though everybody knows I'm his. He makes different rules for his white children and his colored children. He talks about treating us the same, but we're different and he's the same as anyone else in treating us that way."

"What you expect him to do? Go against the law, break all the rules to claim you as his son? That wouldn't do anybody any good. He break all the social taboos, he might as well pack up and leave this state."

"Well, he didn't mind breaking any taboos when he started sleeping with my mama."

"You've got to understand, Paul, that wasn't really a taboo, just something that wasn't discussed in polite society."

"Taboo or not, it makes me different. Cassie and me both."

"So what?" Hammond questioned. "George, Robert, Cassie, you, me, we're all different in our way, but we're still family."

"And what about when I get full grown?"

"What do you mean?"

"Will we still be family then? Can I sit at your table then?"

My brother shook his head. "I don't know, Paul. The world's not made that way, and it's hard for me to imagine it ever will be much different than now, so I'm not going to lie to you and promise you what I can't. All I can say is I truly don't know if you'll sit at my table openly or if I'll sit at yours, but I can promise you'll always be my family. You and Cassie too. I won't deny you or myself that."

I thought on his words. "Know what the preacher was speaking on at church this past Sunday?"

"What's that?"

"How Peter said he'd never deny Jesus either."

"You comparing yourself to Christ?"

I shook my head. "No. Just saying that when it suits a body, anybody can deny anybody, blood or not."

After Hammond and I parted, I walked the woods alone for some time and finally made my way home as dusk began to fall. Home was my mama's house. There was a vegetable garden in the back and a flower garden in front. The house was small and there were only two rooms to it. One was a bedroom that my mama and Cassie had shared. The larger room contained the kitchen, my bed, and the living area. Robert was often at the house as we went about our play and adventures. George and Hammond never came to the house, and my daddy only stopped by occasionally. He never stayed long and I don't recall his ever spending the night. I stopped in the yard and didn't go in right away. The kerosene lamp in the front window was already lit. I knew my mama was waiting for me.

I wasn't ready to face her yet.

I leaned against the old pecan tree that dominated the yard and gazed at my mama's house, thinking on what was between my mama and my daddy. Everybody knew that my mama was my daddy's housekeeper and cook, and he paid her for it. But she was more than his housekeeper and cook, and everybody knew that too. Yet my mama and daddy never flaunted what was between them. I never saw them hold each other. I never saw them show open affection. But there were tender moments between them that I did see, tenderness in the way they looked at each other, tenderness in the way their voices softened in their concern for each other and in their concern for Cassie and me. When there was only family present, my mama spoke frankly to my daddy and sometimes she spoke sharply to him too, as a wife might. But she never sat at his dining table. She said she was there to serve his table, not to sit at it, though I think she was more concerned about how it would look to others if she sat at his table. People hearing that Edward Logan's children of color sat at his table was one thing. A colored woman with her children sitting at his table would have been another; that would have been too bold.

Still, there were times when my mama and daddy did sit together, though not at meals. Sometimes when my daddy came into the kitchen, he would sit at the table and talk to my mama as she worked, and sometimes she would stop her work and join him. She would pour my daddy a cup of coffee or a glass of lemonade or such, and one for herself too, and they would talk of the farm or of my daddy's business or of us children. Though my mama sat with my daddy, I never saw her set a meal for the two of them. Whatever meals they shared together, they shared alone.

I thought on the life my mama and my daddy had made together and the life they had made for Cassie and me. I thought on Hammond and what he had said. I thought on his mother too. I considered how my life would have been if I had had a colored daddy. Boys like Mitchell and R.T. would have been more accepting of me, and I wouldn't have felt so much hurt about not sitting at Edward Logan's table when company came, for I would never have been invited to sit there in the first place. But then I thought about the fact that if my daddy had been a man of color, I wouldn't have had George and Hammond and Robert as my brothers. I thought on a lot of things about my life and in the end decided I had a right to be angry. I had a right to be angry at both my mama and my daddy. I took that anger into the house with me.

I found my mama sitting in her rocker, a splendid rocker made by a man up in Macon, the same man with whom my daddy said he was sending me to study. My daddy had given my mama the rocker. As I entered, my mama glared at me. "You think you grown now?" she asked.

"Ma'am?" I answered.

"You think you grown? I told you not to leave that porch."

"I know you did . . . but I couldn't stay there—"

"And why not?"

I turned on her. "I expect you know."

My mama's voice grew tight. "I knew, I wouldn't be asking you."

"Well, then," I said, feeling my near to twelve-year-old manhood, "maybe you ought to be asking that white man you lying with—"

Now, I was feeling bad about all my angry thoughts against my mama, blaming her for being with my daddy. There was a part of me too that resented the fact that I was not like my brothers, born to their white mother. If I had been, then I could have always sat at my daddy's table and socialized with my daddy's friends. I would have been accepted. Even as I had those thoughts, I felt a mighty guilt, for I loved my mama. Though we clashed because of all my resentment, I wouldn't have given her up for anything. I was all conflicted, and I suppose that's what made me speak the way I did to her, and I was mad at myself for doing so.

But I was no match for my mama about being mad. She jumped up from that rocker quicker than lightning and grabbed the leather strap hanging by the fireplace. "Let me tell you something, boy," she said in a voice I'd never heard from her. "I was your mama when I bore you, I was your mama to you all your eleven years, and I'll be your mama to you 'til I die, and, what's more, I'll be your mama to you 'til *you* die!" Then she laid into me with that strap. I was taller than she was by now, stronger too, and I could have ripped the strap from her hands, but I would never have disrespected my mama in that fashion. Instead, I moved quick, so she only got a few licks on me; still, she kept on flailing that strap. I supposed it was the principle of the thing with her. I had disobeyed her, I had disrespected her, and she wouldn't tolerate that. After all, as she said, she always had been, and always would be, my mama, and I knew that was true. There was no changing that, and in truth, I didn't want to. I remember that whipping in particular, because that was the last time my mama whipped me.

The next day and the days that followed, I refused to eat in my daddy's house. In fact, I wouldn't even enter his house, not even to see my mama. But after a week my daddy changed that. He ordered me back to his table. "You might not like it," he said to me, "but when I sit down to supper with just my family, I expect all my children on this place to be sitting down at the table with me."

"Can't make me," I said.

"I'm your daddy," he said. "You want to test me on what I can do?"

Needless to say, I sat at my daddy's table, but I never forgot why I had been sent from it.

By the time I was dealing with all my realizations about my two families, my sister, Cassie, had moved to Atlanta and was married. At first she had gone to school there, and later she met Howard Milhouse. After their marriage when Cassie was seventeen, she and her husband, who was nearly some ten years older, set up a little store and they were now living in back of it. Since Cassie had married, she had come home only a few times, and I missed her terribly. After that day I'd gotten so upset about not being allowed at my daddy's table, I wrote to her and told her my thoughts, for I figured only she could truly understand how I felt. Cassie didn't write back; she came instead.

"You know, Cassie," I said when we were alone, "there are times I don't feel good about our mama . . . I mean, for being with a white man."

"You're talking as if you think she had a choice about the thing."

I was silent.

"Paul, she was his property, just like everything else around here."

"Well . . . I know at first she didn't have much of a say—"

"*Much* of a say? What about *no* say?"

"But that was nearly twenty years ago, before you were born. Why'd she keep on being with him after we were free? What's she doing with him now?"

"You ever thought maybe it's because she loves him? Besides, it's her life now."

"I asked her once, you know."

"Asked her what?"

"If she loved him, and if she didn't, then why'd she stay with him?"

"And what she tell you?"

"Said she supposed she did love him and, besides, if she ran off and took me with her, he'd come after us."

"Don't you think he would?"

I shrugged. "I suppose."

"He's our daddy, Paul."

"Well, sometimes I wish he wasn't. She raised his family, both sides of it, and what does she have to show for it? This house and this little bit of ground he lets her stay on, while she's still up there taking care of his big house and him."

Cassie studied me before she spoke again. "Paul, you're sounding awfully resentful."

"Got a right to be. I been picked on all my life 'cause of him and her, and don't tell me you don't know how it feels."

"I'll tell you this, little brother. I won't stand for you disrespecting either one of them, not our daddy, not our mama."

I met her eyes and looked away.

"Now, what they done and what they feel, it's their business and they live with it. All I figure we need to concern ourselves with is that they've been good to us and they've taken care of us, both of them. They love us." She waited, as if expecting me to say something to that. When I didn't, she spoke again, her voice sounding a bit harsh. "Don't you think your mama loves you, Paul? Boy, look at me! Don't you think your mama loves you?"

"Course."

"What about your daddy? Don't you think your daddy loves you?"

"I suppose . . ."

"You suppose? Why else you think he did what he did for us? You expect he would have brought us up like he did, taking us into his house, bringing us up with Hammond and George and Robert, if he didn't care about us? You think he would've seen to it we wore clothes as good as our brothers' and that we never went raggedy or hungry? What they ate, we ate too. You forgetting that? You think our daddy would have seen to our book learning, even teaching us himself how to read and write and figure, when it was against the law and he could have been jailed for it, if he didn't care about us? I suppose his taking you all around with him, same as he does Hammond, George, and Robert, so you can learn how to handle business, same as them, that's because he doesn't care about you either!"

"I never said he didn't care," I mumbled.

"Well, you've said just about that."

"Well, maybe it would have been better if our daddy hadn't treated us so well. Maybe it would have been better if we'd grown up hating him and Hammond and George and Robert rather than caring about them. Maybe then I wouldn't feel like I do, like our daddy put a big shiny box all wrapped out there in front of us, making us feel we were the same as his white boys, then just when we reached to open it up, he snatched it away."

"You know what?" said Cassie. "Maybe you're right. Maybe our daddy has made us feel too special, too accepted. I grew up on this place feeling pretty good about who I was and figuring I'd do all right if I ever left here. Then I went off to Atlanta and found I couldn't hardly find a place to fit there until I met Howard. That must have been our daddy's fault. You know our daddy had me staying with that colored preacher and his family, but they weren't accepting of me because I was too white. They treated me nice enough, but they never really warmed to me. I was always a stranger, as far as they were concerned, and they treated me that way. They never treated me like family. In fact, as soon as I'd walk into a room, they'd stop their talking and have little to say to me. Other colored folks weren't that polite. They'd talk about me behind my back and in front of my face too. Things were really awkward and it didn't help matters that our daddy would show up whenever he was in Atlanta.

"Then there were those times the white folks mistook me for white and would act really friendly until they found out who I was. Then they treated me like a leper, worse than they'd have treated a person obviously of color. It was like they had contaminated themselves by treating me the same as one of them. I was trapped there, Paul, between two worlds, a white one and a black one, and neither one accepting me. I even passed a few times—"

"*You what?*"

"Yes, that's right, I did it!" she declared defiantly. "And you know why? Just so I could feel good about myself again! Just so somebody would be accepting of me. I'd walk into stores or in the white part of the city and folks would treat me with respect, white folks and colored folks too, because they thought they knew who I was. That respect they showed, it made me feel good for the moment, but it was all false because it was for who they thought I was, not for who I really am, Cassie Logan. I was miserable, and I was just like you. I got to blaming our mama and our daddy for my misery. Well, not so much our mama, but our daddy. I blamed him for treating me like I was somebody, like I would be treated the same away from this place as he'd treated me here. I was his daughter, but I could never be a part of his world off this place. I was pretty bitter the way I turned my resentment on him, and every time he came to see me, I let him know it too. Then I met Howard at a church social."

"Talking about me?" Howard Milhouse had come in the back door. He had a broken bridle in his hands. Howard was a good-looking young man of medium height and yellow-hued skin. He was quiet-spoken, yet a perfect match to Cassie's outspokenness. Cassie said that in any dispute Howard would sit back quietly while she ranted her views, and once she was tired of talking to herself, he would settle the argument with just a few words spoken. The two of them smiled at each other as only lovers do, and I was happy for my sister.

"Just looking for some leather to tie this together," he said, holding out the bridle. "Figured maybe I could mend it."

Howard liked to keep busy when he came, and was always looking for something to do. He couldn't sit idle. Maybe that's what made him such a good businessman.

"I was just telling Paul about when I first went to Atlanta," said Cassie. "About how folks treated me up there."

Howard nodded as he looked through an open tin of odds and ends my mama kept on a shelf. "You tell him that's how we come to meet?"

"Told him where we met. At that church social."

Howard glanced back at Cassie. "But you didn't tell him why I got my courage up and came over to talk to you?"

"Well, no. I didn't go into all that."

"Well, Paul," said Howard, still looking through the tin, "there were some ladies who were saying some unkind things about our Cassie—mean little jealous kinds of things. They weren't saying them *to* Cassie, but within her hearing. I took one look at Cassie, and I knew she was about to explode. So, before hair got to flying and clothes got to ripping right there in the Lord's house, I went over and started talking to her. I calmed her down and got her out of there."

"He did that, all right," confirmed Cassie, "and just in time too. I was about to let those girls have it, Lord's house or not, 'cause of what they were saying about our mama and our daddy and how I came to be."

"Lucky for me you did come to be," said Howard with a grin, then held up a piece of leather string he'd found in the tin as if it were a prize, and went back out.

"I like him," I said.

Cassie smiled. "So do I."

"Things are better for you now in Atlanta, right?"

"Oh, yes. Not perfect, but better. Folks who don't know about me still shy away if they're colored, and if they're white, I don't try to pass. It's always awkward with them, but they're the ones who have to live with it. Now I've got Howard and his family, and they love me and I love them. Folks are getting to know who I am, and I've made friends."

I nodded. "Still, what you had to go through, the way I'm being treated now, if our mama and daddy hadn't been together, things would be different."

"Yeah, a whole lot different," Cassie agreed with a laugh. "We wouldn't be here!"

I didn't laugh. I frowned at her. "You know what I mean."

Cassie studied me. "When you were a little boy, you never thought this way."

"When I was a little boy, I still had a lot to learn."

"And you still do. You've got a lot to learn about a man and a woman and what goes on between them. You've got a lot to learn about love and and how folks show it. Kisses and hugs aren't all there is when folks are raising their younguns. Spankings and scoldings are about it too. Just because you've had to go up against a few fists over the years doesn't give you the right to blame all your troubles on our mama and our daddy and to go judging them. Didn't give me the right either. I figure they've done what they could, and I'm not faulting them for anything anymore. I've gotten past that."

"I thought you would have understood."

"I understand, all right. I understand you're angry right now because the world doesn't seem to be treating you right. I understand too that anger you've got will pass one day, and maybe then you can see what I see."

"Well, Cassie, I'll tell you this true," I said, meeting my sister's eyes.

"And what's that, Paul?"

"I ever have a daughter, I'll never let her take up with a white man. I never will." I said that, and I've kept that opinion.

"Could be that's the best thing," said my mama. Cassie and I both turned; neither of us had heard her come in. "Long as you talking about me and your daddy, I'm going to tell you a couple of things. First off, I'm not going to apologize to you or nobody else 'bout my life. There's folks who talk about me behind my back, but then grin in my face when they see me coming. I might've been too young to know much of anything what I really wanted when I came into my womanhood but what happened; still, though, I been with one man ever since, and that man has been good to me and to my children. All those folks talking behind my back can't say the same."

Cassie got up and went over to her. "We didn't mean any disrespect, Mama," she said.

I kept my silence.

My mama looked at me. "No matter." She turned slightly as Cassie put her arm around her shoulders. "I'm glad you come home, Cassie. I'm glad I've got both my children here together. There's things I wanna tell you case anything happen to me."

"What do you mean?" Cassie asked. "Something the matter, Mama?"

Now I got up. "Are you sick?"

My mama shook her head. "Just want you to know some things. Y'all all I got, and what little I got belongs to you."

I remember my mama left us then and went off to her room, and when she returned, she was carrying a blue wooden box decorated with bright paintings of all kinds of flowers. She sat down with that box in her hands in the rocker my daddy had given her. She placed the box on her lap and held it close, but she didn't open it. "Old Josh made this box for me," she said softly. "You know, he was like a daddy to me."

Cassie and I both nodded, even though we had never known Old Josh, for he had died before either of us was born.

"All these years I been putting my treasures in it, and that includes whatever little money I could save. You know, ever since I was a girl and first had you, Cassie, I was earning me a little money of my own, not much, but a few pennies here and there, doing extra work. Then that war came and there wasn't much money for anybody, but after that, when things started settling down again, I began receiving wages for keeping your daddy's house and cooking. I also had my garden and a crop of my own. Had some hens and guineas and such, and I sold their eggs in town. Your daddy was always taking care of you, but I done my share as well. It wasn't just your daddy buying all your things. It's not much, but mostly I been saving what pennies I could so there would be something for us, case we need it. Your daddy, he's been good to us, but I never figured to depend on any man. I figured it best I have something of my own.

"Now, that little money I saved, it's right in here." My mama patted the lid of the box. "Another thing in here is a big old watch and chain your daddy gave me long time ago, before the war. He taught me to tell time on it, same while he was teaching me to read and write and figure. Paul, I want that for you. There's a gold locket he gave me, and that's for you, Cassie. Got some other bits and ends in here, things my sweet mama, Emmaline, made me, things not worth anything 'cept to me—little straw bag, a handkerchief she sewed me, a seed bracelet Old Josh made for me when I was little—that sort of thing."

She rubbed her hand across the box. "You know, I never knew my own daddy, 'cause he wasn't bound to nobody like my mama was. He was from the Nation, and he went off with his people. But anyway, Old Josh was pretty much my daddy, and, like I said, he made this box for me. He painted the flowers on it, even put the lock on. He made it for me soon after I came into my womanhood and your daddy started coming around. He told me not to cry about it and to lock my thoughts and my tears and my treasures inside this box. I've done that ever since."

My mama looked at us then, and her voice was soft. "You know I've always wanted both of you to have something of your own. Cassie, you've got your husband, and soon there'll be babies on the way. You've got the beginnings of a good life with

Howard and your store and all. I don't worry about you. Paul, you still got your deciding what you want. There's time enough. But whatever you decide on, I want you to have something of your own. That's important. You gotta have something of your own." She rubbed her hand across the box once more, then rose and took it away without ever opening it.

Betrayal

When the fall came, my daddy, true to his word, sent both Robert and me off to school. He sent Robert to the boys' school in Savannah and me to Macon, where I could go to a colored school and study furniture making. He took me himself. On the journey my daddy said to me, "This man I'm taking you to, he's a decent man, but don't expect him to treat you the same as I do. He's already told me he'll keep you as long as you do the work and don't cause any trouble. He said too he doesn't want you around his family. He's got three girls, and I know that's what's on his mind, so you stay clear of them. Worst thing you could ever do is to go eyeing a white girl."

I looked at my daddy, thinking he had done just the opposite to my mama.

"You understand me, Paul?" he asked.

"Yes, sir."

"You'll be able to go to school and learn a trade as long as you follow his rules, so you make sure you do. It might not be the best living conditions for you, but you'll learn plenty from this man. He's a man of few words, but you listen to everything he says."

My daddy was right. Josiah Pinter was a man of few words, but every word he uttered was direct and to the point. "I know about you," he said when my daddy was gone. "I know about you and your daddy. He never spoke it to me, but folks know, and if a man wants to do that sort of thing, that's his business long as it doesn't get in the way of mine. I've done a lot of business with your daddy, but you lay one eye on any one of my girls, I'll have your hide, your daddy notwithstanding. That understood?"

I looked him straight in the eyes. "It's understood."

He nodded. "You smart as I hear you are, we ought to get along just fine." Then he put me to work.

Now, my daddy was right about another thing: Josiah Pinter certainly did know his trade, and he wasn't stingy in teaching it to me. I put in my morning hours of school each day, and the rest of the daylight hours I studied under Josiah Pinter. He worked me hard and he worked me long, and my school studying had to wait until the late hours after Josiah Pinter had retired for the night. I slept in the shed behind his house and I ate alone; but the man treated me fair. He was one of the best furniture makers around, and I learned what I was sent to learn. I figured I didn't need to sit at his table.

I was a quick study, and I soon was making lamp tables and other small pieces of furniture. In fact, before I left Josiah Pinter's tutorage, I could make just about anything. I had a knack for looking at something and figuring out how to put it together, whether I had been taught how to do it or not. I was still considered an apprentice, but folks said my work was of journeyman quality, and some even said it was more than that. I did well in my school studies too, even though I wasn't decided on how I was going to put all my book learning to use. I was told I could teach or I could go into some kind of colored business, but the truth about the thing was that I wasn't sure what I really wanted. I still had to figure that out.

Though my sleep was little with all the studying and work I had to do, I had no complaints about that; I didn't need that much sleep and I was learning much, both in school and with the carpentry. What bothered me, though, was one of Josiah Pinter's daughters— his middle daughter, girl called by the name of Jessie—and the way she was always looking at me and following me around when her daddy wasn't near. Now, I was coming into my teenage years and this girl Jessie was doing the same, and even though her daddy had told her I was a colored boy, she seemed not to care.

"Doesn't make sense to me," she said. "You're a person, I'm a person. Why can't we be friends?"

I said nothing to that. I didn't want to take the time to tell her.

When I went back home and Robert was there, I told him about Jessie and how she was always trying to talk to me, even though her daddy had said she shouldn't.

"You think she's trying to get you in trouble?" Robert asked. "You know, some girls do that."

"No. No, I don't think that," I answered.

"Well, then, you just got to tell her what'll happen to you if she doesn't stop it," advised Robert. "Tell her exactly what her daddy told you. That he'll have your hide."

I nodded but didn't say anything.

Robert studied me. "Or maybe you like her talking to you?'

"She's been the only friend I've made there."

"Believe me," said Robert, "last thing you need is a white female friend. Why, I've heard stories at school that'd make you puke. Some of those fellas love to talk about what their families have done to Negroes like they were talking about going fishing. One of those boys told me about how his daddy and kin caught a Negro near the outhouse when a white woman was in there.

The Negro, he said he was just passing through the field, but the woman came out and said he was peeping at her through the boards, and you know they strung him up right then and there! That's what they'll do, Paul. You looking white won't stop that, they know you got colored in you. That white boy, he bragged on hanging that man and he laughed about it too. That's what they'll do, all right, so, Paul, you be careful with that girl."

I nodded. Robert was quiet a few moments, then said, "You know, I told you Christian and Percy Waverly go to school up there with me. They go along with the rest of those boys' talk about colored folks."

"Yeah?"

"Yeah, they got their stories too."

"Not surprised."

"Well, me neither. . . . Thing is, though . . . they know about you . . . and sometimes they give me a hard time about it."

"What they do?"

"Mainly they talk about our daddy and say how our whole family cotton to Negroes." Robert moved away from me then, and though I hated to admit it, he seemed embarrassed.

"You let them just talk about our daddy?" I questioned.

Robert turned quickly. "Course not! Gotten into more than one fight 'cause of what they said!"

Now it was I who studied him. "You tell our daddy?"

"What for? He'd figure for me to take care of the Waverlys myself, just like you had to do that time about Mitchell and those other boys. Thing is, though, that school is hard enough as it is, and it just makes things worse for them to go around spreading their stories the way they do."

"I suppose things aren't all that good for either one of us right now," I said.

Robert agreed. "Wish we could've both just stayed here."

"I know. But, Robert . . . I don't figure that'll ever be again."

I took Robert's advice about Jessie Pinter, and when I went back
to Macon, I told her the story Robert had told me. I told her
stories too that I hadn't heard from Robert, but were stories that
were spoken in low voices in the fields and around late-night
fires. I told that girl Jessie that if she thought of me as her
friend, then she needed just to leave me alone. I was there to
study and learn, not there to be friends with anybody. She listened to me and turned away, and made a point from then on of
speaking to me only when necessary.

During this time I was staying in Macon, I got to go home
about once every couple of months. My daddy, George, or
Hammond, if they were home, or sometimes a field hand who
worked my daddy's land, would come to get me. That first year I
was away, I was always looking forward to going home because
I was so homesick. My daddy always tried to arrange for Robert
and me to come home at the same time, and when we saw each
other, we would talk the night away, filling each other in on all
that was happening in our lives. When the summertime came
after the first year, Robert got to spend the whole summer at
home, but I could only stay a few days at a time because of my
apprenticing. But then there came a long string of weeks that I
couldn't go home at all. Josiah Pinter said there was too much
work to be done, and he needed me. He wrote my daddy and
said he'd bring me down himself as soon as the work let up.
Well, Josiah Pinter did take me home, but by the time he did,
Robert had gone back to school, and I didn't hear from him regular like I had the school year before. He wrote only once, a
short letter, and said his schoolwork kept him busy. When I finally did see Robert again, he filled me in on the Waverlys. "You
know they lost their mama a month or so back."

"Yeah?"

"They were out of school for a few weeks."

"Well, you weren't writing, so I didn't know. Were they any better when they came back?"

"'Bout the same."

"Then they're still giving you a hard time."

"Oh, they're not so bad," said Robert.

"What do you mean, not so bad? What's not so bad about them?"

"Well . . . I mean they just regular fellas."

"Regular fellas?" I stared at my brother, then murmured, "Uh-huh," in a way we both understood. Robert looked at me too and turned away. We said no more about the Waverlys.

The next time I got to go home, it was Christmas Eve and Josiah Pinter again took me. My daddy wasn't on the place when I arrived, but would be coming soon. Cassie and Howard were expected, and George and Hammond too. It was going to be a grand Christmas. I was told Robert was already home. "Well, where is he?" I asked my mama.

My mama looked at me as if she wasn't too happy about my asking about Robert. "He went off with them Waverly boys."

"Waverly?" I questioned. "Percy and Christian?"

"They the ones. Came home from school with Robert two days ago." Her eyes narrowed as she looked at me. "Ain't Robert told you they were coming?"

I shook my head. "I haven't heard from him for a spell."

My mama sighed. "Well, anyways, they here."

I was puzzled. "Now, why would he bring them home? He doesn't even like those boys."

"Well . . . things change," said my mama. "Robert wanted to invite them here, and your daddy thinking on them losing their mama this year, he gone ahead and invited their daddy and that younger boy too. Gonna be a lotta menfolks round here this Christmas." She looked pointedly at me. "Hope Robert can find time for you."

"Now, what you mean by that?"

My mama started to speak, then turned away to busy herself with something. "Go on and look for him if you want. That's what's on your mind."

That *was* what was on my mind, so I left my mama straight-away and went to find Robert. I ended up running into Mitchell instead. "Heard you was comin' home," he said.

"Just got back. How you doing?"

"Same as always. How long you here for?"

"Through the New Year."

"Well, that's probably longer than me."

"What you mean?"

"I'm finished with this place. I'm movin' on."

"Yeah?" I said, somewhat surprised. No matter what Mitchell's and my differences, no matter how my thinking had begun to change over the years, I still figured this land was home to both of us. "So, where you going?"

Mitchell shrugged. "Don't know yet. Just figure t' go." At that point Mitchell turned, looking a ways off, and I noticed there was a swelling on the side of his face.

"You been fighting again?" I said, not fearing to speak my mind to Mitchell any longer.

Mitchell looked back at me. "Could say that."

I grinned. "Other fella look worse, I expect."

"Naw," said Mitchell. "I ain't even hit him."

I didn't say anything to that. Mitchell looked at me in an un-derstanding. It was no secret Willie Thomas, too often to my figuring, took a whip to Mitchell. He was known to put a whip to his other seven children as well, and even to his wife. Though I had no love for Mitchell, I had asked my daddy once if he could put a stop to Willie's beatings, but my daddy said no. "That's their business," he said. "Before the war, maybe I would've gotten into it, but now I figure I've got no place in a man's private affairs. Willie's a good worker and I've got no quarrel with him. He runs his family and I run mine."

"Well, I've got t' get goin'," said Mitchell, turning his back to me.

"I don't see you tomorrow, have a good Christmas."

"Yeah . . ." said Mitchell, glancing over his shoulder at me. "You too."

When I first started looking for Robert, it was about midday, so I figured Robert and the Waverlys would be back to my daddy's house for dinner, but they weren't. My daddy was there now, and Mr. Waverly and Jack were with him. I greeted my daddy, then waited on the veranda for Robert. When dinner was served without him and the other two Waverly boys, I went looking for him again. I finally caught up with him, Christian, and Percy walking on a road off our place headed toward home. They had the Appaloosa with them. The Appaloosa's head was bent, there was foam on his coat, and he was breathing hard. Christian held the reins. I didn't even speak to Robert as I hurried over to Appaloosa. "What happened?" I said. I tried to pat the Appaloosa's head, but he reared back, and Christian dropped the reins. I grabbed them, then, talking softly to the animal, I tried to calm him down. "It's me, Appaloosa. It's me, Paul," I said. I didn't have any apple wedges in my pocket, so I just backed him away from the others, talked gently to him, stroked him, then took the chance of laying my head and my chest against him so he could feel me breathing as he breathed.

Christian and Percy laughed. "What the hell are you doing?" Christian asked.

I ignored them. I closed my eyes, holding the horse's head against mine. Appaloosa's breathing was short and hurried at first, but finally it steadied and calmed.

The Waverlys were still laughing when I opened my eyes and asked again what happened. When Robert didn't say anything,

Christian spoke up in his stead. "So, Robert, this is the way y'all teach your niggers to greet folks?"

"I . . . I told you," said Robert to Christian, "we don't use that word."

"Why not? A nigger by any other name . . . but what the hell! We're guests here and we'll try to respect that, won't we, Percy?"

"Most certainly," agreed his brother.

"Robert," I said, ignoring the Waverlys, "what's happened to Appaloosa here?" Now, Robert and I over the years had discussed giving our horse a name, but I loved the sound of the word "Appaloosa" and how it rolled off the lips. I also loved the image of the West and the Appaloosas, and their name had come out of the West. Since the horse was more mine than Robert's—for Robert had never once mounted the Appaloosa since the day we'd won him on the bet—he had gone along with calling him whatever I chose. So we simply called him Appaloosa. "Robert?" I said, when he said nothing, but then Appaloosa neighed as if to answer my question himself. I turned back to him, patted his sweaty coat, and for the first time saw the blood. I looked again at Robert and the Waverlys. "What's this?"

"What you think?" said Percy.

I bit hard on my lower lip, trying to control my anger. "Looks like he's been whipped."

Percy sneered. "Yeah, what of it?"

I turned to Robert. "You tell me what happened!"

"Well . . . nothing, Paul . . . nothing much really," Robert managed, acting himself a bit skittish.

"What do you mean, nothing? Who's been riding him?"

"I rode him," answered Christian boastfully. "So did Percy. First time he's been ridden in a spell by someone knows how."

I glared at Christian, then back at Robert with disbelief. "You let them ride Appaloosa?"

"Well . . . yeah . . . why not? He was theirs once, you know."

"Yeah, once! They didn't know how to ride him then, and they don't know how to ride him now! Just look at Appaloosa!"

"Hey!" cried Percy to Robert. "You just going to let him talk to you this way?"

"I'll talk to him, you, or your brother any way I please!" I spat out angrily. "What you do to this horse? How could you ride him down this way? Use a whip on him? Robert! How could you be so stupid as to ever let a Waverly ride my Appaloosa?"

"*Your* Appaloosa?" said Robert.

"*Stupid?*" exclaimed Christian. "Boy, you calling a white man stupid?"

"You got no need to call me names, Paul!" Robert said sharply.

"Well, what else you call it?" I shot right back. "Look at this horse!"

"Robert, you gonna let this boy talk that way to you?" Percy cried again.

"You don't do something about this smart-talking white nigger, I will!" vowed Christian.

Robert didn't object to the word this time. I took note of that, then turned with Appaloosa and headed off the road into the forest. "Where you going?" Robert demanded.

"What do you care?" I retorted. "You can't ride Appaloosa yourself, so I reckon you don't much care how he's treated or where he goes."

"You leave that horse here!" ordered Robert.

I stopped and looked back at him. "What for? So you and these two other fools can beat him to death?"

"That's it!" cried Christian, and sprang toward me.

Robert grabbed Christian's arm, stopping him. "Paul!" he said. "You watch your mouth!"

I just looked at Robert, then went on with Appaloosa.

"Paul—don't you turn your back on me!"

"Robert Logan, what kind of white man are you?" asked Christian. "You do something about this nigger, or I swear—"

Robert raced after me and yanked me by my arm. "I said to stop!"

"You stop!" I said, and jerked away. I glared at Robert; he glared at me. I took them all in with my gaze, then turned once more toward the forest. This time Robert took hold of my arm with his left hand and, with his right, hit me a sharp uppercut to my jaw. I stumbled backward, dropping the reins. I hadn't expected Robert to hit me. I knew he was mad, and so was I, but we'd been mad at each other before, though not in front of strangers. We'd fought each other before, but not in front of strangers. That's what made this time different. Always before, we'd put our differences aside and stood together when it came to outsiders. Not now.

At first Robert seemed stunned that he'd hit me. Then he came at me again with a vengeance and knocked me to the ground with a wild rage, flailing at me. I gathered my senses, rolled him off, and let him have it, brother or not. I was in a rage too, far greater than I'd ever been, more than I had been with Mitchell or R.T. or any of the others. Robert had turned on me, and it was a hurt more than I could bear. I slammed at Robert with a fury.

The Waverlys pulled me off Robert, and then they began to beat at me themselves, the two of them. All the times I'd had to fight Mitchell came in handy now. Though I was smaller than Christian, I managed a hard punch to both him and Percy, then slipped from their grasp. Holding my stomach with one hand, I grabbed Appaloosa's reins with the other and dashed into the forest. The Waverlys ran after me, but I knew the forest; they didn't. I slipped onto hidden trails and left them behind.

Finally, when I knew I had lost them, I made my way to the creek with Appaloosa. I took him right into the middle of the water and let him drink. When he'd gotten his fill, I took off his saddle and laid it aside on the bank. Then I took off my own bloodied shirt, dipped it in the water, and bathed him down, minding his wounds. "Don't you worry," I told him. "I get you back to the barn and put some salve on you, you'll be good as new." Appaloosa heard my words and neighed as if he understood. I made sure he had some comfort, then tended to my own wounds.

By the time I led Appaloosa back to the stables, the sun was setting in a gray winter's sky. I returned carrying the saddle, with Appaloosa trailing me. My daddy was standing in front of the barn. Mr. Waverly was there too, along with Christian, Percy, and Jack. Robert stood with them. Inside the barn Mitchell and his daddy were tending to the horses. As I neared, I saw that my daddy was tightly holding a strap doubled up in his hand. His knuckles were white.

My daddy looked at Appaloosa. "What happened to him?"

"Ask Christian."

"I'm asking you."

I glanced over at Robert and Christian. "Robert let Christian and Percy ride him, and this is how they rode him."

My daddy didn't even look at the Waverlys; instead, he kept his eyes on Appaloosa and said to me, "He all right?"

"Yes, sir. Except for his markings where he was beaten. He's still bleeding."

"Then let Willie have him. He'll fix him up."

At the mention of his name, Willie Thomas came quickly

from the barn and led the Appaloosa inside. I started to follow, but my daddy stopped me. "No. You stay here." We both watched Willie Thomas as he checked over the Appaloosa; then my daddy turned again to me. "Get those clothes off," he said.

I didn't know what he meant. "Sir?"

"Robert here tells me you hit him. Said you hit Percy and Christian too."

"They hit me."

"I didn't ask you if they hit you," said my daddy. "All I'm interested in knowing about is whether or not you hit them."

"I hit them," I admitted frankly. "But they had it coming. Robert let Christian and Percy ride that Appaloosa, and they—"

My daddy cut me right off. "I don't even want to hear it. Doesn't matter about anything else, about what they did. You've got to learn, Paul, and you've got to learn now, you don't ever hit a white man. Ever."

I stared at my daddy with disbelief and said, "Since when is Robert a man?"

"As of now," said my daddy with finality.

"Then I suppose that makes me a man too," I declared defiantly.

"Not a white man," said my daddy. "You best be remembering, Paul, you're not white, much as you might look it."

"Well, that's not my fault, is it? That's yours and my mama's."

"You leave your mama out of this."

"You didn't."

There was quiet between us. There was quiet all around us. At the back of the barn I could see Mitchell's daddy working on Appaloosa, and even that was quiet. Mitchell stood watching me. The Waverlys were watching me too.

"Paul," my daddy finally said in a voice tight but quiet-sounding, as if he were holding hard on keeping whatever he was feeling inside, "you keep that smart mouth and you're going to end up getting yourself killed. You don't hit a white man and you don't sass a white man. Now, strip down."

"What for?"

"I'm going to teach you a hard lesson and I'm going to teach it to you right now. You get those clothes off, or I'll cut right through them." My daddy said that and unfurled the strap.

I gestured toward Robert. "What about him? Is he getting a whipping too?"

"I'm not worrying about Robert right now," said my daddy. "I'm worrying about you. Now, strip down."

I glanced over at the Waverlys standing there, waiting on my whipping. I looked at Robert too, standing there biting at his lip, the cause of it all, and I said to my daddy, "This isn't fair."

"Who said it was about fair?" My daddy's eyes settled on mine, and I took off the clothes. I stripped bare as they all watched. I stripped bare and felt as I had never felt before, not just naked, but worn and like an old shoe, soleless. My daddy raised his strap, and the strap cut into me good, but I didn't cry out and I let no tears fall. He let the strap fall again and again across my back, and I just stood there in my nakedness gazing out across the land I had once thought was mine, feeling my humiliation and thinking on the family I had once thought was mine. When my daddy finished whipping on me, I slowly picked up my clothing, set my gaze on Robert one final time, then ran off naked into the woods.

I don't know how long I sat alone in those woods. I had dressed, then settled on the creek bank forgetful of time. Darkness was coming on, but I didn't care. I didn't care that my mama was waiting on me and that Cassie and Howard were most likely at the house by now. I didn't care that George and Hammond were probably home too. I didn't care that it was Christmas Eve. After all, it didn't seem like Christmas now. All I had was the darkness. At least it hid my face.

When I saw the lantern coming in the dark, without seeing him, I knew my daddy held it. He walked over to where I sat, and stood before me. The light of the lantern cast a yellow glow over both of us. My daddy set the lantern down, then sat down himself with the lantern between us. He didn't say anything at first, and all there was for a spell were the sounds of the creek, the night wings of the forest, and our own breathing. I started to get up.

"Sit down, Paul."

I sat back down, took a rock, and threw it into the creek. The water splashed, and I threw another. "How'd you know I was here?" I said.

"Don't you think I know where you go on this land?"

I glanced at him, then picked up another rock.

"I know you're angry."

I threw the rock.

"I know you're hating me right now, and I don't blame you for that. But I'm not apologizing for what I did. It's past time you learned these things, and I'd whip you again, twice as hard, if it meant saving your life."

"What life?" I asked. "Walking around every day kowtowing to white folks, even my own brother?"

"If that's what it takes."

I grunted.

"I suppose you think it's easy for me to say that."

"Isn't it?"

"Well, I can't say how it feels to be a colored man. All I can say is how it feels to be the father of one, and I'm telling you, it's an uneasy feeling."

I looked hard at him now. "It was easy enough for you to whip me in front of everybody."

"You think it was? Well, it wasn't." He breathed hard, in a sigh. "All your life I've protected you. Don't you know that? But I just can't protect you in the same way I do Robert, George, and Hammond. I know how white men treat colored men, how white folks treat colored folks, and I know maybe I've been wrong in not making you understand earlier that the way I treat you is not the way every white man is going to treat you."

"I expect I know that already."

"Maybe you know it, but I've always been around to protect you. I know there were some things I've been wrong about in the way I've brought up you and Cassie, but I've tried to do the best I could by you. I've whipped you for doing wrong before. They were always whippings meant to teach you something, make you remember not to do it again. Difference today was I not only wanted you to remember that whipping, but to think on the fact that no matter how bad that strap hurt you today, what can come to you if you go hitting another white man, not just your brother and his friends, will be worse than that. Son, hitting a white man could cost you your life, and it won't necessarily be an easy death. I've seen men lynched. I've seen men quartered. I've seen men burned." He shook his head. "I'd rather whip you every day of your life and have you hate me every day for the rest of it than see that happen to you."

There was silence again between us, and neither of us hurried to break it. Finally, I said quietly, "Robert was wrong."

"To your thinking."

"He was wrong." I wasn't changing my mind about that.

"Maybe. But don't you see it doesn't matter? Wrong or not, he's white. The way it is, he's of age now, and that's all that matters."

"I've had fights with Robert before."

"That was as children. Children, no matter what color, are allowed to have their squabbles. That's overlooked. Now, though,

Robert's of age, and you can't go around hitting him anytime you feel like it. You should've already known that. A black daddy would have made sure his son understood that before now. I expect I put off too long seeing that you understood it."

I threw my last stone into the water and turned to question him. "But why in front of the Waverlys? Why'd you have to whip me in front of *them*?"

My daddy's eyes met mine in the lantern light. "Because they were here, and the thing is, with their being here, there was nothing else I could do but whip you. I didn't chastise you, then maybe they'd figure they'd take care of you themselves . . . now or down the road. But whether they were here or not, it was time I did what I did just the same."

"Something you wouldn't've done if I was white."

My daddy acceded to that. "I wouldn't have had to. I'm going to tell you something, Paul. I know I've had to bring you up differently from your brothers—you and your sister both—but that's because no matter how much I've tried to bring you all up as much the same as possible, the rest of the country isn't about to accept you as the same. You're a boy of color, and if folks know that, that's how they're going to see you. What I've tried to do is give you something to build on, an education and a trade. But for the rest of it—getting through this world alive— you're going to have to use your head. You've got a good mind, son. You're smart. Maybe too smart. You've got yourself a mind like a steel trap, and that kind of mind for a colored boy could get you in a whole lot of trouble. You're my son, but I don't care how white you look, most white folks in these parts will call you and every other person of color 'nigger,' and to them that's all you are. They don't care how white you look, you sass a white man, you hit a white man, they'll kill you."

I turned away.

"They'll do it," he assured me, "and even if you lived here on this land all your life, white folks come after you, I don't know if even I could stop them from killing you, that's what they had in mind." My daddy put his hand on my shoulder and I winced. If my daddy noticed, he didn't mention it. "Paul, listen and hear what I'm saying. Look at me, boy."

Reluctantly, I did so.

"This here is a white man's country, and long as you stay colored, you'll never get anyplace using your fists. All using your fists'll get you, leastways against a white man, is hanged or worse, if you can think on that. So you best be thinking on putting that steel-trap mind of yours to work. Use your head, Paul-Edward, not your fists. You hear me, boy?"

I stood then without answering and moved away. My daddy got up as well. "You go ahead, you stay angry if you want, but you remember what I said." He waited as if expecting me to say something. I didn't. My daddy hesitated. Then he said, "I was going to give this to you tomorrow, on Christmas Day, but I'm figuring I'd best give it to you now." He pulled a ring from his finger and I knew right away which ring it was. It was made of gold and had one stone at its center. "I've given each of my boys a ring, and this one's for you. It's got meaning to it for me, and I want you to have it now."

"What meaning?" I asked.

"It was my daddy's ring." He held it out to me, but I didn't move to take it. My daddy then took my hand and dropped the ring into my palm.

I looked at my daddy and remained silent.

My daddy accepted the silence with a nod. "You keep the lantern and get on home to your mama and let her see to your back. It'll be Christmas soon."

"I don't need your lantern."

"I expect you do. It'll light your way. And remember, Paul, your head, not your fists." My daddy walked away then, and when he was gone, I started to throw the ring as hard as I could after him. But I thought better of it. I gazed upon the ring. I had seen the ring on my daddy's hand, and it had been worn by his daddy. Now it was mine. I didn't want to think on what that meant, not with my back seared through like it was. For a long while I sat by that creek holding that ring and thinking on what had happened. Finally I slipped the ring into my pocket and blew out the lantern light. I saw Christmas in alone.

❧

It was morning when I went to my mama's house. I was aching all over, and my back was stiff. I could hardly walk. The dawn had just broken, but Cassie was sitting there on the front steps waiting for me. She wore her nightgown still, and she had a shawl around her shoulders. Her arms were folded across her chest, and she was shivering. "So you thought you'd make your mama worry about you all night, huh?" she asked as I approached.

I shrugged off the question and put one to her instead. "How long you been sitting out here?"

"Too long. What's the matter with you, staying away all night? Especially after what I heard happened over at that barn yesterday. Don't you think your mama was worried?"

"Wasn't thinking about her."

"Well, that's right plain. Howard and I got here last night, and Mama was sitting here all by herself, just sitting there in that rocker inside with her Christmas dinner cooking, waiting on you."

"Where is Howard, anyway?" I asked, glancing toward the house.

"Where he's supposed to be!" snapped Cassie. "In bed asleep."

"You ought to be in there with him."

"Well, I'd like to be, but how I'm supposed to sleep with you out wandering those woods on Christmas Eve? I started to come looking for you myself, because I knew where you'd most likely be, but Howard and Mama wouldn't let me go stumbling off in those woods."

"I wouldn't think so. Aren't you supposed to be having a baby?"

"You know I am, and don't go changing the subject. I can still whip your little bottom."

I smiled and sat down on the step beside her.

"How you feel?"

"I'm all right."

"You look terrible. You were walking like an old man."

"Thanks. I feel like one."

Cassie pushed my hair back from my forehead. "From what I heard, our daddy used a strap. He couldn't've done this here. Whose fist landed this punch?"

"Tell the truth, I got whipped on so much yesterday, I've got no idea."

"How's your back?"

"Raw."

"We'd better get some salve on it. Course, it would've been better going on last night."

"Too bad our daddy didn't have Willie Thomas bring out a jar while he was whipping me. Willie could have put some on me same time he was rubbing down Appaloosa with it."

"Yeah," said Cassie with a grin. "Our daddy should've thought of that."

I managed another smile myself, then said, "Cassie, you know why our daddy whipped me, don't you?"

"I heard."

"He said it was for my own good."

"Could be he was right."

"How can you say that? Him whipping me like that?"

"Time had come," said Cassie matter-of-factly. "Time had come for you to get an understanding of who you are. Time came for me when I first went to Atlanta, like I told you."

"That still doesn't excuse what he done. Him or Robert either, and I won't forget."

"Well, that's good." I heard the door creak behind us. I turned and saw my mama standing in the doorway. "That's good you won't forget it."

I got up slowly to face her.

"So you decided to come home, huh?"

"Sorry I worried you."

My mama looked at me long, studying me. "Come on in this house and let me get some salve on your back." She then turned to go back inside.

"That's all you going to say about what happened?" I demanded. "Don't you feel anything about what he did?"

My mama turned to face me again, and her look, followed by her words, I'll never forget. "Yes, Paul, I got something to say about what happened. Fact, I got plenty to say. I'm glad your daddy done it. High time he did too. I been telling you and telling you those brothers of yours are white and you ain't. I been telling you that the day was gonna come when things wouldn't be the same between you and them. I been telling you to watch out for yourself and get yourself something of your own. I been telling you, but you ain't been listening. You wanted to believe in them. I been telling you and telling you, and you been resenting me for it, been resenting me for everything that had to do with your making. I been telling you and telling you. Now the day's come. Merry Christmas."

My mama glared at me, and I could feel her anger. But I knew that anger wasn't all aimed at me. She had tried to protect me, and it was true—I hadn't wanted to listen. She had tried to protect me; now she was suffering right along with me. I could see it in her eyes and hear it in her voice. I stared at her, and I felt the tears coming for the first time. My mama's eyes softened as she stood there looking at me, and when she spoke again, her voice had softened too. "Come on in this house, Paul-Edward," she said as she held the door open for me. "Come on, and let me see to your back."

I slept most of Christmas morning, and so did Cassie. I woke to the sounds of my mama finishing up her Christmas dinner, to the smells of roasted ham and a chicken baking, and to the soft talk of Howard's voice and his genial laughter as he kept my mama company. I was miserably sore and aching, but I rose to join them, and later when Cassie was up, my mama put aside her cooking, and we all joined hands and each of us said our Christmas prayers of thanksgiving. Afterward, we gave our presents to one another. My mama gave me my daddy's watch from the box. "Your daddy told me he gave you his ring. You got his ring now," she said, "you might as well have his watch." She kissed me, then hugged me tenderly and squeezed my hand that held the watch. I put the watch away with the ring.

Now, most Christmases Cassie and I spent part of the day up at my daddy's house, but not this Christmas. This day Cassie and I, along with Howard, stayed at my mama's house. My mama, though, went to my daddy's house to finish cooking dinner up there and serve it to my daddy and my brothers and the Waverlys. She said it was her job. Cassie wanted to go with her to help, but my mama wouldn't let her. "It's my job," she said, "not yours. You don't ever have to work in your daddy's house again." Later on, when my mama returned, we had our own Christmas dinner, Cassie and Howard, our mama, and me. I figured this was all the family I had now.

But George and Hammond wouldn't let me be. The next day after the Waverlys were gone, they came down to my mama's house to talk to me. "It's a shame things got so messed up," said Hammond.

"Bound to happen," surmised George. "Tell me something, Paul. If you had to hit a white boy, why didn't you use the good sense to just hit Robert and not the Waverlys? Maybe our daddy wouldn't've whipped you so bad."

I looked at George. "Would you have just hit Robert?"

"Course not," he answered. "I would've beaten all the little rascals black and blue, but there's the rub of it. It wouldn't have mattered about me. I'm so-called white."

"Spite of everything, Paul," said Hammond, "Robert's real sorry, you know."

"Makes no difference," I said.

"S'pose not. But would it make a difference to you if you knew our daddy wore Robert out right after the Waverlys left?"

"He did?"

"Now, he said the whipping was for letting those fools ride that horse," said George.

"But we know it was for more than that," interjected Hammond. "That's got to mean something to you."

George laughed. "Got to mean even more to know our daddy wore Robert's behind out."

Hammond spoke soberly. "You know, Paul, our daddy always said George, Robert, and I were supposed to look out for you and Cassie because you're our blood. Robert didn't do that, so we figure he not only let you down, but all of us."

After they told me that, I realized it didn't mean a thing to me that Robert had gotten whipped. I still loved my daddy and

George and Hammond, even Robert, I supposed, but I no longer felt a part of them. Robert hadn't been whipped as I had been whipped, just for my being a colored boy. He hadn't been whipped naked in front of strangers. He hadn't suffered the humiliation I had. No, that whipping of his didn't mean a thing.

Before I left, going back to Macon, Robert himself came to see me. "I'm sorry about what happened," he said. "I didn't know our daddy would do that. Whip you like he done, I mean." I just looked at Robert, and he said once more, "I'm sorry." He said that, turned, and walked away.

Robert had made his apology. But things were never the same between us. Robert was sorry and so was I, sorry I had lost my brother and, until the betrayal, my best friend. Robert hadn't said anything about being sorry for turning his back on me. He had turned his back on me, his own brother, because of two white boys, and I couldn't forgive him for that. I was thirteen years old by then, and I figured as long as I lived, I could never forgive him for that.

East Texas

When I got to be fourteen, nearing fifteen, my mama died and my brother George came to get me. There hadn't been any kind of lingering illness with my mama. She'd been feeling just fine the last time I'd seen her, and her death came on sudden. Neither Cassie nor I got to see her in the days before she passed. It was the springtime and the warm weather was coming, and folks, once they passed, had to be buried quick, so my mama was washed in scents and laid out in her own house even before I got back home with George. The wake was held that night, the funeral the next morning.

Now, I remember things real clear about that day we buried my mama. First of all, it was a drizzly, foggy kind of day, kind of day right for a funeral. Cassie was there, of course, with her baby and Howard. Robert was there too, as well as George and Hammond and my daddy, and Robert tried hard after we put my mama in the ground to talk to me, but I wasn't listening. I was feeling alone then, like the only real family I had left was my sister, Cassie. Another thing I remember real clear was a group of colored boys coming over and one of them saying to me, "Well, you not so special now, are ya? Yo' mama's dead and yo' daddy'll be takin' himself up with another colored woman soon enough." Then the boys laughed. Mitchell was there when that boy said that to me and the other boys laughed, and Mitchell hauled off and knocked the boy to the ground. "Watch your mouth" was all he said, and the boy got up rubbing his chin. There was no more laughing from those boys or remarks about my mama after that.

Afterward, when the mourners had left us to ourselves, Cassie, Howard, their baby, Emmaline, and I sat at the table laden with food in my mama's little house. We hadn't eaten much. I hadn't wanted any food, but it was warming to know folks had cared enough to bring it. "You know, Paul," said Howard as he finished his coffee, "you're welcome to come back to Atlanta with us. You don't need to stay here alone."

I nodded and kept my eyes on Emmaline, who was more than a year old now and was jumping as I held her.

Cassie leaned over and put her hand on my arm. "He means that."

"I know." I glanced at Howard. "Thank you," I said, then looked again at Emmaline.

"You see Mama in her?" Cassie asked.

I nodded. "Her eyes . . ."

"Eyes, hair, nose, chin. Boy, she's Mama through and through. Sometimes I think I should have gone ahead and named her Deborah after Mama, but you know Mama asked me to name her Emmaline after her mama. Think I'm going to add Deborah to her name now, though, because every time I look at her, I see Mama." Cassie pulled herself up and began to clear the table. She was pregnant again and expected the new baby in the summer.

"Wait a minute, Cassie," I said, starting to stand. "I'll give you a hand."

"Ah, boy, sit down and play with your niece. You haven't seen her in a while. You need to spend as much time as you can with her."

Then, without Cassie's asking, Howard got up and began to help with the table. It seemed a job he was accustomed to doing, and a job he seemed not to mind. The two of them cleared the dishes and the two of them washed and dried the dishes, all while I played with Emmaline. I got on the floor, lay on my stomach, and let her crawl over my back. I gave her horseback rides, stood and lifted her into the air, and let her fly like a bird in my arms. She giggled and had a great time, unaware of the sadness of the day. I laughed too, but the laughter was only for her.

When Emmaline finally fell asleep and was in her bed for the night, Howard decided to take a walk, and Cassie and I were left alone to comfort each other. "I never told her, Cassie," I said, soon after Howard was gone, "I never told our mama I was sorry for those things I said about her and our daddy . . . you remember."

"I do."

"I was sorry . . . I am sorry . . . but I never told her."

"Mama probably figured you were. You didn't have to say it."

"You were right, you know. I had no business trying to be her judge." I then broke down crying and Cassie held me. She took me into her arms and consoled me like the little mother she'd always been to me.

"No, you didn't," she agreed when my tears subsided and I pulled away. "You were too young to go judging anybody. You know, Mama told us both our daddy was the only one. She'd been with only him, and she told me that was to her as if she'd been his sworn wife."

"You think he cared about that?"

"I don't know. I can't get inside our daddy's head."

"Well, whether he did or he didn't, I know one thing, Cassie. I ever have a daughter, I'll never let her go with a white man."

"You said that before."

"I mean it. There's just too much sorrow to it."

"I suppose," she said, her voice dropping. She sighed and then spoke of other things. "You know that box of Mama's, Paul, the one she showed us a few years back? Well, she had me take it to Atlanta with me last time I was here ... almost like she knew. . . . Anyway, there're things in there belong to you."

"You hold on to them, Cassie. I've got no need for them right now."

"I can bring them next time I come, though I don't know when that'll be, now that Mama's gone. Course, you could come to Atlanta and get them. Honey, Howard and I, we've talked about it. You could stay with us. You're my family, and you know how much I'd love it—"

"I know. I know, Cass. But I figure to stay here, at least for a while." I didn't say it to Cassie then, and I'm not sure why, but I wasn't yet ready to leave my daddy's land. Even though I spent much of my time in Macon, I still considered this place home. "Don't worry about it, Cassie. Just you take care of what Mama wanted me to have."

After some while I left Cassie and went down to the grave-yard to say good-bye to my mama alone, but when I got there, I saw my daddy standing over her grave. His hat was in his hands, and I thought I heard the sound of weeping. Maybe I was wrong about that. Anyhow, I didn't want him to see me, so I backed off and I left. I wanted to say good-bye to my mama alone.

I walked for some while in the misty rain and ended up on the slope that overlooked my daddy's land. I sat down on a stump and surveyed the valley before me. My daddy's house was right below and, beyond the house, the yard and flower garden, and beyond the backyard, the vegetable garden. The stables and the pasture weren't all that far from the house. My daddy always liked to have his horses near. Beyond the pasturelands where the horses and cattle grazed were the forests. The cotton fields could not be seen. They, along with all the sharecropping shanties and the people in them, were on the other side of the woods, hidden from view. So was my mama's house. It was mid-spring, and all the grasses were emerald green and all the plants were in bloom. There was only beauty before me.

It was almost dusk, and I could see lanterns beginning to glow inside my daddy's house. Though it was growing late, I continued to sit in the damp, and I didn't stir until Mitchell happened upon me. He gave me a nod and I returned it; then he sat on a stump a few feet from me without a word. Mitchell had gone away some while ago, as he had said he would, but then had come back. I'd heard his mama had sent his brother Jasper to get him, and for whatever reason, Mitchell had returned. "How you doin'?" he asked, breaking the silence.

I shrugged.

Mitchell didn't say anything, and we sat there in silence looking out over my daddy's land together. After a while I said, "One day I'll have a place like this."

Mitchell turned toward me. "What you mean, 'like this'? Figured you t' be here."

"No," I said. "No, I won't be here, not here on my daddy's land. One day I'll have land of my own. I've got to have something all my own."

Cassie and her family stayed on for several days, and I stayed with them, but when they left, my daddy sent me back to Macon. Then, when summer came and school was out, he sent for me again. He said we were heading to East Texas to buy some horses at a horse fair. My daddy had been doing a considerable amount of reading concerning horses coming out of Texas. What with all the wild horses of the West, the Appaloosas and the mustangs, he had heard that horses of some of the greatest speeds were there, and my daddy being the horseman he was, wanted horses of the greatest speed.

Hammond and George were both on their own by now. Hammond was clerking in a law firm in Atlanta, and George was out west somewhere serving in the Army. That left only Robert and me to go on the trip. I was an obvious choice to go because of how I could ride and handle the horses. My daddy decided to take Robert simply because Robert was his son. Everybody knew he would be of no real help with the horses, so it was certainly expected that others would go along as well to help out. Willie Thomas would come along. I figured, though, my daddy would need one more hand, and I asked him if Mitchell could go with us. "He's right good with horses now," I said. "He's gentle with them, and they trust him."

"As I recall," said my daddy, "it was Mitchell who near to crippled Ghost Wind."

"That was a long time ago. Mitchell's learned a lot about horses since then."

My daddy thought on that. "I suppose," he agreed. "How old is that boy now?"

"He just turned sixteen first part of the year."

"Sixteen and he can't ride, can he?"

"That's because you don't let him."

My daddy gave a nod, as if he were considering the matter. "All right, Paul," he said. "I'll keep an eye on Mitchell, and I'll let you know."

At this time, though Mitchell had befriended me more than once in his way over the years, I still did not consider Mitchell a close friend. He was more of an ally than anything else. Seeing that Robert and I were no longer close, I figured I had no real friends. But I also figured Mitchell needed somebody to speak up for him, the same way Mitchell must have figured I needed somebody to speak up for me on the day we buried my mama. As I'd told my daddy, Mitchell was good with horses. He couldn't sit a horse well, but he could care for them well, and he was reliable. I didn't figure I was taking much of a risk in talking to my daddy about him. Only thing that might get both Mitchell and me into trouble with my daddy down the road was Mitchell's temper, so I warned Mitchell my daddy was going to be watching him.

"So?" questioned Mitchell.

"You want to go to East Texas?" I asked.

Mitchell, as was his way, shrugged in answer. "Makes no difference t' me."

"If it makes no difference," I said, "then just go ahead and mess up and end up not going. You figure you want to go, though, then you treat those horses like you always do, and you keep your temper, even around your daddy." Mitchell didn't say anything. He just gave me a look and walked away, but I knew I'd gotten to him.

During the next few days Mitchell did himself and me proud. There was never any question that he'd treat the horses right, but he also held on to his temper. Even when his daddy cursed him and threatened him with his whip, Mitchell kept his silence and my daddy saw. My daddy saw everything, and on the day we set out with the horses to board the train, Mitchell was with us.

When we arrived in East Texas, we found folks from all over the South and the neighboring states at the horse fair. Folks who just plain loved horses and folks who loved the horse racing business had come. First day we got settled, my daddy chose to take a look at the horses available and to show off our horses too. Same day a man from Missouri proposed a wager against one of my daddy's horses, and my daddy took it.

"Well, who's going to be your rider?" asked the man of my daddy.

My daddy looked at me. "This boy Paul here."

The man gave me a look-over and said, "He seems a bit mite to me."

My daddy nodded, as if he hadn't considered that. "Could be you're right. He sits a horse well, though."

"Well . . . it's your money," said the Missourian.

"That it is," agreed my daddy. He and the man shook hands and we prepared to race right then. My daddy and the Missourian found themselves a stretch of road for the race while Willie Thomas and Mitchell brought my daddy's horse, a mare by the name of Starburst, over to the field and the Missourian's folks brought down his stallion. Folks around the fair soon heard about the upcoming race, and as I mounted Starburst, I saw that a goodly number had gathered to watch. My daddy told me to mold myself right into Starburst, to become as one with her, just as I always did when I rode. "Keep that in mind, Paul," he said, "and Starburst'll do what needs to be done. You're no more than a feather on her back."

I glanced over at the other rider. The fellow was older than I, and had the weight of a man on him. He glanced over at me and he grinned, but it wasn't a friendly grin; I knew he was mocking me. "Pay him no mind," said Mitchell. "He's all teeth, nothin' else." I nodded and cleansed my mind of all except Starburst and me. The marks were set, the rules explained, the gun was shot. The race was on. I became one with the mare. Starburst crossed the finish by a full length.

Afterward the Missourian congratulated my daddy and paid him the wager. Other people came around and said Starburst was a mighty fine horse and that I was a fine rider too.

A man out of Alabama, man name of Ray Sutcliffe, told my

daddy I was such a good rider, he wanted me to ride some races for him. "That boy of yours got a mighty light weight on him and he sure enough knows how to handle a horse like he was full grown. I've got myself a good rider, but he's been feeling sick of late, and I need another rider. Could sure use that boy of yours."

My daddy shook his head. "Paul only rides horses he knows."

"Horses I'm talking about aren't wild or anything," said Ray Sutcliffe. "They're my own horses, come straight out of Alabama, not any of these wild, new-breed western horses. In fact, I've got a fine stallion, a grey, I want to race, a real winner if he's got a good rider on his back. I'd pay your boy well. I'd pay you a fee too, on the wager, if I win."

My daddy smiled. "Well, if anybody could ride a horse and win a wager for you, it would be Paul here. But I still have to say no. I don't want this boy or the horse getting hurt. Like I said, my boy rides only horses he knows. I thank you, sir, though, for the offer."

When Ray Sutcliffe left us, I said to my daddy, "You didn't ask me if I wanted to ride that man's horse."

"No, I didn't."

"Well, why not? Maybe I wanted to ride for him."

"Well, if you did or you didn't, I know better about these things," said my daddy. "Some of these horses around here aren't half trained, some of them are skittish, and some of them are just plain mean. Now, I've seen some of that man's horses, and maybe you could ride that grey he was talking about if there were training time, but not just on a first ride. Not all folks train their horses same as we do, and you riding a stranger's horse is just asking for trouble. You could get thrown, you could get run over; in either case possibly get yourself seriously hurt. No, I'm not about to let you ride any horses except the ones we brought here."

"Well, I still say I've got a right to decide what I ride and for who. I'm not your slave anymore."

I remember my daddy got real quiet. If I just hadn't added that last bit, maybe he would have taken the time to talk more to me. Now his mind closed. "Makes no difference about that. I'm still your daddy, and you're still a boy with a boy's judgment. I say no about a thing, then it's finished."

The young manhood in me got my back up. "Well, you didn't tell that man from Alabama anything about you being my daddy, just that I was 'your boy'! Figure that says more than anything else! Now, I want to ride that stallion!"

I'll never forget the look on my daddy right then. There was temper in him and he could have given me a good walloping right there, but he stayed his hand and gave me my warning. "I'm telling you this just once, Paul," he said. "You ride that horse or any other horse I say you don't ride while you're under my care, I'll whip you 'til you bleed. 'Til you bleed, do you hear me? Harsh as that might sound to you, a whipping'll be less painful to you than some crazy horse that could kill you or maim you for life. I'm not going to have that, you understand? That's all I'm going to say about it, so you mind my words."

That said, my daddy walked off from me. I watched him go. I knew my daddy meant what he said, but I didn't heed his words.

It was some three days later when Mitchell and I were brushing down the horses in the stalls my daddy was renting, Mitchell said to me, "That man from Alabama, one wanted you to ride for him, he come askin' me 'bout you. Came to the stables earlier."

I stopped my brushing and peered across the horses at Mitchell. "Did? What he want?"

Mitchell kept on brushing. "Wanted t' know if you were on your own or if you was debted t' Mister Edward."

"What'd you tell him?"

"Told him I didn't know your business. Told him too, he wanna know your business, he best be talkin' t' you."

"My daddy's dead set against my racing that grey or any other horse he doesn't approve of."

"Well, s'pose he got his reasons."

"Said he doesn't want me hurt."

Mitchell grunted.

"Said he'll whip me bloody I ride without his permission."

"Good 'nough reason not t' ride, then. But don't be too surprised if that Alabama man come t' talk t' you."

I wasn't. Early the following morning the Alabama man came to the stables where Mitchell and I were tending to a gelding. My daddy wasn't around. On this particular morning my daddy and Willie Thomas had gone off into the surrounding countryside looking for horses and weren't expected back until late in the day. Ray Sutcliffe came right to the point. "I want you to ride for me, boy."

I looked at him as if surprised.

"I just lost my rider," he explained. "Came down with the stomach flu again or some such thing, and here I've got a race to run by noon. I wanted to speak to the man you work for, but I understand he's gone for the day. I wanted to do him the courtesy of asking him again, but I need a rider now, and you're the best I've seen. Now, I know Mister Logan doesn't want you to ride for anybody but him. He made that clear. But if he's got no hold on you and if you want to ride for somebody else, you can." He looked at me pointedly waiting for a response.

I gave him one. "He's got no hold," I said. Mitchell looked at me, then kept on with what he was doing.

Ray Sutcliffe smiled. "Well, you ride for me today, and I'll make it worth your while."

I glanced at Mitchell and took my time before I asked, "Mister Sutcliffe, what're you figuring as worth my while?"

Ray Sutcliffe seemed surprised that I had put the question to him. More than likely, he was figuring I would just take him at his word about making my riding "worth my while." "You'd be getting my rider's pay," he said. "Same as I'd pay my own rider."

"Well, Mister Sutcliffe, I know what a rider's pay is around here, and it's not worth losing my job because of it. My boss told me not to ride a horse that's not his, so I know I'd be in real trouble with him if I did. No, sir, I thank you for your offer, but I don't figure to risk my job for just rider's pay."

My words seemed to put Ray Sutcliffe on the spot; they seemed unexpected. "Well, don't you worry none about that, boy," he said, talking down to me. "I'll talk to Mister Logan myself and let him know the situation. I'm sure he'll understand."

"He might understand," I said, "but I'll still be in trouble with him. I can't do it."

It was then I saw Ray Sutcliffe's eyes true for the first time. The man was desperate. Maybe he'd made a wager he was counting on winning a little bit too much; I didn't know. All I knew was that he was desperate for me to ride, and I figured him to pay me a good price if I did. "I said I'd make it worth your while, boy, and I will." His voice was now testy. "This here's a good horse you'll be riding, an excellent horse. I've got a considerable wager on him, and that wouldn't be the case if I didn't know what an excellent horse he is. Tell you what. I'll double your rider's wages."

I glanced again at Mitchell, who kept on grooming the gelding, but his eyes did meet mine, letting me know he knew the same as I about this man Ray Sutcliffe. "No, sir," I said again. "Double a rider's pay isn't going to help me out any with Mister

Edward Logan. He says a thing, he means it. I go against his orders and I won't be able to go back to Georgia. I ride for somebody else, then I know I have to go on my own. I go on my own, I'll need more than double a rider's pay."

Ray Sutcliff frowned. "So what're you figuring you'd need?"

I sidestepped answering his question. "Well, first of all, I don't know if I could even ride your horse, seeing that I've never been on him before."

"Well, I tell you what I'm willing to do," said Ray Sutcliffe. "You ride my grey and win that race for me, I'll give you two percent of the winnings. That'd be more than double the pay of my rider."

Now, I knew that this man was not about to count out the total of his winnings to me and let me take my two percent, and I wasn't about to ask him what his wager was. "I don't figure I can do it for that either," I said.

"That's more than enough!" declared Ray Sutcliff. "That's more than a boy like you'll see in any one ride!"

I shook my head, looking as if I was sorry I couldn't take him up on his offer. "No, sir, I just can't do it."

Ray Sutcliffe seemed frustrated. "Well, boy, what do you want, then?"

"Well . . ." I said, as if I were still thinking this thing over, "four times a rider's wages seems fair to me. I'll do the ride for that, if your horse and I can get along."

"Four times a rider's wages!" exclaimed Ray Sutcliffe. "What you take me for?"

I shrugged, as if that was the best I could do for him. "I figure I lose my job, I can get along on that for a while 'til I find another one. Can't do it for less."

Mister Ray Sutcliffe from Alabama did not look pleased. "All right. All right. I'm going to pay you what you asking, this four times a rider's wages—but only if you win, you hear? You lose, boy, and you get nothing."

I was taking a big risk with my daddy, to walk away with nothing for it. But I figured I'd struck the best deal I could with Ray Sutcliffe, and despite the risk, there was something in me that wanted to prove to my daddy not only that I could ride this stranger's horse, but that I was a man now. I nodded. "I understand," I said. "But if he wins, I'll need my money right after the race."

"Agreed. But you'd better ride him well. Come on now to where I got my grey stabled. Time is short."

"I have to finish brushing down these horses first," I said.

Ray Sutcliffe's face took on a look of exasperation. "What? You got a race to tend to, boy!"

"I'm sorry, Mister Sutcliffe, but I told Mister Logan I'd brush these horses down for him, and he taught me a long time ago to do what I say I'm going to do."

"Well . . . let that other boy brush them down for you!"

"I'll be needing Mitchell's help with your horse, sir, and like I said, we're obliged to finish this job for Mister Logan."

Ray Sutcliffe frowned and gave in, though I could tell he didn't like it; he just had no choice. "Best get a move on you, then! My grey's in the next stable over. That race is at noon, and you'd better be there, ready to ride."

"I'll be there," I said.

As Ray Sutcliffe stormed off, I noticed Robert standing at the entry of the stable. When Ray Sutcliffe neared him, Robert stopped him. "Aren't you Mister Sutcliffe?" he asked.

Ray Sutcliffe acknowledged that he was. "And you're Edward Logan's boy, I recall. I saw you yesterday with your father." He held out his hand to Robert. He hadn't offered his hand to me.

"Yes, sir, I am," said Robert, shaking the man's hand. "Mister Sutcliffe, I hear right that you were offering Paul there a job as your rider?"

"That's a fact. My own boy took sick, and I'm in a bad bind with a race coming up in a few hours."

Robert glanced past Ray Sutcliffe to me. "My daddy won't take kindly to this. He told me he wasn't going to let Paul ride horses he doesn't know. He tell you the same?"

"As a matter of fact, he did, young man, and I want you to know I respect your daddy's thinking about that, but I couldn't find him this morning to extend him the courtesy of discussing this matter with him, and unfortunately, I need a rider before he's expected back. Now, I don't know your daddy well, but I'm sure as a horesman he'll be understanding of the situation. That rider of yours said he's not debted to him and he can come and go as he pleases. That right?"

Robert looked at me, then back at Ray Sutcliffe. "My daddy wouldn't think so."

"Well, that'll have to be between that boy and your daddy. As for that boy and me, we got us an agreement for him to ride my grey, so you'll have to excuse me. I've got matters to attend to."

Ray Sutcliffe then left the stables, but Robert called after him. "Paul can't ride your horse—"

"He'll ride!" declared Ray Sutcliffe, not breaking his stride and not turning around. "He'll ride!"

He walked on, and Robert headed for the stalls. I watched him coming, and I was angry that he was interfering in what was my business. When he reached me, he said, "Paul, what do you think you're doing?"

"Obviously," I said coldly, "you heard what I was doing." Then I turned my back on him and started brushing the gelding.

"You know what I mean."

"I could ask you the same thing."

"What?"

I looked at Robert again. "What do you think *you're* doing?" He gazed at me blankly. "Just what are you doing in my business?"

"You know our daddy said you're not to ride that grey."

"It's my business."

Robert shook his head. "You can't ride him, Paul. I've seen that grey. He could throw you."

"If he does, he does. Like I said, it's my business."

"I won't let you do it."

"How're you going to stop me?"

He looked right at me and said, "I'll tell our daddy."

I looked right at him too. "I'd expect you to do that."

"I mean it," said Robert, unapologetic. "I mean it, Paul. I'll find our daddy, and I'll get him to stop you."

I started to turn away. He grabbed at my arm. I stopped and looked hard at him, and I said, "I remember the last time you did that." Those were my last words to Robert. My eyes said everything else. Robert flushed, then let me go, and I went back to brushing the gelding. Mitchell looked my way without uttering a word. Robert turned and left the stables.

When Mitchell and I finished all the work we were supposed to do for my daddy, we didn't go immediately to Ray Sutcliffe's grey. I figured I needed to know something about that horse before I even saw him, so we headed out to find Ray Sutcliffe's rider, the one that was laid up sick. The man was known by the name of Eddie Hawks, and we found him in a livery on a dirty pile of hay where a number of the colored riders were bunked. He looked to be in a bad way, and was suspicious of talking to me at first, but finally he did. "You fool 'nough t' try and ride that horse?" he asked from where he lay.

"I suppose I am," I said.

"You tryin' t' take my job?"

"Just for this ride. You can't ride, I can. Got no interest in the job after this day."

"So what you come t' me 'bout?"

"I want to know how to ride that grey."

"Thought you done said you knowed that already."

"Maybe I should've said I wanted to know how to ride him and win."

Eddie Hawks breathed in short spurts. "Maybe I told you that, I be givin' up my job."

"Told you I don't want it. You can trust me on that." Eddie Hawks closed his eyes like he was thinking on whether to help me or not, on whether to trust me or not. "Thing is," I went on while he was deciding, "your boss came to me. Seems to me he needs this race won, and seems to me if you tell me how to win it, once you're better, you'll have a job to go back to."

Eddie Hawks slowly opened his eyes. "How old you, boy?"

"Fourteen."

"Umph," he grunted. "Say you know horses, huh?"

"Some."

"Well, you don't know none like that ole grey. Ole grey, he got mule in him."

"How's that?"

"Don't know, but he gots it, way he act. He got his own way t' thinkin'. Now, you let that ole horse get out front first, he likely t' rare back and let every other hoss runnin' get 'head-a him. You keep him back some, other horses 'head-a him, and he gets his dander up 'cause he can't stand that! He gotta pass each one. That ole grey, he'll race 'til his heart burst t' git 'head-a somethin' in front-a him already. After that, once he out front, he don't care if they go on and pass or not, 'cause he done figured he done proved hisself. He done passed 'em, done proved hisself already, and he ain't got nothin' else t' prove. You can hold him when he need holdin' and know when t' let him loose when the time come, then you done got that race won."

I thanked Eddie Hawks for his help. Then Mitchell and I went to check out the grey. He was a tremendous-looking horse. "So, you really gonna ride this monster?" asked Mitchell as we took our first closeup look at the stallion.

"I s'pose so. I want that money."

"You know, you could be lookin' for a broken neck."

"You sounding like my daddy now."

Mitchell almost smiled. "Well, don't want that. Thing is, though, Paul, this here's a dangerous-looking animal."

"Dangerous enough for me to reconsider?"

"Well, that's up to you. You the one hafta ride him."

I walked up to the grey and looked into his eyes. "I'll ride him," I decided right then for a fact. "I've got only my neck to lose and four times a rider's pay to gain."

"And a whippin' from your daddy, don't forget that."

I looked at Mitchell. "I win this race and get my money, then I'll be on my own. My daddy won't be whipping me again."

Ray Sutcliffe joined us. "You, boy," he said to me, "you ready to give my grey a try?"

"I'm ready to start getting to know him," I answered. "Not ready to mount him yet."

"Now, what you mean by that? Get on that horse."

"No, sir, I can't. You need to give me some time with him first."

"Well, I don't have none of that."

"It's important. Now, I said I'd ride your horse, Mister Sutcliffe, but I've got my own way of dealing with horses. You want me to win, then I've got to deal with this grey my way."

Ray Sutcliffe looked me up and down, and I knew he hadn't liked what he'd heard from me. But he gave me the leeway. "You just make sure you win. We've got less than two hours before that start."

He left me then with the grey, and I slipped a rope around the grey's neck, took a saddle, a bridle, and a brush, and led the horse off to a shady spot in a nearby pasture, away from the commotion of the stables, away from all the people milling about, away even from Mitchell. I needed to be alone with the stallion.

"You know," I said quietly when we were to ourselves, "maybe this race isn't important to you, but it is to me, so I figure we best get to knowing each other quick. I'm Paul Logan, out of Georgia, and you need to know I've ridden a lot of fine horses, maybe some not as fine as you, maybe some better. Now, I know we don't know each other, but I understand from your rider, Eddie Hawks, you've got a real mind of your own. You like to win if you do it in your own way. Well, that's all right with me, long as you let me ride you and help you out a little bit. See, I figure to prove my daddy and Robert wrong. I figure to ride you, even though I don't know you, and Ole Grey, I figure to win."

I talked on that way to the grey for some while, and after a bit I began to stroke him as I talked. I pulled some apple wedges from my pocket and gave them to him, kept on with my talk, then began to brush him down. When I put the brush aside, I leaned my head against his forehead and I told that ole grey: "I'm going to mount you soon, you hear? Let's see how we work together."

At first I just walked the grey, letting him get used to me. Then I bridled and saddled him and finally I mounted. I let him get accustomed to my weight on his back as he walked around the pasture, then knowing our time was short, I put him through paces, first a trot followed by a gallop before slowing him down and taking him back to the cool of a shade tree. I gave him more apple wedges. I let him drink from a stream nearby before I brushed him again. All the while I never stopped talking to him. "Well, ole thing, I don't know if we're ready or not, but I see that Ray Sutcliffe over there, waving his arms to come on, so I guess we better go. One thing I want you to remember, though. Like I said, I figure to win this race." With that I led the grey over to Ray Sutcliffe and then headed for the starting line.

Now, these few minutes I'd put in with the grey weren't enough for me to truly know him or for him to know me, but it was all the time I had. It wasn't much, and I recognized that and I was nervous, not knowing how this old horse-mule was going to go down the stretch with me on his back. Still, I had done what I could, and I was as ready as I could be in this short time. I figured to prove my daddy wrong and myself a man. All I hoped now, besides winning this race, was that Robert hadn't been successful in finding our daddy. Last thing I needed was for my daddy to show up.

The race course was a country road stretching from the railroad spur line on the east to a stagecoach stop on the west and back again. I was familiar with it. It was the same course I had run the first day on my daddy's mare and had ridden a number of times since, exercising my daddy's horses. The race was to begin and end at the spur line. Two trains were on the spur, and goods were stacked high for loading on the platform. Throngs of people lined the road. Six horses were entered in the race. I was already mounted on the grey when I reached the spur. Now I waited.

When the gun was fired, the grey and I made a slow start. Three other horses were in front of us. According to what Eddie Hawks had said, that was good. The grey's start was all its own, but now as we shot out on the course, I held him back. Eddie Hawks had told me the grey needed a challenge and not to come up too quick on the lead. Now, this was hard for me. I was used to riding horses that came out not only wanting to win, but to lead. I was used to the thoroughbreds that made that run from the start, and all I had to do was just let them rip, right from the gun. After that, all I did was steer the course and hold on. But I respected what Eddie Hawks had said. He knew this grey a whole lot better than I did.

While riding any course I always had markers in my mind to help me keep pace. The first marker was an old shack setting off the side of the road. It was about there that one of the horses trailing us began to pass, and I was surprised to find the grey not willing for that to happen. I could feel the strength of the grey pulling from my grasp, trying to keep that horse at bay, from passing us. And despite Eddie Hawks's warning, I figured it best to let that grey have his way right then. I figured the grey had to know something about winning, and it seemed foolish to me to fall any farther behind. But when the grey neared the third lead horse at the next marker, a huge double-trunked oak by the side of the road, I pulled up hard on the reins trying to keep him in check. I could tell he didn't like that, but I held him. It wasn't time yet to make the run.

The third marker was a fork in the road, with one road leading to the stagecoach station and the other to I don't know where. I made that curve, rounded the stagecoach station, and headed back toward the spur. It was then I let up some on the grey's reins. The grey seemed to be waiting for that. We easily passed the horse directly ahead of us. Passing the next horse, though, took more time than I wanted, but that ole grey kept on pounding dirt and all I did was nudge him on. This part of the course was winding, and it was not my intention to pass the horse coming up on a curve. But the grey's intention was to pass it, curve or no curve, and when the two horses came neck and neck on the curve, I almost fell off. When I gained control again, that ole grey had slipped into second place.

The last stretch of the course toward the train spur was up a steep hill, then a smooth slope down to the spur. Now, uphill on a last stretch is tough on any horse, but this was where the mule in the grey was at its best. All we could see, that grey and I, on that last stretch was the rider ahead and that other horse's rump; we couldn't see anything beyond on the other side. Yet I knew, just like Ole Grey knew, that the spur was there, and the finish line. I loosened up some more on the reins and let the grey have his way. The grey then took charge: climbed that hill, and, with all stops pulled out, passed that last stallion and sizzled like lightning down the hill, toward the spur, and across the finish line.

❧

It was tumultuous, the win. The grey and I slid across that finish line, and Mitchell himself pulled me off in congratulations and gave me a bear hug. As for me, I felt as if I were outside myself, having done the impossible. I hugged that ole grey first, right up around the neck, and he let me, but then folks took him from me and I had no time to talk to him. People crowded near, praising the grey and congratulating Ray Sutcliffe. Ray Sutcliffe, cigar in hand and a big grin across his face, bragged loudly about the win, but made no mention of me. No one else mentioned me either. I stayed by the spur, ignored.

"Well, 'spect that says somethin'," observed Mitchell as we moved away.

"What do you mean?" I said.

"Jus' look. When do you 'spect to get yours?"

I did look. Several of the men standing with Ray Sutcliffe were now paying him money. They were, of course, all white men, and I knew we had to wait until Ray Sutcliffe was alone before asking for my pay. I tried to wait patiently, though Mitchell was restless as we kept a lookout for my daddy and his too. After more than an hour, though, when Ray Sutcliffe was still wallow-ing in his win, Mitchell said, "I can't take no more of this. We got t' get your money and go."

I glanced over at the group of white men. Now, one thing I had learned growing up amidst my white brothers and my white daddy was knowing when and when not to intrude upon a white person's so-called good time, and I knew definitely now was not the time to intrude.

"Come on," said Mitchell.

"No," I said.

"Well, what you gonna do then, Paul? Stand here all day? Wait 'til your daddy come t' whip ya?"

Mention of my daddy made me look around nervously, but I said, "I can wait."

"Well, I can't," said Mitchell. "Man said he'd pay when the ride was done, not after he'd finished jawin' with every cracker in East Texas. I figure it's time he paid." Mitchell said that and headed straight for Ray Sutcliffe.

I yanked on his arm. "It's my money!" Mitchell looked at me hard. I released his arm and looked over at the group of men. I knew if I didn't go see Ray Sutcliffe about this money, Mitchell would. "Like I said, it's my money. I'll get it."

Mitchell nodded to that and let me go without him. I went over to that group of boisterous white men, even though I knew perfectly well this was not the time or the place to confront Ray Sutcliffe, but I also knew it was better I did it than Mitchell. At first I stood outside the group, saying nothing, just waiting until Ray Sutcliffe finished his bragging about the win and took no-tice of me. But that didn't happen. As I kept watch for my daddy, I also kept an eye on Mitchell. I could see he was becoming im-patient. When he started toward the group to join me, I spoke right up to Ray Sutcliffe, interrupting his talk. "Mister Sutcliffe, excuse me please, but I need to talk to you about my pay. I need to get it so I can go."

Ray Sutcliffe looked around and stared at me as if he didn't know who I was. A cigar was in his mouth. He took it out and waved his hand at me as if shooing away a fly. "I'm busy now, boy. I'll take care of you later." He then turned his back on me.

Now, this made me mad. This was the kind of talk I was getting from a man who'd been talking a whole lot different just a few hours earlier, before I'd won this race for him. He'd been desperate then, and he couldn't talk enough to persuade me to ride.

"I need the money now," I said.

Ray Sutcliffe turned slowly and faced me again, and once his gray eyes set on me, I knew I was in trouble.

"What's that you say?"

I didn't want to press this thing, but I was thinking on my daddy and his whip, and on Mitchell coming over if I didn't get my money. Besides, Ray Sutcliffe owed me for this win, something he couldn't have gotten without me. "You promised to pay me right after the race," I said. "I told you I was going to need my money so I can go."

"Nigger, you going to stand there and tell me what I said? Well, I'm going to tell you something right now! I don't know about in Georgia, boy, but niggers in Alabama and here in East Texas watch their tongues. Now, you best watch yours before it gets you into a whole lot of trouble. I'll pay you when I'm ready to pay you."

He started to turn again to his party, but I said, "And when will that be?"

Ray Sutcliffe pointed his cigar-holding hand right in my face. "Could be tonight, could be next week, could be never, you smart nigger! Now get!" He turned his back to me once more, mumbling something about "white niggers," and continued his celebrating.

I was furious, but I had no choice but to leave unless I wanted real trouble. I met Mitchell on his way over. "Well, you get it?" he asked.

"No. He said later." I didn't want to tell Mitchell what else he'd said.

"Later? Later when?'

"Said later when he gets ready."

"Shoot! That could be never, then!"

He was right about that. "Could be," I agreed. "Right now I'm more worried about my daddy coming. It's getting late."

"Well, why don't you worry about your daddy and let me worry about your money. I'll get it for you."

"How? I don't need you making trouble about this."

"Won't be any trouble, long as that man do what he said he was going to do. It's your money and he got plenty of it now, 'cause of you."

"Mitchell, leave it alone."

Mitchell grunted and leaned against a post, then suddenly straightened again. "Ah, doggonit!"

"What?"

"Look."

I turned and saw my daddy along with Willie Thomas and Robert rushing up the pathway from the stables. I didn't wait for anything else. "Let's get out of here!"

"I know one thing," said Mitchell, not moving. "My daddy's not gonna lay another whip on me. I done told him what gonna happen if he do."

I didn't have time to listen to this. I pulled on his arm. "I said let's go!" Then I took off, and Mitchell came behind me. We made our way hurriedly onto the platform in front of the train sitting on the spur and hid behind some cotton bales. We rested a minute. Then Mitchell said, "So what we do now?"

"I don't know, but I know one thing. I'm not taking another whipping either."

We peeked over the bales looking out for our daddies, but when we didn't see them, we settled down behind the bales to wait. "You don't go back and face up to that whippin', then what you 'spect t' do?" asked Mitchell.

I considered. "Suppose I'll go west. Maybe find George. There's plenty of open land out there."

Mitchell scoffed, "For a white man."

"Maybe, but I figure a man of any color can try. I figure to get some of that open land out there, lots of it. Why, I've read they've got mountains that keep snow the whole year long, and the coldest streams filled with fish, and there're all kinds of game out there too. I figure to get me some of that land and have a place same as my daddy with plenty of good livestock on it, horses and cattle."

"Well . . . you dream on."

I knew Mitchell was mocking me, but I didn't challenge him. It was my dream, after all, not his. He could think what he wanted. Instead, I said, "So, what about you? What are you going to do?"

"Go where I can. One place 'bout the same as another t' me. 'Spect it don't matter, long as somebody's not whippin' on me."

"You know," I said, glancing over at the track, "we could take that train west out of here."

"Jus' hop it?"

"Well, I suppose we'd have to. We've got no money."

"You got money. It's jus' in that Ray Sutcliffe's pocket, that's all."

"Well, looks like it's going to have to stay there," I said. "I can't risk going back for it and have my daddy find me."

Mitchell didn't say anything. He just tilted his hat over his face to ward off the scorching sun. I no longer could see his eyes. After a few minutes he hopped up. "Look here, Paul," he said, "why don't you go see what time that train's s'posed t' pull out? I'll be right back."

I got up. "Where you going?"

"I'll be back," he said again, and took off without answering my question. I didn't call after him; Mitchell was Mitchell, and he certainly didn't answer to me.

I left the cotton bales and went over to a platform where tickets were being sold. I found out there were two trains leaving in the next few hours, one going west and one going east. I knew which one I wanted to be on, so I walked the track trying to figure a good car Mitchell and I could hop and hide in to start our journey west. I worried about Mitchell, worried if he had gone back to confront Ray Sutcliffe. I prayed not.

For some while I walked along the cars and no one questioned me. My clothes were good, and I was counting on most folks who saw me to take me for a well-to-do white boy who was fascinated by trains. Still, I wore my cap low over my forehead and was thankful that my hair hung long over my ears and my forehead, somewhat hiding my face.

I continued to walk the track; then I headed back toward the cotton bales to wait for Mitchell. There were a number of folks now gathered on the platform; most of them looked like travelers. Among them were some folks whom I'd seen both times I'd raced. One, a tall, silver-haired woman standing with three younger women, looked my way and smiled, then pointed me out to the others in her group. Quickly, I glanced around for another route to the bales, but I didn't find one before she called to me. "Aren't you the boy who just rode that winning horse a bit ago?" she asked.

I was sorry the woman had recognized me, but I had to answer. "Yes, ma'am," I said.

"And as I recall," she went on, "you won another race a few days ago. My, you are the rider, aren't you?"

She waited for me to reply. "They were good horses."

"Certainly were," she agreed. "I've got a stable of horses myself, and I know good horseflesh when I see it. I know good riders too, and you certainly are one." I nodded my thanks and looked away, ready to be on my way. The woman, however, kept on talking. "I've noticed you've ridden for two different gentlemen. Are you hiring out as a rider, then?"

She gave me no chance to answer.

"Because if you are, I might have a place for you riding my horses. My three daughters here and I are just getting ready to board this train back home, and we've got a couple of new horses to take with us that I'm sure you'd be able to ride. Of course, you need to know I don't put my horses up for as many races as some folks do, but you could do other work with the horses too, training, taking care of them, and such. You think you'd be interested?"

I was interested, but I had other things on my mind. I saw Mitchell coming. He was hurrying up the path, glancing back over his shoulder. I wondered if wherever he'd gone, he'd run into my daddy or his own. I scoured the crowd beyond him but saw neither one. "No, ma'am," I said, rather abruptly, to the silver-haired woman, and backed away. "But thank you kindly, though." I turned quickly and headed toward Mitchell, who left the path and cut across the grassy knoll to meet me. "What is it?" I asked as he drew near. "You run into our daddies?"

"Worse'n that," he said, out of breath. "When's the train goin'?"

"Soon."

"Then we got t' get on it."

I glanced down the track toward the freight cars, all still being loaded. We couldn't jump them right now without being noticed. "Best hide 'til the train starts up."

"Can't hide," said Mitchell. "We got t' get outa here quick!"

"But—"

"Look, I got your money from that Ray Sutcliffe," he said, patting the lower portion of his shirt tucked into his trousers. "Jus' took what was yours. Only thing was, ole Ray Sutcliffe, he wasn't ready t' give it up."

"Ah, Lord, Mitchell, don't tell me—"

"I waited 'til he gone off alone and I jumped him. I had t' knock that fool down."

"Ah, Mitchell—"

Mitchell looked back toward the road. "Got no time t' talk 'bout this now, Paul. They comin'!"

I followed Mitchell's gaze and saw a group of white men headed toward the spur. Not far behind them were my daddy, Mitchell's daddy, and Robert. I looked around frantically. There was no place to hide. Most of the cotton bales were gone now and the loading platform was quickly emptying. I thought about making a mad dash across the tracks, but there was only flat-looking prairie land beyond, and I figured the men would see us before we found cover. I even thought about slipping under the train, but we'd be too visible to folks coming toward the spur. My last thought was as wild as any of the others, but I figured to try it anyway. "Follow me," I told Mitchell, and took off toward the people on the platform. I went right to the silver-haired woman. "Ma'am," I said, "you still want me to ride for you?"

The woman turned, looking around somewhat startled by my sudden reappearance. "So, you changed your mind?"

I nodded. "You still want me to work for you?"

"Well . . . I suppose—"

"Then I can go, long as my friend here can come with me."

The woman looked past me at Mitchell, and I was fearful

what she might think, for Mitchell could look as mean as he wanted to be, and right now he was looking more than mean. I give that woman credit for seeing past that look on Mitchell's face at that moment and sensing something else.

"He's good with horses," I explained. "We travel together."

The woman kept her eyes on Mitchell and slowly nodded. "All right then," she said. "I suppose I can take you both on."

Mitchell nudged me. The group of white men was now spreading along the track and checking the freight cars. "We need to get on now," I told the woman.

"How come?" she asked. Her eyes studied Mitchell and me, and she frowned. "You boys in trouble?"

I looked at Mitchell, then took a deep breath and made a decision that would affect the rest of my life: I decided to trust this silver-haired woman. I told her we had taken the money Ray Sutcliffe owed us when he'd refused to pay, and I told her there were men looking for us now. The woman glanced down the platform at the men searching the cars, then set stern eyes on both of us. "You all hurt that man in any way? Tell me the truth now."

I glanced at Mitchell. There was no expression on his face as he answered her. "Nothin' but his pride and his backside," he said. "I knocked him down."

The woman's voice rose, but not enough to attract attention. *"You hit a white man?"*

Mitchell's silence answered the question.

"Well, that sure changes things," said the woman with a heavy sigh, but she didn't change her mind. "The two of you, pick up those bags and follow us. I never did like a man who doesn't pay his debts. Just do what I say and no one will question you."

She motioned to us, and both Mitchell and I picked up the women's baggage and, with our caps lowered, followed her and her daughters as they climbed onto the train. Just before we entered the car, the silver-haired woman turned slightly and whispered, "When we get inside, do exactly what I say and not a word from either one of you." She didn't wait for a reply, but walked on, expecting us to follow, and we had no choice but to do so. We couldn't go back. I glanced at Mitchell behind me, and I figured he was thinking the same thing as I.

As we passed through the first car, I kept my eyes lowered, not wanting anyone to see my face too directly. But as we entered the second car, I glanced out the window toward the yard. It was then that I saw my daddy, and I stopped. He was standing on the platform with Robert and Willie Thomas, talking to Ray Sutcliffe and two others. Ray Sutcliffe was all red and angry-looking and gesturing wildly. My daddy wasn't red or gesturing, but I could see anger in him too. I could tell just by the way he was standing. There was a stiffness in him, and I knew that was because of me, because of my disobedience and this added trouble that now had men searching the tracks for Mitchell and me. In that moment when I saw my daddy, I wanted to throw down the bags I was carrying and run to him. No matter how angry he was at me, I knew he'd protect me if he could. Yes, he'd certainly whip me, but maybe that was better than this unknown course upon which I was about to embark. But then I thought about Mitchell and our greater trouble. Mitchell had hit a white man and taken his money. There was no easy solution to that.

Mitchell could hang.

All that flashed through my mind as I stared out at my daddy. Then Mitchell gave me a poke, nudging me on, and I seared forever into my memory the picture of my daddy standing on that platform, and walked on. When we reached the women's car, the silver-haired woman motioned us to put the baggage on two sets of seats facing each other. As we did so, she leaned toward us and whispered, "You boys pretend to be arranging the baggage underneath the seats, but leave the bags out, and when

I say so, the two of you slip under the seats yourselves. Pull what bags you can in front of you." The woman and her daughters then took up their hatboxes and their cloaks and began putting them in the overhead rack.

There were only a few people in the car, and I noticed that everyone was busy putting away luggage and preparing for the journey. No one was paying attention to Mitchell and me. They were concerned with their own matters. I hoped none of them would notice if Mitchell and I had come or gone. I suppose that's what the silver-haired woman was counting on. As she and her daughters placed their belongings overhead, a man stopped and offered his assistance. The women accepted. One of the younger women at this point stepped back between the seats, partially concealing Mitchell and me, while the others remained in the aisle. The man arranged the boxes and the cloaks, then asked if he could be of further assistance. The women thanked him graciously and said they could manage now. The man touched his hat in respect to them, then walked on toward the next car. If he had seen Mitchell and me, he paid us no attention.

The women continued to stand, as if postponing sitting for a long journey that would see them seated most of the way. They took out fans from their purses and began gently fanning themselves. After a few minutes the older woman glanced casually around the car and, turning toward one of her daughters in the aisle, smiled at her, then glanced down at Mitchell and me. "Now," she said. With that, Mitchell and I each scooted underneath a set of the wooden seats. The women still didn't seat themselves as they talked about casual matters, while Mitchell and I, stuffed under the seats, tried to adjust to our discomfort. I looked across at Mitchell and met his eyes. There could be no more words said.

After several minutes the women took their seats and arranged their luggage around themselves. Then they hid us from all view with their tremendous skirts. I was shrouded in darkness. I couldn't see Mitchell underneath the seat opposite, and certainly we couldn't talk. It was hot and suffocating as we faced the unknown; but it got worse. Men searching for Mitchell and me had now boarded the train, and Ray Sutcliffe was one of them.

So was my daddy.

I heard my daddy's voice, and I wanted to cry out to him. I heard someone who identified himself as the conductor explain to the four ladies hiding us that a search was being conducted for two boys, one black, one who looked white. The conductor politely asked if they had seen either of us. The older woman politely said they hadn't. The conductor thanked them, and the men moved on—all the men, including my daddy. As they left, I found myself crying. No sound came, just tears. I couldn't afford to be heard; still, I cried. I knew a part of my life was passing now, a part of my life I would never know again, the part of my life that was my daddy.

Some while later the train began to move. I lay still and tense waiting for a sudden halt, waiting for the women to betray Mitchell and me, waiting for us suddenly to be yanked from our hiding places and lynched from the nearest tree. I waited, but the women remained true to their word. When one of them left her seat, the others rearranged their skirts so that they covered any sight of Mitchell or me; no one ever knew we were there.

So that's how Mitchell and I left East Texas, underneath the seats of a train, hidden by the skirts of four white women. It was a long, cramped, uncomfortable journey, but we endured it. We had to. Only thing was, we were on the wrong train. Mitchell and I were headed not toward the Great Plains and the mountains of the West I had envisioned, but east, back into the Deep South.

Manhood

The Land

"'Ey, you boy! Get up from there!"

I looked sleepily at the white boss man who kicked at my bedding, nicking me in the side, and got up. I wasn't happy about it.

The boss man was called by the name of Jessup, and he had a high-pitched voice that rose higher now as he spoke again. "Where's that worthless nigger you always with? That boy Mitchell!" he shouted. All the men who had not yet come out of their slumber began to waken. "Where's he at?"

I glanced down at the bedding beside my own. Only blankets lay there on the dirt floor. The next man over looked at the pile of bedding too, while all up and down the line, sleepy-eyed men stirred with no words said.

"Well?" demanded Jessup.

"I don't know," I told him. "Maybe he stepped outside to relieve himself."

"That boy been gone since midnight check. Seein' you two always together, he gone off, you gotta know 'bout it."

"I'm not his keeper," I said. "Mitchell's a man grown, and if he decides to go off, he doesn't check with me about it." Now, I shouldn't have said that, I know. But I had been roused from my sleep by this coarse man and I hadn't yet reined in my temper. Fortunately for me, Jessup chose to be tolerant, at least tolerant for a white man.

"So, you got a smart mouth on you this mornin', huh, nigger?" he said. "Well, I got somethin' to cut that smartness right outa ya. Seein' you and that Mitchell come in this camp t'gether, you can just do his workload and yours too for the day. That boy ain't back 'fore the day be out and you ain't got your share and his of timber cut, I'm gonna turn you and your smart mouth over to the sheriff. And don't you think of runnin' off on me, 'cause I'm gonna have my eye on you, and my men will too. Now get movin'!" Jessup then turned and looked down the long rows of men bedded on the ground. "All you other niggers, y'all get on up too! The day's a-waitin'!"

The boss man walked to the shanty opening covered only with a sheet of tarp to keep out the damp and cold, then looked back and pointed a finger at us. "And not one of you is t' help that boy there! Today he work alone, less'n that boy Mitchell show up!" He lifted the tarp flap and left as the men began to rise. Several of the men eyed me but didn't speak. I looked back at them in silence, knowing that the boss man had had no need to warn them not to help me, for even without his warning they wouldn't have lifted a finger, not for me.

I turned back to my bedding. I rolled up my gear inside the blankets and tied the roll with a rope. I did the same with Mitchell's gear, then I pulled my pants over my long johns, put on a shirt, coat, and boots, all while the other men milled around tending to themselves and eyeing me still. Their watching made me uneasy. I had spent a lot of my time in the Mississippi lumber camps and this was a particularly rough one. Both the men and the boss, Jessup, were rough. It was known for a fact that Jessup had been the operator of a turpentine camp, a camp set up to drain all the resin from the pines, and many of those bosses could be brutal. It was also known that Jessup had brought some of his turpentine overseers and workers to this camp. Had I known all this when Mitchell and I joined up, I never would have done so, for both Mitchell and I knew about the turpentine camps. We'd been there.

I stepped outside. The dawn had not yet broken. Fog misted through the trees holding the blackness of the night. It was early spring and it was cold. I shivered as I took a deep breath of the damp air and went off to take care of my morning necessities down near the creek. By the time I returned to the camp, the cook had a fire going and pots of chicory brewing and grits boiling. I took a tin and finished off my breakfast before the other men were out. Then, as they emerged from the shanty, I set out up the hillside with my axe to start the day.

Working alone was a weary load. Now, I was considered a good chopper, a man who could chop up to fifteen trees a day, and if I set my mind to it, I could chop twenty. Mitchell could do the same, and for that, we received better pay than for most other kind of work we took on. Thing was, each man had so many trees he had to cut a day and I knew there was no way that alone I could cut the number of trees by day's end as Mitchell and I could cut together, and I understood the consequence of that. But even as the men from the camp joined me in the dense forest and sniggered about my progress, I didn't worry. I figured Mitchell had gone off to give his attentions to some young woman, but I knew he'd be here as soon as he realized the dawn was breaking. He'd never let me down yet.

I was right.

Mitchell joined me just as the fog began to clear. He whacked his axe into a nearby tree without a word, then said, "Heard down the row you was gonna hafta do my work and yours too, I didn't show up."

I finished notching the side of a tree, then walked to the other side of it to hack at the tree until it fell. "I wasn't worried," I said. Before I swung my axe again, I grinned at Mitchell. "Hope she was worth it."

Mitchell looked back at me and grinned too. After that we had no more words as we chopped in rhythm with the sound of my axe against the one tree, then the sound of Mitchell's against the other. We paced ourselves that way until the trees fell. Then we went to work on two more. By midday when the cook's bell rang for dinner, Mitchell and I were already caught up. By quitting time we had chopped our day's worth of trees. That's when the boss man came down on me hard.

"Where y'all boys think ya headed?" he asked as we came from the slopes.

"The bell rung," said Mitchell. "It's quittin' time."

"Oh, yeah, that's right," said Jessup as if he didn't know. "Quittin' time on a Saturday night. Well, boy, you go on and get your pay wit' the rest of 'em. I wanna talk t' this white nigger friend of yours."

Mitchell looked at the boss man, then at me, without moving. I met his eyes, and he walked slowly on, leaving the boss man and me.

"So," said Jessup, "y'all managed to cut all your trees for the day, I see."

"Same as always," I replied.

Jessup spat at my feet. "You know, you one lucky nigger that boy Mitchell showin' up when he did. I was kinda lookin' forward t' callin' the sheriff on you."

I stood there saying nothing, taking the boss man's insults, and knowing he was leading up to something. From the first day I had come into the camp, Jessup had disliked me, and I understood the reason. It was the same reason why the men of color disliked me. I looked too white. Mitchell's being absent in the night gave Jessup another excuse to strike out at me, as if he needed one. He'd said not one word to Mitchell about his absence. He didn't have it in for Mitchell.

Jessup looked up the darkening slope. "You know, Paul Logan, I don't like you. You come in this here camp lookin' and talkin' like a white man and callin' yo'self colored." He looked back at me. "Now, one thing I can't stand is a uppity nigger, nigger thinkin' he good as white folks. Oh, I can tell it in you. You the kind think you good as any white man walkin'. These other boys round here, they don't act that way, none 'ceptin' maybe that boy Mitchell. Leastways he keeps shut, not talkin' citified like you. Well, I figure to teach you a white man's in charge here. I figure you got such a smart attitude, you can just take your white self on back up that slope tomorrow and put yourself in another day's work."

I stared at the boss man, knowing full well he knew the next day coming was Sunday, the only day the camp shut down, but I didn't question him on it; I wouldn't give him the satisfaction.

"And don't think you gettin' paid for any Sunday workin' neither. You gonna put this day in for my satisfaction, and if you don't, I'll make you the same promise I made you this mornin'. I'll call the sheriff on you. You hear me?"

My blood shot hot, but I didn't say the words that were boiling up inside me. All I said was "I hear."

"You best do, 'cause I'm gonna be checkin' on you come first light. And, oh yeah, by the way, I'm jus' gonna keep your week's pay 'til your Sunday workin' time is done." Then, that said, the boss man Jessup turned his back on me and strode toward the camp.

I watched him go, then sat down on a stump, closed my eyes, and tried to take hold of my fury. Ever since I had left my daddy's house, I had been learning and relearning that harsh lesson my daddy had whipped into me when I was fourteen. It was a white man's world, and I had to survive in it. But always constant with me was relearning how to hold my temper. When I had gotten on that train in East Texas, I had decided that I was going to survive, and surviving meant holding my temper. I wasn't going to let this white man beat me down.

"So, Paul, what that ole Jessup want?"

I opened my eyes. Mitchell was walking toward me. "Said I have to work tomorrow."

"On Sunday?"

"On Sunday."

Mitchell cursed. "He done had it in for you since we first stepped foot in this camp, and we both know why."

"Nothing I can do about that."

"What ya mean nothin'? We can leave here right now."

"I don't think so. Not unless you want to see me in jail, or worse."

"For what? Goin' against that pecker's orders?"

"You know there doesn't have to be a reason." Mitchell's eyes met mine and I knew he was thinking of the turpentine camps, the same as I. "Said I'm to work the full day," I went on, "and if I don't, he'll have the sheriff after me. Said too I'm to work the day without pay."

Mitchell cursed again. I felt like cursing myself.

"So what you gonna do?"

"I'm thinking on it," I said.

Mitchell was silent, then looked down the trail toward the camp. "Tell ya what, then. Do your thinkin' in town. That's where I'm headed, and you need t' come with me. We'll go over to Miz Mary's place."

Now, town was no more than a few shacks sitting about three miles down the road. Mainly it was a place where the men from the camp could hear some music, eat some home cooking, see a few ladies, and mostly spend their money. On Saturday nights when the other men went to Miz Mary's place, I went off to some space away from everybody where I could have some time to myself to write my letters and to read. That way I kept my money. "You know that's not how I like to spend my time," I said.

"So what ya gonna do, then? Sit there in that cold shanty, readin' or writin' or workin' on some piece of wood?"

"Only time I have to do it. Besides, I don't go to Miz Mary's, I'm sure I won't much be missed."

"Well, that's a fact." Mitchell was blunt as always. "But you know part of that, that's your own fault, Paul. You keeps yourself separate from the rest, and they thinks it's 'cause you thinkin' you better'n them."

I smiled, thinking of childhood memories. "We've been through that before."

"Like I been tellin' ya, you try socializin' a bit, then folks might see you different."

I thought on that. "I don't know if I could fit in."

"Can't hurt nothin' t' try. Get yo' mind off Jessup."

I considered a moment longer. "Maybe you're right."

"Then let's get cleaned up and get ourselves down t' Miz Mary's!"

❧

I don't know why I let Mitchell talk me into going with him to Miz Mary's. The place was small and dark, lit only with a few table lanterns, and it was rowdy. There was a fellow playing a banjo and a woman was singing, but mostly it was just noise, with men and women talking too loud, laughing hard, trying to shake off the hardships of a week's work. Mitchell was in the midst of it all, but it was not my kind of place. I preferred the quiet. I sat removed from the others in a corner, where a barrel substituted as a table and a box crate as a stool, writing my thoughts to my sister, Cassie.

From the time I had left the train coming out of East Texas, I had been writing to Cassie. I knew after Mitchell's and my disappearance from East Texas, my daddy, Cassie, my brothers too, would be worried, and I needed to let them hear from me. At first, though, I had written letters and not mailed them, for I was fearful my daddy might find out where I was. Then, after a while, I began to take letters, addressed only to Cassie, to the train stops near wherever I was staying at the time and give them to somebody boarding to mail from their destination. I even wrote a letter to my daddy so he'd know I was alive and well, but I mailed the letter in the same fashion as I had mailed letters to Cassie, except I went all the way to Louisiana to do it. I did this not only to keep my daddy from knowing where I was and coming to look for me, but to keep trouble away too. I didn't know how far Ray Sutcliffe might have gone to track Mitchell and me down.

In those early days I didn't put a return address on my letters, so I had no news from home. Later I arranged for a storekeeper in Meridian to collect my mail for me, and though I made a point of not staying near Meridian, I checked on my mail several times a year. Now that I was a man grown, I wrote more openly to Cassie, mailing the letters myself, but I still asked her to keep my confidence and not let our daddy or our brothers know where I was. I also asked her to send word to Miz Edna about Mitchell, for as far as I knew, Mitchell never wrote to his folks. In my letters to Cassie I told her all my thoughts, or most of them. I let her know that I was dissatisfied with the lumber camps; they were fine for some men and that would be all they'd ever know, but I figured for more. I felt I was drifting and I was ready to settle now. I told Cassie that.

"'Scuse me . . . b-but can I talk t' ya?"

I looked up from my writing. A young woman stood before me. I had seen Mitchell talking to her earlier and knew he'd spent time with her. I also knew she wasn't the only woman he'd spent time with.

"My name's Maylene. I knows ya Mitchell's friend."

I stood and pulled out a box crate for Maylene, and she sat down rather shyly. I didn't know what to say to her. We'd never spoken before. "My name's Paul Logan," I said, sitting again.

"I—I know. Mitchell, he done told me."

I nodded, waiting for her to go on. She took her time.

"He done said y'all been knowin' each other since y'all was younguns."

"That's a fact."

"Then . . . I 'spect ya knows him better'n anybody."

"I suppose better than anybody around here."

"Th-then I 'spect ya knows what he likes in a woman."

I readjusted myself on the crate. I didn't like the turn of this conversation. One thing I wasn't about to do was get into Mitchell's love life. He had too much of it for me to keep it straight. "Well, you want to know that, you need to talk to him."

"Can't. I mean, ya knows Mitchell. I asks him a question, and he be tellin' me what I wants t' hear. He be tellin' me the truth, I s'pose, but what I wants from him is more'n jus' pretty words. I wants him t' be my man. I wants him t' settle with me."

I cleared my throat and looked out across the room where Mitchell was talking with two other men beside the bar. "Well, did you tell him that?"

"He knows it, but he jus' laughs."

Maylene looked down at her hands, and her face seemed so pitiful, I felt sorry for her. Now, most women who followed the lumber camps knew not to take the men too seriously, for those men who weren't already married were mostly drifters, ready to move on as soon as the camp moved. "You know," I said, "Mitchell, like most of the fellas, likely isn't ready to settle yet."

"But I needs him."

Just what I was supposed to say to that I don't know. I was saved from having to figure that out by a big fellow from the camp who came over and took Maylene by the arm. The man was called by the name of Johnny B. "Girl, whatcha doin' talkin' t' this white nigger?" Johnny B. demanded, but then didn't give Maylene a chance to answer before he snatched her up. "There's plenty of other fellas needin' yo' company."

At that Maylene got her backbone up. "But maybe I wantin' his."

"You wantin' a white man, girl, you best be gettin' yo'self the real thing."

Maylene jerked from Johnny B.'s hold. "One thing I do know is I ain't wantin' you!"

Johnny B. took hold of her again, rougher this time. The last thing I wanted to do was get in a fight with this fellow, but I figured I had to take up for Maylene; after all, she had been sitting with me. I stood. "The lady made it clear she's not interested in your company right now, so I think it's best you let go of her arm."

The big fellow laughed. "Come on from behind that table, boy, and you jus' make me do that little thing!"

Johnny B.'s challenge was so loud that the music stopped. I came from behind the barrel to stand in front of Johnny B. The room grew quiet, and Mitchell took notice. "'Ey, Paul!" he called. "What's goin' on over there?"

"This here man been grabbin' on me!" hollered Maylene.

Mitchell pushed away from the bar. "That a fact?"

"And he won't let go!"

"Oh, I think he will," said Mitchell.

"Now, you stay outa this, Mitchell!" warned Johnny B. "This here's between me and this white nigger!"

"And that there young lady," Mitchell added, making his way over. "Seem like t' me, ya got a mighty tight hold on her arm there."

"Seem like t' me," said Johnny B., "ya buttin' into somethin' ya got no business." He motioned slightly toward me with his head. "How comes ya wanna take his part anyways?"

"Well, ya see," said Mitchell, when he stood directly in front of Johnny B., "we're brothers. Yeah, that's right. Not that it's any of yo' business, but his daddy and mine was different, anybody can see that. But we're brothers just the same. He come out white; I come out black. So what ya got t' say t' that?"

There was again, for a moment, silence at Miz Mary's.

Johnny B. broke it. "Well, he still ain't like he one of us!"

"That's sho' right!" one of the other loggers spoke up. "Settin' over there in that corner, too good t' socialize!"

I challenged the man. "Why'd you come here from the camp?" I asked.

The man seemed taken aback for a moment. "What's that?"

"I came here to get away from the camp after a week's work. Figure maybe you did the same."

"Yeah," said Johnny B. "But all you doin' is sittin' up there in that corner, all to yo'self!"

"No," I said quietly. "I wasn't all to myself. Miss Maylene there was sitting with me, keeping me company."

Maylene laughed at that, angering Johnny B. further, and he suddenly hauled off and slapped her so hard, she fell back against the barrel upon which I'd been writing. Mitchell grabbed Johnny B. and knocked him down. I helped Maylene up, then looked around just in time to see a man coming behind Mitchell with a broken bottle. I jumped the man and knocked the bottle from his grip. Mitchell turned at the commotion, but then had his hands full again as Johnny B. got up and lunged at him. The two of them then went at it. Another fellow came at me, but I held my own. Two more of the men from the camp jumped into the fray; the rest stayed out of it. Miz Mary herself broke it up. She fired off a shotgun. She ordered Mitchell and me out. Maylene went with us. The rest, Miz Mary said, had better stay put and not follow us if they wanted to set foot in her place again.

Once we were down the road, Mitchell went off with Maylene.

I returned to the camp, but I didn't go directly to the sleeping quarters. Instead, I walked the wooded slopes. Even though I figured the shanty to be empty most of the night, I didn't want to be cooped up inside. I hurt from the fight and I moved slowly, but I needed to be in the open, where the chill of the night and the cleanliness of it could clear my head. After a while I sat upon a stump, breathed deep of the night air, and stared out at the clouds drifting across a full moon. I felt the cold beginning to shroud me, but I stayed where I was. I figured to stay there all night in the cold, if I had to. I had a lot of thinking to do.

❧

Back when Mitchell and I had first left out of East Texas on that train, I had it in my mind that one day I'd go west. Mitchell didn't much care where he went, and when Miz Hattie Crenshaw, the woman who with her daughters had hidden us with their skirts on the train, offered us work and a place to stay, we took it. I figured we could save a little money while with them, then move on. But as it turned out, we ended up staying on at Miz Crenshaw's place near Laurel for almost two years. I trained Miz Crenshaw's horses, took care of them, and sometimes raced them, while Mitchell mainly did whatever needed doing around the place.

Now, I've got to admit that Miz Crenshaw was always fair by me, even though she had plenty of questions to ask. Mitchell and I, however, never told Miz Crenshaw or anybody else much about ourselves. We'd decided from the beginning to keep what was past to ourselves; we didn't want folks, including our daddies, coming after us. When we first started staying with the Crenshaws, they all seemed a bit curious about us, as they had a right to be, and Miz Creshaw was one of the most curious. Once, in fact, she said to me, "That gentleman you were working for, Paul, the one you came with to East Texas, were you with him long?"

I remember looking at Miz Crenshaw and wondering why she was asking me that. I replied to her, "I was born on his place."

"He's the one responsible for having educated you?"

I answered her brusquely. "He saw to it."

"That was mighty generous of him," Miz Crenshaw observed. "Almost like a daddy." She then studied me without speaking further, but I knew she sensed the connection between my daddy and me. After all, she'd seen us together, and except for the differences in our height, I greatly favored my daddy.

"Miz Crenshaw," I said, deciding on a sudden to confide one thing to her, "you ever see him again, I mean like at a horse fair or anything, he can't know where I am. Mitchell either."

Miz Crenshaw kept her eyes on me, then slowly nodded. "If that's what you want, Paul, you needn't worry. My girls and I won't say a thing." That's all she said and she didn't ask me anything more about my daddy, not then or later.

Though Mitchell and I otherwise remained pretty close-mouthed, Miz Crenshaw seemed not to take offense and was always giving us her advice, and particularly to me, since Mitchell showed no interest whatsoever in following any she gave him. When she discovered I had book learning, she encouraged me to read and was always bringing books she thought would be good for me. Later on she arranged for me to do some teaching to other folks of color in the area, and when she learned of my carpentry skills, she took that in hand too. She had some carpentry tools she let me use, and I built her two small lamp tables. She paid me extra to fix things for her, and even sent me up to a man in the area to do further apprenticing.

"You can use this talent too, Paul," she instructed me. "You could go into business for yourself if you wanted. Enterprising men of color are doing that now, I hear. You ever decide to go into the furniture business, I know a good person to see is a man by the name of Mister Luke Sawyer in Vicksburg. He's had skilled wood craftsmen working for him before. He runs a mercantile, and he's a fair man. You could get a good start with him.

But you've got other possibilities as well. You could go to school. There are great opportunities for young folks like yourself these days. Why, you could go to one of the colored schools here in Mississippi or even north to study. You could become one of the great educators of your people or maybe a lawyer or a doctor to them. You could do it, Paul. You've already got the foundation, and you're certainly bright enough. You could do it easy."

Maybe that was so, but I wasn't interested in being a doctor or a lawyer or an educator. I knew Miz Crenshaw meant well, but I never told her what I truly wanted. That I told only to Mitchell. What I wanted was land. I wanted land like my daddy's. In a way, I suppose, I was driven by the thought of having land of my own. In my early years, before I truly realized my two worlds, I had figured that I'd always live on my daddy's land, that my daddy's land would be mine and I'd always be a part of it. When I discovered that wouldn't be, I created my own land in my mind. I knew that land was what I had to have.

During the time Mitchell and I stayed at Miz Crenshaw's place, the will to have my own land grew. Although Miz Crenshaw and her daughters and eventually her daughters' husbands treated Mitchell and me fair, I recognized I was no more than a hired hand, working at somebody else's say-so, and I knew I had no real future there. As a boy, even though I worked for my daddy, I felt my soul was vested in all I did. It wasn't that way on the Crenshaw farm. As nice as they were, the Crenshaws were strangers, and what was theirs would stay theirs; they weren't about to share any of it with me.

Besides that, once Miz Crenshaw's oldest daughters married, their husbands made it quite clear that things would be taking on a change. One of them, in fact, told Mitchell and me outright, "I know you boys have gotten pretty accustomed to having the run of the place. Over the years since her husband and her boys died in the war, Miz Crenshaw's had to depend on a number of folks to keep this place running. Now that she's got menfolks in the family again, she and her daughters won't have the burden of all that worry. You have questions about the place, you come to us. No need to worry them. One other thing too. You boys stay 'way from inside the main house. There be things to discuss, they can be talked about outside those walls. Understood?"

It was understood, all right. Though Mitchell and I were grateful to Miz Crenshaw and her daughters, it wasn't long after that Mitchell and I took to the road, and mostly we stayed to it. I still sometimes dreamed of going west and maybe meeting up with George. I also dreamed of meeting my granddaddy Kanati's people, but none of that happened. Mitchell and I took on jobs and ended up staying for the most part in Mississippi and Louisiana.

First job we took on was in a turpentine camp. In the turpentine camps men of color, many times having their womenfolks with them, set up families and worked in woods far removed from other people. The men were mostly rough, sometimes coming into the camps from whatever they were running from. Some admitted to being escaped convicts. Some even admitted to murder. The bosses didn't care. They just wanted workers. Besides, sometimes the bosses were murderers or convicts too. In the turpentine camps the men, called chippers, chipped the pines year after year draining from them all that was good, resin for turpentine, resin for tar, resin for medicine. Then, when there was only a shell of the tree left after five years or so, the camp moved on. I didn't like what was done to the trees. They were hacked out to a slow death, drained of all their treasures until they were worthless. They couldn't be used for lumber and were left like ghosts to stand hollow and fragile until knocked down in a storm, or a fire consumed them.

Mitchell and I were only seventeen and sixteen years old when we joined up with the turpentine camp, and we thought we knew more than we did. We soon found out differently. The white boss man was in full control. What he said was absolute law and usually there was no other law around. Even if there had been, it would have made no difference. Whatever the white boss man said, the white law would have gone along with him. Once we saw one man of color kill another man of color in the middle of a dispute. The boss man told the chippers to bury the dead man and sent the other man on back to work, and that was all there was to it. He didn't care. But then there came the day a boy of color not much older than Mitchell and me beat one of the white operators of the camp until he was bloody, then ran away. The bosses and their hounds hunted that boy down, killed him, dragged him back to the camp, and left him there to rot. They wouldn't even let us bury him. They wanted us to be reminded daily of who was in charge. Mitchell and I got out of that camp as soon as we could, and we didn't make the mistake of working again in the turpentine camps.

After that, I took on teaching jobs and carpentry work, and sometimes I trained and raced horses. But mostly, Mitchell and I went lumbering, working long hours in the Louisiana and Mississippi lumber camps. I didn't have to go to the camps to find work. I went because of Mitchell. He liked the camps, the excitement of them, and the danger. When Mitchell asked me to work in a camp with him, I did so because he asked, and Mitchell was now family to me, the only person near I could count on. I was the only person Mitchell could count on too.

Now, being small built and so white-looking, I always had to prove myself in the camps, and I worked as hard as any man to pull my own load and didn't let anybody beat me. Mitchell had no problem in pulling his own. He was tall and muscular, a good-looking young man to the womenfolks, and other men respected him on sight. Mitchell was just that kind of person. However, he still had his quick temper and sullen ways, and that meant trouble too many times. Seeing that Mitchell and I always backed each other up, like at Miz Mary's place, I sometimes found myself in a fight when the matter had nothing at all to do with me and many times made no sense to me either. I didn't like brawling, and I figured the best way to stay out of needless trouble was to stay out of places like Miz Mary's. Now I was angry at myself for letting Mitchell talk me into going there in the first place.

The longer I sat on that stump in that night chill, I thought that maybe it was a good thing I had been caught up in another senseless fight. Maybe it was a good thing the boss man Jessup had taken such a strong dislike to me and pushed me into working for him for nothing. Maybe I needed this anger that had built up in me to get me moving in another direction. It was my nature to always look at what seemed a setback as being something from which I was supposed to learn. I figured everything that happened was supposed to be telling me something, and I always figured there was something good that was supposed to come out of the something bad, if I just took the time to study on what it was. Well, I was taking the time now, and I had made up my mind about one thing. This kind of life wasn't what I wanted, and it was time for me to move on.

I rose from the stump. I'd been sitting there for the better part of the night, but I had things figured now. First thing I did was gather up some firewood, then I headed back with it to the shanty. No one was there. It was dark and cold in the shanty, with not even the fire that dimly lit the room on work nights. There wasn't even moonlight shining in, for there were no windows. I laid the wood on the floor, then tacked back the tarp over the door to bring the moonlight in. I found my bedroll packed with my gear. I unrolled it and took out one of the blankets. I placed logs in that blanket, rolled it carefully up again, and tied it with rope, so that it looked as if all my gear was still inside. I did the same with Mitchell's gear, then placed the blanket-wrapped logs where our bedrolls had been. I re-rolled the rest of our gear and took it with me back to the woods, where I hid it in the brush. Then, without a blanket or a fire to warm me, I settled on the damp ground and went to sleep.

That morning I rose with an aching head and a swollen jaw. It was another foggy morning, and though I had on long johns under my pants and wore a coat over the heavier of my two work shirts, I shivered uncontrollably. My body was stiff from sleeping in the damp, but I took up my axe from the tool shed and headed for the slope. It being Sunday, there was no breakfast. The cook had the day off. When I got to the chopping line, I found Mitchell sitting on a stump, waiting for me.

"What you doing here?" I said.

"Waitin' on you. Time t' go t' work."

"This is my load," I contended. "It's not on you."

"Not on me? You know Jessup just used me bein' away the other night as an excuse to come down on you. 'Sides, anythin' on you, it's on me. You know that."

I knew that, all right. I had expected Mitchell to come sooner or later, for if the situation were switched, I would have been there for him. I acknowledged his words with a nod, then said, "I decided, Mitchell."

"What's that?"

"I can't stay working here."

Mitchell jumped up. "Then let's go! We get our gear and head outa here right now!"

"Can't do that, not yet. Jessup'll be watching, and he won't hesitate to put the sheriff after us."

"Then what we do? Work here all day for nothin'?"

"That's right."

"Ah, naw—"

"We put in this day's work, Jessup won't figure us to be going off come nightfall. He would be figuring if I were going to run, I'd've done it last night. If we leave at nightfall headed back toward Miz Mary's, nobody'll question us. Lot of the men'll be staying up at Miz Mary's sleeping the night through, so there'll be no question either about us not being in camp come nightfall. Now, I figure we can both work this day if it means putting some ten or more hours between us and them."

Mitchell nodded, mulling over what I was saying. "Thing is, I just don't like the idea of givin' this man a day's work for nothin'.'"

"It's either that or we take off right now and end up with Jessup's dogs chasing after and most likely catching us."

Mitchell conceded to my thinking. "Well, I ain't leavin' without my gear."

"Don't worry. I've got it already and I've got it hid, all except for one of your blankets. Had to leave one of yours and one of mine."

"I gotta leave my good blanket? Why ain't you brung it?"

"Because I wrapped those blankets around some logs. Had to leave something looking like bedrolls. Figured as long as they thought our gear was still here, they'd think we were too."

Mitchell wasn't happy. "First a day's pay, now my good blanket!" He slammed his axe into a tree. "That boss man, he better stay clear of me this day! He done made me mad!"

Maylene arrived unexpectedly at noon riding one of Miz Mary's mules and bringing us dinner. She surprised both Mitchell and me with a feast of fried chicken, ham hocks and collard greens, corn bread, and even pecan pie. She brought hot coffee too, the real thing, not the chicory we'd been drinking in the camp. It was a Sunday feast. I thanked Maylene and took one of the drumsticks and a piece of corn bread.

"Girl, where you get a chicken t' fry?" Mitchell asked her.

"Miz Mary," Maylene said shyly. "I done tole Miz Mary

how Paul Logan done had t' work this day and how you done said ya wasn't gonna let him do this work by hisself, and how you was gonna work too. Tole her wasn't no food served on Sunday here at the camp and she done tole me I could bring part of this here chicken up to y'all."

Mitchell grinned. "Yeah? That a fact? Never knowed Miz Mary was so generous."

"Had t' do some tradin' too," said Maylene.

"What kinda tradin'?"

"Nothin' much. Jus' tradin'" She looked at me as she reached into a sack she held. "These papers here, they yo's," she said, handing them to me. "Found 'em on the floor last night where ya been sittin'."

It was the letter I had been writing to Cassie. "Thank you," I said.

Maylene accepted my gratitude with the same shy smile with which she had first greeted me, then admonished, "Y'all eat up now. I'm a good cook."

She started away, but Mitchell pulled her back, putting his arms around her waist. "Ain't ya gonna eat with us?"

"Naw. I gotta get back."

"I don't think so." Mitchell smiled down at her, and she glowed in his smile.

I interrupted the lovers. "Mitchell, I need to talk to you a minute."

"Now?"

"Now, before Miss Maylene goes," I said, and walked away, still holding my chicken and corn bread. After a minute or two, Mitchell followed.

"So, what is it, Paul?" Mitchell asked when he reached me.

I glanced over at Maylene, who was kneeling on the ground spreading out our dinner. "I was just thinking that, seeing Maylene rode up on a mule, if she carried our gear back with her, we wouldn't have to worry about our being seen walking the road carrying it ourselves. You think she'd do it?"

Mitchell glanced over his shoulder at Maylene. "She'd be wantin' t' know why."

"Then tell her."

"And get her in my business?"

"We could use her help."

Mitchell shook his head. "Don't trust a woman ain't my mama."

I shrugged. "All right, then," I said. "That's how you feel."

"Course," said Mitchell as I turned away, "you could be right. I mean, we get stopped on the road carryin' our gear, there'd be hell t' pay."

I waited, letting him make up his own mind about the matter.

He glanced once more toward Maylene. "Where's the gear?"

"In the bushes near that stand of three pines we figured to cut last at the end of the day."

"All right," Mitchell said. "I'll talk to her, but I best do it alone." He then walked back to Maylene. He took her hand and led her beyond my view. I sat down and ate, then waited. When Mitchell reappeared, Maylene wasn't with him. "Maylene, she took our gear," he said as I joined him.

"What you say to her?"

Mitchell sat on the ground and took up a chicken wing. "Jus' told her I needed t' trust her on somethin'."

"That's all?"

Mitchell glanced at me, the wing in his hand. "She seem t' think it was enough."

❧

Mitchell and I finished off only part of Maylene's dinner, then set the rest aside for later. We figured we'd need it come nightfall. As we got back to our chopping, one of Jessup's men came to make sure I was working. Another came up later, and at the day's end the boss man himself showed up. "See ya done had some help," he said, eyeing Mitchell. "Must be good t' have friends."

"Bell ain't rung," said Mitchell sullenly. "Is it quittin' time?"

"It's near dark, ain't it?" the boss man replied. "Nobody rings a bell on Sunday." Jessup then looked at all the timber we'd cut. "Reckon y'all can go on. Looks t' me ya put in a good day's work. Maybe I'll have ya do it again come next Sunday." He laughed, then paid me my money for my week's work, but not for my Sunday.

Mitchell and I took up our axes without a word and left Jessup on the slope. As we walked away, he called after us. "'Spect y'all headed on back t' that Miz Mary's, huh, like all the rest? Well, y'all jus' make sure ya get them axes back t' that shed 'fore ya do. You leave them out t' rust, and the cost of new ones comin' outa your pay!"

Mitchell started to turn, and I figured him to vent his feelings about what the boss man could do with his axes, but I warned him off. "Let it be," I said. Mitchell cut me a sour look and walked on.

"Enjoy Miz Mary's!" hollered the boss man, and laughed. Those were the last words we heard Jessup speak. We put the axes in the tool shed, then left that camp. We made the three-mile walk up to Miz Mary's and met Maylene out back. Maylene had a small leather bag hanging from her shoulder and I glanced from it to Mitchell. I hoped that she didn't think she was going with us. She gave Mitchell a hug, then led us into the woods. "I got yo' stuff hid," she said.

We retrieved our gear and I thanked Maylene. "Hope your helping us won't cause any problems for you."

"Naw. Don't ya worry none 'bout that. Nobody seen me."

"Well, I do thank you."

Maylene seemed to blush under her chocolate skin. "Got y'all some more food."

She handed over the leather bag to Mitchell. "More fried chicken and corn bread."

"What! No greens?" Mitchell teased as he took the bag.

"Ah, go on!" laughed Maylene, and playfully pushed at him.

I moved away with my gear. "I'll say good-bye now. And thanks again, Miss Maylene."

Maylene smiled and gave me a nod, then turned all her attention to Mitchell. As I gave them privacy for their farewells, I heard Maylene say, "I sho' wish ya could stay here." Then she began to cry. I didn't hear what Mitchell said to console her.

❧

"So where we headin'?" asked Mitchell when we were again on the road.

"Figure north toward Vicksburg."

"There lumbering up there?"

"Heard about a camp south of Vicksburg. Thing is, though, Mitchell, I'm figuring I'm finished with lumber camps for a while."

"What ya gonna do, then?"

"There's a man Miz Crenshaw used to talk about who lives in Vicksburg, man name of Luke Sawyer. Runs a mercantile. Miz Crenshaw said he was a fair man, and I plan to see if maybe he and I can do some business."

"What kind of business?"

"See if I can make some furniture for him to sell."

"Well, if you doin' the furniture makin', what ya need him for?"

"I don't have all the tools I need to make the better pieces, and I don't figure to use my money buying more tools either. I figure maybe Luke Sawyer can make that investment."

"Then what ya gonna do with your money? You sure ain't

hardly been spendin' none of it." Mitchell looked at me knowingly and his eyes smiled. He knew when it came to my money I was pretty closemouthed, even with him, and he sometimes laughed at me because of it. He knew I had saved most of my money and that I'd put that money away in a bank in New Orleans. He teased me, but he didn't fault me, even though the way he saw things, there was only today, so whatever money he had, he might as well spend and enjoy it now, and he did.

"Got something else I want to spend it on," I said defensively.

"What's that?"

"Land."

Mitchell laughed. "You back t' that again, huh?"

"It's always been on my mind."

Mitchell just shook his head.

It was already nightfall by the time Mitchell and I had started out. We walked the night through. Mostly we kept to the trail except for when we heard someone coming, then we slipped into the woods for a spell. But the woods were dense with overgrowth and black with the night, and we didn't stay long in them. When the morning came, though, the woods were where we stayed. We moved cautiously as we kept north and out of sight. We walked steady, but we didn't run. If anybody had seen us running, the first thing they would've wanted to know was why we were running. It was a dangerous thing for a black man to be running if he couldn't explain his reason for it. Several times we stopped to rest, but we didn't linger long at any one spot, for we both were thinking on that boy from the turpentine camp, and we wanted to put as much distance between Jessup's camp and us as we could before nightfall. We kept on moving and we didn't complain. By midday we figured we were far enough away to take time to eat some of Maylene's fried chicken and corn bread.

"That Maylene," said Mitchell as he stripped a chicken bone clean, "she was right 'bout one thing. She sure 'nough can cook."

"She seems to have a good heart," I commented.

"Yeah, thing is she gone and got it tied to mine."

"Well," I said, "that happens a lot with you and women. You got yours tied to hers?"

"Naw. Womenfolks jus' seem they give they hearts easy like."

"And they get broken easy like too," I observed.

Mitchell grunted. "Well, I don't promise 'em nothin'. How they end up feelin' is they business."

I was quiet to that. I munched on my corn bread and took some water. Then I said to my friend, "You given any thought to settling?"

Mitchell laughed his deepest laugh. "Me? Look here, Paul, jus' 'cause you wantin' t' set yo'self on some land, don't get the idea that's what I want. All I want is what I'm doin' right now."

I studied him. "But what'll that get you?"

"Freedom t' move and freedom t' be. That's all I want."

"Nothing else? You've got to want more than that. You've got to have some dreams too, Mitchell."

Mitchell scoffed. "Like you goin' west? Like you havin' land like yo' daddy's? Shoot! What dreams get ya? You still a black man in this white man's land, and you got no freedom 'cept for what you make for yo'self. You put in yo' time and you die, and I figure t' keep my freedom 'til that day come."

We finished our eating, then pushed on. By nightfall we were exhausted, and we finally found ourselves an open spot on a ridge to sleep. "How far you think we come?" asked Mitchell as he slumped exhausted to the ground.

"All I can say is we're a day closer to Vicksburg."

Mitchell tugged at his boots. "That may be, but my feet tellin' me we done put in more'n ten times a trip to Vicksburg."

I agreed and slipped my pack off my back. We made a fire to keep ourselves warm, but both of us were too tired to eat any more of Maylene's good food. Mitchell spread his blanket on one side of the fire and placed his gun, which he always kept handy, under the blanket where he could reach it easily, and I spread my blanket on the other side of the fire with no weapon but my knife, and we lay down. "Sure wish I had me my other good blanket," Mitchell grumped as he settled himself, but within a minute or so was snoring. I closed my eyes and fell asleep myself.

"Y'all niggers get up from there!"

I woke with a start and sat up. Men with shotguns stood just beyond the dying fire. The shotguns were pointed at Mitchell and me. I heard rustling at my back and saw two more figures behind us. Mitchell sat up too, but he did so slowly. I glanced his way and cautiously stood. Mitchell stayed put. "What's this about?" I said, showing my face full in the waning firelight. The men stared at me, and I could see in their faces I was not what they had expected.

"Who are ya?" one of them asked, his shotgun still pointed our way.

"Man traveling," I answered, figuring to hold my own with them.

The man waved his shotgun toward Mitchell. "Wit' this nigger here?"

I glanced over at Mitchell. He was sitting like stone, but I knew that under his blanket he had hold of his gun. "We came out of Georgia together," I answered truthfully. "He worked for my daddy. Now we're headed west." I took a chance on what those men were thinking about me. "I don't know what my business has to do with yours. Why don't you tell me why you've got those shotguns pointed at us?"

"We after a chicken thief!" exploded a man from the darkness. "Damn niggers been stealin' our chickens!"

"That a fact?" I said. "Well, we've had no part in that."

"How we know?" The question came from behind me. I turned slightly. I couldn't see the man's face clearly, just his slight figure, and I noted the smell of liquor. "You coulda done been puttin' that there nigger up to the stealin' while you hung back!"

"You see any chickens here?" I asked.

From the other side of the fire came another voice. "You coulda done sold 'em already and I'm figurin' sellin' 'em, eatin' 'em, they all stole jus' the same!"

"When were the last ones stolen?" I asked, surprising myself at how calm I sounded.

"Jus' this night!" came a voice from the back. "Two of mine!"

"And you figure we have them?" I motioned to the fire. "You see any chicken cooking here? You see any feathers around or chicken bones, for that matter?"

The men were silent for a moment, then the lead man motioned toward the darkness. "Check it," he ordered.

From behind me one of the figures came closer and peered down, inspecting the ground. It was at that moment I was grateful Mitchell and I had been too tired to eat before we slept; otherwise there would have been chicken bones in that fire. I just hoped the men wouldn't go looking in our gear and find Maylene's fried chicken. Even though it was cooked, they might figure it was stolen chicken cooked elsewhere. My eyes met Mitchell's and I knew he was thinking the same. We both kept our eyes off the leather bag.

"Well?" questioned the man across the campfire.

The figure shook his head. "Don't see nothin' here." He turned then, and as he did, I could see he was merely a boy with a man's height. He hesitated a moment, looking at me, then moved back into the darkness. I decided not to let his look bother me. I went on acting my part.

"You mind my asking from where these last chickens were stolen?" I asked, presuming my right as a man free, as a white man free, talking to other white men.

"Told ya, my place!" bellowed the man from the back of the group.

"As I said, we're traveling through, so I don't know where that'd be."

The man thundered his reply. "Back east there, no more'n two miles!"

"Well, does it make sense to you for two men who just stole two chickens to walk no more than two miles, then lie down and go to sleep? Does it make sense to you that there are no feathers and no bones near here? And there would be if we had killed the chickens and eaten them. Do you think that there would be anybody near here to whom we could have sold these chickens, seeing that I'm sure everybody within ten miles knows everybody else? Would any of you buy chickens from some stranger knowing there's been chicken thieving going on?"

There was no answer from the men. Some of the men looked at one another and lowered their shotguns. But then the man standing behind Mitchell and me said, "Or maybe ya jus' done been sellin' t' niggers."

Without turning, I said, "We didn't take the chickens." My words were steady, strong, but quietly spoken.

"Yeah? And why we s'pose t' believe that? We don't know you!"

I took a moment, turned, and stared into the darkness as if I could pierce the man's unseen eyes. Then, in a tone I'd heard my daddy use to lesser men, I said, "You questioning my word?"

There was silence. I didn't move. I didn't even look at Mitchell. I figured Mitchell was ready to do what needed to be done. The man in the darkness said nothing. The lead man finally lowered his gun and said, "Y'all figure t' be gone come mornin'?"

I turned to him and nodded. "I figure so."

"Ya best stick t' that," he warned. "We don't take easily t' strangers round here." Then he and the others moved away without another word.

Mitchell and I stayed put, listening to the sounds of their footsteps fading, then the sounds of the forest natural. It took a few minutes before I could breathe normal again. Mitchell got up. He was holding his gun. "That was close."

"Too close," I said.

"Figured for sure them lumbermen done come after us," he said, dismissing the chicken hunters.

I didn't say anything to that. Men looking for chicken thieves and men looking for two men of color who had left their job were all the same to me, as long as those men were white. I turned to my bedding and started rolling it up.

"Whatcha doin'?"

"Getting ready to move out of here."

"Tired as we are?"

"I suddenly got myself some new energy."

Mitchell stuck his gun into the waist of his pants. "'Spect I have too."

After he'd packed his gear, Mitchell said, "Ya know, Paul, I 'spect we best be splittin' up."

I glanced over at Mitchell, reading him before he said his next words; still, I asked, "Why's that?"

"You know why. You lookin' white in the night done saved us this time, but them men catch a white-lookin' man and a black one for sure on the road walkin' t'gether come light, they might have theyselves a change of mind 'bout our thievin'. We be separated and they come on us, they won't remember one of us from anybody else. Same goes if the lumbermen got folks after us. We travel t'gether, folks take too much notice."

I knew Mitchell was right. I had already thought it myself. "I could help get us out of a mess, though, we get stopped."

"Can't help me, you swingin' from a tree yo' own self."

I sighed.

"They figure you got colored in ya, Paul, that's what's gonna happen sure. You be swingin' 'fore I do."

"All right," I said, not liking the truth of any of this but knowing it was so. "You going to head on up to the camp?"

"Yeah, figure t' do so."

"I'll be going to that Luke Sawyer's store."

"We can meet up there. Say, in a month or so?"

I nodded, and the matter was settled. "But you send me word before then," I said, "and I'll do the same." Mitchell agreed to that. We figured it would ease both our minds to know that the other hadn't gotten caught by Jessup or been mistaken again for a chicken thief.

We stayed on by the campsite awhile after that, waiting for the men to move farther away from us. But before the morning came, we took to the trail again, still headed due north. Couple hours after the dawn we went our separate ways.

❧

I was dead tired; still, I walked all that day. Mitchell and I had split the last of Maylene's food, and I ate the final piece of chicken for my dinner shortly past noon. I figured to save the corn bread for my supper. By nightfall I was looking for a place to lay my head in some kind of peace. The moon was rising and I still hadn't found a spot. The darkness came, followed by a full moon. The land opened up into meadow, and I left the trail, crossed the meadow in part, and found myself a hillside to climb. There were some trees, but no dense brush. Out beyond the slope I could see the outline of a forest in the moonlight. There was no man-made light, and I took solace from that. I took off my gear and set it on the ground beside a good-sized rock and wondered how far Mitchell had gotten in his travel. Then, without rolling out my bedroll or checking around that rock for rattlers or any other such thing, I lay down and went to sleep.

Next morning when I woke, the sun was already high, shining bright in my eyes. Having not had much sleep in the past days, on this morning I had slept long, and even peacefully, despite being in a place I didn't know and without Mitchell to keep watch with me. I shielded my eyes from the sun, gave them a rub, then looked out upon the day.

I was awed by what I saw.

All around me was emerald green, and above that, God's own bluest skies, blessed only with two or three perfect rolls of pillow-like clouds. A meadow lay all around me, and a forest of longleaf pine dotted with oak and hickory circled the meadow. Gazing from the slope where I sat beside the rock, I felt I was sitting where God Himself must have once sat and been pleased with Himself.

I got up and began to walk the land. I trod down the slope, circled the meadow, and lastly went into the forest along a cow trail laden with dung, to a glade that held a pond as its center. A fallen tree lay beside the pond, and I sat upon it as the morning light slit through the trees and shone everything golden. For the first time since I'd left my daddy's land, my heart soared, higher than any mountain I'd ever imagined, up to God's own perfect clouds, and I felt a peace come over me.

"'Ey, boy! Whatcha doin' here?"

I turned, startled, and stood quickly. I'd been sitting on the log for some time and the sun was now directly overhead.

"I say, whatcha doin' here?"

An old man stood before me, a stick in his hand for support. He was a man of color.

"Just sitting," I said.

"You ain't from round here, is ya? Ain't seen ya before."

"No, sir. Just came here this morning. Slept up on the slope yonder last night."

The old man's eyes narrowed and he came closer. "Who you? What name ya go by?"

"Name's Paul Logan," I said, feeling a sudden familiarity with the old man, as if he were a part of home. "I come out of Georgia."

"And here ya is way over here? Ya don't know it, boy, this here's Mississippi!"

"Yes, sir. I know that."

The old man eyed me again, then sat down on the log. I took my seat beside him. "Whatcha doin' way over here in Mississippi?" he asked me.

"Heading toward Vicksburg."

"T' do what?"

I smiled at the old man's curiosity. "Maybe get a job."

"Umph" was all the old man had to voice to that.

"It's right pretty country here," I said.

"That sho' the truth."

"You know who owns it?"

"Oughtta. Man done bought it from my Old Master Morris Granger. Old Master done had t' sell a bunch of his land for taxes, or so that's what folks say. After that war he ain't had no money. Now, I been on this here place from time I was a youngun. Old Master tole me that done been way more'n three score and ten, and I ain't never figured nobody else be puttin' they name t' this land outside Old Master's people. Young Master Filmore, he in charge now. Old Master gone on t' the Maker, but I still here."

I nodded in appreciation of that fact. "Well, who owns this land now?"

"That there'd be Mister J. T. Hollenbeck. Come down from somewheres north and done bought it after the war. Bought near t' all the land round in here."

"You think he'd be willing to sell some of it?"

The old man turned and stared at me through milky-looking eyes. "Now how's I s'pose t' know somethin' like that? Ya wants t' know that, then ya needs t' be askin' him."

I rose. "Then I expect I will. Where can I find him, this J. T. Hollenbeck?"

"Jus' follow that there trail back t' that meadow, then ya head yo'self straight north. Turn t' the east ya come t' a creek, and a forked road. Follow that right fork, and ya find him."

"Well, I thank you."

The old man nodded.

I started away, then stopped to look back at him. "May I ask your name?"

"Elijah," he said. "That's what he called me, Old Master did. Elijah. That's all."

I thanked him again, then left him there, sitting by the pond.

I went back to the slope, got my gear, and headed out. I followed old man Elijah's directions as far as the creek and stopped there to wash up. I had myself one spare shirt and a spare pair of pants, and after I'd cleaned myself, I put them on. I brushed my teeth with a sweet gum stick and combed my hair back straight. Then I continued on my way to see J. T. Hollenbeck. I wasn't dressed Sunday-go-to-meeting, but I was clean.

❧

When I presented myself to J. T. Hollenbeck, I let him know right off I was a man of color. I figured it was best I not misrepresent myself concerning this land. If I did business with him, he'd eventually find out anyway, since I wasn't trying to hide the fact, and I didn't want any chance I might have of buying this land to backfire in my face. Thing was, as it turned out, J. T. Hollenbeck wasn't interested in selling, no matter what color I was.

"If you really want land," he told me, "the man to see is Filmore Granger. I know he's made a few small land deals in the last few years, but I can tell you from experience, dealing with him won't be easy. Now, you say you're a man of color, so I can't guarantee you that Filmore Granger will even do business with you. But if you're interested in buying some land in these parts, you need to at least talk to him. Tell him I sent you, though I don't know how much of a recommendation that would be." He smiled. "I don't know whom Filmore Granger despises more, white Yankees or free Negroes."

"Well, I thank you for your advice," I said, trying to hide my disappointment about the land. "I'd be much obliged, though, if you ever do decide to sell any of your land, you'd keep me in mind."

J. T. Hollenbeck looked me over, scrutinizing my worth, I suppose. "I ever do think on selling, I'll probably be asking cash money. You'd be able to do that?"

"Well, that'd be depending on your price."

"It'd be fair, but it wouldn't be cheap. Most men of color couldn't afford it. Where would you get it?"

"Well, that wouldn't be your worry, Mister Hollenbeck," I said, speaking direct, "long as I meet your price."

J. T. Hollenbeck smiled again. "I'll keep that in mind, Paul Logan." Then J. T. Hollenbeck told me how to get to the Granger house, but when I left him, I kept to the trail toward Vicksburg. I had no interest in seeing another piece of land right now. I had seen the land I wanted, and it was that land that stayed on my mind.

Caroline

When I got to Vicksburg, I went straightaway to find Luke Sawyer's store. When I found it, I told Luke Sawyer that Miz Hattie Crenshaw out of Laurel had suggested I look him up. I told him that I was a wood craftsman and that I was looking for a place to start up my work again. I told him that I could make just about anything when it came to wood furniture; then I handed him the yellowed sheet of paper Miz Crenshaw had written on my behalf when I'd left her place. The fact that I was a man of color was in that letter. Luke Sawyer looked solemnly at the letter, then glanced over his spectacles at me. "How you know Miz Hattie?" he finally said.

"I worked for her a few years back."

"Doing woodworking?"

"Some."

"You learned woodworking at her place, then?"

"No, sir. I apprenticed with a man in Georgia, but I finished up with a man outside Laurel."

"You got tools?"

"Just what I can carry with me. Not all I need."

"So how you expect to make furniture if you don't have all the necessary tools?"

"Well, Miz Crenshaw said you used to have a cabinetmaker working out of your store, so you'd most likely have access to the tools I'd need. What you don't have, maybe I could make."

"You'd want to buy the tools from me then?"

"What I'd like to do," I said quite frankly, checking his eyes, "is go into business with you. You supply the major tools and I'll make the furniture."

Luke Sawyer studied me. "And how do I know you can do what you say you can?"

"You got something you want made?"

Luke Sawyer gazed at me in silence before pulling out a notebook from below his counter. Then he turned and motioned for me to follow him. He led me outside to a shed that was set back a ways on the west side of his store. He unlocked the door and showed me in. There were some tools hanging on the wall, a fireplace was in the corner, and a lathe sat in the middle of the floor. Planks of lumber were leaning against the wall and dust was settled around the room. "It's been a good while since I had anybody working in here," said Luke Sawyer as he coughed from the dust. Then waving the dust away, he opened his notebook and thumped his forefinger on a page showing a picture of a night table. "Can you make that?"

I studied the picture, then glanced around the room at Luke Sawyer's tools. "Long as these tools of yours are good, I can make it."

"Well, I know a lady who mightily wants an oak night table like this and a chifforobe to match. I'm not going to risk my wood on a chifforobe just yet, but if you can make a night table to satisfy her, then I'll consider a proposition with you and I'll pay you for the table. You turn out a poor piece and mess up my wood or my tools, I'll put you to work chopping wood or anything else needs doing 'til I figure you've paid me in full for them. Agreed?"

"Agreed," I said. "But I'll tell you right now, Mister Sawyer, there'll be no need for me to chop wood."

"How long you figure it to take you?"

I looked again at the picture. "I can start today, finish in about a week, maybe less. After that, I'll have to put a finish on. If I use linseed oil, it could take several weeks for a nice finish. Just a couple of days if I use shellac."

"Shellac'll do," said Luke Sawyer. "You got a place to stay?"

"Not yet."

"Then you stay the night here, if you want. There's the fireplace over there in the corner you get cold, and some firewood out back. Just don't burn my place down."

"It'll be here in the morning," I said.

Luke Sawyer grunted and left me to my work.

It had been late afternoon when I arrived at Luke Sawyer's store. I cleared away the dust, then settled down to making the night table. I worked the evening and into the night, slept a few hours, then woke before the dawn and started on the work again. It had been some time since I had set my hands to finished wood, but the touch of it, the smell of it, was the same as it had always been, and it was satisfying to me. I worked the morning long without any food or drink, except for some water from Luke Sawyer's pump out back. About noontime I stood up from my workbench and went outside.

The day was crisp and sunny, and I took my first food of the day in the outdoors. I had bought some cheese and bread from Luke Sawyer's store, and I ate on the bench that set next to the door of the shed. I ate my fill, wrapped the remainder of the cheese and bread, which I figured to save for my supper, then went to stretch my legs.

Now, Luke Sawyer's store was set on a large triangular piece
of land, with roads on every side. It was a good location. Folks
came from every direction to the store. There was no way a
body could have missed it. I walked midway down the stretch of
the store's side yard and stood looking out at the surroundings.
The greenery of Vicksburg was all around, and I breathed it in,
feeling good in the sunshine of that springtime day. But then I
heard a commotion rising near the front of the store, and I walked
a bit farther to see what it was. Before I got to the road, I stopped
beside a big oak tree that bathed me in shadow.

On the road were five boys about the ages of eight or nine,
four of them white, one a boy of color. The white boys were circling the colored boy and yelling obscenities. The colored boy
stood with his head bowed, crying and wordless. Though I
chose to stay out of other folks' business, it bothered me to see
those four boys taunting that one, and I started from the shad-
ows to stop it. But then I heard someone yelling at the boys, and
I stayed put. Turning, I saw that the yelling was from two young
women coming up the road. "Y'all leave him be! Y'all leave him
be right now!" cried one of the young women, and the white
boys grew silent. At first they seemed startled by the order; then
when they saw from whom it came, they began to laugh.

The young women kept their stride. One wore a light-blue
dress. The other wore a similar dress, but in gray. They were no
more than girls, actually, looking to be in their mid teens or so. I
couldn't tell which was older. Both were tall and stately, with
pretty faces and skin the reddish brown of pecans. Both wore
long braids, and they each carried a covered basket and bore one
between them. I figured them for sisters. There was no laughing
from either one as they approached the boys and stood before
them.

"So, what y'all want?" asked one of the smart-mouthed boys.
"This ain't y'all's business."

"You messin' with this boy here, it is," said the girl dressed in blue.

"Gal, you best stay outa this."

"I'm not a gal. I'm the person tellin' you to leave this boy be."

"You best be watchin' yo' mouth!"

"You best be watchin' *yo's*," warned the young woman, undaunted. "I said leave this child be and I mean it. Come on with us now, Henry."

Another one of the sassy-mouthed boys stepped forward in front of the boy of color. "He ain't goin' nowheres 'til we say so!"

The young woman glanced away for a moment, and the expression on her face told me she was tired of fooling with these children. She set down both of her baskets, then looked again at the boys. "Now, look here," she said, "I know each and every one of y'all's mamas." She stared each boy right in the face. "Lloyd James, you know my daddy just saved your cow in birthin'. And Harold Thomas back there, *yo'* mama been buyin' pies from my mama for years. Jamie Struthers and Conrad, I see y'all too, and you know I know your mamas, and I know for a fact not a one of 'em would 'low y'all to be down here doin' such a thing, makin' fun of this here child." The young woman then placed long-fingered hands on her hips. "Now, go on and get 'fore I have to go tell them 'bout y'all."

"And if this girl here don't tell y'alls mamas, y'all can rest assured I will!" hollered someone from the porch of the store. I turned. It was Luke Sawyer. He stood in the store doorway, a large forbidding presence holding a bloody butcher knife.

The boys looked up fearfully. The young woman, however, without looking around at Luke Sawyer, had the last word. "Now, y'all get!" she ordered once again.

The boys took off.

The young woman watched them go; so did Luke Sawyer. Then he said, "Girls, them baskets for me?"

Both girls replied, "Yes, sir."

"Got some more of them good pies and cakes from your mama?" Luke Sawyer grinned. "Well, bring 'em on in."

"Yes, sir, Mister Sawyer, in just a minute," said the young woman who'd done all the talking. She put her arm around the boy, Henry. "Soon's we tend to this boy here."

"Suit yourself," said Luke Sawyer, turning back to his store, then stopped and looked around again. "Where's your papa? He bring y'all into town?"

"Yes, sir, he did," answered the same young lady. "He over at Mister Crane Cooper's place."

"Tendin' to that ole mule of his, I reckon."

"Yes, sir."

"Um. Cooper oughtta just shoot that mule and be done with it. But long's your daddy can keep fixing him up, I s'pose he won't."

The sisters laughed. "S'pose not," said the one.

"Well, y'all come on in when you ready," said Luke Sawyer, and went back into his store.

The young woman then turned to the crying boy. "Now, hush up, Henry!" she ordered. "Don't you be cryin' 'bout them ignorant boys. Don't you know their words can't hurt you none, 'less you let them! They tryin' to make you feel little, but they can't make you feel little if you feel big inside. No matter what they do, they can't do that. You hush up that cryin' and go on home to folks who care 'bout you, and don't you be hangin' round this here store where these ignorant boys can make fun of you. You hear me?"

The boy nodded and wiped at his eyes with his arm. He turned slightly, but his arm hid his face. He started down the road.

"Wait up just a minute there, Henry!" the young woman called, stopping him. She dug into her basket and pulled out a good-size cookie. "This here's for you, Henry, and can you carry yo'self a pie without droppin' it?"

The boy spoke for the first time. "Pie?"

"That's right. A pie."

The other young woman now spoke up. "Caroline, you can't go givin' this boy one of these here pies!"

"Hush up, Callie!" snapped Caroline. Then in a softened voice she said to the boy, "Now, you take this here sweet-potato pie to yo' mama and tell her that's yo' pie. But you be sure and share this pie with yo' mama and yo' sisters, ya hear me?"

"I hear," said the boy, Henry, and turned full toward me. Now I could see his face clear. He had a bad cleft lip, which no doubt had been the object of the boys' taunts. But that didn't seem to matter to him at the moment, as his lips curled into a wide grin. "Thank ya."

"Well, you sure 'nough welcome," said Caroline. "But you better make sure that pie get all the way home! Yo' mama can bring me back that tin come church time Sunday."

"Yes'm, I make sho'." The boy headed down the road, and the two girls picked up their baskets and started for the store entrance.

"Owww, girl," said the one called Callie, "Mama's gonna whip the livin' daylights outa you 'bout givin' 'way that pie! You know we s'pose t' be sellin' these here pies!"

"Well, you know what, Callie?" said Caroline. "I don't care! That boy needed somethin t' make him feel good 'bout himself, and if a little ole sweet-potato pie can do that, then that's what I give him. Mama can jus' whip me if she wanna!"

"Well, she'll wanna, all right!"

Caroline shrugged off her words. "Ya know what, Cal? I've gotten my share of whippin's before. 'Spect I can take another one." With those words she entered the store, and her sister followed. I headed back to the shed with a smile on my face.

I went back to my work. I labored steadily on the night table the rest of that afternoon and several days after that, sanding it, making the edges rounded and smooth, making it perfect. When I finished, I was satisfied. I got some shellac from Luke Sawyer's store and he looked at me with a raised eyebrow. "You done already?"

"Soon as it's stained," I said, and returned to the shed. I brushed on the first coat of shellac, then settled back waiting for it to dry before coating the table with another. While I was waiting, Luke Sawyer came out to the shed. "It's not dry yet," I said.

Luke Sawyer nodded and walked around the night table without touching it. He studied the drawers sitting separately on a shelf, and I could see admiration in his eyes. "If these drawers fit in that table as good as they look, Paul Logan, then I don't figure you to be chopping wood."

"They'll fit," I assured him.

Two days later, with an additional coat of shellac dry on the night table and the drawers smoothly slid inside, Luke Sawyer had me bring the night table into the store. Soon after, he sent a boy over to the house of a Miz B. R. Tillman, wife of one of the bankers in town, with the message that a night table like the one she'd admired in the catalog was available if she'd like to take a look. Miz B. R. Tillman came late in the day, just before closing, with her husband, Mister B. R. Tillman. Luke Sawyer called me from the shed, and I stood aside as the Tillmans looked over my work.

"I understand you're a colored boy," said B. R. Tillman.

I looked at him in silence.

"That right?" he questioned, looking for confirmation.

"I'm a man of color," I said, quietly correcting him. I was no longer a boy.

B. R. Tillman nodded. "Well, I've heard some mighty good things about your woodworking from Mister Sawyer here. Some mighty good things. Now, if this be the kind of work you do, those good words were true, all right." He walked around the table inspecting it. "Say you made this in just this last week?"

"That's right."

"Um-hum," murmured B. R. Tillman admiringly, and continued his inspection.

Meanwhile, Miz B. R. Tillman had already made up her mind. "Benjamin Roy," she said, "I want this night table! Best work I've seen in a while by anybody around here. I want a chifforobe with the same design. Get them, please!"

B. R. Tillman protested a bit. "Now, Miz Tillman, that's going to be depending on what Mister Sawyer here is asking for it—"

"He'll be reasonable," said Miz Tillman.

"Now, precious—"

"Won't you, Mister Sawyer?" she asked.

"Well, Miz Tillman," said Luke Sawyer, "I always try to be."

"Well, if that's your attitude," said B. R. Tillman, "we ought not have a problem. What you asking?"

The haggling over price took more than an hour, and both men seemed to enjoy it immensely. Finally a deal was struck, with B. R. Tillman paying what Luke Sawyer had already told me he would for the table, and a price agreed for the chifforobe if the piece met the Tillmans' approval. The Tillmans, especially Miz Tillman, went away happy with their purchase. Luke Sawyer locked his store and turned to me. He picked up the money the Tillmans had paid and said, "I suppose now we need to determine how we're going to split this. I wanted you here because I wanted you to know exactly how much I was getting for this piece of furniture. I mean to treat you fair."

"I believe that."

"But you know I've got a lot of expenses connected with this woodworking plan of yours. I've got the wood to pay for, the tools, and don't forget the shed you're working in—and staying in, I might add. So seeing that you're using my tools and my shed and customers who come through me, as well as the fact that I'm supplying the lumber, I figure that I'm heavy on the expenses end. Now, you talk like an educated young fella. You understand percentages?"

I nodded.

"Good. Well, I figure to pay you twenty-five percent for your labor, and I'll keep seventy-five percent for my overhead and profit."

I looked at Luke Sawyer, and had he been a man of color, I would have laughed, and he no doubt would have laughed with me. Instead, I shook my head somberly. "I'm afraid those terms won't do, Mister Sawyer. I'm a master craftsman and I've been at my trade for some years now. Without my experience there'd be no night table worthy of selling to the likes of the Tillmans, or a chifforobe on order, so I figure my investment of time and skills are as important as your investment of your tools and your supplies. Thing is, I figure any piece that's made, the cost of supplies needs to already be figured. As for my staying in your shed, I appreciate your offer, and it would be convenient for me, but I believe it would be convenient for you too. I'm the kind of man who, once I make a commitment, I stick to it. If I stay in your shed and I say something is going to be done by a certain time, I can work through the night if need be. If you want to charge me rent for the shed, we could do that, or if I need to find a separate living space, I can do that, but I figure fifty percent of any transaction is the least I can take."

Luke Sawyer studied me in the dim light. "Equal partnership, eh?" he asked, and his wording was not lost on either of us. "What about my customers? Remember, you wouldn't be getting any orders for furniture if folks didn't come to me. They trust me, and I'd have to be standing behind your workmanship. That's a lot on me."

I nodded. "I appreciate that, and I believe that as long as I make quality pieces, there'll be satisfied customers who'll let other folks know about pieces they can order through your store. I think that fifty percent would be profitable for each of us."

"Um ..." murmured Luke Sawyer, thinking that over. "Maybe even more profitable for you, if you start taking on customers that come direct to you without bothering to come through me."

"If you're concerned about that, Mister Sawyer, I can tell you right now that as long as we have an arrangement, I'll take only customers who come through you. I'd figure, though, to set my own hours."

"Set your own hours? How do I know then that my orders'll be done when I figure they ought to be?"

"They'll be done, and on time."

"Well, if they're not, I'll charge you on them. Five percent of what's coming to you for each day the work's not done."

I agreed to that, but added, "Of course, I'll need to know beforehand what the piece is and have a say in the time it's going to take me to make it."

"Long as it's reasonable. Don't forget, I know about how long it takes on a piece."

Again, I agreed.

"So, set your own hours, consult with you before I make my deals, what else you want?" Luke Sawyer asked dryly.

"Nothing," I said. "But there is something you need to know. I'm looking to buy land and once I do, I'll be working it. If it's agreeable to you, I'd contract to work with you for a year."

Luke Sawyer stared at me in silence, and I didn't know what he was thinking in that quiet moment. Then he laughed, outright and loud. "Thought I was supposed to be the businessman here! All right, then, Paul Logan," he said. "We'll try it this way for a spell, but I tell you one thing right now. I start losing money or you don't live up to your end of things, then this deal's off. Agreed?"

"Agreed," I said.

"I s'pose I owe you some money, then." The look on Luke Sawyer's face was solemn as he gave me my money, but then he extended his hand to me and I shook it, and I remembered that, for he was the first white man to shake my hand since I had left my daddy's land.

❧

About two months after I started working with Luke Sawyer, Mitchell showed up late one Saturday evening. I had already quit my tools and settled down to my reading when he knocked on the shed door. As we had said we would, we had both sent word about our safe arrivals, but we hadn't been in contact further. Course, I'd known he'd come eventually, but his sudden appearance gave me quite a surprise. "I must say, it's about time you showed up," I said. "I've been thinking about coming to look for you."

"Good to see you too," said Mitchell. "First time I've had to get away."

"So, where're you working? Still at that camp I sent word to?"

"Naw . . . was. Got a job there few days after we split up, but I've moved on to another camp now. Place called Mud Creek."

I had heard of the camp. "What happened?" I said. "Why'd you leave the first camp?"

"Same as usual. Folks just don't seem t' want t' get along with me for some reason."

"Another fight?"

"Wouldn't call it a fight," grumbled Mitchell. "It was over with in less'n a minute. Fella couldn't even hardly make a fist.

But then he went and made such a fuss, I figured it was best I find me another place."

I tried to hide my smile. "What was the fuss about? His woman?"

Mitchell looked at me. "What else?" He suddenly laughed, and I laughed too. It was good to be with him again.

I hadn't cooked much for my own supper, just some collards and onions with a bit of ham hock, but I had some potatoes in store, as well as a side piece of bacon and some eggs, and I happily cooked them up in celebration of Mitchell's arrival. Mitchell cooked up some poor corn bread too, and we sat down at my cleared workbench and ate hungrily, as if we had before us one of my daddy's Christmas feasts.

"So, you're working just a half day away from here?" I said.

Mitchell was concentrating on eating, and he only nodded.

"Things okay with you there?"

Mitchell glanced across at me, swallowed, then took a gulp of his milk. "You got reason t' think they wouldn't be?"

"It's just that last time I saw you, we had those Mississippi lumbermen after us, as well as that band of men looking for chicken thieves."

Mitchell smiled. "Well, I 'spect they still lookin'." I smiled too, and Mitchell added, "Ain't heard no more 'bout 'em, and ain't lookin' to hear no more 'bout 'em. My job ain't bad. Pay's 'bout the same. Boss man 'bout the same like the rest I known. Ain't nothin' much different, 'ceptin' I ain't got nobody watchin' my back." Mitchell looked pointedly at me, and I understood. I felt the same. Thing was, though, I was in a different situation now and not having to worry about a camp full of men turning on me. I was feeling like instead of watching over my shoulder, I was looking ahead. "Look like you makin' out all right," Mitchell observed, glancing around at an unfinished table and a cabinet that took up a corner of the room.

"For now," I said.

"So, what kind of deal you work out with Luke Sawyer?"

"Worked out a fifty-fifty partnership with him. He lets me use his tools, his shed, and his lumber, and I make the furniture his customers want."

"You could've done it on your own, Paul. You ain't needed no white man. Yo' work good 'nough on its own self."

"Wasn't interested in putting what money I got into all the tools I'd need for making furniture. What I was interested in was someone to put up the tools for me and I could still be my own boss."

"Yeah . . ." murmured Mitchell, "less this here Luke Sawyer see different."

I shrugged. "It's only for a short while anyway. You forgotten what I really want?"

"How I'm gonna forget? You been talkin' 'bout the same ole thing ever since we left outa East Texas."

I grinned wide. "Well, I found it."

"Land?"

"Land. Same day we went our separate ways, I found it. I walked late that night and I was so tired, I didn't give any thought to where I was. I saw what looked to be a safe place on a hillside and I just put down my head and went to sleep. But come the next morning, I woke to an amazement. Mitchell, I was sitting on the most beautiful spot of land I've ever seen. I can't even begin to describe it to you, because words don't hardly fit, but it had meadows and a virgin forest, and a pond too. When I saw it, I couldn't believe it. I got up and walked all around the place. I can't explain it, but that land just drew me to it, like I belonged there. Mitchell, it felt like home."

Mitchell studied me across the workbench. "So, what you do 'bout it?"

"What do you think? Went to see if I could buy it."

Mitchell scoffed. "From a white man?"

"What makes you think a white man owned it?"

Now Mitchell laughed. "'Cause a black man couldn't afford land good as you describin'!"

I let Mitchell finish with his laughter, then said, "There's something about that land, Mitchell. I mean to have it."

"The man willin' t' sell?"

"Said he wasn't . . . not right now anyway. But I figure I can wait."

"Wait how long? A year? Ten? Waitin' on a white man t' let loose of his gold ain't what I call right smart."

"Well, maybe not," I conceded, "but I'm thinking on maybe buying some other land and working it while I'm doing my waiting."

"And what 'bout your woodworkin'?"

"Never intended to make a lifetime of it. You know that. I told Luke Sawyer the same when I struck my bargain with him. It's land I want, not a carpentry shop."

Mitchell nodded. "So when you 'spect t' get this other land?"

"Well, one thing I promised Luke Sawyer was a year's work with him. I'll need to live up to that, so I'll wait awhile."

"This Luke Sawyer, he a fair man?"

"Seems to be."

"Don't count on it."

Mitchell again gave me that pointed look, and I understood. After all, Luke Sawyer was a white man, and even if he had been a man of color, there wouldn't have been much trust as far as Mitchell and I were concerned. The two of us had learned long ago to trust only each other. "I get a piece of land," I said, "you're welcome to come in on it with me."

Mitchell laughed again. "Told you before, Paul, I ain't wantin' t' be no farmer. "'Sides, a man get hisself some land, he must be figurin' t' settle, get hisself a wife and younguns and tied down." He shot a quzzical look at me. "You found yourself somebody?"

I shook my head. "Been too busy to look."

"Seem, though, you given thought to it."

"Won't deny that," I admitted. "I figure it's time I settled."

"What you doin' wit' your free time? You seeing any young ladies?"

"You know I don't have time to court."

"Well, anybody courting you?"

I smiled.

"So—who is she?" demanded Mitchell.

"Well, there've been one or two young ladies who've invited me to supper."

"Least that's something," said Mitchell. "You go?"

"Too busy."

Mitchell grunted.

"But what about you?" I asked. "I know you must be seeing somebody. You always are."

"Yeah . . . but they all just the same to me. Course, I did meet myself a couple of real nice girls, pretty too, a week or so back. They come to the camp with their mama, but I ain't tried to court 'em or nothin'."

"Why not?"

Mitchell eyed me as if I should already know the answer to that. "'Cause nice girls, they always be 'spectin' you to settle, and you know that ain't me. I don't intend t' settle."

"Never?"

"Yeah . . . when I'm dead."

Mitchell stayed the night in the shed, and we talked through most of it. Next morning, right after breakfast, Mitchell headed back to the camp so he could reach it early enough to see one of the camp women who'd taken a liking to him. Once Mitchell had gone on the road, I started back to work. I had long ago given up the notion of the Sabbath as a day without toil. Even though I read my Bible, I didn't attend church. The store was locked and quiet on a Sunday. Luke Sawyer's house, on the same piece of land, was just as quiet, for Luke Sawyer and his family were all-day Christians and spent most of the day in the white church across town. I had no one calling me, no one demanding my time. For me, Sunday was a good day to work.

"So, you been holding out on me, huh?"

I looked up in surprise from my workbench to find Luke Sawyer standing in the doorway. It was late on a Monday afternoon and Luke Sawyer was dressed in the long white butcher's apron he often wore during store hours and, as usual, that made his already large frame appear more threatening. I felt caught off guard and I grew tense at the tone of his voice. "What?" I said.

Luke Sawyer waved a letter toward me and stepped into the shed. "You know what this is? A letter all about you!"

I put aside the piece of pine I'd been planing and rose slowly, readying to defend myself against whatever accusations he was about to make.

"That's right! It's all here!" Luke Sawyer held up the letter for emphasis as he stood opposite me. "Why didn't you tell me you knew about horses?"

"What?" I said again.

"This letter here is from Miz Hattie Crenshaw. I wrote her about you when you first came—I like to know who I'm dealing with/ Seems she's been away and didn't get my letter 'til recently. But anyway, I just now got this letter from her and she tells me you not only know carpentry, but you're about the best horseman she's ever seen! She says you can ride the best there is, and you can train them too. Even the wild ones!"

I turned to get a chisel from one of the shelves. I didn't want

Luke Sawyer to see the look of relief I was sure showed on my face. "How is Miz Crenshaw?" I asked.

"She's fine, fine."

"I'm glad to hear that."

"Well, what about it?"

I turned back to him with the chisel in hand.

"What about the horses?" he went on excitedly. "About what she said? You that good?"

"I've done quite a bit of work with horses," I admitted.

"Miz Crenshaw says when you worked for her, you were so good, she loaned you out to some of her neighbors who needed help with some of their finer horses. Says you even raced for her and some others, and every race you rode, you won! I think you're being too modest, Paul."

I smiled slightly. "Well, I've always loved horses." I sat back down on the bench and again took up the pine.

"So, how come I had to hear all this from Miz Hattie? How come you didn't tell me yourself?"

I looked up at him. "I came to you about making furniture, not riding horses."

Luke Sawyer studied me, then said, "Come with me." At that, he turned brusquely and left the shed. He expected me to follow and I did. He led me behind his store past a stable, where he boarded horses and kept some for hire as well, then down a trail through woodland to an open pasture. A corral was at the far end of the pasture and a herd of horses was penned inside. We crossed to the corral, then Luke Sawyer leaned against the gate and motioned toward the horses. "So, what do you think?" he asked.

I glanced at the herd. They looked to be mostly mustangs. But there was one who was different and right away caught my eye. It was a stallion. He looked underfed and there was dried blood on his coat, as if he had been in battle. He hadn't been cleaned up, yet he stood apart from the others. He was a palomino. Both he and another stallion, a black one, had been tethered on opposite sides of the corral. "They're from out west?" I asked.

Luke Sawyer nodded. "Man brought them in a few days ago on a barge 'cross the Mississippi. They're supposed to be bronco-busted, but that's all, and from the look of some of them, seems like the job wasn't too well done. Still, he's looking to make a sizeable amount on them. He's boarding them here while he tries to round up some buyers to look them over. He says he'll give me first pick if I'm interested in buying."

I looked at Luke Sawyer. "And are you?"

"Depends," he said. "I've done business with the man before, but only to buy a couple of everyday kind of horses for hiring out to folks around here. I've never bought any real quality animals from him, and he swears most of this bunch is quality."

I turned again to the herd. "Could be. Mustangs are known for their speed."

"Well, to be truthful, I've got my eye on one in particular. That black beauty of a stallion tethered yonder on the far side. Don't know what kind of quality he is, but he sure is a beauty."

I nodded in agreement.

"I want you to check him out and let me know what you think."

Again I nodded.

"Fact to business," said Luke Sawyer, "I want you to cut out the best six of the bunch."

"That'll take time," I said.

"Know that. But I need for you to check out all these horses and let me know what you think in the next two days. Man's expecting buyers to be coming in after then."

I frowned. "Don't you have somebody to do that kind of work for you already?"

"Never needed anybody. Took care of it myself. This here's different, though. I've got a chance to get some real quality animals at a low price, and if I get the right ones, I can do right well in selling them later. I hadn't given much thought to this until Miz Hattie's letter arrived. If you're as good with horses as she says you are, then maybe I'll buy them."

I fixed my eyes on Luke Sawyer. "On my word?"

Luke Sawyer fixed his eyes on me too. "On Hattie Crenshaw's," he said.

I took a few moments to stare out across the corral before turning back to him. "You know, Mister Sawyer," I finally said, "if I take the time I'll need with these horses, I'll lose time on the furniture you've got contracted."

"I'll take care of that. I always give myself a little leeway in dealing with my customers, and I'll give you two extra days on the orders we've got."

"I understand that, Mister Sawyer, but I could be losing money."

"Not really. I'd pay you for your time, same as I'd pay my stable boy."

I wanted to laugh at that, but of course I didn't. I remained sober. "So, all you want me to do is pick out the best six for you?"

"That's right."

"And what if there aren't six good ones?"

"Then you pick out whatever there is. Course now, I'm going to have to approve of them."

"I understand that, but like you said, these horses are only bronco-busted. You planning on giving them more training before you sell them?"

"Well, that would make them worth more, so I'd think so."

"You've got somebody in mind to train them? Somebody who's trained horses like these before?"

Luke Sawyer's glance at me was coy. I figured he knew where I was leading with this. He put on his bartering face. I'd seen it often enough to know. "There are some fellas around."

"Might be a good idea then for them to take a look at the horses as I cut them out."

"Was thinking on that." Luke Sawyer pursed his lips. "Was thinking too, if you'd like the chance, I'd let you see what you could do with one or two of them."

I shook my head. "Well, I thank you, Mister Sawyer, but I've contracted with you to make furniture, and if I spend my time training a horse at a stable boy's wages, I'm definitely going to lose money. I can certainly check over the herd and take out the best for you, but I figure I'll need to get back to my workbench after that."

"Suit yourself," said Luke Sawyer and turned away.

"When do you want me to start?"

"Now."

I did just that. After Luke Sawyer left, the first thing I did was sit atop that fence and study each horse from afar. There were fifteen horses all together. I watched the movements of each and the way they were with one another. I noted the ones who stood together and the ones who stood apart. Several times I let go shrill sounds and banged tins. Some horses were nervous and bolted. Others became more alert, their ears perked, but remained in place. By the time I got down from that fence, I already had a good idea of the horses I'd be cutting out for Luke Sawyer.

Next thing I did was to build a temporary chute into which I could put one horse at a time. Then I enlisted the aid of Luke Sawyer's stable boy and two of his friends with the promise of a day's wages for each, and had them help me in roping the horses and leading them into the chute. We were able to get a few of the horses in without much difficulty, but most, including the palomino, gave us trouble. Still, I was able to get a close look at each of them, and I studied them carefully, front and rear. I checked their ears, their eyes, their abdomens, their legs, and their hooves. I should have checked their teeth too, but I chose not to be bitten. I took note of the weaker horses.

That night I spent on the ground outside the corral, talking to the horses, singing to them. I spent all the next day with them, observing them, and the next night as well. The following morning I cut seven from the herd, including the black stallion Luke Sawyer had his eyes on. He had been right about the stallion. Not only was he a beauty, but he seemed to be of fine quality. I led each horse with a rope around the meadow several times. I didn't try to mount any of them. By the time I finished, Luke Sawyer had come down to the corral. "So, you've made your cut?" he asked.

"I've picked out the best seven."

"Seven? I thought I told you six."

"You did, but I'm thinking of buying the seventh one myself."

Luke Sawyer looked surprised. "Didn't know you were interested in buying yourself a horse."

"Well, as you know, there're some mighty good ones."

"Which one you want?"

I hesitated and hoped Luke Sawyer would prove to be the man I thought he was. "Mister Sawyer, you asked me to find you the best six horses. I've chosen you the best seven. After you choose your six from this seven, I'll take the remaining one."

Luke Sawyer looked at me askance. "They're all that good?"

"Like I said, they're the best in the herd."

Luke Sawyer turned toward the seven horses. "Then I expect I'd best go take a closer look at them."

The stable boy, Luke Sawyer, and I put each horse into the chute and Luke Sawyer studied all of them. He didn't examine the horses as thoroughly as I had done, but he did check their teeth, legs, and hooves, and he questioned me about each one. When he'd checked the last of the horses, he turned to me. "I'll ask you again, which one do you want?"

"I said—"

"I know what you said. You tell me which one you want, and it better not be that black one. He's mine."

I looked out over the horses. "Well, if I had my choice, it would be that palomino yonder. The bay also looks fine."

"The palomino, huh? Well, I'd just better take him myself."

My face didn't change. I knew what Luke Sawyer was doing. "As I said, Mister Sawyer, I picked out what I figured to be the best seven. Your choice comes first."

"Miz Hattie said you know horses as well as you know carpentry. You figure that's true?"

"I believe that to be so," I replied.

"Well, I know you know carpentry, so I'll figure your horse skills are up to the same quality. If I buy these horses, I've decided I want you to train them for me."

I shook my head at that. "Don't see how I can, Mister Sawyer. I've got my furniture-making contract with you to honor—"

"And, I know, you can't work for a stable boy's wages. So, what do you figure you can work for? Maybe that horse you want?"

"I'd figured to buy him myself."

"You did, huh? Well, I don't think so. I think you want to bargain me into paying you with him. That's what I think. Well, I'm willing to do it, but on one condition."

"What's that?"

"I'm going to set a selling price this day on every horse I buy, and if after you've trained these horses and I don't at least get my asking price on every single one of them, I'm going to take that palomino back."

"Palomino?" I questioned. "But I thought you figured to keep him."

"Naw. He's too scrawny-looking for me. Besides, if he's the one you really want, then maybe you'll do even better at training the rest to have him. Agreed?"

"Agreed."

"And one other thing, Paul. I'll give you to the end of our work year agreement for you to have them properly trained and for me to sell. Another thing too. Any furniture we agree to do, that still has to be done."

"As long as I've agreed to the orders," I stipulated. "I know how much I can do."

"You'd better," said Luke Sawyer.

As he walked away, I smiled. I knew how much I could do, but so far Luke Sawyer didn't.

❦

That man from across the Mississippi sold his seven horses to Luke Sawyer, but not at the price he had in mind. I'd told Luke Sawyer the faults of all the horses, and that trader must have known them too, for even though he threatened to wait until the other buyers were present and put them up for bid, in the end he didn't hold up Luke Sawyer about the price. Luke Sawyer said afterward he had done too much business with the man for him to chance losing any further business. The trader sold the balance of his horses as well, some at higher prices, but I figured the buyers would one day regret that.

Right after Luke Sawyer bought the horses, I took on the training of them one at a time. I worked with one horse, keeping it separate from the others for as long as it took, and when that horse was trained, Luke Sawyer would sell it, and each time he got his price. Luke Sawyer was mighty pleased, and so was I. Throughout the time I was training Luke Sawyer's horses, I was also training the palomino. I nourished him. I fed him the best of the grains, and he gained weight and his coat healed. He became a magnificent-looking animal. I didn't neglect the others, but the palomino was special. I already considered him mine, and I trained him to race. And he was fast, faster than any horse I'd been on in quite a while. He was so fast and spirited that when I rode him, it was almost like riding Ghost Wind again. I named him Thunder. But I didn't let my feelings get close to Thunder, not like I had Ghost Wind and Appaloosa, for I knew I had to sell him one day, and I didn't want to have to give up another thing I loved.

"Looks like I made a mistake letting you keep that horse," said Luke Sawyer good-naturedly after he'd seen me ride Thunder.

"He's a fine horse, all right," I admitted.

"That he is." Luke Sawyer leaned against the corral fence and stared out at the palomino. "How'd you like to race him?"

"Race him? Where?"

"Here in Vicksburg with some gentlemen I know. I can sponsor the horse. After all, he still belongs to me. You can ride. You win, we split the purse. How does that sound to you?"

I considered.

"You can make yourself some extra money."

"All right," I said. "I'll let you know when I think he's ready."

It wasn't until near winter that I raced Thunder. He was plenty ready by then; he won. Luke Sawyer claimed the purse and that was all right with me, for unlike Ray Sutcliffe, Luke Sawyer kept his word. He split the purse with me, right down the middle, and I put that money away. It was to be the first of several races and the first of several profitable purses.

I saw Mitchell again at Christmastime. He came and stayed Christmas Day, and left right after. I saw him only once during the next few months, but then, I hadn't expected to see him much more than that. Mitchell knew where I was. I knew where he was. Each of us had his own work and his own pursuits, and both of us knew if one of us needed the other, he'd be there. I missed Mitchell, but I wasn't lonely. My work filled my days and much of my nights. There was no time for socializing, even if I'd been inclined to do so. In addition to the horse training, the furniture orders had been steady, and folks were pleased with the furniture I had made, and those folks included B. R. Tillman and his wife. I had made their chifforobe for them and they had been mighty pleased. That meant, of course, Luke Sawyer was too. Things had worked out well for both of us. Luke Sawyer could now provide his customers with a new service, and he had increased his business. As for me, I had a roof over my head, food to eat, and most important to me, a few more dollars accumulating. The winter passed quickly.

Spring came and settled toward summer. It was during this time that a man by the name of Sam Perry came to see me. Luke Sawyer brought him to the shed. Sam Perry had with him two of his children, a boy of about twelve called Nathan and a young lady named Caroline. I smiled when I saw the young woman. She was the same young woman who had helped the harelipped boy the day after I'd arrived in Vicksburg. I rose from my bench to greet them. Sam Perry was a big man, tall and muscular, dark in coloring, and he wore a huge mustache. I shook his hand and gave a nod to the boy, Nathan, and the young lady, Caroline. I noticed that Caroline's hair was not in braids this time, but was tied with a ribbon and hung long down her back. Caroline returned my nod, and I looked into her eyes for the first time. They were intensely brown and seemed to smile.

"Now, Sam Perry here," said Luke Sawyer after the introductions, "come to see you 'bout making him a piece of furniture."

"That's right," said Sam Perry. "Heard 'bout you, seen some of yo' work too. It's mighty fine."

"Thank you," I said.

"Seems he thinks it's so fine," Luke Sawyer interjected, "that he's thinking on having you make his wife a rocking chair."

Caroline hooked her arm into her father's. "Mama's been wantin' a really fine one for the longest time, ain't she, Papa?"

"That's a fact," Sam Perry confirmed with a loving glance at his daughter. "Sho' has. Had an old rickety one 'til a few years back, and I kept mendin' it best I could, but finally wasn't no more I could do with it but chop it up for firewood. Now I figures t' get her one made, if we can come t' some understandin'."

"And it's got t' have tiny little flowers painted on it," specified Caroline, "right 'cross the back top of it on the headboard. I seen a rocker like that once, and it was sure pretty."

I looked at her. "I'm afraid I don't do that kind of paint work."

"Well, I do."

I liked her outspokenness, but I frowned. "You'll do it?"

"Yes, suh. When you get finished with yo' part, I'll do mine."

I was silenced.

"Well, before we go to talking about any decorations, we best get us an agreement about price first," said Luke Sawyer, always the businessman. With that, he and Sam Perry got down to the specifics of the wood and style of the chair. Luke Sawyer asked me how long I figured it would take to make the rocker. I told him, and then he and Sam Perry began to haggle price. Now, Luke Sawyer always set his price within fair limits, though a little high because most folks, when it came to having something made, didn't like set prices. They liked to bargain so they could have some say-so and feel in the end that they had themselves a fair deal. When an agreement was reached, they felt good about the price and figured they'd gotten themselves a bargain and were happy.

I always stayed out of this part of the transaction. I listened and learned from Luke Sawyer, just as I had learned from my daddy, but both Luke Sawyer and I were in agreement that haggling price was his domain. I noticed, though, that the young lady, Caroline, took great interest in the price debate and greatly influenced her father in the terms he was asking. She stood right by his side and shook her head at Luke Sawyer's price demands and backed her daddy up with a nod when he pointed out the unreasonableness of each price Luke Sawyer set and countered with a price of his own. I smiled, amused, then moved away and sat again at my bench. I picked up a table leg I was sanding and went back to work.

"Whatcha doin'?"

I looked up. It was the boy, Nathan. He was staring curiously at the table leg.

"Doing some sanding to make this table leg smooth as possible. I'll do the same with the other legs too, then attach them to the tabletop over there."

Nathan moved closer and ran his fingers along the wood. "Sho' is smooth. How you do that?"

"With sanding paper," I said. "It's quite rough, like sand. Some folks use sand instead of the paper, but I prefer this. You ever used it?"

Nathan shook his head.

"Then try it," I said, giving him a piece.

Nathan grinned and took it. He rubbed the rough paper with his fingers and grinned again.

I smiled. "Why don't you take that table leg from the shelf there and have a seat on the bench." Nathan got the leg, and when he was seated, looked at me for further instructions. "Now, just rub the paper over it like this," I said, continuing my sanding of the table leg I held. "Just a little at a time, back and forth, but go with the grain of the wood and not too hard."

Nathan watched me, then timidly began to sand. He did a few motions back and forth, then looked over at me for approval.

"That's right," I said, and went on with my own sanding.

A few minutes later Luke Sawyer and Sam Perry reached an agreement, and Luke Sawyer went back to his store. Sam Perry and Caroline then came over to the bench. Sam Perry put his wide hands on his hips, and laughed. "Look like ya done took up yo'self a helper."

I glanced at Nathan and smiled. "Looks that way."

"Let me see," said Caroline, stooping over the boy's shoulder to take a look at his work.

"Feel," said Nathan. "Right here." Caroline ran her long fingers over the sanded wood. "Done that with this," the boy proudly announced as he held out the sanding paper.

"Umm . . ." Caroline murmured with approval. "Feels good." Then she felt the paper. "Here, let me see that," she demanded, but Nathan shrugged his sister away and went back to his sanding. Caroline gave him a soft thump to the back of his head in playful annoyance, then turned to me. "You got another one of these I could try, Mister Paul Logan?"

I nodded, somewhat taken aback that she'd used my full name in addressing me. I reached for another sheet of sanding paper, but Sam Perry said, "Not today, daughter. We gotta get in that store and get them things yo' mama wantin'. Come 'long now. You too, son."

"But, Papa—" protested Nathan.

"Son, we been here long 'nough. Mister Logan, he got work t' do. 'Sides, it's gettin' late. Time t' go."

"Come on, boy," Caroline said to her brother, pulling at his arm, and Nathan reluctantly stood and laid the table leg on the bench. "Thank the gentleman," she ordered.

Nathan looked at me with regret at leaving. "Thank ya."

Caroline too looked at me. "I'm glad you gonna make my mama's chair. You do fine work."

"Well, thank you," I said.

"Remember, though, I'm gonna do them flowers when you finish."

"I'll remember."

Sam Perry extended his hand to me, and I stood to shake it

again. "My daughter's right 'bout that," he said. "Ya does mighty fine work, and I'm gonna be lookin' forward to that rocker, Mister Logan."

"I'll do my best and hope your wife likes it," I returned.

Sam Perry ushered Nathan and Caroline out of the shed before him, but when his own great frame filled the doorway, he turned back and said, "I understand from Mister Luke Sawyer that you a man of color."

I met his eyes. The words were almost a question, though they were forthright and without fear. "That's right."

"Then I'd like t' invite you to our church up at Mount Elam come Sunday next, then have dinner with my family after church. My wife's a fine cook and we always got plenty."

I hesitated, not knowing exactly what to say to his invitation. "Well, I thank you, but I pretty much stay to myself."

Sam Perry didn't seem surprised or put off by my reply. "Understand that. But if you changes yo' mind, you be welcome any Sunday you choose. All you hafta do is show up. You be welcome." With that said, he gave me a nod and left.

I sat again on my bench thinking on the invitation and on the Perrys, particularly Caroline. Then I picked up the table leg Nathan had been working on and started sanding again.

By the time the next Sunday rolled around, I had thought aplenty on Sam Perry's invitation, but I didn't make up my mind to go until I walked out into the sunshine of that morning. Before Luke Sawyer and his family left for church, I asked Luke Sawyer if I could hire out the palomino. He said I could just take Thunder; he wouldn't charge me anything. After all, the horse was practically mine. I said I'd rather pay him for the horse. Though I didn't say it to him, I wanted to keep everything business between us. I didn't want Luke Sawyer doing me any favors. He told me to suit myself, and I paid him fifty cents for the day.

Now, if the Mount Elam church had been in walking distance, I would have gladly walked, but I had learned that it was some miles away and I needed a horse to cut the time. But even on horseback the distance was long, and I found that I had misjudged how long it would take me. I had no intentions of racing Thunder over the badly rutted roads, and the leisurely pace made my arrival at Mount Elam much later than I had intended. Since services had already begun, I chose not to go in, for people were often put off by me at first and I didn't want to have to explain myself. So instead I dismounted and stood outside listening to the sermon through the open windows. When the services were over, I led Thunder into the woods. I figured to stay there until the churchgoers left, then to head back to town without letting Sam Perry know I had even been at Mount Elam. I found a creek lined with brush. Both Thunder and I drank from the creek, then I sat on the bank gazing out at the water while Thunder grazed. Soon I heard voices nearby. I looked around. Two young women had entered the woods and they were arguing. One of them was Caroline Perry.

"Listen here, Val," Caroline said, "I ain't hardly interested in that little Negro of yours, and if you had any sense, you wouldn't hardly be interested in him either."

"I seen him lookin' at you!" declared the one called Val.

"Well, what he do with his eyes just ain't my business," stated Caroline.

"I know you, Caroline Perry! You tryin' to take my man away from me!"

"What!"

"You know it's the truth!" Val accused.

"Girl, if you ain't the silliest—"

"Well, you can't have him!"

"Shoot, child, I don't want him!"

"You do so!" thundered Val, then in a rage lurched for Caroline's massive head of hair.

Caroline, not caught off guard, promptly grabbed Val's arm. "Val, girl, don't you mess with me!" she warned. She thrust the girl back.

Val chose not to heed the warning. "I'll mess with you long as you be messin' with my man!" she vowed, and lunged again at Caroline. Caroline at that move pulled back and, with a right hook as solid as any man's, knocked the girl right across the jaw. Val fell flat.

"Now get up!" Caroline ordered. She put her hands on her hips. "And stop actin' so foolish!" She waited for her orders to be carried out. But Val didn't get up. She lay there not moving. From where I sat, I couldn't see if Val's eyes were open or closed, but I could see the look on Caroline's face. "Val?" Caroline said, and her voice was changed. "Val!" She knelt over her stricken friend. "'Ey, Val . . . Val, you all right? Val!"

I got up and headed toward them to see if I could help. Caroline turned as I approached, but she said nothing. She just looked at me. I looked down at the girl Val. Her eyes were closed. I checked under her jaw with my fingers and found her pulse was strong. I didn't figure Val to be bad hurt, just knocked out. I pulled away and said to Caroline, "I think she'll live." Now, I don't know if it was the look on Caroline's face at that moment or what I had witnessed of this striking young woman that made me tease her, even though I wasn't a teasing kind of fellow. "You don't tell, I won't tell."

Caroline glanced at me, finding no humor in my words, then back at the motionless Val. She softly patted at the girl's face. "Come on, Val, get up. Val, you know I ain't meant to hurt ya, so you wake up now." It was an order, and it seemed from her tone she expected to be obeyed, but Val still didn't move.

"Maybe a wet, cold cloth might help," I suggested. I took out my handkerchief, went to the creek and dipped it in. I squeezed out the water and brought the handkerchief back to Caroline.

"Thank ya," she said without looking at me as she kept her eyes on her friend. She dabbed the handkerchief over the stricken girl's face.

Soon Val began to groan. She sat up slowly with her hand holding her jaw and glared accusingly at Caroline. "What ya do t' me?"

"Nothin' you ain't deserved," declared Caroline unremorsefully. "Here, come on, get up. I'll help you back t' the church." Val stood shakily, without even noticing me, and Caroline put her arms around her waist to support her. Then she looked at me once more. "I'll let my papa know you here. He'll be 'spectin' you for dinner."

"No, I wasn't going to—"

"He'll be 'spectin' you," she repeated. "I'll tell him."

"Thank you," I said, and smiled.

She didn't smile back. She turned with Val and went back toward the church. I watched them go.

❧

When I met up with Sam Perry, I told him what I had tried to tell his daughter, that I was heading back to Vicksburg and wouldn't be staying for dinner. Sam Perry, however, wouldn't hear of it. "You done come all the way out here and now you leavin' without Sunday dinner?" he questioned. "No, suh! You comin' on home with me!"

I protested, but Sam Perry insisted. Now, I know if I had had a true mind to leave, nothing would have persuaded me otherwise, but the truth was I was wanting to be with a family again. I had been without mine for so long. Sam Perry told me his family had gone on ahead of him to take care of chores, and that he had a bit of church business to settle before he headed home, and he asked me if I didn't mind waiting. The wait was fine with me, seeing that I was a bit nervous about sitting down to dinner with folks again.

It took Sam Perry about an hour to finish up at the church, and it was then I learned he was on foot, so I walked too, holding the reins to the palomino. Sam Perry, as soon as he had seen Thunder, looked him over and gave his approval. "Heard 'bout him and them races you and him been winnin.' He's a fine horse, all right," he said. "I know animals, and he's mighty fine." For some reason, his approval pleased me.

As we walked, I found myself very much enjoying Sam Perry's company. He was a storytelling man, and a good one at that. The minutes passed quickly and almost before I was ready, we were at Sam Perry's farm. The house was small and had the look of a sharecropper's shack. There was a shed to one side of it and the two buildings were connected by a breezeway. I figured the smaller structure to be the kitchen. Several long-legged boys sat in the breezeway. "Ya know my boy Nathan," said Sam Perry. "Them other two is Elliott and Jonah. Boys, this here's Mister Paul Logan."

I nodded at the boys and they did the same toward me.

"You boys now, y'all come on down and take this fine horse of Mister Logan's t' the pasture. Give him some water and feed."

The boys hurried to obey their father's orders. I thanked them, then watched as they led Thunder away.

"Don't worry. He be fine," said Sam Perry. "Pasture's fenced. That horse, he ain't goin' nowheres. My boys take good care of him."

"I don't doubt it," I said.

Sam Perry led me up a path toward the porch. On either side of the path was a multitude of flowers, petunias and snapdragons, marigolds, pansies, and even roses. I stopped to admire them. "They somethin', ain't they?" said Sam Perry. "They my wife's and the Lord's doin'. Lord sends the seeds, the rain, and the sunshine, and my wife, she do the plantin' and the tendin', and she mighty good at it too. She don't 'low no weeds. Ole weed show his face, he be yanked outa there 'fore he know'd what hit him." He laughed and motioned toward the porch. "Why don't you rest yo'self up here a spell. It'd be cooler than inside. I'll see 'bout gettin' us somethin' t' drink and let my Rachel know ya here."

"Well, I thank you," I said, "but I think I'll just admire your wife's flowers a bit longer."

"Admire all you want," said Sam Perry with another laugh. He went into the house and I remained on the pathway taking in the beauty of the garden. The flowers were splendid, planted knowingly to bring out the best of each. The tallest were in back, the most delicate, the smallest in front, and there was a pattern to them, with rows of purples and reds and oranges and yellows arranged in intricate designs. Each side of the flower yard was bordered neatly with stones. The garden made the little shack look almost grand. An artist had been at work here.

"So, you like flowers, do ya, Mister Paul Logan?"

I turned. Caroline was standing at the side of the house holding a bucket of water. I smiled and tipped my hat. "Yes, ma'am, I do."

"Well, good," she said, "'cause one thing we sho' got plenty of, it's flowers. Might not have much else, but we sho' got plenty of them." She glanced at the porch. "Papa with you?"

"Yes. He went inside to let your mama know we're here."

"Then he be back in a minute, I reckon," Caroline said. She switched the bucket to her other hand as if to alleviate its weight. "I got to carry this bucket on to the back of the house."

I moved toward her. "I'll be happy to carry it for you."

"No, sir, thank ya. This water goes to the kitchen, and one thing my mama can't abide is a lotta folks in her kitchen." She then looked toward the house and called, "Papa! Papa! You comin'?" She received no response and looked at me again. "You go on up t' the porch there and wait outa this sun. Papa won't be long."

Her words were an order, and for one so young she seemed mighty sure in giving orders. I tipped my hat to her again and started up the path just as Sam Perry opened the porch door and came out holding two large tin cups. Caroline glanced at me with a smile, then disappeared around the side of the house. I stepped onto the porch and took both the cup and the seat Sam Perry offered, and he sat down beside me. Just about that time several of the Perry children came onto the porch. Two of the youngest, who looked to be about three or four, immediately climbed onto Sam Perry's lap, while the older ones stood barefoot, leaning against the posts and staring at me.

Sam Perry laughed. "I got me quite a houseful, ain't I? And this here ain't all of 'em. Got me a baby crawling in the house and another boy older'n Sylvester and Calvin there, and course I got my girls, Callie and Caroline. Now they's all the ones still at home. Got two others, my oldest boy, Hugh, and my girl Risten, married and on they own. Eleven in all! Got me three grandbabies, and this here's one of 'em." He tickled the neck of the little boy sitting on his knee. "This other one here with these big eyes and pretty smile, she's another one." He grinned wide and the little girl giggled, then hid her face. Sam Perry laughed.

Before dinner was ready, all the Perry children appeared on the front porch. I figured I was a bit of a curiosity to them, and they mostly just stared at me with only mumbled words to say. Caroline came out, and so did Callie, to order all the children to the back porch to wash up, and their older sister Risten brought a bowl of fresh water, a towel, and some soap for their father and me. Of all the Perrys, only Miz Perry didn't make an appearance on the porch. When dinner was announced, Sam Perry ushered me into his house.

The main room of the Perry home was small and full. A bed sat in a corner, a fireplace was on one side, and a long table took up the middle. A bench was on either side of the table, and a chair was at each end. The table was laden with food—butter beans with crowder peas and rice, biscuits and corn bread, fried chicken and beef spareribs in gravy, plus pickled preserves of onions, tomatoes, and cucumbers. There were vinegar beets too. It was a grand spread of food and hardly looked like the table of a sharecropper's family. Both Callie and Caroline were busy circling the table pouring tall glasses of cold buttermilk as Sam Perry continued to make me welcome, and there was even hot coffee poured for Mister Perry and me. Sam Perry smiled with pride as he gazed down the table to where I was seated at the other end, and I had the feeling he had read my mind. "You know it taste even better'n it look," he said. Then he let out a loud holler. "Rachel! Rachel! Where you at? Come on now! Come on in here, sugar, so's we can thank the Lord and show Him how much we thanks Him for His good food!" He then turned to the rest of the Perrys. "All y'all old 'nough t' sit with company, find yo'selves a seat. Rest of y'all stand back for prayer, and then yo' mama and yo' sisters'll see t' yo' plates."

Caroline and Callie, along with Nathan and the older brothers still living at home, and the two married children with their spouses, all took seats at the table. But Sam Perry's wife had not come in, and Sam Perry called to her once more. When Miz Perry still did not appear, he turned to Nathan. "Boy, go get yo' mama and tell her we waitin' on her! Tell her not t' be stayin' off in that kitchen all through this dinner. We wants her here at the table."

Nathan hurriedly carried out his father's command. He returned shortly, followed by his mother carrying one last dish, which she placed on the table. Then she put her hands on her hips and stared down at her massive husband. "What you doin' wit' all that hollerin' at me, Sam Perry?" she fussed. "I come when I got all my food ready. Ya knows that!"

"Wanted you t' meet our company, Miz Perry," said Sam Perry in explanation. "This here's Mister Paul Logan from outa Vicksburg. I told you 'bout him."

I stood as Miz Rachel Perry seemed to take note of me for the first time. "Miz Perry," I said in greeting, "I thank you for having me to your home. You've certainly prepared a beautiful dinner here."

Miz Perry said nothing. She just stared at me while I stood awkwardly waiting for some response. Rachel Perry was a small woman, not at all like her husband in stature. She was a good-looking woman too, pale in coloring, but weary-looking. There seemed to be no laughter in her.

"Mama?" said Caroline, and Rachel Perry finally gave me a stiff nod in return for my words.

"Go on have a seat there, Mister Logan," said Sam Perry, offering no apology for his wife's cold greeting, "and let's join hands in prayer." He stretched out long arms and grasped the hands of his children on either side of him, and all at the table grasped the hands beside them. I did the same.

After the blessing was asked, all the women, including Caroline, rose from the table and took the children with them to prepare their plates in the kitchen. After some time Caroline and Callie, along with Risten and their sister-in-law, returned. The children, they said, were eating on the porch. Rachel Perry too returned, but she didn't sit down. She refilled dishes throughout the meal, but she never looked once at me.

Despite that and the uneasiness I felt at Rachel Perry's attitude, I still found that I was enjoying myself. As Sam Perry had said, his wife was an excellent cook, and he hadn't exaggerated that point. I hadn't tasted food like what was spread on that table since my mama's own good cooking. The main meal filled me up, but when the layered pecan cake and the sweet-potato pies were brought to the table, I couldn't say no. In addition to all the good food was the warmth of being with a family. Throughout the meal Sam Perry, his sons, and his daughters kept up a lively conversation punched by laughter and good-natured teasing, and at the end of the meal we all sat for a while longer as Sam Perry told stories. When the children had finished their meals on the porch, they ran in and out and gathered close, and I felt the warm circle of family. But eventually Miz Rachel Perry appeared and announced, "If y'all finished, then I gots t' get this table cleared and this food left over put away. Caroline, Callie, Risten, y'all give me a hand."

All the Perry girls, as well as their sister-in-law, stood and began to help their mother. At that, Sam Perry invited me outside. "Look like the womenfolk done made it clear we got no further business in here!" All the men and boys then went outside, and once on the porch Sam Perry offered me some tobacco. I took it and filled my pipe, and for a while we sat enjoying the smoke. I had picked up the habit of pipe smoking in the lumber camps, and it was the only frivolous thing on which I spent my money. I enjoyed the aroma of the tobacco. It reminded me of my daddy. As I listened to Sam Perry's talk and his laughter, I was already thinking on the day's end and not wanting it to come. Still, I didn't want to overstay my welcome, and as it grew late, I put out my pipe and made ready to go.

"Now, don't be hurryin' off," objected Sam Perry. "It's feedin' time for my stock. Why don't ya come 'long wit' me and my boys and take a look at 'em. I'm just gonna change my pants and get my work boots on." I agreed to that, and after Sam Perry had changed, we headed toward his pasture. "Got me plenty of fine animals for a man as dirt poor as me, I reckon," he said.

"May be a sin to be so proud, but God gonna hafta forgive me for that, 'cause there's three things I ain't shame t' 'mit I'm right proud of—my wife, my children, and my animals."

I figured he had a right to be proud. He had a fine family. He also had chickens and guineas, several cows, a pen full of hogs, and two mules.

As we stood outside the hog pen, Sam Perry said, "I s'pose you been wondering how a man like me come t' have animals like these here. S'pose ya been wondering too how I could 'ford fried chicken and spareribs on my table. Well, I works hard and I puts my faith in the Lord, and the Lord done give me a gift. I got the gift of healin'. Learned 'bout healin' when I was a boy, and that's how I made my way through slavery, healin' the white folks' animals. Now, I might not have much far as land goes, 'cause this here land belongs to that white man up the road. But I got me a fine family and I got these here animals and plenty t' eat, and I thanks God for 'em all 'cause He done give me the gift of healin' His creatures. Folks call me t' tend they animals. White folks come, black folks come, well-t'-do and poor folks too. Folks that can, they pays me sometimes with their litter runts. God and me, we take care of them runts and brings 'em up strong. So if I'm proud and sinful, I figure that's partly God's fault too," he laughed, "'cause He done give 'em all t' me!" He turned from me then and hollered to Nathan and another of his sons to bring the slop buckets.

While his boys went to get the slop for the hogs, Sam Perry opened the pen gate and stepped in. "Now, you best stay on that side the wire, Mister Logan," he advised. "These ole hogs can get t' be a bit ornery. 'Sides, you ain't dressed for it." He glanced past me as a noise arose across the yard. I turned and saw Caroline, a basket looped over one arm, yanking at the gate to the chicken coop. "Pull it hard, sugar!" Sam Perry called. "One of these here days I'm gonna make myself another gate," he mumbled, more to himself than to me. "That there one's always get-tin' stuck." He hollered again to Caroline. "Pull up on it and give it a yank!"

"I'll go see if I can help her," I volunteered.

"Well, I 'preciate that. I ain't already been in with these hogs here, I'd take care of it myself."

"Glad to be of help," I said, and crossed the yard. Caroline was still pulling at the gate when I reached her. "You mind if I try?" I asked.

She put her basket down and hit at the gate with her hand. "Papa been sayin' he gonna fix this thing, but he ain't got round to it." She hit the gate again. "I ain't had on this here Sunday dress, I'd just jump it."

I glanced at her. I imagined she would. "Let me take a look," I said, and she stepped aside. I studied the rusty latch. "Well, here's the problem. One of the screws is out, so the latch slipped a bit and it's not fitting right." I looked at the ground, searching for the screw.

"Don't ya be worryin' none with it," she said. "We take care of it t'morrow. All I want now is to get in there and gather these eggs. You like eggs, Mister Paul Logan?"

"Yes, but—"

"Y'all get it open?" Sam Perry yelled from across the yard.

I looked again at the latch and leveled it up with my hand. I was then able to release the tongue of the latch, and the gate opened.

"We got it now, Papa!" answered Caroline, and Sam Perry waved his hand in return and turned his attention back to his hogs. "I sure do thank you, Mister Paul Logan," Caroline said, picking up her basket.

"You're welcome," I said. "But tell me something."

"What's that?"

"Why do you always address me by my full name?"

Caroline smiled at me without any hint of shyness. "'Cause I likes the way it sounds. Always did like that name Paul. It just sounds nice, don't ya think?" She didn't wait for an answer as she went into the chicken pen. "You come on wit' me and see some of our layin' hens. And be sure and close that gate behind ya so's these chickens don't get out. The younguns already fed 'em, so it's their beddin' time now, but we got some hens that lay late, so I gotta check for eggs."

I did as I was told and followed Caroline through the yard and into the henhouse.

"S'pose you 'bout ready t' be quit of us and all our family," Caroline teased as she went about checking under the hens. "There's sure a lot of us."

"No, actually, I've enjoyed being here. I haven't seen my own family in some time, so this has been a good day for me. One thing, though. It seems to me your mother doesn't much care for me."

Caroline brushed away my comment with a wave of her hand, as if fanning away a fly. "Ah, don't you mind Mama. She ain't meant no harm. It's just that she done had a hard life and it done got into her soul. Ain't nothin' you done."

"But there's something about me, isn't there, that made her that way toward me?"

Caroline was more open than I had expected her to be. She looked straight into my eyes when she answered. "Nothin' more'n the fact you lookin' like a white man."

I gazed at her in silence.

"That there, that's what it is," she said, and turned back to gathering her eggs.

"But didn't your daddy tell her about me? About me coming to dinner?"

"Oh, he told her, all right. He done told her he invited Mister Paul Logan, but that's all. He didn't tell her anythin' 'bout what ya look like. Ain't said nothin' 'bout you lookin' near white. He shoulda done told her that, knowin' how Mama is, but he ain't, so my mama ain't 'spected you t' be lookin' like ya do, and it took her by surprise a bit. When she done seen ya, other things come to her mind."

"Other things?"

Caroline diligently continued to gather her eggs. "Things 'bout when she was born. Things 'bout when she was a baby. Things 'bout slavery days."

"Now, what could seeing me have to do with that? Certainly I'm not the first near-to-white-looking person she's seen."

"Not sittin' at her table," Caroline retorted. She stopped and fixed her deep brown eyes on mine. "You see, t' my mama ya might's well be white. That there's what she sees, and she can't get over that."

"Well, I'm not white," I said.

"Partly you are. Anybody can see that. But that don't matter. Part of it you are, my mama done seen it." Caroline's eyes were still fixed on me. "She done seen that and not nothin' much else. She done seen that there man called hisself her master when she seen ya, and she done seen the white woman that was his wife too." She turned from me and walked on.

"Well . . . I'm not them," I said softly.

Caroline glanced back. "Course you ain't. But Mama, she ain't thinkin' on that. She thinkin' on the folks takin' away her name."

I watched her without words.

Caroline continued on with her talk, gathering eggs all the while. "Ya see, my mama was a baby only a week old when she found her name gone."

"Her name gone?" I followed her again. "How?"

"The white folks done took it," answered Caroline matter-of-factly.

"Took it?" I questioned. "A name?"

"That's right. Just took her name. Ya see, this here's how it was. My mama was born into slavery belongin' t' some white folks by the name of Means. Now, my grandmama Rose, she done picked out a name for my mama even 'fore my mama was born, and that name she done give to my mama was Rachel. My grandmama Rose, she done took pride in that name 'cause that there was the name her mama done held. So come the day my mama was born, my grandmama Rose, she give my mama that name of Rachel, and that was the way everybody was thinkin' of her, the name when she got born, just simply that. Rachel."

Caroline pulled one last egg from under a protesting red hen and put it in her basket. Then she fixed her eyes on me again. "But my mama wasn't 'lowed to keep her name for long. Come a week after her birth, that white woman married to the white man who had hisself papers to my mama said no baby on her place could be callin' herself Rachel. Said no baby born, 'ceptin' hers, was t' have that name, 'cause that was what she was namin' her baby born a few days after my mama, and she wasn't gonna 'low no colored child carryin' the same name as her child.

"Well, my grandmama still gone on callin' my mama Rachel, 'ceptin' when the white folks were around. But then some years later that white woman heard my grandmama Rose calling my mama Rachel, and she got mad. She tried to stop my grandmama from callin' my mama by her name. My grandmama told her ain't nobody got a right t' take my mama's name away. Well, that ole white woman figured she had the right, so she had my grandmama took to the yard and she whipped my grandmama 'cause she wouldn't give up my mama's name. She whipped her, but it ain't done no good, 'til she gone and threatened my mama. Then my grandmama Rose gone and done what them white folks 'spected said in their hearin'. Whiles they was around, she called my mama 'Daughter' or 'Sister,' nothing else. But to my grandmama, my mama's name remained the same: Rachel, and that's what she called her when they was by theyselves. That was her name. Name she was born. Name now." Caroline gave me a pointed look. "So, Mister Paul Logan, that's what she be thinking on when she see you. That's a fact," she said with a nod, ending her story. "Just hope you don't hold how she be actin' 'gainst her."

"No . . . no, I don't. Fact, I can somewhat understand how she feels. A given name's important. My mama didn't have to suffer about my name, but she had a name for me too—my daddy's name. She couldn't give it to me officially though, because my daddy said it wasn't fitting that I be called by his name."

"Why not?"

"Because my daddy had three other sons and none of them had his name." I hesitated, then added, "They didn't have his name and they were white."

Caroline nodded in understanding. "Well, what was the name?"

"My daddy's name is Edward. My mama used to call me that sometimes, along with my given name of Paul, when it was just her and me and my sister, Cassie, around. Even my daddy sometimes called me by it when it was just the two of us."

"And how'd you feel 'bout that?"

"What do you mean?"

"How'd you feel 'bout not having your name spoken open?"

"Well, I suppose I felt like it was a secret. But the fact was, I wasn't a secret. Everybody knew I was my daddy's son. I just think my daddy didn't want to hurt my brothers by speaking my name so open, not to mention the fact it wouldn't've looked right to his white friends. But I've got to admit, whenever he called me by his name, I always felt a pride in it."

Caroline's dark eyes studied me without another word. Then she put her basket down, turned, and looked around as if she were searching for something. After a moment she went to a corner and brought back a small burlap sack. She stuffed it with straw, then placed half a dozen eggs inside. She held out the sack to me. "You take these. They're for you."

"What?"

"You said you liked eggs, ain't ya?"

"Well . . . yes . . ."

"You got yo'self a layin' hen?"

"No . . . but I can't just take your eggs."

"Yes, you can."

"Well, what do I owe you for them?"

She smiled a bright smile at me. "Jus' a good rockin' chair for my mama. Now, take 'em."

There she was giving orders again. I took the sack and thanked her for the eggs. "Are you always this generous?" I asked.

"Whatcha mean?" she said, picking up her egg basket again. "You seen we got plenty. Nothin' generous 'bout that."

I thought on how she'd given the harelipped boy one of her mama's sweet-potato pies. "I happened to be at Luke Sawyer's store the day you and your sister brought pies to sell, and you took a little boy's part who, as you said, was sorely in need of something 'to make him feel good.' From the smile on that boy's face, I think that pie you gave him was just what he needed."

Caroline halted and laughed outright. "You was there? You seen that?" She sounded somewhat embarrassed; then, if there was embarrassment, it fled quickly. "Yeah, Henry, he enjoyed that pie, all right."

"But what about you? What did your mama have to say about her pie when you got home?"

"Don't tell me you done heard that too? You heard me and Callie talkin' 'bout Mama and that whippin' I was sure t' get?"

I nodded. "Anybody standing near heard it."

She laughed again. "'Spect you right. Well, I gotta admit I worried a bit all the way home 'bout how Mama was gonna get after me, but when I got back, she wasn't so bad. She fussed a lot, mind ya, but then again she always fussin' 'bout how I'm too much like my papa, always givin' stuff away and how we never gonna have nothin' 'cause we ain't got the good sense t' realize we poor." Caroline was still laughing as she ushered me out of the henhouse.

I gazed out across the pasture, west of the barn, at the cluster of animals. "I'd hardly call you poor."

"Well, when it come t' money we ain't got much. But we thankful for what we got. What you see out in that there pasture, though, is 'cause of my daddy's healin' hands and God's grace."

I nodded, understanding from Mister Perry's words what she meant.

"God give him the power in his mind and in his hands t' heal critters when he was in slavery, and that blessin' made his life and ours some easier. Fact, his knowin' healin' saved him from hangin' during slavery days."

"How was that?" I asked.

"Well, seems like there was a time my papa tried runnin' away from that man called hisself his master. He done already run away two times before then when he was still a boy and was so-called belongin' t' another man. But he was now property of this man called Perry, and he ain't run off on him before. Now, this Perry fella thought well of my papa 'cause of all he knew 'bout healin', and he let my daddy go off his place t' court my mama, who was livin' on somebody else's plantation. Well, on one of those times my daddy went off courtin', he run away. He was figurin' t' get hisself free, then get my mama free. But then the white folks caught up with him and they was ready to hang him, but that ole master wouldn't let them do it. He said, 'I need this here boy. He more'n valuable t' me. He got the healin' in his hands.' So them white men whipped my papa, but they ain't hung him."

Caroline looked at me and gave a nod. "That's a fact. Tell ya somethin' else 'bout names too. In them slavery days my papa got called by the name of Sam for Samson 'cause he was so strong. White folks, they call him that still, and when he doin' business, he go by that. But he had hisself a Christian name of Luke, like Jesus' disciple, and his folks and all the colored folks called him by that, and my mama, when she and my papa was courtin', she called him Luke too. My papa, he liked that. My mama says my papa's a healer and he got the blessin', and she's right proud of that. Well, what I'm right proud of is, my daddy say of all his younguns, I got the blessin' too and he be teachin' me."

"You like the healing?"

"I surely do," she admitted. "May be selfish of me t' say so, but I'm glad, of all my daddy's children, I was the one got the gift."

I knew Caroline was saying exactly what she felt. I had nothing to say in return to her honesty. I just smiled as I opened the gate.

When I left the Perry farm, it was almost sunset. As I mounted Thunder, I had with me not only the eggs Caroline had given me but a helping of food for my supper and for my breakfast too. All the Perrys saw me off, including Miz Rachel Perry. I thanked her for having me and for the wondrous food she had cooked. All she gave me for my words was a nod in return, and as I rode off, I realized that during all the hours I had spent at the Perry home, Miz Rachel Perry had not spoken one word to me.

It was in the next month that Sam Perry brought Caroline to the shed to paint her flowers on the rocker. Nathan was with her. Sam Perry left them both while he went off to tend some ailing horses on the other side of town. I felt a bit awkward at first, having the brother and sister in my work space, but when

Caroline saw the rocker, she put me at ease. "Oh, Mister Paul Logan, it's lookin' mighty fine!" she declared as she slowly slid her fingers along the sanded grain of the chair's rounded back, then rocked it gently. "Oh, it's just so fine!"

"It sure is," Nathan agreed.

"Why don't you try it out?" I said to Caroline. "Go ahead and sit in it."

Caroline shook her head. "Oh, no, thank ya."

"Well, then, I'll try it," declared Nathan playfully. But before he could sit down, Caroline shoved him away.

"Ah, naw, ya don't! Nobody sits in this rocker 'til Mama do. She gonna be the first one."

"Ah, Caroline—"

"It's hers, and right is right!"

Nathan laughed, shrugged, then knelt on the floor to study the rocker more closely. He felt along the curves and looked at me. "Mister Logan, how you get this here wood t' do like this so this here chair rocks?"

I pointed to a long wooden box in the corner of the room. It was supported with legs at one end, while the other end was set across a giant kettle. The kettle was set over a fire and was filled with boiling water. Nathan turned to where I was pointing and his eyes grew big as steam drifted from the box. "That's called a steam box," I said. "I soak wood I want to bend in water, then I put the wood in that box. You see how half the kettle is closed and the box is sitting over the other half? Well, there are openings underneath the box so that steam from the kettle can get inside." I got up. "Come on, I'll show you."

Nathan followed me over to the steam box. I opened the loading door at the end of the box over the kettle, and Nathan jumped back, startled, as steam blew out. Caroline, still by the rocker, laughed, and Nathan himself smiled. "I should've warned you about that," I said, then waited until the steam cleared.

Once it had, I pointed out the two pine cuttings already inside. They lay across rods set several inches from the floor of the box so that the steam could circulate around them. I closed the door and went to the other end of the box, and showed Nathan the vent holes. "The steam goes in from the kettle, circulates around the wood, and comes out here. After the wood's been in the box awhile, it's soft enough to bend."

Nathan's eyes showed his amazement as he walked around the steam box, studying it.

"Mister Paul Logan, you mind if I get started now?" I looked over at Caroline, who had been patiently watching us. "I don't want t' be in yo' way."

"You won't be," I said.

"Good." She patted the headboard of the rocker. "I'm gonna put Mama's flowers right here, and then when Mama sit down and rest her head, it'll be like she lyin' right in her flower bed." She smiled. I smiled back as she began pulling out several small jars from her basket and placing them in a neat row on the workbench. "These here are my paints," she said. "I got them from the store. I saved for them with my own pie money." I brought a work stool over and placed it beside the rocker for her. She smiled her thanks, then sat down and went to work. I stood watching her.

"Mister Logan," called Nathan "can ya show me how it's done? How ya bends the wood, I mean?"

I nodded, glanced once more at Caroline as she began to lightly sketch an outline of her flowers onto the headboard, then went over to Nathan. I pulled one of the pine cuttings from the steam box and slowly bent it for another rocker, so that Nathan could see. He was fascinated. I then returned to the cabinet I was making. Seeing that Nathan was so eager to learn, I let him help me. But even while I was instructing Nathan on how to fit the dowels of the boards for a drawer together, I was aware of Caroline across the room delicately painting bright splashes of yellows and reds and greens, oranges and blues, creating the bright flowers and the grasses too of her mother's garden. She worked in silence at first, but as the garden of flowers grew, she began to hum, and I didn't mind the sound of it. I was used to working in silence, with just my own thoughts for company. Caroline's presence made the morning pleasant. When she stood, I knew she was finished, and I regretted that she was.

"Well, what y'all think?" she asked, grinning widely. "And if ya don't like it, keep yo' words to yo'selves."

Nathan went over to the rocker and leaned close to inspect it. After a moment or two he looked at his sister and teased, "It's okay, I reckon, but whoever told ya you could paint?"

Caroline laughed and playfully swatted his arm. "Boy, told ya t' keep yo' words t' yo'self."

Nathan laughed. "Ah, it'll do. Main thing, Mama's gonna love it."

"Yeah, she gonna, ain't she?" Caroline beamed and leaned against her brother's arm as they both admired the rocker. She then glanced over her shoulder at me. "You ain't said what you think 'bout my flowers."

"Well, maybe he was thinkin' same as me," said Nathan, "so he keepin' his words to hisself."

Caroline turned on him. "Was I talkin' to you?"

Nathan laughed. I smiled. "You said flowers would brighten up the rocker. Well, you were right." I left my bench and went to take a closer look. The flower garden was spread all across the headboard. It was wild, alive, and inviting. "You do good work," I said.

"Thank ya," she said. "So do you."

I smiled at her again, then walked around the chair. "I'll put several coats of linseed oil on it to bring out the natural beauty of the wood, and when it's dried, it'll be ready for you to give to your mother."

"How long that gonna be?" asked Nathan.

"Could be several weeks for a good linseed stain. To me, linseed oil on wood looks better than shellac."

Caroline's disappointment showed on her face. "I was hopin' we could take it home t'day."

"It takes a while for a good coating," I said, "and I want to make sure each coat is totally dry before applying another one."

"Well . . . we want it right."

"I'll bring it out when it's ready."

"You ain't gotta do that. We can come get it."

"That's all right. I've got some business out that way I've been thinking on taking care of, so it won't be any trouble. I'll just check with your daddy about it when he comes back."

"Well, whenever you bring it, we'll be ready for it." She smiled happily now. "I can't hardly wait!"

I returned her smile.

❧

When I finished staining the rocker, I spoke to Luke Sawyer about taking it to Sam Perry, and he said that was fine by him as long as I collected the remaining money that was due. I said I'd take care of that. Luke Sawyer told me to take his wagon, so I covered the rocker with a tarp and set it in the back of the wagon and tied it down. Then I headed out for Sam Perry's farm. I didn't tell Luke Sawyer I had other reasons for wanting to deliver the chair. I wanted to see Caroline again, but I figured to keep that to myself.

When I got to the Perry place, I halted the wagon some distance from the house and went on foot to find Mister Perry. I wasn't sure how he wanted to present the rocker to his wife, and I didn't want to spoil his surprise. I came across Nathan first. I asked him to get his daddy for me and told him I'd wait at the wagon. Nathan ran off to do my bidding, and when he returned, not only was his daddy with him, but several of his brothers and sisters, including Caroline.

"Ow, let's see it!" said Caroline joyously, clapping her hands together like a little girl.

I smiled at her and untied the rope as all the Perrys crowded near. I lifted the tarp from the rocker and a raucous shrill rose from them all.

"Ah, my good gracious, that there's sho' fine! That there sho' is!" exclaimed Sam Perry as he walked around the wagon admiring the rocker from every angle. "Can't nobody say nothin' 'gainst yo' work! Ya done us proud!"

Callie had words too. "Ain't never seen no furniture this fine and pretty," she said. "Mama's gonna jus' love it!"

"It sho' is a beauty, all right," joined in Nathan. "Jus' look at that wood!"

"Just look at the flowers," I said, and looked pointedly at Caroline. Caroline beamed back at me.

"My girl, she sho' done dressed it up, ain't she?" said a proud Sam Perry.

"That she did," I agreed, my eyes still on Caroline, but she seemed not to notice now as she competed in chatter with her sister and brothers about the rocker.

Amidst it all, Sam Perry dispatched Nathan and another of his boys to get his wife, who, I learned, was with Risten at her place. "Tell her I need her here now, nothin' else!" he ordered. He also sent someone to gather the rest of the Perrys from the fields to the house. Then he laid his hand on my shoulder. "Why don't you and me finish up our business," he said. I nodded and pulled out the bill Luke Sawyer had written and handed it to him. Sam Perry glanced at it, then called to Callie and Caroline to come over. With no embarrassment, he openly admitted, "Can't read. All my younguns of school age can. I done seen t' that." The young women read the bill to their father, and Sam Perry nodded in agreement to the balance due, then pulled out a tiny sack from his pants pocket and counted out the money due. "Can't read," he laughed, "but I sure 'nough can count!" I smiled and wrote "Paid" across the bill, along with my signature, and handed it to him again. "Now, you don't mind, Mister Logan, let's drive on up t' the house and put this here rocker on the front porch. I want it there waitin' when my Rachel show up!"

Sam Perry and I re-covered the chair, then climbed onto the seat of the wagon and his children climbed onto the back, surrounding the rocker, and we rode to the house. When we reached it, all the Perrys jumped down, and I pulled the tarp from around the chair. Sam Perry then gently lifted the rocker from the wagon and set it on the porch. There were then more words of praise for the chair as more Perrys came in from the fields. I chose to go at that point, but Sam Perry wouldn't hear of it. "No, suh!" he exclaimed. "You done made this chair, and ya got a right t' see how much my Rachel gonna love it. You stay right here!" At first I protested, but the truth is I wanted to see Rachel Perry's face when she saw the chair. Though I did stay, I wasn't figuring Rachel Perry would be any too pleased that the rocker so special to her husband and her family had been made by me.

After a bit, a wagon came rattling up the trail. The wagon held the eldest Perry daughter and her family, Nathan and his brother, as well as Rachel Perry. "What's the matter?" Rachel Perry cried, standing up before the wagon was stopped. "Them boys ain't said! Ah, Lord, one of my babies hurt! That's what the matter, ain't it?"

"No such thing!" denied Sam Perry, going over to the wagon. "And stop all that hollerin', woman! Ain't nothin' wrong!"

"Then how come you t' send for me like that?"

Sam Perry helped his wife from the wagon. "Ah, sugar pie," he said soothingly as he placed his arms around her. "Jus' wanted you t' come."

Rachel Perry pulled away furiously. "And you hafta go and send for me like that?"

"Now, don't be mad, Miz Perry. No need t' be mad! No need for worry neither . . . 'cepting for what's on that porch!" He then put his massive arm around his wife again and pointed her toward the rocker.

Rachel Perry stared at the rocker and her mouth opened, but no words came out.

"You love it, Mama?" cried Caroline.

"Ah, naw . . ."

"So, you don't love it?" teased Sam Perry.

"Ah, Luke . . ."

"Done had it made special for ya, baby, jus' for you. Man here done made it, and Caroline done painted them there flowers—"

"All your favorite flowers, Mama!" exploded Caroline. "Every kind you done planted in your garden—your petunias and your marigolds and snapdragons, even your roses!"

"Your pansies too!" added Callie. "Ain't they fine?"

Rachel Perry shook her head, unbelieving.

"Well, come on!" ordered her husband. "Don't jus' stand way back here gazing at it. Go on, take a closer look."

"That's right, Mama!" cried Nathan. "And sit in it! Caroline ain't let me."

"It's your chair, Mama," said Caroline with a chiding glance at Nathan. "Ain't nobody sat in it yet. You be the first."

"Come on, sugar," said Sam Perry, and with his eldest son, Hugh, led Rachel Perry to the rocker as if she were a queen. Gingerly, Rachel Perry touched the arms of the chair. Then she touched the headboard and slipped her fingers across the flowers.

"You like it, Mama?" asked Caroline eagerly.

"Ah, sugar . . . it's jus' . . . it's jus' too much."

"Well, go on! Sit in it!" ordered her husband. Rachel Perry obeyed.

All the Perrys clapped.

"Ain't it grand, Mama?" asked Caroline, kneeling on the porch floor beside her. "Ain't it jus' too grand?"

"Ah, yes, sweet-pea." Rachel Perry smiled and folded her hands over the knuckles of the chair. "Ah, yes." Then she began to rock. Again all the Perrys clapped.

Sam Perry grinned. "So, I takes it ya like yo' rocker, huh, Miz Perry?"

Rachel Perry grinned too. "Well, what you think, Mister Perry?"

"Well, if ya likes it, then you gots this man here t' thank for it!" Sam Perry then extended his arm toward where I stood near the side of the porch. "'Cause Mister Logan, he the one done made it!"

Rachel Perry turned to look at me, and I truly believe she saw me then for the first time. She stared at me coldly, without a word. I returned her gaze, then turned away and headed for my wagon. Sam Perry seemed not to notice as his children continued to chatter, but Caroline rushed over to me. "Thank you, Mister Paul-Edward Logan," she said. "You done made my mama mighty happy."

I took a moment. "You called me Paul-Edward."

"Yes, sir. Yes, sir, I did. I been thinkin' on what you told me 'bout your name and I been figurin' you a lot like my mama 'bout her name. I figure Edward was a name what yo' mama wanted you t' have, and yo' daddy too, and to my way of thinking, I figure you deserve your name. So, I decided that's what I'm gonna call ya from now on. I'm gonna call you Paul-Edward. Mister

Paul-Edward Logan." Her eyes probed mine. "That all right with you?"

I nodded. "It's all right," I said, and turned away, feeling a lump rising in my throat. I climbed onto the wagon.

Sam Perry took note and came over. "Now, get on down from there, Mister Logan, and stay for supper!"

"I thank you," I said, "but I've got a lot of work still, and Luke Sawyer'll be looking for his wagon and mules back soon."

"Well, you know you're welcome."

"I believe that," I said, then put my hand to the brim of my hat in good-bye and quickly backed up the mules and headed out. I didn't want to stay longer. I was an outsider in a family time, and I didn't want to spoil that. I didn't belong there among the Perrys in all their warmth and love. I was alone, and as I thought of Caroline's words to me, I felt something I hadn't felt since my mama had died. Throughout the time I had been making the rocker for Miz Rachel Perry, I had thought about my mama and her rocking chair. I had thought about my daddy too, because he had given it to her. Now, after Caroline's words, I thought on them again and I realized just how alone I was and, among all this family, how much I missed my family. I missed Cassie. I missed my daddy. I missed Hammond and George, and even Robert. But I could never return to them. My life was here now, and as I rode back to Vicksburg, I decided it was time for me to settle. It was time for me to buy land. It was time for me to buy land, settle down, and have a family of my own.

The Bargain

I asked Luke Sawyer about land. I figured what with his being a businessman and knowing just about everyone there was to know in and around Vicksburg, he'd know what land was for sale, or at least who was willing to sell, and at what terms. I told him too about my interest in J. T. Hollenbeck's land. Luke Sawyer stroked at his neatly trimmed beard as I broached the subject with him. "You planning to quit on me already?" he said.

"I told you I'd stay a year, and it's past that now. I figure it's time for me to go looking for land."

"And you want me to help you?" He laughed. "Want me to shoot my own self in the foot?"

I shook my head, giving him no smile in return. "Just want to know where maybe I can look."

Luke Sawyer sighed and turned away from trying to cajole me into furthering our bargain. I had kept my agreements with him, about making the furniture and about the horses. Luke Sawyer had sold five of the horses and received offers on the black stallion, though he still talked of keeping the stallion for himself. He had received offers on Thunder too, but he had been true to his word. He said Thunder was spoken for. All the sales had been at the price Luke Sawyer had set and now the palomino was mine. Luke Sawyer had signed papers saying so. "You've done some mighty good work," he said, "and you've been a good man to work with, but you set on having land, Paul Logan, I'll think on it and check around. You realize, though, not just everybody would sell to you, once they know you're a man of color."

"I know," I said.

"Long's you do," Luke Sawyer finished, and no more words about land were said between him and me for several weeks. Then came one day in late August when he brought a man and his young son back to the toolshed. The man's name was Charles Jamison, and his boy was called Wade. "Fella I was telling you about, Mister Jamison," said Luke Sawyer.

"Yes. I've seen him ride. That's one fine horse you have, Paul Logan."

"Thank you," was all I said.

"You interested in selling him? Luke Sawyer tells me he's signed his interest in that palomino over to you."

I glanced over at Luke Sawyer, then back to Charles Jamison. "Not at this time."

Charles Jamison nodded to that in acceptance and walked around the shed, looking at the finished pieces and the ones on which I was still working. His son, ten or so, followed him, touching the wood in quiet wonder much as Nathan had done. "I can indeed see," said Charles Jamison when he'd made his way around the room, "that you weren't exaggerating about his work, Mister Sawyer." He looked directly at me. "It's fine work."

"Thank you," I said.

"But I understand you're interested in something besides horses and woodworking. Understand you're interested in buying some land."

I nodded. "That's right."

"Understand too you've seen some of J. T. Hollenbeck's land that you'd like to buy. Well, that's good land. My family lives here in Vicksburg, but we also have a small place near Mister Hollenbeck, so I know the area quite well. In fact, I've got an interest in that land myself."

I guarded my words, but I had to know. "Is Mr. Hollenbeck thinking of selling now?"

"He's talked about it. His wife, who was a Southerner, died recently and their children died before her, so he no longer feels obliged to hold on to that piece of land, or to stay here, for that matter. But if he sells, I figure it won't be for a while yet." Charles Jamison studied me. "You willing to wait awhile for Hollenbeck land?"

I took a moment before I answered. "I'd be willing to wait a spell for the piece of land I saw, and if the price was right. In the meanwhile, I'd like to get some land to work now."

"One thing I know. When and if J. T. Hollenbeck decides to sell, he'll be wanting cash. You ready to pay cash for some land now?"

"Rather not," I replied. "Not if there's another way."

"Well, there's another way, all right, if you're willing to put in some mighty hard, bone-breaking work."

"And what would that be?"

"Clearing land in return for the title to it. You willing to do that and work out terms for it, you can go see a man name of Filmore Granger."

"I've heard that name before."

"You've been here a year, then you should have. The Grangers own the biggest section of land around the town of Strawberry. In fact, at least half the land J. T. Hollenbeck now owns once belonged to the Grangers."

I received that information as if learning a new fact. I said nothing about the old man Elijah, who had already told me the same.

"You willing to put in the time and the work, if you want land, Filmore Granger is the man you want to see. Just remember, though, if you do business with him, he can be a hard man."

I thanked Charles Jamison, and after he and his son were gone, I mulled over his words and slept on them. That next morning I mounted Thunder and headed south to talk to Filmore Granger. I figured if Filmore Granger had land to sell in exchange for the work of clearing it, I had the strength and the will to do it. As for J. T. Hollenbeck's land, I figured I'd bide my time about that, and if the Lord was willing, I figured to one day have that too.

I found Filmore Granger and his boy, along with a colored workman, grooming horses in the Granger stables. I told Filmore Granger who I was and why I had come.

"Land, you say?" Filmore Granger glanced at me and went on tending one of his mares. "What makes you think I'm interested in selling any of my land? Harlan," he said, addressing the boy before I had time to answer, "bring me that brush." The boy looked at me, then hurried to do his father's bidding.

"Well," I said, "I spoke to Mister J. T. Hollenbeck and Mister Charles Jamison, and both of them mentioned you might have land for sale. They suggested I come see you."

"They did, did they?"

"Yes, sir, they did. I'm interested in thirty or forty acres to get myself started and settle down, but seeing that I'm a man of color, it might be difficult for me to get a bank loan to buy a parcel."

"You mean to say you're a nigger?" exclaimed the boy. Filmore Granger said nothing. The workman looked at me now and met my eyes.

I ignored the boy and went on as if I had said nothing amiss, though I felt my anger rising at his using that word to me.

"Both Mister Hollenbeck and Mister Jamison said maybe you'd be willing to work something out with me. Mister Jamison said you might consider exchanging the land for clearing it."

Filmore Granger glanced my way, then took his time about speaking again. When he finished with the mare, he gave me his attention. "You ever thought about sharecropping? There's an advantage in that for you. I supply all the seed, animals you need. I take all the risk. You just put in the labor. We share the crop."

I guarded my words in my answer to him. "Mister Granger, I wouldn't own the land if I were to sharecrop, and it's land I want."

Filmore Granger studied me a moment. "So you know what land of mine you want?"

"No, sir," I said. "I didn't know what land might be for sale."

"Well, I got a piece of land in mind. You want to see it, I'll show it to you."

"I'd be obliged," I said.

Filmore Granger then turned the remainder of the grooming over to the workman, and saddled the mare. He told the boy to saddle a bay, then the two led the horses outside. As I untied the reins to Thunder, the boy suddenly stopped. "Where'd you get this horse?" he demanded.

"It's a fine-looking horse, all right," said Filmore Granger, eyeing me as if I had no business with Thunder. "What are you doing with him?"

"He's my horse."

"Yours?" questioned Filmore Granger. I'd seen that look before. "Who'd you get him from?"

"Mister Luke Sawyer. He owns a mercantile up in Vicksburg." I told him that truth and no more.

"He know you got him?" asked the boy.

I stared coldly at him. "He knows," I said.

Filmore Granger nodded. "Then get on him and let's go."

Filmore Granger then mounted the mare and started off. The boy quickly mounted his bay and did the same. I followed them.

For nearly an hour we traveled over a rutted road, which finally meandered off into a trail in the middle of the forest. Filmore Granger halted his horse and got down. "This way," he commanded, and started down a footpath too narrow for the horses. I dismounted and once again followed him and his son. The trail led to a small glade near a creek, where the Grangers stopped. "This here's the center of this section," Filmore Granger said. "You want, a house could go right up there on that slope, and then you'd have your water just a few feet away."

I looked around. It was a land dense with trees and brush, dark, with little light shining through. There was no magic here.

"Now, a good part of this land would have to be cleared to get yourself a crop. My family's owned this land the last sixty-odd years, and far's I know, none of these timbers have been cut. It'd be a lot of hard work, and I'd be expecting no less than seven hundred trees a month until it's cleared. You got somebody to help you?"

"Well, I've never been afraid of hard work," I said truthfully. "As for help, I've got somebody in mind." I was figuring that Mitchell and I together could turn this place into something. Later on, after we'd cleared the place and put in a few years of crops, we could sell it and buy something better.

"What about oxen?" Filmore Granger said. "You'd have to supply your own. You got that kind of money?"

"I was figuring on mules."

"Oxen are better for logging."

I knew he was right. But when Filmore Granger said this to me, I had already thought about what animal I would use to help in the logging. I had done enough logging to know that oxen were sturdier and that their short legs were less likely to break than the legs of a mule. They had an even temperament, unlike some mules who could be as stubborn as any man, and they had the strength to pull logs through mud and rain. Still, I figured a mule could hold its own on this kind of land. I didn't figure the soil to become too sodden, not by the moisture I saw now at the end of what had been a rainy few weeks, and it looked to me a mule could manage logs across it. Besides that, I was thinking about after the logging was over. A mule could travel as fast as a decent horse, so therefore was good for riding. Mules could pull a plow and they could pull a stump; oxen could as well, but most farmers preferred mules over oxen, so I figured to buy four mules, then sell three of them without much trouble when the logging was over. That was my thinking. I just hoped I wouldn't regret it.

I met Filmore Granger's eyes. "I can manage with the mules," I answered quietly, without addressing his question about my money.

Filmore Granger pursed his lips, eyeing me again, and after a moment went on.

"Now, you say you're interested in thirty or forty acres. Well, it would have to be forty. But you'll have to chop all the trees that are at least sixteen inches in diameter at the smaller end, that's sixteen or more straight across the tree. The lumber company won't take any trees less than that. The rest you leave in the ground."

I nodded my understanding as my eyes took in the forest of virgin longleaf pines and white oaks. While Filmore Granger talked, I was figuring how many acres Mitchell and I could clear in a year.

"You clear all the trees I want," Filmore Granger went on, "all forty acres become yours. You don't, you forfeit the whole forty. Now, all the timber you cut is mine. I expect that timber to be stripped of branches and stacked here along by this creek."

"Who'd take it out of here?" I asked.

"I'll take care of that. I'll bring up a crew of rafters each month and run the logs down creek. You just chop the trees and get them to that bank yonder."

"What about crops?"

"I'm not interested in your crops, just these trees. Whatever else is in the ground is yours. Once the land is yours, you can clear all the rest of the trees, for all I care. You do after a few years, give them a chance to grow, then you'll have yourself some good cash money."

I nodded, then walked across the glade, figuring how long it would take Mitchell and me to clear the forty acres. I could see that some of the land was sloping and that could be hard on us and any mules we had. Also, some parts of the forest looked to be denser than others, but seeing that this was a virgin forest, I was figuring three-fourths of those trees were likely to be sixteen inches or more diameter. Still, when I looked up at the massive trees, I decided with Mitchell and me each being able to fell about fifteen to twenty trees a day, more if we had to, we could do it. We could clear Filmore Granger's forty acres of timber for him and have ourselves forty acres of good farming and grazing land afterward, and we could do it in two years. I walked back to face the Grangers. "If I take this on," I said, "then I'd want the first timbers I cut to be for a cabin. If I need to put some other buildings on the place, shelter for my animals or for my tools and such, I would want to cut timber for that as well. I wouldn't figure you to charge me for it."

Filmore Granger studied on the matter. "Well, I don't know about that. You'd be taking money out of my pocket by using my timbers."

"The thing is, if for some reason I don't get the land cleared, you'd already have buildings standing here."

Filmore Granger nodded but did not accept my terms. "I tell you what. You go ahead and cut the timbers you need for your shelters, but only trees less than sixteen inches. I'll be checking to see that you do. You cut down any of my trees sixteen or more inches, then you're going to have to answer to me. Another thing, don't you dare to cut off this section. One thing I won't stand for is you pilfering my trees to line your own pockets."

I took offense to that, but I didn't let Filmore Granger know. "I wouldn't do that," I said before accepting his terms. "All right, Mister Granger, I can agree to what you say. But I would like a map to help me with the boundaries and I'd like to walk the land off with you to see exactly how many trees there are and to mark the boundaries, so I'll know how far out to cut."

Filmore Granger agreed to that. "But you need to know I expect the first trees you cut to be out along the trail yonder to the road there. I need a road across to this glade so I can get my men and wagons in and out. That comes first, before any building you do. Fact, I'd expect a roadway clear in two months. I figure to bring in men about then to run the first logs down the creek."

"I understand," I said, then took a moment adjusting my thoughts, for I knew I had to put my next words just right. "Mister Granger, after we walk off the place and mark the tree line, if it's agreeable with you, I'd like to have a written agreement stating our terms."

Now, I'd expected some objection from Filmore Granger about this, but it was the boy who spoke up, not his father. "What you need a piece of paper for? My daddy's word good enough for a white man, it sure ought to be good enough for you!"

I glanced at the boy but addressed my words to his father. "I meant no offense. It's just that I know that sometimes things get a bit muddled and folks sometimes forget certain things when they aren't written down as fact. I figured a written agreement would keep me alert as to what I need to do in order to own this place."

Filmore Granger eyed me coldly, but I knew he understood what I was saying, even though I knew he didn't like it. I was willing to risk his withdrawing his offer if I didn't have a legal paper. I'd learned long ago a white man's word didn't mean all that much when he dealt with people of color. Ray Sutcliffe had taught me that. "All right, boy, you can have your paper. You come back in the morning," he said, "and we'll mark a tree line and walk off all forty acres."

I tried not to study on the fact he'd called me a boy, even though I was a man grown. "That'll be fine," I said, my voice even, "but if you don't mind, Mister Granger, I'd like to make the terms of our agreement dated to take effect in thirty days, at the end of September. I've got work to finish up in Vicksburg, but once I come back, I can start right away."

"You sure are demanding for a white nigger," objected Filmore Granger at what he no doubt thought was my arrogance. "All right, thirty days. I'll draw up your paper too stating 'our' terms, as you say." He turned to leave.

I kept my anger to myself and called out to him. "Mister Granger, if you don't mind, I'd like to spend the night here seeing we'll be walking the land in the morning. It'll give me a chance to see more of the place."

"Suit yourself," he said. I thanked him, but Filmore Granger had no more words for me as he and Harlan headed back up the trail.

So I stayed that night on the first piece of land I figured to own. I walked it, studied it, and checked out the density of the trees and the underbrush. The next morning at dawn I met again with Filmore Granger, and he and I, along with the boy Harlan and the colored workman, walked off the land and marked the tree line for cutting. When that was done, Filmore Granger handed me a paper with all the terms we'd stated. It was already signed. "You keep it," he said snidely, "so you can remember the terms and your mind don't get 'muddled.' As for me, I keep the terms and every specific about them right here." He thumped the side of his head with his forefinger, gave me a hard look, and left with his son and the workman.

When they were gone, I again walked the forty acres. This

was to be my start, but this piece of land gave me no real pleasure. One day I figured to own the land I really wanted, land like J. T. Hollenbeck's meadow. But for now I'd go back to Luke Sawyer's store, finish up my work there, and buy what I needed to work this place. When I returned, I was counting on Mitchell being with me.

❧

Once I was back in Vicksburg, I let Luke Sawyer know I had struck a deal with Filmore Granger and that I would be leaving at the end of the month. "Well, you know I'm sure sorry to lose you, Paul," he said, "but I'm figuring you to still do what orders you can for me."

"I was figuring on that too," I said. "I can always use the cash money, especially since I'll be looking to buy a couple of mule teams, supplies, and such."

"Well, you want yourself some good animals, you best go see Sam Perry. He's the best man I know for getting you what you want and at a good price."

"I'll do that," I said, and when I had just about finished all the orders for Luke Sawyer, I headed out for the Perry place. I told Mister Sam Perry what I was planning, and he took me straightaway to a white farmer who had mules he figured the farmer would be willing to sell. The two of them haggled over the cost for some while, longer than I wanted to take, but Sam Perry won out in the end. It seemed he'd helped the farmer in the birthing of his mares, and he made the farmer feel so guilty about the price he wanted to charge that the farmer finally relented. When we left, we had the mules. Same thing happened when we went looking to buy another pair of mules and a wagon—the same long haggling with the same results.

"I thank you, Mister Perry, for all your help," I said when we were back on his place. "I'll pay you for your services."

"No need for pay. Was glad t' help ya. But I am gonna ask

somethin' of ya I been thinkin' on. Now, you ain't gotta agree t' this, 'cause I woulda helped you out in any case. That's jus' what one man'll do for another."

"Well, I appreciate that . . . but just what are you thinking on?"

"Ya gonna need help workin' that land of yours?"

"I figure I will. But I don't figure to hire on anybody."

"Can understand that. What I'm askin' 'bout is if you'd be willin' t' take on my boy Nathan t' help ya. Nathan's only twelve, but he's big for his age, strong too, and he could be of some mighty real help t' ya in exchange for you teachin' him yo' craft."

"Woodworking?" I said.

"That's right. The boy taken quite a shine t' both you and yo' work, and I figure it t' be a good craft for him t' learn. He get t' be good as you, he could make hisself a good livin'."

I studied on the prospect and on this man Sam Perry. More and more I was seeing my daddy in him. "Well, to tell you the truth, Mister Perry, I hadn't thought to be responsible for anybody, let alone a twelve-year-old boy."

Sam Perry whittled at a stick and said, "Let me tell ya somethin', Mister Logan. 'Fore I learned ya was gonna have yo' own place, I done give a lotta thought t' yo' takin' on Nathan and teachin' him. I don't know much 'bout ya, and you ain't been in these parts but for 'bout a year, but I got me a good feel for knowin' folks, and one thing I got me a feelin' 'bout is who you is. Now, I done talked t' Mister Luke Sawyer and some other folks who been seein' ya regular, and I know ya t' be a hardworkin' man who mostly keeps t' hisself. Heard ya live quiet like and ya keeps ya word. Now, that ain't all t' a man, and I ain't fool enough t' think it is. All my children, each and every one of them eleven, they precious t' me and I takes what happens t' each one serious. You take my boy with ya, I be entrustin' him t' ya care and I be expectin' ya t' treat him right and not be leadin' him into no ungodly ways. I done prayed on this long and hard 'bout askin' you t' teach my boy your craft and the good Lord, He done put in my mind this here's the right thing for Nathan, you willin' t' do it. Comin' t' this woulda been a whole lot easier on me if you was gonna be stayin' in Vicksburg, not way off past Strawberry, but I still feel it's the right thing for my boy, you willin' t' take him on."

I was silent, mulling over what Sam Perry had said before I spoke again. I thought on the work that Nathan could do. I hadn't figured on a third hand, just on Mitchell and me, but Sam Perry was right. Nathan was big for his age and strong. Another hand would make things a whole lot easier. "All right," I finally agreed. "I think that if the boy's willing, it'll work out well."

Mister Sam Perry smiled. "Oh, he'll be willin', all right. Two things, though, 'fore we shake on this. First be, boy won't be able t' start wit' you 'fore another few weeks. I need him here t' help me get my crops in."

"That's fine," I said.

"'Sides that, my girl Callie gonna be gettin' married in an-other couple weeks or so, and his mama wants him home for that. Weddin' gonna be at the church, but we gonna celebrate afterward right here. You sho' welcome to come join us."

"Well, I thank you, Mister Perry, but I won't be back this way until I've got a roadway cleared, and that could take me more than a month. Congratulations, though."

"Thank ya. My Callie, she's marryin' herself a fine boy. Now, one other thing 'bout Nathan goin' with ya," he said, getting back to the business at hand. "I wants you to keep in mind I'm still his daddy, and I be holdin' ya responsible for him bein' treated same way I'd treat him in my own house."

"You don't have to worry about that," I said. "I'll treat him right."

"Then we's in agreement," said Sam Perry with a wide grin as he put out his mighty hand to me. I took it. I figured this to be a good deal for both of us.

When I left Sam Perry, I didn't go directly back to Vicksburg. Instead I headed for the lumber camp at Mud Creek. I wanted to tell Mitchell my news. When I got to the camp, though, I learned that Mitchell had taken off for a few weeks. Evidently he had told the boss man that his daddy was sick and needed him. But I knew that was a lie. Probably the boss man did too, for he added that he was only letting Mitchell come back because he was the best worker he had. I didn't know where Mitchell had gone, but I wasn't worried about him. I figured he'd just gotten it in his mind to go off with some lady friend. I knew he'd be back. I was just disappointed that I couldn't count on him to return with me to the forty acres at the end of the month.

In the next days I finished the furniture Luke Sawyer had on order. Then I said good-bye to Luke Sawyer, leaving word with him to let Mitchell know that I'd be back in Vicksburg in about five or six weeks if he came looking for me, and I set out on my wagon filled with supplies and drawn by my team of mules, headed for the Granger plantation. I had left the palomino in Luke Sawyer's care. I figured that was better than my taking him to the forty. I didn't figure to work Thunder like a mule, and there would be no time for racing. Also, I didn't figure it the best thing for me to show up on a fine horse, not right now, when I had to deal with folks the likes of Filmore Granger and his boy.

I reached the forty before dark, put up a shelter of tarp and poles at the head of the trail, then got myself a good night's sleep. The following morning I got started clearing the trees along the trail to make a road. I also made a cartlike carrier using large wheels I had bought in Vicksburg, to hitch to the mules so that one end of the logs could be placed on the cart and the mules could more easily drag the logs to the creek. It was slow going with me working alone, but I figured the hardest part was yet to come—I still had to get the stumps up, or at least level them to the ground so that animals and wagons could pass, but I decided not to worry about the stumps for a while. I had two months before Filmore Granger brought his work crews in and the stumps would have to be gone. I just prayed that Mitchell would be here by then to help me out.

Soon after I arrived on the forty, I took the time to barter myself a couple of laying hens and a rooster, and I got myself a dog too. I had brought tinned goods, bags of flour, cornmeal, sugar, and chicory, that sort of thing, with me from Vicksburg. I had brought coffee too. After all the years I'd spent in the lumber camps with only chicory and water to drink, I wanted coffee. It didn't matter to me that coffee was more expensive than chicory. I wanted the real thing and I figured that on occasion I'd have it. I brought seed from Vicksburg as well, for planting a garden in the spring. For right now I made do with the rice I had brought with me, and for vegetables whatever was growing wild. I loved mustard greens and had already discovered that there were plenty of them and other greens too throughout the forest. As for meat, there were plenty of deer for venison, possum, raccoon, rabbit, and squirrel. On top of that, the creek was filled with fish. I didn't figure I'd go hungry.

During those weeks I spent alone, I thought often on Caroline Perry. I liked the way she thought, I liked the way she looked, and I liked the way she stood up for herself. She had touched me deeply, and by the time I returned to Vicksburg to get Nathan, I had made up my mind. I figured to ask Sam Perry if I could court his daughter. But before I headed out to the Perry farm, I went to see Luke Sawyer. I took him two small tables I had finished during the evening hours on the forty, and he was pleased. "Now, I know you got it in your mind to farm, Paul," he said, "but I tell you the truth. You got a gift with wood, and if you settled down to just doing that, I could have more orders for you than you could take."

"I thank you," I returned. "But you know my thinking on this. Long as I can do some pieces I can work on at the place, I can sure use the cash money. Thing is, though, I've got to put this land first."

Luke Sawyer nodded to that. He'd heard it before. "Just want you to know, it don't work out, then you always got a place here."

I thanked Luke Sawyer again, took my payment for the tables, and took on two more orders. I got the wood for the orders, then bought some of Luke Sawyer's tools I would need to do the work. Luke Sawyer said I could just take his tools; he trusted me to bring them back. But I preferred to buy the tools. I felt the same way I had when I had rented Thunder from him. I couldn't be beholden to Luke Sawyer.

I left Luke Sawyer after that and set off for the Perry farm. When I arrived, I learned that Nathan wasn't there, and neither was Caroline.

"Sorry, but Nathan's out with Caroline and their mama deliverin' pies," explained Sam Perry. "They be back 'fore time to fix supper." I didn't say anything, and he went on. "Ain't knowed the 'xact day you was comin', else I'd a done had Nathan here and ready t' go."

"It's no problem," I assured him, though I was disappointed about Caroline. "We can get started when he comes in."

"Naw. Be too late by then. Best y'all spend the night here, start out early mornin'."

I agreed to that.

"'Sides, I know for a fact, Nathan's mama gonna wanna keep him close long's she can." Sam Perry smiled at that.

"Well, that'll work out fine," I said. "I've got a friend I want to see who works in a lumber camp south of here."

Mr. Perry looked around at me. "Camp over by Mud Creek?"

"Yes, that's the one."

"Say you got a friend there?"

"That's right. Want him to help me work this forty acres I've taken on, but I haven't heard from him in a while. Figured maybe I could swing by there before heading back toward Strawberry."

"Ya do, maybe ya see my family on the way. They deliverin' some of their pies down along that way."

"That a fact?"

Sam Perry laughed. "Them men at that camp, they get one taste of my wife's pies and cakes and they can't seem t' get enough. Every pie and cake my womenfolks make, they buys."

"Well, I can't say that I blame them. Your wife's an excellent cook."

"My girls too!" proclaimed Sam Perry, then laughed loudly at his bragging. "Even if I do say so myself!"

I smiled. "Well, it is the truth."

"Yeah . . . these young men love my daughters' cookin'! S'pose that's one reason why they get spoke for so quick!" He laughed again. "Callie's and Risten's husbands, they already enjoyin' good cookin' and pretty soon now, Caroline gonna have a husband enjoyin' hers too."

The smile left my face. "What's that?"

Sam Perry nodded proudly. "Said they all gonna be married ladies soon. My Caroline, she jus' done give her heart to a fella she met not too long ago. Fact to business, he work at that same camp as yo' friend. I don't know that much 'bout him. Seem nice 'nough, but he got no family round here. Told Caroline she wanna marry this man, she gonna hafta pray on it 'til next sum-

mer. After that, the boy still round and he done proved hisself t'
be a good worker, then I figure him t' be serious 'bout this thing.
For young folks, near a year's a long time, and it's hard on 'em and
they got t' keep theyselves in check, but for a lifetime of livin', it's
worth it to pair right. My Caroline's a strong-willed girl, and I
know she gonna keep that boy in check. She agreed t' what her
mama and me said, and he done too, so she official spoke for."

I was numbed by the news. Yet something nagged at the back
of my mind. "I think I'll go see my friend," I said abruptly, needing suddenly to be off alone. "I'll most likely spend the night
and come back for Nathan in the morning first thing."

"Suit yo'self, but ya know ya welcome t' spend the night here."

"I know," I said, "and I thank you for that. You don't mind,
though, I'll just take one of the mules and leave the wagon and
the others here with you, along with my dog."

"Nothin' t' mind. You jus' be sure and be here time for breakfast come mornin'. My wife, I know she gonna have a few words
for you."

I left with nothing more to say, and went about unhitching
the mules. I put three of the mules out to graze, and mounted
the fourth. With directions from Sam Perry on how to reach the
lumber camp, I set out to find Mitchell. As I rode, I pondered
on the fact that Caroline was now spoken for, and I kept thinking on Mitchell's words about the pretty girls who'd come to the
camp. I hadn't figured on Mitchell to settle and marry, and
Mitchell surely hadn't either, but Caroline Perry was the kind of
girl who could change a man's mind about a thing like that, even
a man as set against settling as Mitchell. I thought on them both
all the way to the camp, and before I reached it, I had no more
doubts. I knew it within my bones. I suppose I had known as
soon as Sam Perry had told me the news; maybe that's why I
hadn't even asked the name of the fellow who had spoken for

Caroline. I didn't really want to know. But I did. It was Mitchell who was going to marry Caroline Perry.

❧

"'Ey, Paul!" exclaimed Mitchell when he saw me. "Man, whatcha doin' here?"

"Come to see about you," I said. "It's been a while."

"That's sure the truth."

We slapped each other on the shoulders, then Mitchell led me over to a space where we could talk, away from the other loggers.

"Where'd you go off to?" I asked when we were alone.

"How'd ya know I was gone?"

"Came by. Didn't anybody tell you?"

"Ya know they ain't, else I'd've been up t' Vicksburg by now! What ya want when ya come by?"

I noted Mitchell hadn't answered my first question yet about where he'd been, but I answered his. "Same as now," I said. "I've got some news for you."

"What's that?"

"I've got myself some land."

Mitchell laughed in congratulations. "Ya don't say! That land you was talkin' 'bout?"

"No, I'm still waiting on that."

"Well, what land you got?"

"Forty acres near to the land I want. I made a deal didn't call for any money."

"How'd you pull that off?"

"I clear forty acres of trees sixteen inches across or more in two years for the man who owns the place, and the forty acres are deeded over to me."

Mitchell looked skeptical. "I s'pose the trees on the place is Mississippi thick?"

I smiled. "You're right about that."

"And you figuring you can clear forty acres in two years?"

"I'm figurin' I can . . ." I met Mitchell's eyes. "With your help."

Mitchell smiled. "Now, how my name get into this? I don't recall sayin' anythin' 'bout any land. You the one wanted land."

"Well, to my figuring, if you came in and helped me on this, we could split the acreage. You take twenty, I take twenty."

"What I'm gonna do with twenty acres?"

"Farm it."

Mitchell considered. "You gonna do the same?"

"For a spell. Figure, though, to sell the timber on it for cash money eventually and buy a better piece."

"You mean that land you been wantin'.'"

"Yeah . . . that land."

"What 'bout supplies? You got everything you need?"

I nodded. "I bought four mules, wagon, axes, saws, rope, food. Yes, I think I've got everything we'll need."

Mitchell turned his back on me and stepped away, considering. Then he turned again to face me. "'Fore I decide on that, there's some news I gotta tell you."

"I think I know," I said.

"What's that?"

"You're getting married."

Mitchell looked at me in silence, his lips slightly agape.

"So it's true."

Mitchell made a hissing sound, expressing his surprise that I already knew. "How'd you find out? Who told you?"

"Well, just so happens I was doing some business with the family of the young lady you proposed to. Her daddy told me."

Mitchell shook his head and let out an embarrassed laugh. "Who'd've figured, huh? Me? Fella wasn't never gonna get tied down."

I smiled at his predicament.

He became suddenly serious. "But this one, Paul, she special."

"I know," I said. "I've met her."

"Did?"

"Met her whole family. Her daddy came in one day up to Luke Sawyer's place wanting me to make a rocker for her mama, and I met the young lady then. She's a fine young woman."

"Ain't she, though?" Mitchell grinned at his good fortune. "I first seen her back last summer when she come t' the camp with her mama selling pies, but I ain't started 'changing many words wit' her 'til the spring." He laughed. "I s'pose she kinda scairt me!"

"Is that why you went off?"

"Ain't ya heard? My daddy was low sick."

"Uh-huh."

Mitchell laughed again. "Ya right, Paul. I was tryin' t' get her off my mind. She's young, but she's sure got a woman's hold on me. I figured t' take up my time with somebody else and put some distance between us, but it ain't helped. All I could think 'bout was her." He looked at me a bit sheepishly as he confessed that. Then he said, "So, ya seen her, huh? Ain't she somethin'?"

I nodded and was honest with my friend. "I was on the verge of asking her daddy if I could court her myself when he went and told me she was spoken for."

"That a fact?"

"It's a fact, all right. I reckon I was just too slow getting up my nerve to try and court her."

"Reckon you was," said Mitchell; then he hesitated. "You liked her that much, huh? I got reason t' worry?" Mitchell studied me close, no longer laughing. "You got any problem 'bout me and her? You do, you tell me now."

I shook my head. "You spoke for her. She accepted. Whatever feelings I had, or I've got, I'm letting them go. I've got no part in it now, except as your friend." I said that, and I meant what I said, though I was feeling a hurt I'd never felt before.

Mitchell looked at me long, accepted my words, and sighed. "Who'd've thought it, Paul? Me, with a fine young lady like that? I don't know if her daddy care much for me, but I promised him he got no cause to doubt me. I'm gonna take care of Caroline. I'm gonna take care of her fine."

"I expect you will," I said. "Especially if you've got yourself twenty acres of good farmland."

Mitchell let go a raucous laugh. "You really tryin' t' get me 'bout this thing, ain't ya?"

"You going to turn me down?"

Mitchell was silent. "You know I done had my share of the womenfolks, Paul, and you know jus' 'xactly where I come from and where I been, so I 'spect you know what I mean when I say Caroline Perry the best thing ever come into my life." He looked at me, and I answered him with a nod.

"You just make sure you take care of her," I said. "She's too fine to be thrown away."

"Don't worry," said Mitchell. "I know that. I know you've seen how I've done before, but you can believe this, Paul. I won't ever do that t' Caroline."

I accepted my friend's words and went on. "So, what about the land? Are you going to work it with me?"

"Wouldn't be able to work it with you for another few weeks. I'm flat broke and I need me some cash money from this camp. Soon as I leave from here, I'm even plannin' on sellin' my gun t' put some money in my pocket."

"But you'll come in with me on this?"

Mitchell grunted. "You asked me and I need it." He extended his hand. "You're a true brother to me, Paul. Always done been."

I took Mitchell's hand. "And you know, you're more a brother to me than any of my blood." We shook hands, and the deal was sealed. That night I wrote out the terms of our agreement even though Mitchell didn't want any part of any written paper. We had shaken hands on the deal, and that was enough for him. But I figured it was the fair thing to do, for if anything happened to me before our two years were up and there was any question about the forty, Mitchell would need some written word about our agreement. I wrote it and signed it, and against his objections, Mitchell signed it too.

☙

That next morning I left the camp early while it was still dark in order to reach the Perry farm in time for breakfast. When I got there, I found my heart racing upon seeing Caroline. She looked even prettier than I remembered. As we sat down to breakfast, I said, "I've just come back from the lumber camp over by Mud Creek. I was visiting a friend of mine there. Turns out the two of you know each other."

Caroline's eyes seemed to dance as she looked at me. "Do?"

"Yes. . . . His name's Mitchell Thomas."

"*My* Mitchell?" exclaimed Caroline.

"Ya don't say!" added Mister Perry.

"You really know my Mitchell?" Caroline almost squealed with delight.

I nodded. "Since we were boys. We came into Mississippi together from East Texas. We grew up together on my daddy's land in Georgia."

"Well, ain't that somethin'!" said Sam Perry. "You hear that, Miz Perry?" he asked his wife. "What ya say t' that? Mister Logan here knowin' the young man our Caroline gonna marry?"

Miz Rachel Perry glanced at her husband, then to my great surprise turned to me and spoke. "You think he a good man?"

I looked straight into her eyes. "Yes, ma'am, I do. Since the day he became my friend, he's never let me down, not even one time."

Miz Rachel Perry kept her eyes on me a moment longer, looked at her beaming daughter, then back at me again, and nodded. She had no more words for me right then, even though the rest of the family had plenty as they asked question after question about Mitchell and me. But after breakfast was over and Nathan and I were packing to go, Miz Rachel Perry pulled me aside. "Mister Logan," she said, "I wants t' thank you for my rockin' chair."

"No need," I said. "It was your husband's doing."

"But he ain't made that rockin' chair. You done that. I know he done paid ya for it and it was yo' job t' make it, but still I'm thankin' ya for it. It's a finely made piece of furniture and I 'preciate that. I always 'preciate good work and I wants ya t' know that."

"Well, I thank you, Miz Perry. You know, though, I can't take all the credit for that chair. It was your daughter Caroline painted the flowers."

"I know that. I know." She looked away for a moment, pressed her lips together, then turned back to me. "I wanna 'pologize t' ya too."

"Apologize?"

"That's right. My husband and my daughter Caroline, they both done told me I ain't been the best I coulda been when you come for supper that Sunday. But they ain't had t' tell me that. I know'd I wasn't bein' a Christian woman, welcomin' a stranger t' my house. It wasn't nothin' t' do with anythin' ya done I acted that way, and I wants ya t' know that. You seems t' be a fine young man and ya does fine work. You welcome here . . . anytime."

I was overcome by Miz Perry's words. I'm not sure why. Maybe it was because I saw my mama in her. Maybe it was because I saw her pride and felt her pain about her name and what her mother had suffered to give it to her. I was so overcome, all I could do was nod, and she accepted that without another word. She looked into my eyes, and I believe she saw what I felt.

On the way back to the forty acres neither Nathan nor I had much to say to each other. I had my thoughts on Caroline and Mitchell, and clearing the trees in time, and I reckon Nathan was already missing his family. By the time we reached the forty, it was nightfall. I halted the wagon at the head of the trail because of the stumps, then Nathan and I unhitched the mules and led them to where I had built a shed. We fed and watered the mules and the dog too; we unloaded the wood and my tools, and set them in the shed along with all the other supplies. Once all that was done, Nathan and I settled in the shed as well. I had made only one bed, a crude one at that, and I let Nathan have it. I built a fire, rolled myself into a blanket, and lay on the ground beside the fire. Nathan was already snoring. I was tired, but it was way over in the night before I could fall asleep. The news of Caroline and Mitchell had hit me hard, and now with only my mind for company, that's all I could think about.

The next morning before the dawn, I rose before Nathan and rekindled the fire. Then I woke the boy and sent him to the creek for water. When he returned, I put on a pot of chicory and unwrapped the biscuits and ham Miz Perry had given us, and we settled down to breakfast without a word. Afterward I began to show Nathan what a day's work on this place was going to be. I had already cleared the roadway. Now I set Nathan to leveling the stumps that lined the roadway while I chopped more trees. The work was hard, but Nathan didn't complain. In the afternoon I began chopping trees to build a cabin, for it was already fall and we would soon need sturdier shelter. As soon as the trees fell, I had Nathan hack off the branches, and when the evening came, we gathered all the branches and burned them.

Finally we sawed down a circle of stumps for sitting, dug a fire pit in the center to do our cooking, and sat down to eat more of the good food Miz Rachel Perry had sent. After supper I kept my end of the bargain I'd made with Nathan's father. Or at least I tried to. I started on the cabinet I'd contracted with Luke Sawyer, and it was my plan to have Nathan help me with every step. But Nathan, though his interest was there, was too tired to do anything much after such a long day. Finally I told him to go on to his bed. Maybe, I decided, the teaching would have to wait awhile, at least until Nathan was accustomed to his new job of logging.

A few days after Nathan and I settled into our work routine, we had an unexpected visit from Charles Jamison's boy, Wade. He was on foot. He came right up to where we were working on the slope. I was chopping a tree at the time, but I had given to Nathan the less hazardous job of sawing the branches from the fallen trees. Both of us were hard at work, our attention only to the job at hand, when Wade suddenly announced his presence.

"Hello!" he called.

His words were shouted above the buzz of everything else. Both Nathan and I stopped our work and looked toward the sound and the boy who'd issued it.

"Hello!" Wade hollered a second time, and waved at me up the slope. "Remember me, Mister Logan? I'm Wade Jamison!"

I remember thinking he was a boy sure of himself. I gave him a nod.

"My daddy and me, you know we've got a place right up the road, so I figured I'd come see 'bout the neighbors."

"That's obliging of ya," said Nathan, not sounding at all impressed.

"Not at all," said Wade, taking no offense, it seemed, to

Nathan's tone. He looked around. "My daddy said you're clearing all the trees through here. Forty acres of them. Got your work cut out for ya."

"Yes, we do," I said.

"Y'all need some help?"

"We've got help coming," I replied.

"Well, I'll let y'all get back to it," said the boy. "Just wanted to say hello."

"We appreciate that," I said.

"Oh, I'll be stopping by again." He turned to go, took a few steps, then turned around. "'Ey!" he said, looking at Nathan. "What's your name?"

"Nathan."

"Well, Nathan, you like t' fish?"

"Yeah . . ."

"Well, how 'bout us goin' fishin' sometime?"

"I work mos' the time."

Wade nodded like a wise old man in understanding. "But you ever get a break in your day and wanna go fishing on a Saturday, when I'm out of school, I got some poles and I know some real good spots. I'll check back sometime when I'm on my way to the Rosa Lee. That's what we call the creek yonder. That be all right with you?"

Nathan glanced back at me, then looked again at Wade and gave a nod.

"All right!" said Wade with a smile. "See y'all, then!" He waved us a good-bye and went on his way. Nathan and I returned to our work.

A week later on a Saturday morning Wade Jamison was back again, and this time he had his fishing poles with him. "Can't go," said Nathan when Wade asked him to join him.

"Well, ya know, fishing is really good this time of morning," said Wade.

"Know that," replied Nathan. He hesitated. "But I got too much work t' do."

I looked at Nathan eyeing those fishing poles, and I knew he was longing to go. He had been putting in nearly the same hours as I and without complaint. I figured he needed some enjoyment and to be with someone near his own age. "Nathan," I said, "some catfish would sure taste good for supper. Why don't you go on with Wade and catch us some?"

"But what 'bout the branches?"

"They'll be here for you when you get back. Just make sure you're here come noon."

Nathan grinned wide. "Yes, suh, I'll do that." Then he went off happily with Wade. Each boy was holding tight to a fishing pole.

After that, every Saturday Wade Jamison showed up with his fishing poles and I let Nathan go with him. I limited the fishing to just that one morning a week because of all the work to be done, and neither Nathan nor Wade pushed for more. But despite Wade's showing up just once a week for fishing, we saw him more than that. Every day or so he was on the forty after school, wanting to help if he could. I politely declined his help; still, he often stayed awhile keeping Nathan company as he worked. Since Nathan's work wasn't slowed by his presence, I saw no harm at first in his being there. But then as Nathan began to look forward to Wade's visits and began to parrot Wade's words to me, with "Wade said this" and "Wade said that," I decided to speak to Nathan about keeping his distance with this new friend.

"I don't think it's a good idea for you to be getting too close to Wade Jamison," I said when the day's work was done and we sat at the outdoor fire eating our supper.

Nathan glanced away, then back at me again. "Why not? He nice enough."

"Nice enough, yes," I agreed. "But he's white."

Nathan's eyes went downward and he studied his cup. "Ain't nobody round here much, 'ceptin' us. Wade, he seem t' like me and he smart. I don't see nothin' wrong bein' friends with him."

"Maybe you don't," I said. "But in my life I've found there's no such thing as a lasting and equal friendship between black and white." I thought on my brother Robert. "If you're colored, that white man's going to always think of you with your color in mind, and I don't care how close you think you are, if that white man figure it's in his interest to turn his back on you, that's just what he's going to do."

Nathan shrugged off my words. "All we do is go fishin'."

"Fishing?" Again I thought on my brother. I thought on the fishing poles nestled near the creek in that mound of rocks on my daddy's land. I knew it had to be hard on Nathan being in this place with only me, working this land without his family. I knew what it meant to have a friend when a boy was his age. I knew that kind of blind trust. I knew also about betrayal. I could have told him about Robert, but I chose not to do so. Maybe for a while this boy Wade wouldn't hurt him. "Fishing," I repeated. "It's a good passing of time with a friend," I said. Then I looked pointedly at Nathan. "Just don't pass too much of it with Wade Jamison."

Nathan eyed me resentfully, and I figured he was regretting his daddy's admonition to do what I told him. "I gotta go fetch water for the mornin'," he said, and got up. As I watched him heading for the creek with a bucket in each hand, I knew I hadn't gotten through to him. I took one last sip of my chicory, then tossed another log on the fire. I decided Nathan would have to find out for himself what it meant to have a friendship with a boy the likes of Wade Jamison, a friendship with a white boy.

❧

It wasn't long following that talk with Nathan that I came down from chopping and found Wade working alongside Nathan hacking off branches. I called Nathan aside. "How come you've got Wade working with you?"

"He jus' helpin' me out, that's all."

"Well, you thank him and tell him to go."

"But—"

"Do as I say!" My words came out sterner than I'd intended.

As I walked away, I heard Wade say to Nathan, "You get in trouble 'cause of me?"

And I heard Nathan say, "Forget it. He don't understand."

I heard that, and I knew unless I talked to this boy about how things were, about how things had been between folks as close as my brothers and me, I knew he would go on trusting folks he shouldn't, folks he couldn't. So I went back on what I'd decided earlier about Nathan learning for himself how the world was, and that same night, after the day's work was done and the brush was burned, I sat with Nathan again at the outside fire and told him about Robert. "You might know this already," I said, "that my daddy was a white man. Well, my daddy had five children, far as I know. Two of those children were with my mama. That was my sister and me. The other three were boys with his white wife. My daddy raised my sister and me with those boys, and he acknowledged my sister and me, that we were his. He made those white sons of his share everything of theirs with my sister and me, and that included their learning.

"Now, of those boys who were my brothers, I was closest with the youngest because he was the same age as me. The two of us, we did everything together. We weren't only brothers, we were the best of friends. We couldn't've been any closer. Then there came the time when we were both thirteen, entering our young manhood, when white friends of his from school came to visit. They were boys we'd both despised when we were younger, and we'd stood together against them. But on this visit my brother wanted only to please them, and he turned his back on me to do it."

I stared out into the black night and felt that old hurt welling up within me again. "He was my brother, my best friend, but he turned his back on me so he could face his white friends. I learned a terrible, painful, hurtful lesson the day he did that, and I keep it with me in remembrance. We weren't just friends, we were blood. Still, he turned his back, and I learned right then that white folks are going to be white folks, no matter how close a person of color is to them. White folks, they're going to look out for their own, and that's other white folks."

I had said my words, and when they were finished, I sat in silence. For a while Nathan sat in silence too, before he turned to me, his face unaccepting. "Well, that was you," he said quietly.

"Yeah, it was him, all right!" boomed a voice from the darkness. "And you best take t' heart what he been tellin' ya!"

Nathan and I both jumped up and looked out toward the creek. The voice was unmistakable, and I grinned as Mitchell stepped from the night into the firelight. Then I laughed, delighted to see him, and so did Nathan, who clearly idolized Mitchell. "Didn't hear you come up," I said.

"I know that. Man, you need yo'self a dog!"

"Got one."

"Then where he at?"

"Over yonder," said Nathan.

"Then ya need t' shoot him and get yo'self another one," surmised Mitchell with a laugh, and sat down beside the fire. He glanced at our empty supper tins. "Any food left?"

There was a bit of corn bread, but not much else, for Nathan and I, after a grueling day's work, had eaten the most of what was cooked. We had eggs, though, and collards, and we quickly cooked them up for Mitchell as well as another pan of corn bread as he told us about the lumber camp and about his travel here. But most importantly, he told us about Caroline and the rest of the Perrys. "Seen 'em just yesterday," he said, "and they sent plenty of love t' you, Nathan. Got a letter from them too. Caroline wrote it."

Nathan beamed as Mitchell handed it to him.

"Don't you read it just yet," said Mitchell. "I got somethin' t' speak t' you 'bout first. Now, I heard what Paul here was sayin' t' you when I come up. He was telling you 'bout his family, his family of white folks. Now, Paul, he ain't had to do that, but seein' he done it, you oughtta have the good sense enough to listen to him. He told you all that and done warned you 'bout how white folks'll be and I heard you say some fool thing 'bout 'that was you.' So ya tell me, boy, you figurin' things gonna be different for ya and any white so-called friend you got?"

Nathan was silent.

"I ain't talkin' t' the air out here."

"Wade, he's my friend," said Nathan stubbornly, not looking at Mitchell.

"Wade, huh?" Mitchell glanced at me, then fixed his eyes on Nathan again. "Well, you jus' keep on believin' that, believin' this white boy Wade's your friend. You'll learn on yo' own one day, and it won't be easy. Hardheaded folks can't never be taught nothin' the easy way. They gotta go learn it for theyselves, and I oughtta know. I was as hardheaded as they come." Nathan stared out into the night without a word and Mitchell gave him no more mind. Instead, he turned to me. "So tell me 'bout the work here, Paul. How we doin'?"

As Mitchell ate his supper, I filled him in on all the logging, and after that, though we were both dead tired, we talked yet another hour or so. Nathan soon stretched out beside the fire and fell asleep in the night. When Mitchell and I could no longer keep our eyes open, we did the same.

The next morning before the dawn I rose first as usual, woke Mitchell and Nathan, and after a cold breakfast of leftover corn bread and some hot chicory, the three of us set to work. Now that Mitchell was with us, I knew there was no doubt about getting all the trees cut. In the days that followed, Mitchell and I, along with Nathan, put in the longest hours we'd ever worked, even more than the hours we'd worked at the camps. Up long before each dawn, we tended to our morning chores of feeding and watering the mules, then tended to our breakfast. With the fires still hot, we cooked a pan of corn bread along with a pot of whatever vegetables we'd gathered, with salt fatback thrown in for our meat, and set that food aside. It was our dinner and our supper. We didn't want to waste daylight hours cooking.

By the grayest of light we were at the trees chopping. At midday we took our dinner. Supper didn't come until after dark and all the animals were watered and fed. But the day did not end with darkness. At night we built a huge fire and burned the branches we'd chopped from the trees. By the time the fire died, it was past midnight, and we often fell asleep still in our clothes. There was not much rest for any of us. We didn't attend the local church gatherings, and we broke the Sabbath every Sunday. The Lord might have been able to rest on the Seventh Day, but Mitchell and I didn't figure we could. During the first weeks Mitchell was on the forty, we spent our Sundays working on the cabin and putting together some make-do furniture, as well as laying a bridge across the creek for easier crossing. We also tended to personal chores, like washing our clothes or mending, and I took the time to write my letters to Cassie, do my woodworking, and teach Nathan. After the cabin was finished, we chopped trees on a Sunday too. Christmas came and went and still we chopped. We kept right on working and we didn't complain. We figured we were young and strong and healthy, and we could do whatever it took to get our forty acres.

Once a month, right on schedule, Filmore Granger would arrive with Harlan, along with workmen to move the timber down the Rosa Lee. We always had his logs stacked and waiting, and Filmore Granger seemed pleased. Once the Grangers had taken possession of their timber, Mitchell would bathe in the creek, put on his other set of clothes, and mounting one of the mules, go off to see Caroline. He would leave on a Saturday, spend his Sunday with Caroline and her family, and return before dawn on Monday morning, ready to work, even without sleep. Sometimes Nathan went with him, and while they were gone, I continued to work. Come sunrise Monday morning, Mitchell was always ready to chop the trees. He never let down on any of his work with me while he courted Caroline, and I had no complaints with him. I even joked with him that he had finally become a church-going man. I didn't begrudge Mitchell his time away. I knew folks in love needed to be with each other. Still, there was regret in me that it was Mitchell going off to see Caroline and not me. But I didn't dwell on it, and after a while I became accustomed to his monthly trips. Then, late one Sunday night upon Mitchell's return, he brought back news I hadn't expected to hear.

"Robert's been in Vicksburg," he announced as he sank onto a chair before a low fire.

I turned to him in silence.

"Heard he'd come through Vicksburg last week with a work-man."

"Robert? What was he doing in Vicksburg?"

"Maybe lookin' for you."

I was silent; so was Mitchell.

Finally, I said, "How'd you hear about him?"

"Mule threw a shoe, and I had to go to the livery and have another put on. Man there was talkin' 'bout a fine horse that was brought in by a Robert Logan from round Macon. Said he was deliverin' it for purchase."

"You think he's still there?"

"Don't know. Got no need t' think so, though. Maybe he was

just passin' through." Mitchell glanced over at me. "You gonna go find out?"

I thought on it, then shook my head. "Robert wants to see me, and if he knows where I am, he can come here. I'm not going looking for him."

Mitchell looked at me with a nod and turned back to the fire.

That night as I lay on my cot, as tired as I was, I couldn't sleep. I kept thinking on Robert. I thought on George, Hammond, my daddy, and, of course, Cassie. It had been so long since I'd seen them, and I wanted to see them. Even with the letters from Cassie telling me about our daddy and our brothers, about Howard and her children, I felt the ache daily of missing them. I longed to see them all, but I didn't think I could, not yet. I wondered about Robert, if he really had come looking for me. I figured in my next letter to Cassie I'd ask her about it. Robert. I wondered if he'd changed as much as I.

It was early spring by the time I went again to Vicksburg to take the furniture I had made to Luke Sawyer. Mitchell and Nathan went with me. Nathan was eager to be home, for Mitchell had brought back the news on his last trip that Risten had had another baby while he was there and that Callie was expecting. As soon as we reached the store, Mitchell and Nathan unhitched the mules from the wagon and headed off for the Perry place. I declined to go with them, giving the excuse that I had to tend to Thunder, who was still being boarded at Luke Sawyer's stable, and that I had to see to my orders. The truth was, though, I was not yet ready to see Caroline again.

I figured to spend the night in the shed, and that was fine with Luke Sawyer. As always, he was pleased with my work and he paid me as agreed. I took on several more orders, though not as many as he would have liked. Afterward, I went to the shed to select the wood I would need and read the letter from Cassie that Luke Sawyer had been holding for me. I had written Cassie about Robert and she said, as far as she knew, Robert had no idea that I was in the area. Our daddy had sent him to Vicksburg on some business and that was all there was to it.

I was relieved.

※

As the next weeks went by, Mitchell began preparing for his marriage to Caroline. He bought himself a suit and a new pair of shoes. He made a bed for the two of them and asked me to build a small cabinet where Caroline could put some of her things. He'd promised Caroline a house and he drew up a plan for it. He picked out the site and together we figured on just when we could build the house. Mitchell wanted it up before the wedding. We figured there to be time for that. But all Mitchell's plans were soon disrupted by the unexpected arrival of Filmore Granger, who announced to our surprise that he needed more trees. As usual, his boy Harlan was with him. Seems he took that boy everywhere.

"Well, Mister Granger," I said, after a glance at Mitchell, standing somewhat apart from us, "we'll have half of this forty cleared before a year of our contract's up."

"That's not what I'm talking about," said Filmore Granger. "I need more trees cut a week, more than you been cutting."

I frowned. We had produced as many logs as we could in a day's time. There was no way we could increase that unless we took on more help. "How many more?"

"Eighty."

I shook my head. "I don't know how we could do that, Mister Granger. We're putting in more than fourteen hours a day as it is to produce the logs we've cut so far."

"I know that, and you've done a good job. I had my doubts you could do it, but you've done it. Now I'm going to need those extra trees."

"Well, eighty's a lot."

"Know that, but I've got a new contract I've got to meet, and that contract calls for so many board feet a week. So, that means more trees, and you'll just have to figure a way to cut those eighty more. You can't do it, then I'll just have to get me somebody who can."

I looked straight into Filmore Granger's eyes. "Our agreement calls for cutting all trees sixteen inches or more in diameter at the smaller end within two years."

"And that's still what it'll be, just that there'll be more trees cut sooner rather than later. Course now, that agreement's only good if you get all the trees cut, and you know now how many I want cut and when."

I wasn't fool enough not to know when I was being threatened. We didn't cut these trees for Filmore Granger, we could lose the forty. "How long would we have to keep this up?"

"'Til I figure I got enough to fill my contract."

"I need to know how long if we figure to do this."

Filmore Granger was silent, and his eyes narrowed at my questioning him, but then he gave a little. "Well, let's just say until you've finished cutting twenty of these forty acres. You figure you can do that? Look at things this way. Sooner you get these acres cut, sooner you can get to your plowing and your crops."

Throughout this exchange Mitchell had said nothing. I looked at him now. "What do you think?"

Mitchell's eyes were on Filmore Granger, and I think his gaze made Filmore Granger uneasy, for a sudden scowl crossed his face when he found Mitchell's eyes upon him. "I think," said Mitchell, "we've put months of sweat into this land that's 'bout t' go for nothing. It's up to you, you wanna let it go. I go 'long with what you decide."

I turned back to Filmore Granger and remembered the warnings both J. T. Hollenbeck and Charles Jamison had made concerning him. Mitchell was right. We had put months of sweat in the land, too much sweat to lose the forty now. "All right, Mister Granger," I said, "somehow we'll cut the extra eighty."

"And another thing," he added, "I'll be bringing men in here every two weeks instead of once a month to run the logs down creek. Be sure you've got the logs I need."

"You'll have them."

"Good boy," said Filmore Granger as if complimenting somebody's dog. I knew how he felt about doing white man's business with me, and I knew how I felt being treated like somebody's dog. My mind raged and my blood went rushing, but I held my words. My daddy had taught me that. I wasn't going to let this man beat me down.

When the Grangers were gone, Mitchell slammed his axe into a tree. "You shoulda done broke his head open for that."

I gave Mitchell a look. "That's right, and then have a whole bunch of white folks come snap my neck with a lynch rope?"

"I don't trust that scound'," was Mitchell's reply.

"I don't either. But I've got a written agreement with him, and I mean to have this land."

"And jus' how you figure we're gonna cut and log another eighty trees a week? Good-a choppers as we are, we can't hardly do that."

I shrugged. "Sleep less, I guess."

Mitchell grunted. "Not me. I need what little sleep I get."

"What do you suggest, then?"

Mitchell looked away for a moment, then back at me. "I know a man by the name of Tom Bee. He done lumberin' with me up at that last camp I was at, but he done quit that camp 'fore me. He's a good man. He's older'n us and got a family, but he knows how t' chop. Can't chop good as us, maybe ten, twelve trees a day, but he could help and we could make up the rest between us. Seein' he got his family down in here, maybe he be willin' t' come in with us."

I frowned. "He'd be wanting cash money."

"Wouldn't you?" admonished Mitchell.

I eyed Mitchell and did some figures in my head.

"You got that kind of money?" Mitchell questioned.

"Well, I hadn't figured on having to pay out cash for workers," I said. "I had other plans for my money."

"'Spect ya did," said Mitchell. "But you wanna give this man Filmore Granger what he want, how you 'spect t' cut all them trees without some more help? I ain't got much, 'ceptin' part of that last month's pay from the camp, but what I got, I'll put in. You know I bought my wedding suit already."

I considered and gave up on my figures. "All right," I said. "But this Tom Bee, he best be up to working longer hours than he's ever seen in a lumber camp."

"Same pay as there?"

I met Mitchell's eyes and agreed. "I'm not about to cheat any man when it comes to his work. I figure to pay him according to how many trees he cuts, that and meals."

Mitchell nodded. "All right then, Paul, I'll go see if I can't find him first thing come light in the morning. You oughtta know, though, he's a talker, so don't go blamin' me for that."

Mitchell caught up with Tom Bee, all right, and later that same day Tom Bee showed up ready to work. Problem was, he had a white boy with him. The boy looked to be in his mid teens, and he seemed mighty familiar to me.

"What's he doing here?" demanded Mitchell as soon as he saw him.

"Name's John Wallace and he jus' like my shadow," said the talkative Tom Bee with the boy standing right in hearing distance. "Come on him 'bout a year ago 'bout t' drown in swampland when that foolish boy done tried t' cross it. I come on him and I says t' myself, 'Lord have mercy! That boy 'bout t' drown!' An' I ain't thought nothin' 'bout nothin' 'ceptin' some poor fool was 'bout t' go down. Ain't thought nothin' 'bout no color, nothin' like that. Lord jus' done throwed all that out my mind and I gone flyin' int' that there swamp and I done dragged that boy out. Boy so grateful, he done been wit' me 'bout ever since. Come outa Alabama where his folks is, but he left them and met up with a no 'count brother of his round Biloxi, stayed wit' him awhile, then was headed on up this way when I gone and pulled him outa that swamp. That brother of his, he come round sometime and sometime that boy go off with him, then he come on back. When John round here, where I go, he pretty much do the same."

I looked again at the boy, and it came to me where I'd seen him before. He had been the boy on the ridge, the same boy who had come with that group of men looking for the chicken thieves. The boy looked at me too and said, "Ain't I seen you b'fore?"

"Not that I recollect," I answered.

He took a closer look at me. "Ya seems familiar somehow."

"We'd met, I'd know it," I said.

"But seem like—"

"Hush up, boy!" ordered Tom Bee. "Now, you stop botherin' this man and get on over there yonder 'bout yo' business so we can talk here!" The boy took another look at me, then obeyed Tom Bee and moved away toward the creek.

Mitchell eyed the distant boy with suspicion. "What you bring him 'long for? What you 'spectin' him t' be doin' here?"

"Same as me," answered Tom Bee. "Cuttin' this here timber."

I shook my head. "I only figured pay for one man."

"Ain't gotta pay him no extra. Jus' meals. He stay up at my place most the time anyways. He work or he don't, that there be up t' him. He don't work, then he go off this place. He work cuttin' them trees, then I figure he be payin' me for all I be doin' for him. He won't be no trouble."

Mitchell shook his head. "I ain't likin' this."

I agreed. "Me neither. I can't have a white boy working on this place."

Tom Bee nodded and looked out to the slope. "Seem like t' me, ya already got one.

I followed his gaze. There at the top of the slope was Wade Jamison hauling brush. I sighed. "That boy," I said, "he just keeps coming back."

"So what 'bout that boy John?" asked Tom Bee. "Where I go, he jus' go. He won't be no trouble," he repeated. "I see t' that."

I glanced across at Mitchell, then answered Tom Bee. "What he does, that's going to be up to you and him. You want to pay him wages out of your wages, then that's up to you, but I don't intend to pay wages for another hand."

Tom Bee nodded. "Me and John, we work it out."

"Fine," I said.

But Mitchell grunted and got up. "Look like t' me we gettin' too many white folks on this place." He looked at me and walked away. I didn't give him any retort. I was feeling the same way.

I got up and followed Mitchell. When we were alone, I said, "That boy yonder was on the ridge that night."

Mitchell turned and stared at John Wallace now talking with Tom Bee by the creek. "Then I know he best go. White boy round here anyways gonna only mean trouble. He seemed t' done recognized you."

"Well, he sure looked at me rather curiously."

Mitchell laughed. "Who don't? Most likely, he was tryin' to figure out just what you are."

I didn't laugh. "Tom Bee's set on looking out for this John Wallace, and the boy wants to be with him. If we tell Tom Bee that John Wallace has to go, the boy might get more suspicious of me."

"But he don't know for sure it was you on that ridge. He stay round here, he might get sure."

"I figure we'll have to take that chance."

Mitchell shrugged. "Well, it's up t' you, but I got my eye on him. He do one thing don't look right t' me, we won't hafta worry 'bout him again. I'll take care of it."

I stared hard at Mitchell. "Don't you touch him," I warned. "That boy gets hurt, who do you think they'll come looking for?"

Mitchell eyed me and looked away. From that moment, I stayed worried.

We settled down to work, the five of us, Mitchell, Nathan, Tom Bee, me, and John Wallace. John Wallace continued to bother me. I knew that if he could place me clear, he could bring everything crashing down around us because of that one time I'd assumed to try and pass the color line. But though he was on my mind each day, he made no trouble while he worked with us. Except for words passed during the course of logging, Mitchell and I didn't have many words with him. Neither did Nathan, and I found that somewhat surprising since they were close in age. All of us pretty much just let John Wallace be and he seemed satisfied with that.

Summer came and the heat began to settle. The insects came too, and so did the rain and the snakes. We were drenched from our own sweat and we itched from insect bites. Living became miserable. The land began to muddy and the mules had a hard time of it pulling the logs through the muck. I began to think that maybe I had been wrong about buying the mules instead of oxen. Oxen with their short legs would have held in this kind of weather. Maybe I'd thought myself too smart. I just prayed that none of the mules broke their legs. But I didn't pray about the snakes, and that was a mistake. One of them bit a mule and one bit Nathan. Fortunately, neither snake was a rattler, because if it had been, we would have had to shoot the mule and we might have lost Nathan. The Lord blessed us on that.

For more than two months the five of us kept up a pace that would have felled weaker men, men with less determination than Mitchell and me, and though Tom Bee did his share of complaining, he worked hard, and so did Nathan and John Wallace. As the time drew near to meeting Filmore Granger's latest timber orders, we cut our sleep back even more, working the full seven days of the week, and all the days felt blended together. We worked such long hours that Mitchell grew concerned about the time needed to build a house for Caroline. "You know her daddy put almost a year on us before we could marry. Well, that time's about up, and I don't intend to wait one day longer. I gotta figure out how I'm gonna build that house."

"Well, you bring her on here," I said, "and you two take the cabin. Rest of us can stay in the shed. Soon as we get all the acreage cleared, there'll be time enough to build the house you want."

Mitchell agreed to that. "S'pose that's all we can do."

Within two weeks of our finishing the cutting of Filmore Granger's first twenty acres, it began to storm daily, and we were forced to stop our work. There was nothing we could do in the face of it. Even Mitchell and I, who kept the work going in rainy weather, were forced inside as the brunt of the storms brought winds so hard, we couldn't even see what was before us. The storms kept up for the better part of a week, putting us behind in the number of trees left to cut to fulfill our agreement with Filmore Granger. As soon as the storms cleared, we were at the trees, chopping even through the night by lantern light.

Throughout all this, John Wallace worked with us, until one

day when his brother showed up. We already knew from Tom Bee that John Wallace's brother went by the name of Digger, and as soon as I saw him, I figured Digger Wallace to have also been on the ridge that night. He was a small-built man with worn clothes and eyes that were bloodshot and hands that shook. He looked to have had too much drink, and even from where I stood I could smell the liquor on him, the same as I had smelled liquor on one of the men who had come looking for the chicken thieves. A whip was looped at his side, hanging from his belt, and he kept his hand on it as he talked.

"I come for my brother," he announced. "Where he at?" Digger Wallace turned directly toward Mitchell, who was on the bank hacking at branches that had been left on some of the logs. I was a few feet away with Tom Bee and the mules, stacking logs to be run down the creek.

Mitchell glanced up but said nothing. At that, Tom Bee greeted Digger with a wide wave. "'Ey there, Mister Digger!" he called. "Say ya lookin' for John?"

"Yeah, that's right. Where he at?"

"He back there in them woods choppin' branches wit' 'nother boy," answered Tom Bee.

Now, it was an unfortunate thing that Mitchell was the one standing closest to Digger, for Digger looked from Tom Bee to him again and said, "You, boy, go get him. Tell him I wants him down here." That was Digger Wallace's first mistake.

Mitchell had an axe in his hand, and I knew how dangerous that could be. He just looked at Digger and kept on with his work. I left what I was doing and started over.

"'Ey, nigger! I'm talkin' t' ya! I told ya t' get my brother!" That was Digger's second mistake.

Mitchell turned to face him. "I ain't nobody's errand boy," Mitchell said. "You want him, then you follow that nose of yours through them woods 'til ya find him."

Mitchell again turned back to his work. He was holding his temper. Digger Wallace, though, didn't hold his. He untied the whip from his belt and uncoiled it to strike. "Nigger, ya do what I say!" he cried, then flashed the whip toward Mitchell, his final mistake.

Mitchell grabbed hold of the whip in midair and yanked it from him. "Don't nobody whip on me no more!" he declared. "And you call me nigger again, I'm gonna lay this whip right 'cross you!" Then Mitchell cracked the whip hard in front of Digger's face.

Digger jumped back fearfully and, as he did, wet his pants.

Mitchell sneered at Digger's mishap. Then he said, "Now, you get yo'self off this land!"

Digger stood trembling and humiliated. "Ya gonna pay for this!" he threatened. "Ya gonna pay!"

Mitchell stepped forward, the whip still in his hand. "Yeah, I know. Now, get!"

Digger backed away. "I wants my brother!"

"I'll get him for ya, Mister Digger!" cried Tom Bee, and hurried off into the woods.

Digger, now some feet away from Mitchell, said pitifully, "I wants my whip."

Mitchell tossed it at him. The whip landed at Digger's feet. With shaking hands, Digger picked it up and tried to muster some dignity. "Tell my brother I'm waitin' on him down yonder by the bridge!" he said loudly, giving one last order, and walked away.

I went to Mitchell. "We could face trouble about this. I can't swear to it, but I believe he was on that ridge too."

"Ah, he ain't nothin' but a drunk."

"A white drunk," I said.

"Don't forget, coward too. I wouldn't put it past him, if he was on that ridge with his brother, t' been doin' all that chicken thievin' his own self. He look like the kinda scound' t' do some-thin' like that, then come lookin' for a black man to hang it on."

I watched Digger Wallace's slim figure as he headed for the bridge, and I thought on what Mitchell said. Could be he was right, but that didn't change my thinking about Digger Wallace and trouble.

When John Wallace came from the woods, both Nathan and Tom Bee were with him. "Where's Digger?" John Wallace asked.

"Yonder by the road," I said.

John Wallace glanced over at his brother, then went to talk to him. When he returned, Digger stayed put. "He says he headin' back t' Alabama and he figures best I go with him. I'll get my things." He went off to the shed, and Tom Bee went with him. A few minutes later John Wallace, his bedroll across his back, came over to me and he said, "Ya know, Paul Logan, you sure look like another fella I done seen a while back on a ridge south of Strawberry. A white man." The boy kept his eyes on me. "I done told Tom Bee you looked familiar from that place, but he the only one and he won't say nothin', 'cause he already done told me not to. If you was there, ya got no reason t' worry 'cause-a me . . . you or your friend. Ya done treated me right fair." Then John Wallace went to join his brother.

I didn't see John Wallace again until he came back into these parts some years later and a man grown. By that time he was changed, but he never mentioned either of us being on that ridge again, at least to my knowing. But it wasn't John Wallace I was worried about that day as he left the forty. It was Digger. I worried, for no matter how drunk and cowardly Digger was, he was still a white man.

The day after John Wallace left, Mitchell and I came from chopping and found Wade Jamison helping Nathan hack branches from the fallen trees. We called Nathan over. "What's that Jamison boy doin' here again?" demanded Mitchell.

"He helpin' wit' the brush," mumbled Nathan.

"How come?"

"Said he wanna help."

"There's no money to pay him," I said.

"He don't care. He jus' said he wantin' t' help us out."

"I don't like it, Paul," said Mitchell. "We already had that one white boy round here, and look where that got us."

"I'll talk to him," I said.

"Don't make him go, Paul," pleaded Nathan. "Wade's my friend."

Mitchell scowled down at him. "Friend? Boy, you still carryin' that foolishness round in yo' head?" Nathan didn't say anything, and Mitchell walked off in disgust.

I looked at Nathan, then went over to talk to Wade. "Your daddy know you're doing this?" I asked.

"Yes, sir."

"He ask you why?"

"Yes, sir, and I told him about how hard you all are working and I didn't want you to lose your land."

I looked long at Wade Jamison, then said, "Why should you care?"

"Because you make good neighbors," he answered without hesitation.

"I suppose you know about my agreement with Mister Granger."

"Yes, sir, I do."

"Nathan told you?"

"Told me, all right, but my daddy already knew."

I was silent. I didn't like everybody knowing my business. "I can't have you working here. I appreciate your willingness to help us, but I can't have it."

"I don't need pay," said Wade.

"Maybe not, but everybody works here gets paid in some kind of way, and the thing is, I'm not figuring on paying another hand."

"But you don't pay Nathan."

"Not in money."

"I know. He told me about you teaching him cabinetmaking."

"Nathan's told you a lot."

"We're friends."

"Uh-huh."

"I was thinking, you let me work here this summer, you could teach me cabinetmaking too. I'd like to learn. That could be my pay."

I studied the boy with his blond hair and his blue eyes. He looked much like Robert. I shook my head. "I can't do that."

"'Cause I'm white?"

The boy was blunt. I decided to be the same. "That's right."

"I don't understand."

"I think you understand enough. What you don't, ask your daddy."

Wade Jamison looked at me. "Can I stay on 'til it's time for the next load to go down the creek?"

"Why would you want to do that?"

"Like to complete what I start. I'd like to help out until Mister Granger doesn't need so many trees, and Nathan said the next time Mister Granger comes with his men, you'd have all the extra trees he's been wanting chopped by then."

I thought on it. "It's important to you?"

"Yes, sir."

"All right. You tell your daddy what you're doing, though, and make sure it's all right with him."

"Yes, sir."

"And, Wade—"

"Yes, sir?"

"I'll pay you wages for this week's work."

The boy's lips parted as if to object to that, but then he seemed to sense my need to pay him for his work, and he nodded. "Yes, sir," he said, and went back to chopping the branches.

The day following that talk with Wade, Charles Jamison himself rode over to the forty. He looked around and commended me. "You've certainly gotten a lot of clearing done. Looks like you'll soon be ready to do some farming."

"I hope so," I said.

"You know, my boy Wade's taken a real liking to working here on your place."

"He's been a big help. But I told him his being here had to be all right with you."

Charles Jamison nodded to that. "Understand you told him too you didn't want him working here."

I thought on my words. From all I'd heard and from my few dealings with Charles Jamison, he was a fair man. Still, I couldn't get over the fact he was a white man. One unwise word and I figured I could find myself in deep trouble, Charles Jamison being a fair man or not. "I decided not to take on another hand right now," I said. "We've just about got all the trees we need cut for the next run down the creek."

Charles Jamison nodded. "Understand that. He told me. Wade, though, is figuring this is something he needs to be doing because of what all's happened in the past. Now, understand me, I'm not apologizing for anything. My daddy farmed and he had slaves, and his daddy did the same before him. It was considered all right then. By the time I was a boy, thinking was beginning to change, and by the time of the war I already knew that things couldn't be the same, and come the end of the war and the changes came, I accepted those changes because I had to. Besides, it was time. But Wade's been coming up feeling like folks

are folks, and he's wanting to make some amends. I'm not feeling the same. What's done is done. My granddaddy and my
daddy cared about our land and the folks who lived on it, and
I'm not about to apologize for anything they did. But I'm re-
specting my boy and his feelings, and I'm learning from him,
just as I learned from my daddy, who was thinking before the
war of eventually emancipating his slaves."

"But it didn't happen," I said, a little too bluntly and a little
too bitterly. My daddy hadn't freed me either.

"No, it didn't," said Charles Jamison, looking me over. His
voice didn't change. "The war happened instead, and we're all
still recovering from that."

I didn't say anything.

"We being neighbors, I figured these things needed to get
said. I'm wishing you luck. You need my help on anything, you
let me know."

I thanked Charles Jamison for his offer, but I didn't figure to
ask his help on anything. I liked him and I liked his son, but I
didn't intend to be beholden to any white man. Not again.

Wade Jamison stayed working for another week on the forty,
and when the Grangers came again for their timber, he was
there. He watched as the logs were rolled into the creek, then
went back to hacking off branches. I watched as Filmore
Granger's boy, Harlan, followed him, and I heard Harlan say,
"Thought the Jamisons were supposed to be quality folks."

"What you mean by that?" asked Wade, stopping his work.

"Quality, and here you doin' a nigger's bidding."

Wade Jamison took his time and said to Harlan, "My granddaddy logged trees, even while the Indians were here. Nothing's
wrong in logging and nothing's wrong in taking orders from a
man who knows logging."

"But you here working for these niggers on Granger land!"

"Thought this was suppose to be Logan land after these trees are cut," challenged Wade. "Now, I'm working for myself, and even if I weren't, I don't see nothing wrong with what I'm doing."

"Then you a fool," said Harlan.

The boy Wade stared at the boy Harlan. "Not if I don't think so," he said, and turned again to his chopping. As agreed, when the last logs were headed down the creek, Wade Jamison left. I admired the boy and hated to see him go, but my thinking was much the same as Mitchell's. A white boy on the place could only lead to trouble.

With the demands of the Grangers lessened now, Mitchell again turned his attention to his upcoming marriage. He and Nathan readied the cabin for Caroline's arrival. They cleaned and swept it, and Mitchell bought some pane for me to make a window so that Caroline could have the sunshine inside. Nathan and I moved our few things to the shed, and when all that was done, Mitchell, Nathan, and I hitched two of the mules to the wagon and headed for Vicksburg. I had arranged for Tom Bee to watch out for the animals and to keep chopping, so I had no worries about the place. It was my first journey off the forty in more than three months.

❧

Mitchell married Caroline on a hot day in August at Mount Elam Baptist Church, and I stood up as his witness. Mitchell was nervous and Caroline was beautiful. She wore an ivory dress, and her hair hung long, graced with baby's breath from her mother's flower garden. As she and Mitchell exchanged their vows, I couldn't keep my eyes off her, and despite my loyalty to my friend, I had to fight a heaviness in my heart at seeing Caroline marry someone else, even if it was Mitchell.

After the ceremony, all the people from the church followed the flower-covered wagon carrying Caroline and Mitchell to the

Perry farm, where Caroline's family had laid out a tremendous table of hams and fried chicken and roasts, vegetables and breads of all kinds, pies, cakes, and puddings. It was a true feast, and Miz Rachel Perry herself brought me a plate of food. As I stood enjoying her good cooking, Caroline came over and gently touched my arm. "Mister Paul-Edward Logan," she said, "I understand me comin' to the forty is gonna put you outa your house."

"No such thing," I said. "And, please, no more calling me 'Mister' Paul-Edward, all right? Paul-Edward will do just fine. Even Nathan calls me Paul. After all, we're like family in a way now."

She smiled. "I know Mitchell says y'all like brothers."

"That's a fact."

"Still, I feel like I'm puttin' you outa your house."

"Well, don't feel that way. It won't be a problem, really. It'll only be for a short spell, just 'til we get your house built."

"But I hate to think of all y'all havin' to sleep in the shed."

"Don't worry about it. I've slept in a whole lot worse places."

"Ain't that the truth!" said Mitchell, coming up behind Caroline and slipping his arms around her. "Like Paul said, don't worry 'bout it. We'll get you a house built soon enough." He kissed her cheek, and Caroline glanced back at him with a smile. They looked good together.

That next morning after the wedding, Nathan and I headed back to the forty. We left the wagon and one of the mules with Mitchell so that he could bring Caroline and her things. Nathan rode the other mule. I rode Thunder. I had decided it was time to have the palomino with me. After all, I was paying board money to Luke Sawyer I figured I could now save. Besides that, although Thunder was allowed to graze in Luke Sawyer's pasture and was getting decent feed, he wasn't getting the exercise he needed. No one but I, so far, could ride him. There were enough trees now cut on the forty so that there was open land

and plenty of grass. I figured to graze Thunder on that grass and to race him too, at least on the forty. It felt good to be riding him again.

Mitchell stayed a week with Caroline at the Perry farm and that was fine with me. We were on schedule with the trees, and I was figuring by this time next year we'd own the forty outright and have ourselves a crop. When Mitchell came back, I knew we'd have to work hard to make up these few days missed if we were going to stay on schedule, but I figured a wedding was worth it. Most folks only got married once, and what was before Caroline and Mitchell was a lifetime. They might as well start it right.

The Promise

Caroline's arrival changed many a thing. It wasn't just that she now occupied the cabin with Mitchell, but more it was her presence that was felt all across the forty. One week after Mitchell brought her from her parents' farm, Caroline had a new and much larger garden planted, and it was a garden for which she had broken ground herself. She asked no help from any of us. Right away she had taken over all the household chores too, and that in itself made a big difference, for it freed Mitchell, Nathan, and me for more chopping time. The most welcomed change, though, was in our meals. After Caroline's arrival, there was no longer just grits with a cup of hot chicory for our breakfast, but also eggs, crusty biscuits and sausages, gravy and preserves, and fresh milk. It was that way from then on, for Caroline had brought with her a store of her mama's preserves and canning, as well as her daddy's meats from their smokehouse. She had also brought a rooster and two laying hens, two piglets, and a milking cow. They were all presents from her family to her and Mitchell. Dinner and suppertime were no less than the breakfast, with vegetables and corn bread, preserved beef or venison, and a pudding or a cobbler of some kind. Whatever Caroline cooked was a feast; she was as good a cook as her mother, and no matter how busy Mitchell, Nathan, and I were, Caroline insisted we come eat her good food. "How y'all 'spect t' keep your strength, y'all don't eat. Lots of trees up there still, and I 'spect y'all can cut a few more y'all got good fueling in ya!"

I found Caroline was a precious kind of young woman. She was strong-willed and outspoken. She was loyal. But she also had a temper, and she proved that more than once. I'd already seen her slam her knuckles into her friend's jaw at Mount Elam. Soon after she was on the forty, she let that hand go again across another young woman's face. The young woman, I soon found out, had made the mistake of speaking ill of Mitchell, and she'd made that mistake to Caroline's face. The woman's name was Minnie Scott, and it just so happened that I was coming from chopping when I witnessed Caroline's confrontation with her. This time I didn't hear what was said. I just saw Caroline suddenly haul off and slam Minnie Scott with the flat of her hand. When I got into hearing distance, Caroline was ordering the woman off the forty. Minnie glanced up at me, turned, and hurried away without a word. Caroline, hands on her hips, watched her go, then picked up her hoe. That's when she saw me. She glanced back over her shoulder at the retreating Minnie, and looked at me again. "'Spect you seen that, huh?"

"I did," I said.

"'Spect you must be thinkin' all I do is go round hittin' on folks."

I shrugged. "Not my business." I started to walk on.

"She done said things . . . things 'bout Mitchell." I stopped and gave her my attention. "I don't 'low nobody t' be sayin' things 'gainst folks I care 'bout, they be true or not."

"You figure what she said was true?"

Caroline's jaw hardened. "Woman was talkin' 'bout Mitchell's wild ways 'fore we got married. Said she heard it from Mister

Tom Bee." I nodded, and Caroline softened. "I know Mitchell been with women 'fore me, but he ain't with nobody but me now, and that's the truth."

Again I nodded.

"That Minnie, she talked one time too many outa turn when she said he was out tommin' round on me, 'cause I know different, and even if I ain't, I ain't gonna have her runnin' up here t' me with her tongue."

"Well, I guess you won't have to worry about that again."

Caroline smiled. "I always done had me a temper. Took after my mama, and she always gettin' after me 'bout it. I gotta ask the Lord t' help me 'bout that." She looked a bit contrite.

I smiled as well. "That might be a good idea. I just hope you don't ever get mad at me."

"Jus' stay on my good side," she warned with a grin, "and you got nothin' t' worry 'bout."

I laughed and Caroline went back to her hoeing.

Despite having a temper when crossed, Caroline was good for Mitchell. I could see that. She kept him in check, and with her will for work she sometimes seemed to press him to do a little more than he was willing. More than once I heard her after him about one thing or another concerning the forty, and the thing she most worried him about was planting a crop. "What I wanna know," she said one dawn as we finished our breakfast, "is when we gonna get this land plowed and planted. Good day for it today."

"Well, right now," said Mitchell, "you ain't noticed, we kinda busy choppin' trees."

"I know that!" said Caroline. "But I thought you and Paul-Edward said you was goin' t' do some plantin' on them acres you done already cleared. We could pull up some of them stumps and have ourselves a nice little field."

"We're figurin' on that," said Mitchell. "But we talkin' 'bout next spring. Right now I'm figurin' we got more tree clearin' t' do 'fore we can get to the plantin'."

"Wait too long," said the all-knowing, farm-wise Caroline, "we gonna be too late to plant anything."

"Well, woman, what you gonna plant? It's here late summer already."

Caroline was ready with an answer. "Can get us in some collards and spinach and cabbage. Maybe some sugar peas too. I got seed from home. Can get them harvested 'fore real cold weather set in and I can take 'em t' the market in Strawberry t' sell."

"Won't have time for plantin' or harvestin'," objected Mitchell. "We got trees to cut."

"Could be, Mitchell," I interjected, "maybe we can do both."

Mitchell turned to me. "How you mean?"

"Maybe we can split the work. You and I, we can still be cutting the trees, and Caroline can work the fields and Nathan can help her out sometimes. Maybe we can even get Tom Bee back to work with us a couple of days a week."

Mitchell questioned me on that. "You ready to let go more hard money for another hand?"

"Did it once before," I said. "Maybe it's time I did again."

"Ready to let go for a plow too?"

I nodded. "I've already set aside for that. Could be we'll make a little money from the vegetables. In any case, it won't hurt to break the ground early. It'll make it easier for spring planting."

"Good then," said Caroline. "We can get started."

Mitchell gazed quizzically at her. "Can you handle a plow?"

Caroline laughed. "Sugar, seem like I been plowin' and hoein' since I could walk, so I ain't hardly 'fraid of no plow."

Mitchell too laughed as he looked at her. "Baby, you ain't hardly 'fraid of nothin'!"

Caroline got her fields. I've got to admit, though, she and Nathan didn't do all the plowing. They didn't do all the stump-pulling either. Mitchell and I took turns helping with that. But she and Nathan did all the planting, and when the vegetables began to grow, they took care of the weeding too. Yet with all that and the household chores Caroline had taken upon herself, she still found time to help in hacking off branches and burning the brush.

I hired back Tom Bee for a few days each week during that late summer and early fall as we settled into what would become our life on the forty. Things looked good for us, and I gave no worry to getting the rest of the trees felled. We worked hard as always, chopping the trees and now even pulling up more of the stumps, but with more than twenty acres cleared and part of it ready for plowing, I knew that by the next fall, the acreage would be ours. We took time for a bit more leisure.

Caroline, who believed in keeping the Sabbath, refused to work on that day, outside of making sure the animals were fed and we were too. There was no colored church building close by, but folks met down by the Creek Rosa Lee for church services about twice a month, and Caroline always went to join in. Sometimes she even got Mitchell to go with her and saw to it that Nathan did as well. But I never did. On those days I took the time to do my woodworking or write to Cassie. My not going to church, however, didn't keep a little bit of church from coming to me. Caroline brought it to the forty when several of her new acquaintances, young women about her age, came to join Caroline in Bible reading on the Sundays when there was no service at the Rosa Lee. One of the young women was a Miss Etta Greene. She was pretty, kind of quiet, and seemed to take a liking to me, and with Caroline's urgings, I saw her home several times from those meetings, and even upon occasion went to call on her. Mitchell teased me that it looked like it wouldn't be long before I too would be hitched. "Yeah," he said, "Miss Etta got wedding plans for you, boy!"

Nathan laughed and I smiled as we sat around the night fire at the end of the day when the brush had been burned. Caroline, sitting close to Mitchell, pushed him gently in reproach. "Now, you stop that, Mitchell! What's between Etta and Paul-Edward is they business."

Mitchell turned and stared at her. "They business? Who been puttin' 'em t'gether?"

"All I done was introduce 'em t' one 'nother. They becomin' friends was they idea."

"Um-hum," murmured Mitchell with a grin. "Paul, ya might's well start plannin' on it now. Caroline ain't gonna be satisfied 'til she got another woman on this place."

Caroline cut her eyes at Mitchell, and I said, "Well, I'm afraid that's going to be a while yet. I've got some more things I want to get done before I go commit to marrying somebody."

"So you saying Miss Etta ain't the one, huh?" questioned Mitchell.

"Well, she's nice enough," I hedged.

"But she ain't the one! 'Cause if she was the one, you couldn't hardly wait t' get hitched, plans or no plans. Jus' look at me. Here I was thinkin' I'd go t' my grave single and free, and here comes Miz Caroline into my life and changes all that right quick." Mitchell turned to her. "Gone and changed that forever."

Caroline smiled at Mitchell and slipped her arm around his.

"Thing that gets me, though, Paul," Mitchell said, turning back to me, "is you was the one talkin' marriage long 'fore me. I was the one declarin' I wasn't never gonna marry, but you was sayin' it was time you got yo'self a family. Now, here I am married for life and here ya puttin' it off."

"You leave him be," ordered Caroline. "He ain't ready t' get married, then don't be pushin' him 'bout it."

"But he the one—"

"Leave him be!"

"Thank you, Caroline," I said.

"You welcome," she said.

"Well, ain't this somethin'!" cried Mitchell. "You two done joined up against me! My wife and my friend!"

Caroline, Nathan, and I laughed. So did Mitchell.

"What I'd like t' know," said Caroline, nudging closer to Mitchell, "is how the two of y'all come t' be such good friends in the first place."

"Didn't he tell you?" I asked.

Caroline made a guttural sound feigning exasperation with her new husband. "This man, he don't tell me nothin'!"

"Now, woman, you know that ain't true," denied Mitchell. "Thing is, this here wife of mine just after me all the time t' tell her everythin' from the moment I was born, and I keep tellin' her I ain't keepin' track of things like her."

"Gotta keep track, I keep tellin' you," said Caroline in a business kind of way before she smiled her love at Mitchell. "How we gonna pass things on t' our children, we don't keep track? I wanna know everything."

"That's sure the truth," grumbled Mitchell.

Caroline playfully slapped at his shoulder, then looked back at me. "So, how'd it come 'bout? You and Mitchell 'comin' friends?"

I waved any response off to Mitchell. "So, what did you tell her?"

Mitchell shrugged. "Told her I was born on yo' daddy's land."

"That's all? You tell her about who my daddy was?"

"What else I need to tell? Caroline's a smart woman. One look at you and she done figured out who your daddy was."

"Well, Paul-Edward, he already done told me that," interjected Caroline. "But what I'm wantin' t' know is how y'all came t' be so close. Mitchell ain't said, so, Paul-Edward, you tell me."

Caroline's eyes pierced mine across the fire. I glanced at Mitchell, and he shrugged as if resigned to his bride's demands. I smiled. "He beat me into a friendship with him."

"What!" exclaimed Caroline.

I grinned. "Well, see the way it was, when we were boys, Mitchell there was always beating up on me—"

"How come?"

"Jus' ain't liked him, that's all," said Mitchell.

"Told me," I said, "'cause he wanted to."

Caroline cast a disapproving eye on Mitchell, and Mitchell threw the look over to me. "Watch it, Paul."

I laughed. "It's the truth!" I vowed. "Mitchell was always picking on me, and he knows that's the truth! One time he just up and hit me on the head, and when I asked him why he did it, he said right out without cracking a smile, 'Felt like it.'"

Caroline turned abruptly to Mitchell with a hand on her hip, as if to chastise him. "You mean t' tell me you done that? You was that kinda youngun?"

"Paul doin' the talkin'," said Mitchell, straight-faced. "Let him tell it."

"Not talkin' t' Paul-Edward now. I'm talkin' t' you."

"Then I guess I done that," he admitted with a laugh. "I s'pose I was kinda mean."

"Kind of?" I retorted. "You had me scared to death of you! I had to even go to my daddy and my brothers about you!"

"Yeah . . . but I whipped ya still."

"Yeah, you sure did."

"Them brothers of yours, though, I had t' think on them 'fore I done it."

"Did?"

"Yeah. That Hammond, I liked him pretty well, and Robert, I

could take him or leave him. He ain't done nothin' t' me. But that George, I was kinda scairt of him."

"You were?" I asked, somewhat surprised.

"Yeah. Respected him too. Kinda would've liked t' gone head t' head with him."

I smiled, thinking of the match.

"So how y'all get t' be friends?" Caroline asked again.

"We made ourselves a deal," I replied.

"And jus' what was that?"

"I said I'd teach Mitchell to read and write, and Mitchell agreed to teach me how to fight."

Caroline nodded. "Good deal for both of ya, then, huh?"

"Course now, I got the better of it," said Mitchell. "I learned how to read and write, but Paul there, he still can't fight." We all laughed, and then Mitchell added, "Ah, he do all right sometimes, I s'pose. I gotta admit he done helped me outa more'n one scrape, startin' back from that time he saved my hide when I gone and rode Ghost Wind."

"Ghost Wind?" questioned Nathan, taking an interest.

"Yeah. That was a stallion Paul's daddy had. Done bought him special jus' for racin', and that man, he was sure proud of that horse!"

"That's the truth," I agreed.

"My daddy, he was the one s'posed t' take care of that stallion, brush him down, take care of his ailments, stuff like that, but nobody was 'lowed t' ride that horse 'ceptin' Paul's daddy and Paul. Well, I was 'bout thirteen at the time, and that didn't sit well wit' me. Fact t' business, I kinda resented the fact Paul got t' ride that horse and I let my feelings be known t' him too. So Paul, one day when his daddy wasn't round, he up and let me ride Ghost Wind. Now, up to this time I ain't rode nothin' but a mule, let 'lone no creature had the speed in him like that Ghost Wind. I got on that horse's back, and that horse knowed I ain't had no business whatsoever sittin' up on him! That horse looked back at me one time, then took off—WHAM!" Mitchell shot his hands together, then extended one arm straight ahead. "I'm tellin' y'all, I thought I was gonna die!"

We were all laughing now.

"Well, that sure made two of us," I said.

Mitchell shook his head. "Ah, Lord, I thought that horse was gonna kill me, and he jus' 'bout done it too! There we was flyin' through the woods, and I'm gettin' hit all upside the head with branches and leaves and whatever else was hangin' from them trees, and all I was thinkin' was tryin' t' get that horse t' stop while Paul there was chasin' way 'long behind us yellin' for me to rein in Ghost Wind. Like I could!"

"Well, what finally happened?" Caroline asked.

"Yeah," said Nathan, "how ya finally get him t' stop?"

"Ain't," said Mitchell. "That ole stallion jus' done got tired of me and throwed me off his back!"

The laughter grew louder. But right after, I noticed Mitchell sobered and I knew his thinking. I sobered too.

"Thing was," Mitchell went on, "I ain't knowed what I was doin' and ain't had no business on top of that horse in the first place. That stallion got bad cut, hurt his leg. Paul, he caught up wit' us and we took that horse limpin' back t' the barn. My daddy, he done took one look at that horse and one look at me, and he done pulled out his whip."

Nathan leaned forward. "So ya done got a whippin', huh?"

"Well, seem like t' me you mighty well deserved one," observed Caroline. "Runnin' that animal down like that."

Mitchell looked at Caroline. "Woman, you sure are hard on me, ya know that? But the truth be told, that time I done deserved a whippin'."

Nathan laughed. "I bet yo' daddy done wore ya out, huh, Mitchell?"

Mitchell looked at the boy and shook his head. "Naw. Naw, he ain't."

"Well, how come he ain't?"

Mitchell gave a nod toward me. "'Cause Paul there said he done it. He said he rode that horse."

Caroline looked at me, and there was a soft expression on her face. "You done that?"

"How come?" questioned Nathan.

I shrugged. "Truth is, I questioned that myself. I'd always wanted Mitchell to get a good whipping because of his beating up on me so much."

"He done it," explained Mitchell, "'cause he ain't wanted me to get a whippin' 'bout ridin' that horse. That's what it was. Lord only knows why."

"Wasn't being noble," I said. "Just guess I was feeling guilty because of my white daddy."

Nathan glanced from Mitchell to me. "So you the one got the whippin'?"

I shook my head. "No, I didn't get a whipping."

"He got punished, though, just the same," said Mitchell.

Nathan was curious. "And what was that?"

I was silent, letting Mitchell answer. "Paul, he couldn't ride Ghost Wind no more."

Caroline's eyes were soft upon me. "And that was hard on you?"

I smiled somewhat sadly, remembering. "It was hard, all right. There was nothing like riding that horse, Caroline. Riding Ghost Wind was better even than riding Thunder. I'd rather have taken my daddy's whipping."

Mitchell snorted a laugh. "You wouldn't've wanted t' take that whippin' so bad it had've been my daddy dishin' it out!"

"Well, you sure took plenty."

"Ain't that the truth! That was the only one of two times my daddy ain't wore on me when he had a mind, and he would've done it then if Paul's white daddy hadn't've told him not to, and my daddy wasn't 'bout to disobey Paul's daddy. Only other time he ain't laid on me with that strap when he had a mind was when I was fifteen and I done grabbed that strap 'way from him and told him he wasn't gonna beat on me no more. I was full growed by then with the same height I got now, near the same weight, and he ain't argued wit' me none. Jus' done told me I could jus' get then, and I went."

Nathan was intrigued. "So that's when you come here, you and Paul on that train?"

"Naw. I gone off for a few months, but then my mama sent my younger brother Jasper t' beg me t' come back. Jasper, he done had welts all over him, and he done said our daddy'd been puttin' a strap regular t' all the younguns and my mama too. Now, when I was home and my daddy got a mind t' take out that strap of his when I was round, I'd jump in and take the beatin'. Ain't mattered who he done pulled that strap out for, my mama or one of the younguns, I'd jump in and make him so mad, he'd beat me instead. But I got tired of him beatin' on me. That's how come I left. When I gone back, I told my daddy I was there for only one reason, and that was t' keep him from raisin' that strap one more time 'gainst my mama or the young-uns. I told him he did, I was gonna kill him."

Mitchell stared into the fire. I stared across at him. In all the years I'd known Mitchell, he had never told me this. Caroline gently rubbed his back. "That's a hard thing."

Mitchell looked at her. "I meant it, Caroline, and he knowed I meant it. Long as I stayed there, my daddy, he ain't never raised his hand or that strap t' none of us again."

❧

Caroline's field of vegetables grew well, and she along with Nathan made several trips to the market in Strawberry to sell them. The vegetables made a small crop and we didn't get much for them, but the money helped pay Tom Bee. We put the remainder of the money aside for next year's seed. In the spring we figured to plant cotton.

Christmas came soon after Caroline's last trip into town for the year, and this Christmas was like none I had seen since I was a boy. There was no disregarding Christmas this year, for Caroline was in charge. She ordered Mitchell to kill a goose and a coon. Along with the goose and the coon, she baked one of her daddy's hams, corn bread and biscuits, pies and cakes, and fixed up all kinds of vegetables. The spread she put before us on Christmas Day was as fine as any set by her mama, Miz Rachel Perry. Mitchell and I told her that, but Nathan teased that she still had a long way to go to rival their mama's cooking, even though he had seconds and thirds of everything. After all that eating, he pulled out the harmonica Caroline had given him for Christmas and began to play. Caroline laughed and was happy. She had invited Tom Bee and his family, and there were quite a few of them, to join us for the day and enjoy all the fine dinner fixings. Now they enjoyed the music too. The children lit up the place.

January came and the new year brought with it the expectation of finally owning the forty. Mitchell and I had until the end of September to finish cutting Filmore Granger's trees, but I figured to have them all down before then. I wanted title to this place as soon as I could get it. Only then could I call it my own. I could be satisfied with this piece of land for a while, since by now, I had pretty much put the Hollenbeck land out of my thoughts. I hadn't even gone back to it since I'd been on the forty. It was another man's land and there was no sense in daydreaming. But then one day in late February Wade Jamison came again to the forty. At first I thought he had come to fish with Nathan on the Rosa Lee. He hadn't. He had come to speak to me. "My daddy sent me to see you," he said.

My brow furrowed. "What about?"

"He said he remembered you were interested in Mister Hollenbeck's land. He was wondering if you still are."

"Why's that?"

"'Cause Mister Hollenbeck is selling now. He's getting ready to move back north."

For a moment my breath caught and I couldn't speak.

"My daddy's buying the most of his land," Wade went on, "so that means we'll be double neighbors, on two sides of you."

I studied the boy. "When did Mister Hollenbeck put his land up for sale?"

"Well, he's been thinking about it for some time, according to my daddy," said Wade. "But he just made up his mind. He offered all the land he'd bought from the Grangers back to Mister Filmore Granger first off, but Mister Granger wasn't interested. Mister Granger said he wasn't about to buy back land at a robber's price that rightfully already belonged to him, so Mister Hollenbeck, he came to my daddy."

My mouth went dry. "He's selling all of it?"

"Far's I know. He said it's time he headed back north. He's got family there. All the family he had here are either dead or gone."

"Wade, you said that your daddy's buying most of Mister Hollenbeck's land. What about the rest of it?"

"Well, a lot of folks are interested in that land, so Mister Hollenbeck, he's keeping aside some of it to sell to them. My daddy figured you'd be interested in knowing that."

"I am," I said, and hurriedly thanked him before turning away.

"Is Nathan around?" Wade called after me. "I was wondering maybe if he is, we could go fishing?"

"Fine with me," I said, my mind on the land, and feeling only gratitude toward the boy as I hurried off to saddle Thunder. I didn't return to the slopes, but rode Thunder down the Granger trail to J. T. Hollenbeck's land. We crossed the splendid meadow and passed the hillside where I had spent my first night in these parts. We crossed that meadow without stopping and headed straight to J. T. Hollenbeck's house.

"Mister Hollenbeck," I said, upon my arrival at his front porch, "I'm Paul Logan."

"Yes, I recall you," said J. T. Hollenbeck. "I heard you took my advice about seeing Filmore Granger and you're working his land now."

"That's right. But as you might recall, when you gave me that advice, I was interested in your land at the time."

"Yes, I recall that too." His gaze left me and settled on Thunder, tied to one of the horse posts. "That your horse?"

I glanced at the palomino. "Yes, sir, it is."

"Fine-looking. Mighty fine," he commented. "If I weren't moving north, I'd consider trying to buy him from you." He looked back at me. "So, what can I do for you?"

"Well, Mister Hollenbeck, I still am interested in that land of yours."

"That a fact?"

"I understand you're selling some of your land now. If that meadowland and pond about a mile south of here are available for sale, I'd be interested in buying it."

J. T. Hollenbeck studied me. "Just how many acres are you talking about?"

"That depends on your asking price."

"Between twelve and fifteen dollars an acre for anybody buying less than a thousand, ten for a thousand or more."

I shook my head. "That's a lot of money. Most acreage around here goes for between seven and nine."

"Well, that's most acreage. But I've got some special land here. If I didn't, I wouldn't have already sold the most of it and have people waiting to buy the rest. I admit some parts have more value than others and that meadowland is some of the best. It'll go for fifteen. I figure my price is fair on that. Only reason it's not already sold is because Charles Jamison reminded me you were interested in buying some of my land. He told me if you don't buy that piece of land, he will."

"I understand that you're a fair man, Mister Hollenbeck, and that this is good land, but still, fifteen dollars an acre to a man who can't afford to buy a thousand acres is mighty high."

"You're saying it's not fair?"

"I'm not saying that, Mister Hollenbeck. I'm just saying a man who can't afford a thousand acres can't afford five dollars more an acre."

"And what would you think this man could afford?"

"Same price as the man buying a thousand."

"You say you're willing to pay me ten an acre?" J. T. Hollenbeck smiled, as if not taking me seriously.

"Yes, sir, I am."

"So at ten dollars an acre, how many acres would you be wanting?"

I didn't have to think on that. I already knew. "Four hundred," I said.

"Four hundred? You're aiming high."

I didn't say anything to that.

"I'll be wanting cash money," said J. T. Hollenbeck. "You got cash money for four hundred acres of Hollenbeck land?"

"How soon would it have to be paid?" I asked, warding off the question.

"Soon as we've got a contract. I plan to have all this land sold before I leave here come fall." He looked at me pointedly. "So, you still think you're interested in Hollenbeck land?"

"I'm interested."

J. T. Hollenbeck looked again at the palomino, and was for some while silent. "All right then," he finally said. "But I want you to know I don't usually go around losing myself money. If you can meet the ten dollar price, those four hundred acres are yours."

"I can let you know next week."

"No, you let me know before this week's out. I've got other folks waiting for my land. You come back here by then, we can do business. You don't, and I get another offer after that, I won't hold one acre for you."

"I'll be back," I said.

J. T. Hollenbeck gave me another nod, and that was the seal on our agreement.

When I left J. T. Hollenbeck and recrossed the meadow, I lingered awhile. I walked up the slope, knelt beside the rock on which I had rested my head that first night, and I prayed to have this land. When I finished my praying, I sat there on that rock for a long while looking over the land, then I walked down to the pond, gazed up into the trees for a spell longer, then finally headed back to the forty. As I neared the place, a slight man smelling of whisky stepped from the dense woods onto the trail.

It was Digger Wallace.

He stopped and stared up at me with bloodshot eyes. "I ain't know'd that horse of yours," he said, "I'd've done thought you was a white man comin'. But I been seein' you ridin' round on that there horse and folks tell me it's yours. Seen that boy Mitchell on him once too ridin' 'cross that field down yonder." He spat on the ground in front of me and his spittle was the color of stale tobacco. "Horse like that oughtta not be rode by no niggers." His eyes met mine, then he crossed the trail and slipped back into the woods.

I watched him go, then rode on. When I reached the cabin, Tom Bee was there, but was preparing to leave as I rode up. "Jus' come by t' let y'all know I done seen that Digger back round these parts," he told me. "That John Wallace boy, he come by on his way t' Vicksburg. Said he was goin' t' find a job up there. Said Digger, he come back wit' him and he still round."

"I know," I said, dismounting from Thunder. "I just saw him."

"Did?" asked Mitchell. "Wish he'd show his face to me."

"Ah, he ain't gon' do that," declared Tom Bee. "Not less'n he got a whole buncha other white men wit' him, and he be too shamed t' tell 'em what ya done t' him t' bring 'em round. I figures y'all best be keepin' an eye out for Digger, though. He's a scound'!"

"S'pose we know that already," said Mitchell.

"Then ya watch out for him!" Tom Bee warned, and walked away.

As he left, I said to Mitchell, "You worried?"

"What 'bout?"

"Digger being back."

Mitchell just looked at me and laughed. He was being truthful with that laugh. I knew he wasn't afraid of Digger. But I was.

"So ya back," said Caroline, smiling at me as she came to the doorway of the cabin holding a stack of plates in her hands. "We was wonderin' what done happened to you."

"Yeah," said Mitchell. "I was 'bout t' come lookin' for you. You decided to give yourself a day off, huh?"

I just smiled, and Caroline said, "He work hard 'nough. He deserve his day. Now both of y'all get washed up for supper. I'm 'bout to set it on the table."

"Yes, ma'am!" Mitchell exclaimed, and grinned at her before she turned back into the room. Then he and I went to the side of the cabin where we kept the water barrel, and poured water into the two washbowls. "Well, you gonna tell me where you gone off to?" asked Mitchell as he lathered with soap Caroline had made while still at her parents' house. He grinned again. "Maybe to pay a call on Miss Etta?"

"No," I said. "Better than that."

"Better?"

Now it was I who grinned. "I went to see J. T. Hollenbeck."

Mitchell sobered. "J. T. Hollenbeck? Now, just what business you got with that white man?"

"What you think?" I leaned toward him. "The land, Mitchell, the land. He's ready to sell."

"And you figure you can buy it?"

"I figure to try."

"How much he askin'?"

"Was asking fifteen an acre. Got him down to ten."

"How many acres?"

"Four hundred."

At another time in his life, Mitchell would have laughed. He didn't now. He frowned instead. *"Four hundred?* You got that much money?"

"Figure to get it."

Mitchell grew quiet, then said, "You plannin' on askin' yo' daddy?"

I met Mitchell's eyes. "You know better."

Mitchell nodded. "Then what ya gonna do?"

"Going to see if I can borrow it from a bank."

Mitchell was again silent before he spoke. "You plannin' on going up to Jackson and passin'?"

"I'm going to Vicksburg."

"They know you there."

"Good, because I don't plan to pass."

"Then you can forget 'bout that loan. You think one of them crackers gonna loan a colored man money for a prime piece of land like that?"

"J. T. Hollenbeck said he'd sell it to me. That's my chance. I'll get the money somehow."

Mitchell just looked at me.

"I'll be heading for Vicksburg before light in the morning."

Mitchell grunted.

I laughed. "Trouble with you, Mitchell, is you've got no faith."

Mitchell too laughed. "Well, you and Caroline, y'all both carry enough between y'all to carry me too." Caroline called us in for supper and the two of us went in still laughing.

❧

Much later that evening after the brush had been burned and both Caroline and Nathan had gone inside the cabin, Mitchell and I sat by the outside fire talking, and sipping at some chicory. "You know, Paul," Mitchell said, as it grew late, "I got me some good news too."

"Yeah? What's that?"

Mitchell grinned wide. "Caroline's gonna have a baby."

For a moment I was silenced.

"You heard me right."

"You? Somebody's daddy?"

"I know. It's somethin', ain't it?" Mitchell spoke softly, as if awed himself by the fact.

"You'll make a good one." Mitchell just looked at me. I smiled. I meant what I said. "When you expecting the baby?"

"Late summer. Right about when we get deeded these forty acres, I reckon. Caroline just told me last night."

"It'll be a wonderful beginning, then," I said. "A baby and a deed to this place."

Mitchell nodded. "I figure it t' be a boy."

"Why's that?"

"Just do, that's all." He looked down at his cup and kept his eyes on it. "It be a boy, you 'spect I'm gonna do him like my daddy done me?"

"Why would you? Boy deserve a whipping, you'll give it to him, no more than that."

Mitchell looked up. "I sure deserved some of 'em, ain't I?'

"Yeah, you sure did," I agreed.

"Ya know, it's too bad you ain't feeling nothing special for Etta or some other young woman, 'cause it'd be good if we had children round this place t'gether. Be good to have yours and mine grow up with one another."

I smiled. "Why? So they could fight all the time like we did?"

"Yeah, that . . . and so they could watch out for one 'nother too." He looked over at me. "Maybe you change yo' mind 'bout Miss Etta."

"I don't think so."

Mitchell shrugged and got up. He tossed the remainder of his chicory into the fire. "Look here, Paul, Miz Caroline's waiting, but there's one more thing I need to talk t' you 'bout."

I got up too. "What's that?"

"I was thinkin', things don't go like you wantin' 'bout that bank loan, I want you t' do what you think best 'bout these forty acres."

"What do you mean?"

"You figure you can use these here forty acres in some way to get that land you want from Hollenbeck, then you do that."

I shook my head. "No. Your twenty acres, they stay your twenty. I need to use any of it, I'll use my half."

"Look, Paul, I wouldn't be having the twenty, you didn't figure this deal with Filmore Granger in the first place. You hadn't've figured this deal, I wouldn't've had no home t' give

Caroline. You need to sell this forty acres to help get that four hundred, then seem like t' me, there'd be room on that four hundred acres for Caroline and me."

I smiled in jest. "You expecting two hundred acres, then?"

Mitchell's face was blank. "No," he said seriously. "Just my twenty."

I grew serious too. "It'd be a risk you'd be taking."

"Done took plenty of 'em before."

"Not with a baby on the way."

Mitchell shrugged. "I trust ya, Paul. Been trustin' ya ever since we got on that train t'gether. You the smartest man I know, and if you want that land, then I figure you'll find a way t' get it." He reached into his pocket and pulled out a folded wad of paper, which he handed to me. "Here, take this."

"What is it?"

"Jus' my writin' sayin' you got my rights to the whole forty and that's okay by me." Mitchell grinned. "I wrote it out real good, just like you taught me, and I wrote it on that piece of paper you figured I just had t' sign when you come out to the lumber camp that time and made yo' offer to me." He stepped away.

"You sure about this?" I called after him.

"Said I was. Whatever you gonna do, Paul, I back you up."

"You always do," I said.

Mitchell grunted. "Same as you." He turned with a wave of his arm to me and walked toward the cabin. "See you when ya get back. You come back here with a contract in hand for that land of yours, then we gonna do us some real celebratin'!"

I stuffed the paper into my pocket. "Hope to bring good news."

"You will," said Mitchell. He grinned one last time back at me. "And here you and Caroline sayin' I ain't got no faith." He laughed loudly and went into the cabin.

I laughed too, and sat again by the fire.

The next morning long before daybreak and the others were up, I mounted one of the mules and rode to Vicksburg. After my encounter with Digger Wallace, I had decided it was best to leave Thunder on the forty and not rouse the jealousy of more white folks, especially when I was trying to borrow money.

I didn't stop to see Luke Sawyer but went directly to see the banker, B. R. Tillman. He seemed surprised to see me, but he showed me into his office. He didn't offer me a seat. "My wife been raving about that chifforobe you built for her, Paul," he said as he himself sat down. "Shame you not doing that kind of work full time anymore. You've got a gift." B. R. Tillman glanced through some papers on his desk as I stood hat in hand before him. Finally he turned his attention to me again. "So, now, Paul, why you come to see me?"

I didn't like standing before this man, hat in my hand, but I said clearly what I had to say. "I've come about seeking a loan on a piece of land I'm interested in buying. It's four hundred acres and located near Strawberry."

B. R. Tillman straightened in his chair. "That wouldn't be J. T. Hollenbeck's land you're talking about?"

"That's right," I said. "It is."

"Four hundred acres?"

"That's right."

He got up from his chair, came to the front of his desk, and leaned against it. He folded his arms across his chest and fixed his eyes on me. "That's some mighty impressive land."

I nodded in agreement.

"Yes, it's good land, all right. Used to be Granger land, one of the finest plantations in this part of the state."

"I understand that," I said.

B. R. Tillman looked at me over gold-edged spectacles. "Now here you looking to buy it?"

I knew what he was thinking as soon as he said that, but I figured he could think what he wanted. "Yes, but I'm going to need a loan to do it," I continued. "The section'll cost four thousand dollars, and I'm looking to borrow thirty-two hundred of that amount."

"*Thirty-two hundred?* What about the other eight?"

I looked straight into B. R. Tillman's eyes. "I'll provide that myself."

"You?" He looked at me with disbelief. "Most colored folks don't have two nickels to rub together. They're lucky if they even see a hundred dollars in a year, and here you're talking about you've got eight hundred to put on some land? Just where did you get that kind of money?"

I took my time before I answered. It was true that most colored folks, at least the ones I knew, and white folks too, for that matter, didn't see a hundred dollars in cash money in a year, and folks sharecropping mostly saw none at all. But I had lumbered and I had trained and raced horses and I had made quality furniture. I had received fair money for all that work, and I had saved the most of it. Adding to that, I had made my deals with Luke Sawyer. I could have told B. R. Tillman all that, but I figured he would still have questioned me more, and I had no intention of disclosing my arrangements with Luke Sawyer. We were keeping that to ourselves. "I saved it," was all I told B. R. Tillman.

"Saved it?" He smirked. "Young fella like you?"

I just looked at him and he didn't press me further.

"So, you want to borrow thirty-two hundred dollars. How you expect to pay it back?"

"The same way I earned the eight hundred dollars to put down on it," I said, maybe too cockily, being a man of color talking to a white man. I attempted to correct myself. "I still will be doing work for Mister Luke Sawyer and I'll be selling the forty acres I've contracted to clear for Mister Filmore Granger down near Strawberry. After the first year, I'll have crops I can sell. I was figuring cotton, corn, sugarcane."

B. R. Tillman walked back around his desk and sat down. "So, what are you proposing to me then, Paul? Even if you sell those forty acres of Mister Granger's for, say, four hundred dollars— and that's high figuring—that still leaves a lot of money owing. If you want the bank to loan you money to buy this land, what do you have to give us in collateral?"

To me the answer was obvious. I expected it was obvious to B. R. Tillman as well, or would have been if I hadn't been a man of color. "The land," I said.

"The land?" he questioned. "*The land?* And what's on it? There a house? Crops? What? How will you farm all that acreage? You got money to take on sharecroppers? What other kind of collateral are you offering me besides that land if I make you this loan?"

"A house in one year," I answered. "Crops in one year. In addition, as you know, I'm a woodworker. Anything in wood anybody wants made, I can most likely make it. I've got an understanding with Mister Luke Sawyer concerning that. What-ever I make from my woodworking I can pledge to this bank. When I get my crops in, I can pledge them to the bank as well . . . then, of course, there's always the land itself. As you said, it's good land, and I figure it can stand as its own collat-eral."

B. R. Tillman stared at me. "Now, why you want four hun-dred acres of land you can't afford when you already got yourself forty acres contracted? If you could produce a crop yearly on this here four hundred acres for a number of years and sell that crop at a price equal to pay your debt to this bank, plus all your taxes, then I'd consider making you a loan. But, Paul, I know there is no way in hell that you can do that. I know this payback notion of yours is all in your head. You have no financial record here. You have no farming background here. That four hundred acres is good land, all right, but it's a white man's kind of land, too expensive for you. Why, it wasn't so long ago it was against the law for a negra, I don't care how white-looking, to even own farmland in the state of Mississippi, and here you are talking about buying Hollenbeck land?" He shook his head. "I'm afraid I'm going to have to say no. It's too much for you to take on, and we have no desire to have to come take that land from you when you're not able to meet your payments. If you were talking about twenty or forty acres like what you're working now, maybe we could work something out. No, my advice to you is keep working that forty acres you got and be satisfied. It'll make you a good living."

I left B. R. Tillman. I went to other bankers, but they pretty much said the same thing. I wasn't ready to accept defeat. I went to see Luke Sawyer, got a couple orders from him for which I already had the wood, and spent the night in his shed before leaving Vicksburg. On the ride back all I was thinking on was how I could still buy the land. Nothing came to me. I bypassed the forty and headed toward Hollenbeck's meadow. I had another day before I had to let J. T. Hollenbeck know if the deal was set. I rode to the pond and let the mule water. Afterward, I rode back to the meadow and settled on the slope where I'd first spent the night. I slid my gear off the mule's back and settled down to look out over the land beside what I now considered my praying rock, and I prayed to be shown a way to have this land. I sat there until nightfall before I finally rolled out my blanket and lay down. I put everything into the Lord's hands. In the middle of the night I woke, took my coat, and by the light of the full moon, ripped one of its seams and pulled out a thin wallet I had made from calfskin. I put the wallet in my pocket, then went back to sleep. The next morning I woke with a plan, and it was that plan I took to J. T. Hollenbeck.

"You said you wanted to have all your land sold before you leave and you wanted cash for it," I said as I sat with J. T. Hollenbeck on his front porch. He had been doing paperwork on the porch when I arrived, and he had invited me to join him there. He had even offered me a seat. Not every white man would have done that.

J. T. Hollenbeck nodded, and puffed on a cigar. "That's right."

"Well, at your asking price of ten dollars an acre, I'd be figuring to buy two hundred acres of that section we talked about."

"Thought it was supposed to be four hundred."

"It was," I admitted. I met his eyes. "It's two hundred now. But it still includes that meadowland centering near that hillside and the pond."

J. T. Hollenbeck studied me a few moments, as if deciding whether or not it was worth his while to hear me out. "Go on," he finally said.

"Now, at ten dollars an acre, I could make you a down payment of twenty-five percent on contracting the land," I continued calmly, trying not to sound anxious that he might reject my offer. "That would be five hundred dollars on signing, and I could pay twenty dollars a month for the next six months. In the seventh month, I'll pay the rest that's due, thirteen hundred eighty dollars."

J. T. Hollenbeck stared at me, then smiled slightly. "Now, how are you going to get thirteen hundred eighty dollars in half a year's time? You have yourself a bank loan?"

"Not a bank loan," I said. "I plan on selling off the forty acres I'm working."

"But I understand you don't have title on that land."

"I will by the time your note would be due."

"What about the remainder of the money? That forty acres won't bring you near enough to pay for my two hundred acres."

"I understand that. But I plan to plant cotton too. I've already bought my seed, and if cotton prices stay the same as in this past year, I figure to earn about four hundred dollars on the crop. Also, I can have as many orders to make furniture as I can handle from Mister Luke Sawyer up at the Vicksburg mercantile and I figure in the next seven months I can earn two hundred dollars for my work."

J. T. Hollenbeck slowly shook his head. "That still doesn't seem to me like that'll bring enough."

I had held back my final source of income. "I also figure to sell my palomino."

J. T. Hollenbeck studied me and was silent. He drew on his cigar, then took it out. "Six months, you say?"

"Seven months," I answered, correcting him.

J. T. Hollenbeck's eyes narrowed. "Now, why should I have to finance you for my own land for that period of time? I told you I wanted cash money on this transaction. Could be it'd be better for me to sell outright that piece of land you want."

I agreed. "But you've got a lot of land here to sell, and I'm willing to buy. You'll have five hundred dollars when we sign. You'll be getting a payment every month, and the land will stand as its own collateral." I paused. "I fail to make any payment to you on time—monthly or the last one—I'm willing to pay a penalty." Now, it might not have been very smart of me to volunteer to pay even more money if I didn't need to, but I was hoping to persuade J. T. Hollenbeck of my commitment to pay him his money, and on time.

J. T. Hollenbeck stared at me, then thrust his cigar back between his lips and walked the length of the veranda to the other end and stared out, his back to me. I waited patiently. J. T. Hollenbeck took his time. Finally he turned, took the cigar out of his mouth, and pointed at me with the hand that held the cigar. "The down payment would have to be eight hundred fifty dollars, not five hundred, and that monthly payment would have to be twenty-five dollars, plus five dollars for me carrying you. Seeing that it's already the end of February, payments would begin next month and the final payment of one thousand dollars will come due the end of September. According to what you've said, you should have title to that Granger piece of land by then. If you're smart enough to work a deal with me, then I figure you're smart enough to have found a way to sell that forty acres of yours in time to pay me. I'll give you seven months, not a day more.

"And you certainly will pay a penalty if you default on this agreement. I've given you the lower price on this land because I admire what you're trying to do. Not many men, black or white, would have taken on what you've already done, or been so persistent in what you want to do. I admire that too. I believe in giving people with your kind of motivation a chance. But you'll pay hard if you've been wasting my time. I'll treat all the money you've paid me as earnest money, and if you default, you'll lose it. I figure that's fair, seeing I should be selling that land at fifteen dollars an acre to begin with, not ten. If you keep your bargain with me, I'll take the loss. If you don't, you'll take it. That means you won't get back one cent. Now, can you live with those terms?"

They were some hard terms, all right, and I should have walked away, I know, but J. T. Hollenbeck's land was the land I wanted, and if I didn't agree to his terms, I wouldn't have a chance of getting it. Agreeing to his terms, though, meant I could lose all my savings. Still, I knew that J. T. Hollenbeck was giving me a chance. I also knew that most white men would not have given me such a chance, would not even have talked to me about my buying such a piece of land. It was a bad deal for the person who didn't figure to have the balance of the money. But it was a great deal for the person who figured to have it.

I figured to have it.

So I made the gamble. I accepted his terms and forced myself to keep from shouting my joy. When I'd been doing my figuring, I'd figured high and I'd figured low. I had made my low offer to J. T. Hollenbeck so that I could have some bargaining room. I had savings enough for Hollenbeck's eight hundred fifty dollars in down payment. I had enough money too for some of the monthly payments. What I didn't have, I figured I could get. I wasn't worried about the final thousand dollars. I had the forty and I had Thunder. By the time the seven months were up, I would have orders for Luke Sawyer finished and a crop as well. I might even end up with some money left over. "I can handle it," I told J. T. Hollenbeck.

J. T. Hollenbeck walked back up the veranda. "Good," he said. "I'll need to have your eight hundred fifty down before the end of the week."

I felt the calfskin in my pocket. "If we can do the written work, I can pay it now," I said. "I've got a blank draft that can be drawn on a bank in New Orleans."

J. T. Hollenbeck smiled. "New Orleans money is as good as anybody else's. Come on in and we'll write up the papers."

I was jubilant. My head was up there right in the clouds as I headed back toward the forty. Every now and again I laughed, and I even sang, as I rode along on the mule, just thinking on the reality that the land was now going to be mine. There was part of me that couldn't believe it, that I was going to have land just as grand as my daddy's. It didn't matter that the acreage was much less; it was the land I wanted. There was part of me too that wanted to let my daddy know I was going to have this land as grand as his, and I was going to get it for myself, without him. When I thought on that, though, when I thought on my daddy and on my brothers, I felt a sadness, but I refused to let thinking on them spoil my joy. I could hardly wait to get to the forty to tell Mitchell and Caroline the news. I raced that mule the last three miles toward home. I raced him as if I were atop Thunder.

Before I reached the cabin, I saw Nathan running toward me. I figured he was eager to hear my news about the land, and I waved happily to him in recognition. I was grinning wide by the time he neared, but when I saw his face clearly, I knew something was wrong. As always on a workday, dust caked Nathan's face, but today tears had streaked that dust. I leaned forward. "What is it?"

"Mitchell!" he sobbed. "He bad hurt, Paul!"

"What happened?"

"Somebody done shot him in the back, jus' as a tree was 'bout t' fall! Tree done fell on Mitchell and he all broke up inside and bleedin'! We don't think he gonna make it!"

"Where is he?"

"Up at the place."

I grabbed Nathan's arm and he swung up behind me. I spurred the mule into a gallop once more. Before the mule was fully stopped at the front of the cabin, I leaped down and raced to the door. Tom Bee sat on the stoop, his head back against the logs. He'd been crying too. He looked at me but said nothing. I flung the door open, then just stood there. Mitchell lay unmoving on the bed, and everything seemed to be in blood. Caroline and an elderly woman called Ma Jones sat beside him. Seeing me, Caroline got up. She saw in my eyes my question, and she answered it. "He been waitin' on you." She added nothing more, just walked past me and out the door. Ma Jones followed her.

I went over to the bed. Mitchell lay so still, I was fearful he hadn't waited long enough. Then he opened his eyes. "So, how'd it go?"

I stared at him. "What?"

"You get the land?"

I nodded. Mitchell closed his eyes and almost smiled. "Um . . . knowed ya would. Course, I never done thought one of them banking men would loan a colored man no money."

"Didn't," I said, speaking as normally as I could, about what no longer mattered. "Gave me some advice, though. Talked to me like I was some boy. Told me J. T. Hollenbeck's land was a white man's kind of land and to be satisfied with what I had."

"Then how'd you get it?"

"Doesn't matter. Save your strength."

"Wanna know."

"Already paid Hollenbeck the down payment. I'll pay the rest during the next seven months."

"You had that much money?"

I nodded mutely.

Mitchell managed the smile this time. "Well, I shoulda knowed."

I sat down, wanting to take his hand but fearing Mitchell would know my fear if I did. "Nathan said a tree fell on you. How'd that happen?"

Mitchell grunted. "Like t' know that my own self." His breathing was hard.

"You get careless?"

He looked straight at me. "Coulda done gotten foolish. Ain't never got careless . . . 'specially when somebody firing at me." Every movement was labored. "Got shot just as the tree was 'bout t' fall. Must've stumbled in front of it."

"Who shot you?"

"Digger."

"Digger? You sure?"

"It was him, all right."

"Well, you forget about Digger Wallace right now. Right now you just save your strength."

"Got no strength t' save. I ain't comin' outa this."

"Course you are."

"Naw, I won't. Don't start lyin' t' me now. We been through too much t'gether."

"Yeah, we have been, some as bad as this, and we both sur- vived, so I know you'll be all right."

Mitchell again grunted, closed his eyes, then, as if by sheer will, forced them back open. "That girl Etta you been seeing, you meant what you said 'bout her?"

My lips parted, not sure why he was asking about Etta at a time like this. "What do you mean what I said about her?"

"'Bout you ain't got feelings for her. That's what you said."

I nodded. "Yes, I meant that. But why—"

"Then good."

"Good?"

"Then I can ask you what's on my mind."

"And what's that?"

"Want you t' marry Caroline."

I gazed at Mitchell, figuring now his mind was going. "What's that?"

"You just shut your mouth. . . . You got plenty time t' talk. . . . I ain't. Can't keep repeatin' myself. Said want you t' marry Car- oline."

I shook my head, not knowing what to say to his rambling. "Well . . . that's not possible, Mitchell . . . you're married to her—"

"Want you t' take care of her for me. Want you t' take care of her and my boy."

"Mitchell, no . . . I can't let you talk like this—"

Mitchell grabbed my hand, and there was in his grasp an

amazing strength. He raised himself up on his elbows. "Paul, you gotta do this for me. You gotta do this! I ain't gonna rest easy 'less you say you gonna do it. You, me, we always back each other up, you know that. So you take care both of 'em for me. You promise me that, Paul. Promise me!" His grip tightened in his urgency, and I could feel the time slipping away.

"I promise you, Mitchell," I said, and I felt as if Mitchell had squeezed the words right out of me with his final moments of strength, for once the words were spoken, the promise made, he fell back flat and his hand slipped away.

"Good. Knowed I could count on you, Paul. Knowed I could. You won't be sorry. I promise you that."

They were Mitchell's last words to me. He closed his eyes again and this time he made no effort to open them. His breathing grew even more halted, and he did not answer when I called to him. For some while I gazed down on my friend, thinking on all we'd been through together, on the unreality of his lying there, on words that needed to be said but maybe not. I squeezed his hand, then I went to the door, opened it, and called Caroline.

She came quickly and glanced at me, and I went outside. Tom Bee was still sitting on the stoop. "It was that Digger Wallace, ya knows that, don't ya?" he said to me. "It was Digger shot that boy. No 'count scound'! Shot that boy and yo' horse too!"

I turned as if in a sleep. "What?"

"Yeah. Thunder, that there fine horse, he lying dead in the pasture out yonder. That no 'count scound' shot Mitchell, then the horse. I done seen him do that, shoot the horse, I mean. Ain't seen him shoot Mitchell, but I done seen him shoot that horse. Why you 'spect he done that, Paul? Shoot that horse like that?" Tom Bee looked up at me, searching for answers. "That horse, he ain't been hurtin' nobody."

I just shook my head, with no answers to give, and left Tom Bee. I walked past Nathan, who was standing with the mule, and without a word to him headed up the slope with an axe. I walked to the cutting line and began to whack at a tree. With each whack of the axe I thought of Mitchell: of Mitchell standing on my daddy's land facing Hammond and George with an axe, ready to use that axe on my brothers and on me; of Mitchell beating up on me every time it moved him to do so until we came to our understanding; of Mitchell hitting that white man to get my race money; of Mitchell and me under the seats of that train. I couldn't think on Thunder, only Mitchell. I whacked at that tree until it fell. Then I started on another one.

About dusk Caroline came and got me. "You needs t' be there, Paul-Edward," she said as she hugged her arms to her body. "You leave these here trees be. You his family. You needs t' be down there with him."

I nodded, left the axe, and followed her down the slope. With Nathan and Tom Bee, Caroline and I sat the night through at Mitchell's side. That next morning, just before the dawn, Mitchell died. My friend, my brother, was gone. ᴐ

Family

I made a coffin for Mitchell. I had some good, strong plank oak-wood that I'd gotten from Luke Sawyer to make a cabinet on order, but I figured to worry about that cabinet later. Right now I needed the best wood I had to bury my friend. All day I worked on that coffin, and Caroline with Nathan's help washed Mitchell's body in scents and herbs. We dressed Mitchell in his wedding suit, put his boots beside him, and lined the coffin with a quilt Caroline had made for their wedding bed. As the sun set, we buried Mitchell under an oak tree and marked the spot with a cross. We said our prayers over him, and then we left him to his rest.

Right after the burial I asked Tom Bee to make the ride over to the Perry farm and let Caroline's family know about Mitchell. "Tell them I'll be bringing Caroline over when she's ready," I told him. Tom Bee said he'd set out first thing the next morning.

When Caroline, Nathan, and I were back in the cabin and all the folks who had gathered were gone, I said to Caroline, "I'll take you and Nathan home whenever you say." Caroline looked at me and was silent. We were seated at the table, and what food folks had brought, Caroline had set before us, but only Nathan was eating. "I know it's been a long day and you haven't had much rest, so you just think on it and let me know." I waited for her to say something, but she didn't, so I finished off the coffee I'd been sipping and got up.

"Ain't you gonna finish your plate?" she asked.

"Not much hungry," I said. "I'll just cover it and put it in the food safe."

"Leave it. I'll take care of the food."

"No," I said, finding a clean cloth. "You don't have to wait on me. I'm used to doing for myself."

"Then suit yourself," she said.

I put the covered dish away, wished both Caroline and Nathan a good night's rest, and turned to go. "Paul-Edward," Caroline said as I opened the door, "I'm stayin' here."

I looked back at her. "What was that?"

"I said I'm stayin' here. I ain't goin' anywhere."

"Well, we can wait a while," I conceded. "It's just that I thought you'd want to go back home to your family."

"This here's my home now."

I shook my head. "There's no home here."

"Mitchell told me I get his half of the forty."

"Well, you do, but—"

"Then I got a home here."

"No. You can't stay."

She got up. "Who say I can't?" She eyed me, waiting for an answer, then began to clear the dishes.

"I wasn't expecting you to stay, not with Mitchell gone."

"You figured 'cause-a that I'd be gone too, huh? Well, ain't gonna be that way. I'm stayin'."

"But I told Tom Bee to tell your folks I'd be bringing you home."

"You ain't oughtta told him that. You oughtta done asked me first."

"Maybe so, but I didn't figure you'd want to stay."

"Well, I am."

I took a deep breath. "What about Nathan?"

Nathan stopped eating and looked over at his sister. "You hafta ask him," Caroline said. "But he stay or he don't, I'll still be here."

"Now, that wouldn't be right," I protested. "A man and a woman not married here on the same place, it just wouldn't be right."

"I said I'm stayin'. I've got a baby comin', and I plan to have somethin' for this here child. Part of this land belong t' Mitchell belong to his child now. His daddy worked right 'longside you t' get it, and now you got some seven months 'til the time's up t' do all the work need doin' for us t' keep it. I'm gonna work right 'longside you now, Paul-Edward, jus' like Mitchell done, 'til this land be truly ours. I done promised Mitchell. 'Sides, how was you plannin' on doin' all this work by yo'self?"

I didn't know what to say to her. Tell the truth, I was just too drained and tired to argue with her about it at that moment. I hadn't slept, and my mind was no longer clear. "We can talk about it in the morning."

"Nothin' else t' talk 'bout."

I just looked at Caroline. She looked at me, and I left.

That night, despite my weariness, I couldn't sleep. I had my mind on Mitchell and on Caroline too. I passed part of the night in restless thought, then finally rose and lit a lantern and settled down to writing Cassie to tell her about Mitchell. I wrote a second letter as well, to Mitchell's mother, and enclosed it for Cassie to deliver. Before the dawn broke, I stuffed the letters in my pocket, took up my shotgun and my shells, and headed up the slope where Mitchell was shot. I found the fallen tree and the ground soaked red with Mitchell's blood. I placed my hand upon the bloodstained earth, then slumped upon the ground,

and for the first time I cried for my friend. I remained there
until the sun was high, then I took my shotgun and my letters
and headed across the forty. I passed the spot where Tom Bee and
Nathan had buried Thunder, but I didn't linger there. Tom Bee
hadn't understood why Digger had killed the palomino, but I
did. Digger was a little man who had nothing. Out of his own
meanness he had killed that magnificent animal because he had
belonged to me, a man of color. He had killed my horse and he
had killed my friend. I left the forty and kept on going. I was
planning on hunting Digger Wallace down.

❧

I headed straight for Tom Bee's place, which sat on the farther-
most edge of the Granger plantation. Even though I knew Tom
Bee wasn't there, I figured what with John Wallace having
stayed there, Tom Bee's family would know something of the
Wallaces and their whereabouts. They said John Wallace had already gone to Vicksburg and they had only heard about Digger
being back. I thanked them and asked that they let Caroline
know I'd be gone for a while, then went on my way again. I
asked every family of color I came upon about the Wallaces, and
they all had the same to say. They hadn't seen them. I took cau-
tion and didn't ask any white folks directly about Digger. I didn't
want them to see me with my shotgun. What few colored folks I
put faith in, I asked them to inquire about Digger and they did
that, but the word they brought back to me was that Digger was
nowhere around, and neither was John.

I didn't accept what word they brought back, and I kept push-
ing on, looking. I went into Strawberry, mailed my letters, and
asked more questions. Mitchell was constantly on my mind.
Some white man had killed him, and I didn't figure either
Mitchell or I could rest until that white man was dead. I lived in
a daze. I wandered that countryside making inquiries about Digger, always hiding my shotgun before I began my questioning so

folks wouldn't know I was hunting. But every time I asked, the answer was always the same: "Ain't seen him. Most last we heard, he gone back t' Alabama." A day and a night passed, then a second and a third of both. I lived on restless sleep and a black-rage anger. I killed squirrels and rabbits and cooked them in the woods, not from hunger, but just to keep up my strength to hunt out Digger. But there seemed to be no Digger to be found.

Finally I headed up to the ridge where Mitchell and I had first seen Digger that night the men had come looking for the chicken thieves. I stood there on that ridge rethinking that night and how close Mitchell and I had come to trouble. I'm not sure why I went back there. I didn't really expect Digger to still be lurking around, as he had that night with his brother John. I was now thinking Mitchell had been right, that they had been the ones who were the chicken thieves. Like Mitchell, I didn't put it past Digger. I settled on the ridge and spent the night. I didn't light a fire. I didn't sleep. I just sat there on that ridge and thought on my life and Mitchell's. The hours passed. The wind rustled the trees, and a soft rain came, and still I sat there. The rain passed and the clouds cleared and a full moon shone, and still I sat there. I was exhausted. Every forest sound drummed in my head, but I took no note of them. I needed sleep, but I couldn't rest. I couldn't do that until I'd found Digger.

"Paul Logan?"

I opened my eyes and jumped up. The moon was fixed directly overhead. I couldn't have drifted off for more than a few minutes, yet that had been long enough for me to lose sense of myself and for someone to come up on me.

"So there ya is! We done been lookin' all over the place for ya!" Tom Bee stepped forward, and with him was Sam Perry. I stared at them without words. "If I ain't know'd 'bout this place, we never woulda done found ya!"

"Tom Bee?" I said, still somewhat in a stupor. "How'd you think to come here?"

"That boy John Wallace. He done tole me he 'spected he seen you and Mitchell up on this here ridge one night some time back. He done said everybody done thought ya was a white man." Tom Bee eyed me knowingly. "I figured maybe ya thought Digger hung 'bout these parts, so that's how come we headed over this way."

Sam Perry placed his massive hand on my shoulder. "How's you holdin' up?"

I just nodded.

"Miz Caroline, she done sent us t' look for ya," explained Tom Bee. "Mister Perry here and his wife, and some of his family come back t' the place wit' me, and Miz Caroline, she said ya done took off and ain't even said word one t' her 'bout it."

"I sent word."

"Uh-huh, she done told us 'bout that. Long wit' that so-called word come folks tellin' her ya been out lookin' for Digger."

"Ya find him?" Sam Perry asked me.

"No."

"Then that's good. I was 'fraid maybe ya had."

I sat down wearily. "Everybody says he's most likely gone back to Alabama."

"Course he done that!" exclaimed Tom Bee. "Ole low-down nothin' of a coward! I coulda done told ya that 'fore I done gone t' Vicksburg!"

Sam Perry sat down beside me. "Best this way, Paul."

"He killed Mitchell."

"An' you go kill him, you gon' die too."

I said nothing.

"So what ya gon' do now, Paul Logan?" asked Tom Bee. I

looked up at him and Tom Bee exclaimed, "Ya ain't thinkin' 'bout a fool thing like goin' off t' Alabama after that no-good scound'?"

I took a moment, then said, "If that's where he is."

"Naw," said Sam Perry, "naw. Ya go get yo'self killed, then what's gonna come of that land ya worked so hard for? Y'all boys done put near t' a year and a half in that place. Ya gonna end up throwin' it all away for a no 'count like this Digger Wallace?"

"Listen t' him, Paul Logan!" ordered Tom Bee. "Ya knows good and well ya can't go killin' a white man if ya don't figure on hangin' yo' own self! Onliest way ya don't get lynched is for ya t' run, but I knows no matter how fast ya runs, they most likely catch ya!"

"It's yo' land and it's yo' life," said Sam Perry. "But I'm gonna tell ya, son, ain't nothin' ya can do for Mitchell now, 'ceptin' t' see good on that land. My girl, she dependin' on that."

I looked at him and my mind turned to Caroline. "She going back with you?"

"She said she ain't."

"I told her she couldn't stay, not the way things are."

"Well, that gonna be up t' her."

"I promised Mitchell I'd take care of Caroline."

"Then ya 'spect t' keep that promise, ya best be forgettin' 'bout this Digger. Ya can't go keepin' promises from the grave."

Sam Perry and Tom Bee talked to me through the rest of that night, and I began to focus on Caroline, on Caroline and her baby, and on my promise to Mitchell, instead of my own grief. They talked until there was nothing more to say. That next morning at daybreak we left the ridge and headed back to the forty.

It was nightfall by the time we reached the cabin. I didn't go in to greet Caroline or Nathan or the rest of the Perrys, but went straight to the shed, took off my boots, and lay down. Within minutes the shed door opened and Caroline stood looking down at me.

"So ya back, huh?" she said. Her hands went to her hips. "Well, next time you take off, I'd 'preciate you tellin' me face-to-face. I done lost my husband, now I gotta go worryin' 'bout you too? Don't ya do this t' me again, Paul-Edward Logan. Ya hear me? Not again." The order given, Caroline turned and left the shed, closing the door behind her. I smiled for the first time in almost a week, and then I fell asleep.

I slept the night through for the first time since Mitchell had been shot. I was so tired, my sleep was a deep one and undisturbed. I slept way past the dawn until midmorning. When I woke, it was to the sound of a baby crying. The sun peeping between the logs was harsh against my eyes, and I got up. I opened the shed door and saw Sam Perry with Nathan and Hugh leading the mules who were dragging logs to the creek. I shielded my eyes from the sun with my hand as I gazed out.

"So you up!" called Sam Perry before I could speak. He laughed and gave a wave. Hugh and Nathan waved too.

"What're you doing?" I said.

"What it look like?" returned Nathan with a grin. "We gettin' these trees down t' the creek."

Sam Perry nodded agreement. "My girl Caroline said you was gonna sleep all day, we best get t' it!" He let out another hefty laugh. "You best get on in that cabin. Womenfolks been done had breakfast for ya."

"I see," I said. "Well, I'll join you soon as I can."

"No hurry on that," said Sam Perry, moving on. "Jus' make sure you get your food first. You don't, those womenfolks gonna be mighty mad!"

I nodded absently as I looked toward the cabin. "I thought I heard a baby crying."

"Most likely did," Sam Perry affirmed. "My grandbaby's in there!"

"Yeah, Callie, she done brung her baby with her!" said Nathan.

"Ain't got time for jawin' now!" Sam Perry called good-naturedly. "That Tom Bee, he waitin' t' send more logs down t' the creek, so we best get movin'! But you, son, you take your time. No rush on you!" The three of them waved once more, then moved on toward the Rosa Lee. I turned back into the shed to find my boots. Before I could get the boots on, Caroline came again to the shed.

"Heard you was up," she said, standing in the doorway as she had the night before, but this time with her hands clasped before her. "Ya wantin' breakfast?"

I adjusted my eyes to her silhouetted there. "Heard you were keeping it for me."

"Won't be hot."

"Doesn't matter."

"Then ya come on in and get it."

I nodded and she turned to go. "Caroline," I called.

She stopped and looked back.

"I'm glad your folks are here."

"Well, I'm glad too," she said.

"Hope you're going back with them."

Now those clasped hands of hers loosened and settled once again on her hips. "What give you that idea? Thought I done told you my mind 'bout stayin' here."

"You told me. But seeing that they came for you—"

"They come to give me comfort."

"And to take you back."

"Well, like I done told ya, I ain't goin'."

I hesitated, figuring already how Caroline would take my next words. "I want you to know, Caroline, I don't think it's right for you to be here, even with Nathan. I'm here a single man and you're a widow, and it doesn't look right—"

"You see me worried 'bout that?"

"Well, I promised Mitchell I'd take care of you."

"And so how you figurin' on doin' that if I ain't here?"

"Well . . . my plan is first of all to secure this land—"

"And jus' what I'm s'pose t' do while you doin' that? Stay sharecroppin' on my daddy's place when I got twenty acres of my own right here? Now, that don't make no kind of sense to me. Mitchell might've made you promise to take care of me, but I figure the best way for you to keep that promise is for you to help me take care of myself."

I took a moment to accept her reasoning and to gather my words for what had to come next. I fumbled with my boots and finally got them on. Then I straightened and looked directly at Caroline. "That be the case," I said, "and you set on staying, then what I think we need to be thinking on after your mourning period is our getting married."

"Mitchell told you t' do that too, huh?"

"He said . . . to take care of you. That's what he wanted."

She grunted. "I know what he wanted. Told me same as you. Well, I loved Mitchell and I'm carryin' his child, but he can't tell me what t' do from the grave. Ain't nobody gotta take care of me, Paul-Edward Logan, and Mitchell can't make me marry you or nobody else."

I heaved a sigh at her stubbornness, and I suppose at my own relief. "So you're just going to stay on here?"

"Look here, Paul-Edward, I ain't tryin' t' put you out or make you break your promise t' Mitchell. I'm jus' tryin' t' do for myself and for my child."

"You're not going to change your mind?"

"Nope, I ain't."

"Then what about the baby when it's time? Who's supposed to help you through that? It's best you're home with your folks."

"You forgettin' Ma Jones jus' a few miles from here? All I gotta do is send for her."

I sighed again.

Caroline waited, as if seeing whether or not I would say more on the matter. When I didn't, all she said was "You comin' t' get yo' breakfast?"

"I'll be in."

She nodded and left. After a few minutes I followed her. I figured to leave the rest of my talking up to Caroline's family. I figured if anybody could persuade Caroline to leave this place, the Perrys could.

In the days following Mitchell's death while I was away hunting Digger, a number of people had come by offering their condolences to Caroline. Among them, I was told, were Charles Jamison and Wade. A day after my return, Filmore Granger and Harlan came to the forty, but offering condolences wasn't what was on their minds.

"Understand that boy Mitchell up and got himself killed," said Filmore Granger as he and Harlan stood with me near the creek.

"He was killed," I said flatly.

"Heard a tree fell on him."

I nodded to that, and that was all. I didn't add anything about Digger.

"Well, he was a good worker."

At least he gave him that.

Filmore Granger glanced around the clearing, then out toward the woods beyond the fields. "You still got quite a bit of cutting to do. How you expecting to get all my trees down without that boy?"

"It'll get done," I said.

"You got seven months, no more."

"I understand that."

"Long as you do."

Filmore Granger was silent a moment as he looked past me toward the cabin. "Who are all these people?"

I glanced around. Rachel Perry and Callie were hanging wash. Sam Perry and Hugh were leading the mules with a load of logs to pile them on the bank of the Rosa Lee. "Mitchell's family," I answered, and that was all.

Filmore Granger grunted. "Where they from? Don't seem to know any of them."

"They're not from around here." I told him nothing more.

Filmore Granger stared curiously at the Perrys. "They planning on staying?"

"I don't know."

"Well . . . long as my trees get cut."

"There are logs ready now, if you'd like to run them down the creek."

Filmore Granger gave me a hard look. "I'll come get them same time as always."

I nodded. It was up to him. My look said it all, and I knew he didn't like it. He and Harlan mounted their horses. "Just make sure the number of logs you've got for me is the same as always," he said. "I won't stand for a run being short, just because that friend of yours is dead."

"It won't be," I said.

Filmore Granger spurred his horse, and he and Harlan rode away. I stood staring after them, thinking on Digger. Sam Perry came over and joined me. "Understand from Caroline that there's the boss man own this place."

"Not for long," I said. "We've got seven more months, then it's ours clear."

"You gonna be able to cut all the trees ya need?"

"Yes, sir, I'll get it done."

"Wit' jus' you and Nathan and Tom Bee?"

"It'll be hard," I admitted, "but it's been hard before. Mitchell and I, we can—" I stopped myself and there was a long silence between Sam Perry and me.

Finally Sam Perry said, "That's right, son. You ain't got Mitchell no more." He laid his hand on my shoulder. "But I believes ya get it done. I believes ya will." He took his hand away and sighed before looking out toward the cabin. "Jus' wish we could stay on here and help ya with it."

"Your helping these last few days while my mind was off elsewhere has already helped save the place. With what Mitchell, Tom Bee, and I had already cut, we've got enough now for the creek run."

"S'pose that boss man be happy 'bout that."

"I don't know," I said. "I get the feeling sometimes he'd like nothing better than for me not to live up to that contract we signed now that he's already gotten the bulk of his trees. He's getting his timber money from the lumber company. He's getting a clear field for planting too. He'd probably like nothing better than to take back the forty, but he won't, because I'm going to live up to that contract. Every tree he's marked will be down before the date we set."

"Well, I sure believe that," said Sam Perry. "One thing I want, though, is for ya not t' be worrin' on teachin' Nathan yo' craft right now while ya tryin' t' cut these here trees. Ya hafta keep yo' mind on one thing, and that there's on clearin' this land. Ya wait on teachin' Nathan. There ain't gonna be time right now."

"No, sir, Mister Perry," I said. "That's mighty generous of

you, but we made ourselves a bargain. Nathan's been a great help in getting the trees cleared. I don't know how Mitchell and I could've managed without him. I intend to keep my end of the bargain."

"And ya will! Only thing is, we needs t' wait 'til after all these trees ya done promised t' this man are down and ya got yo' land papers. Ya don't get them papers, then my Caroline got nothin' for herself and her baby. Now, Nathan and I done talked it over. He ain't wantin' t' leave from here. He wantin' t' stay on and help ya get this land and he wantin' t' put all his time int' that. He already done told me he ain't gonna do no woodworking even if you do. He gonna spend his time choppin' them trees, choppin' branches, doin' whatsoever need t' be done t' help clear this forty. 'Sides all that, in a way ya kinda like family now. We gots t' pull t'gether."

My eyes met Sam Perry's and I knew he had faith in me. I figured to live up to it. I decided not to fight him; he was right.

I looked out at the woods still thick beyond the fields, and my mind set on the deal I had made with J. T. Hollenbeck. I could keep the forty, but without Mitchell, and without the palomino to sell, I didn't know how I was going to keep the land.

I had been wrong about the Perrys being able to persuade Caroline to return home with them. Sam Perry talked to Caroline, Callie talked to Caroline, and so did Hugh. The only one who didn't talk to Caroline, at least not in my hearing, was Rachel Perry. The others, however, seemed to make up for any silence on her part. But the more they talked, the more stubborn Caroline became. Finally she said to them outright: "Papa, you and Mama, y'all talked me into waitin' near a year 'fore marryin' Mitchell. But this time nobody talkin' me into nothin', not even you, Papa. I loves you, Papa, and I respects you and what you say, but my mind's made up 'bout this thing. Now, y'all take

Nathan on home if you got a mind to, but that won't change my mind none 'bout stayin' here. Callie, Hugh, I'm tired of hearin' 'bout leavin' from the two of you. I know y'all loves me and wants what's best, but this here what was Mitchell's land is mine now, and I'm stayin' on it." After that there were few words said about Caroline leaving.

The Perrys stayed on for several more days. Sam Perry and Hugh put in the long hours with Tom Bee, Nathan, and me, and we made up for the days missed when I was off looking for Digger and Tom Bee had had to come searching for me. But hard work wasn't all the Perrys gave. They brought some normalcy back to our lives and even a bit of laughter. Having the Perrys on the place lifted all our spirits. As the family consoled Caroline, and Nathan too, I took note of Callie's child. She wasn't quite a year old, but she made her presence felt in everything she did. I watched her and thought of Mitchell's child and how much life he could bring to the forty. Still, I didn't see how that could be. Caroline had to leave.

The night before the Perrys were to head home, I went directly to Rachel Perry with my worry about Caroline. "It'd be best she go," I said.

Rachel Perry studied me in silence, then asked, "Why?"

I was taken aback. All she'd been hearing were reasons why for the past several days. She waited, staring at me.

"The baby, for one," I said. "With Caroline being pregnant, there's no telling what kind of problems she might have."

"Caroline done told me there's a woman two or three miles 'way can help her."

"I just thought she'd want to be with her mother."

"Well, 'cordin' t' Caroline, this here Ma Jones could take care of anythin' I could. What other reasons you got for her t' leave?"

I was silenced. It was obvious.

"Well?"

"We'd be two unmarried people on this place, Miz Perry. Even with Nathan here, there could be talk."

Rachel Perry nodded and sighed. "No matter what ya do, folks talk. Seem some folks got nothin' better t' do. Now, I'm gonna tell you somethin', Paul Logan. I gots my worries 'bout Caroline stayin' on here, but I ain't been tryin' t' get her t' leave. That's my husband's doin'. I ain't tried t' get her t' leave 'cause I agrees wit' her. This here's her place now. She needs t' keep it. She needs t' work it. She needs t' be on it. I wants her t' have somethin' of her own."

Rachel Perry's words moved me into another time and another place

"Now, far's this other thing 'bout you and her livin' up here not married, Caroline done said you willin' t' marry 'cause that's what Mitchell wanted. Well, Caroline told me she wasn't marryin' nobody jus' 'cause Mitchell said t' do it, so don't you worry 'bout it. One thing I want you to know, though, Paul Logan. I liked Mitchell. He had a way 'bout him. But I figure you t' be a steady man, and I be proud t' call you my son, things work out that way. I don't think my girl could do no better." Rachel Perry's eyes met mine, and that was all she said.

The next morning at dawn Sam and Rachel Perry, Hugh, and Callie with her baby got onto their wagon and headed back to Vicksburg. After they left, Caroline, Nathan, and I went back to our daily business of chopping the trees, hacking the branches, and burning the brush. We said few words among us, even though our thoughts were on Mitchell and missing him. That night we sat at the outdoor fire for a spell before turning in, and Caroline said to me, "In all this time I ain't asked you 'bout the land."

"Land?"

"The land you was wantin' from J. T. Hollenbeck. You'd gone

off t' Vicksburg t' see 'bout gettin' money for it," she reminded me.

I nodded. "Seems so long ago now."

"I know," Caroline agreed. "Whole lifetime."

"Well, didja, Paul?" asked Nathan. "Didja get it?'

"I got it."

"Knowed ya would!" he exclaimed, sounding much like Mitchell.

Caroline smiled. "Mitchell done told me anybody could get it, you could."

I smiled too. "And he used to tell me he didn't have any faith."

"Well, he sure done had faith in you. He told me he give you a paper for his half of the forty t' use as you seen fit."

I nodded. "Is that all right with you?"

"I ain't worried 'bout it."

"I intend to put the forty up for sale. It'll help me pay for Hollenbeck's land, that along with a crop. I'd figured to sell Thunder for the rest of the money." I glanced across at her and she met my eyes. "I'll have to figure something else."

Caroline only nodded. For some time we sat in silence. Then Caroline said, "Mitchell know 'bout you gettin' Mister Hollenbeck's land?"

"First thing he asked me."

"Well, I'm glad."

"One thing I always intended was for Mitchell to see it—the land, I mean. But seemed like we were always too busy. I regret that. It's truly something to behold."

"Well, maybe his baby and me, we can see it for him," she said.

"I hope that too," I murmured.

Soon after, the three of us fell into silence, but that was all right. After a bit we all went off to our sleep. We'd gotten through another day without Mitchell, and somehow the next day we went on with another one.

☙

In the days and weeks that followed, I don't know how I would have made it without Caroline and Nathan. Each day I woke, I thanked the Lord for Caroline's stubbornness and her determination to stay. Having her still on the forty gave me the will to go on, and having Nathan gave me some of the help I needed. Thing was, though, I figured I'd have to hire on another man to provide at least part of the work Mitchell had done. But I put off doing that. I kept Tom Bee on, and exhausted myself with the kind of hours Mitchell and I had put in when Filmore Granger had demanded more trees. Caroline objected mightily to the amount of work I was doing, but I didn't heed her words to slow down. I figured I knew better than she what it would take to ensure that all the trees I'd contracted with Filmore Granger to cut would be off this land by the date we'd agreed.

I had since Mitchell's death thought things through about J. T. Hollenbeck's land. I had already paid eight hundred and fifty dollars and made the first monthly payment of twenty-five dollars, plus the five-dollar interest charge. If I gave up on buying the land, I wouldn't be getting any of that back. J. T. Hollenbeck had made that clear. More than losing the money, I didn't want to lose the land. I loved that land. It touched my soul. I intended to keep on paying the notes. To help pay the final thousand, I had planted more cotton than I had figured to do before, and added to that, I was planning on selling all but one of the mules once the timber was cleared. Maybe, just maybe, if cotton prices were good, and I could get a good price for the mules, I could make up some of my loss.

I counted my money. What with paying the monthly note to

J. T. Hollenbeck and already paying Tom Bee, I knew I'd be out of cash before I took over ownership of the forty and could sell it. When I'd made my deal with J. T. Hollenbeck for the monthly payments, I'd figured on Mitchell, and I'd also figured on being able to finish several pieces of furniture for cash money. I finished two lamp tables I had taken on order from Luke Sawyer and took them to him. Out of the money he paid me, I paid him for the oak I'd used for Mitchell's coffin and let him know it would be a while before I could make his cabinet or anything else. I told him I regretted I couldn't keep my bargain with him about the cabinet, but I no longer had the time for furniture making. It was the first time since I had left my daddy's house that I had broken my word, and it pained me that I was breaking it to Luke Sawyer. I asked him to send his orders to another furniture maker, and he wasn't happy about that. I also asked him about possible buyers for the forty acres. He said he'd ask around.

Now there was no more money coming in. I let both Nathan and Caroline know that, but I didn't tell them about how low my cash was. I figured that was my problem and somehow I'd solve it. But in the meantime, in order to keep up with the logging, I had no choice but to hire on another worker. The man I hired, was a young friend of Tom Bee's by the name of Horace Avery. Right after I hired him, I went all the way up to Jackson and I sold my daddy's ring. That next month, I went to Jackson again and I sold my mama's watch. Both were hard things for me to do. The watch and the ring had more meaning to me now, and I thought long before selling them, and I looked for a way not to have to do it. But in the end, I knew that my mama, and my daddy too, would have done the same as me. I had no choice. I had to stretch my money. I had to save the land. When the note came due again on J. T. Hollenbeck's land, I went to Vicksburg to sell my furniture tools to Luke Sawyer.

"So what's going on down there?" Luke Sawyer asked as he

looked over his spectacles at me, much the same as he had done the first day I'd met him. "You don't look good."

"It's difficult without Mitchell."

"'Magine so. But things so bad now you got to go sell your tools?"

"I've got to make ends meet until I've paid off my debt on the Hollenbeck land. I'll get more tools after that."

Luke Sawyer gave me a long look, then shook his head at my predicament. "It's a shame," he said, "'bout that palomino."

I nodded in agreement.

Luke Sawyer pressed his lips firmly together and he seemed angry when he spoke once more. "You could've gotten a good price for him. That was one fine horse!"

Again I nodded.

Luke Sawyer cleared his throat, as if to relieve his anger. "You told me once, Paul, you'd sell that horse when the time was right. To my figuring, you might have thought the time was right when you signed for that Hollenbeck land. Am I right?"

I met Luke Sawyer's eyes. "Selling him was in my plans."

"Makes sense to me. How much were you counting on him bringing?"

Now, Luke Sawyer was a good judge of horse prices, and I knew his questioning me was not just out of curiosity. "He could race and he could win, and he looked to be only about five or six years old. I figure he could have brought me just about as much as that forty acres I'm chopping."

"That much, huh?" Luke Sawyer rubbed his chin. "That'd be about four hundred dollars, then. That's a lot of money."

"I know."

"Well, I've got one good bit of news for you. Found a man who's interested in that forty acres of yours. His name's John Lawes, and he'll come down and take a look at it. If he says he'll buy it, you can count on it."

"Good," I said.

Luke Sawyer looked at me closely. "I suppose. But what about the rest of the money you need? I understand the banks turned you down."

I took a moment. I hadn't told Luke Sawyer that. "I'll figure something. Right now, though, all I'm trying to do is keep up my payments on the land note and get title to the forty so I can sell it."

"You've taken on a lot, Paul."

I half smiled.

"And like I said, you don't look good."

I shrugged.

Luke Sawyer suddenly grinned. "You could come back to work with me. Full time."

"That wouldn't get me the money I need."

"S'pose not," Luke Sawyer agreed, "not 'less I get in another herd of horses fine as that batch brought in three years ago, and that ain't likely."

I conceded to that with a nod, looked down at my tools, then back at him. "What I need now is cash money, Mister Sawyer, and I figure these tools can bring me some. I've come to you because I thought you'd appreciate their worth."

"So what if I need for you to make me some furniture?"

I shook my head. "I couldn't do it. I just don't have the time. That's why I asked you to get yourself another furniture maker."

Luke Sawyer sighed. "All right, all right. I ain't liking this, not one bit, but I'll buy your tools. You just think over what I said. If you decide to come back and work with me, the door's open."

I thanked him for that.

"Now I suppose we gonna hafta haggle price."

"Just give me your best offer," I said.

Luke Sawyer studied me over the spectacles, and without even looking at the tools, he made his offer. There was no haggling. I knew he was giving me more than the tools were worth.

I worked seven days each week. I chopped the trees and I tended cotton. I worked with fever and I worked with pain. I worked as I had with Mitchell before Caroline came on the forty. I pushed myself until I could push myself no further. Everything in me needed to keep my promise to Mitchell and to myself. I needed to secure this acreage so that I could buy J. T. Hollenbeck's land, and I needed to have a place for Caroline and her baby. Once that was done, then I figured I could take the time to rest. It wasn't until I woke one morning with a fever burning so high, I almost passed out, and had the dysentery and legs so weak, I had trouble standing, that I recognized the Lord had put a halt to my working.

"Maybe ya listen t' me now!" Caroline fussed as she tended me. "Told you long time ago, Paul-Edward Logan, t' stop all this hard workin' like ya do!"

"But, I've got to—"

"Ain't gotta do nothin' but rest like I tell ya to. I'm in charge now."

"But the trees—"

"They get cut, don't ya worry," she said as she hovered over me with a cool cloth. "I see t' that. Don't be forgettin' this here's my land too."

Well, Caroline did see to it. I stayed on my cot for almost a week with my weakened body, and from the dawn on until late nightfall, I heard chopping outside the shed. When I finally was able to get up, Caroline warned me, "You bein' bedridden, it's the Lord's way of lettin' you know you ain't in this by yo'self, Paul-Edward Logan. He got His hand in it too, and He tellin' ya t' slow down. Y'all'll get it done, but in His time, not yours."

I smiled at her. "But I'm sure He expects me to do my part."

"Just don't you die on me," she ordered. "I can't hardly carry on for both you and Mitchell."

Once I was back on the slopes, I learned from Tom Bee that it was not only he, Horace, and Nathan who'd been cutting the trees, but Caroline too. I began to worry even more about her and the baby. Even once I had my full strength back, Caroline continued the work she'd begun when she'd first come on the forty. She plowed, she planted, she weeded, and she burned the brush—that in addition to all the daily house chores she did. All she gave up at my insistence was chopping the trees.

As the days and weeks since Mitchell's death had passed one into another, more and more I had begun to look forward to the evenings after the brush was burned, for there were many nights when Caroline and I sat at the outdoor fire and talked late hours into the night. Sometimes Tom Bee was with us and sometimes Horace Avery on the nights they stayed over, but mostly it was just Caroline and me, and I liked things that way. Nathan would always sit with us as long as he could, but then sleep would drift over him and he would lie down, curled on the ground near the fire, and we didn't disturb him to go off to the shed until we too rose to go to our sleep. I'm not sure what Caroline's thinking was on not sending Nathan off, but it was a comfort to me knowing Nathan was right there in our presence, and maybe the same was true of Caroline.

More and more I thought on my promise to Mitchell, that part of my promise to marry Caroline. I hadn't broached the subject with Caroline again since the day after my return from the ridge; still, I thought of it and no longer just because of Mitchell. Although from the beginning I had been attracted to Caroline, once Mitchell had spoken for her, I had let thoughts of her pass. I refused to dwell on her. I admit there were times I thought of Caroline, but I fought those thoughts and let them go. She had become my friend's wife, and that's how I had seen her. I had always expected to fall in love and find the right woman to work the land with me, and I knew I couldn't do better for a wife than Caroline. But at first following Mitchell's death, I didn't feel anything except my own sorrow and rage, and I knew Caroline felt the same. I had asked her to marry out of obligation to Mitchell and she'd made it clear that Mitchell was not about to rule her from the grave. The passing months, though, had begun to heal our wounds, and I began to wonder if her feelings for me were growing beyond our friendship, as mine were for her.

Each day as my feelings grew more, I worried more. Caroline's baby was soon due, and I worried about not only its coming but Caroline's continuous work from before the dawn until the late-night hours. I tried to get her to slow down, but she only laughed.

"You think my mama had a choice 'bout slowing down before she had me?" she asked one evening, when only she and I were left awake at the fire. Nathan lay asleep beside it. "No, suh! She worked straight 'til she had me, and once she did, she got back t' the fields soon after, and I'll tell ya somethin', Paul-Edward Logan. I figure t' be strong as my mama."

I smiled at Caroline across the fire. "I don't doubt it."

She smiled back. "Better not."

I was silent.

She studied me. "What's the matter?"

"Can't help but worry."

"Told ya, you got no call to worry 'bout me." For a moment she too was silent. "What else you got worryin' you?"

I met her eyes and had a sudden flood of needing to tell her what she wanted to know: I wanted to tell her how my promise to Mitchell was eating at me. I wanted to tell her how much the land I was trying to buy from J. T. Hollenbeck meant to me. I wanted to tell her how low I was on money and that I didn't have enough to meet the next monthly payment on the note. All I had was enough to pay Tom Bee and Horace Avery. I had made sure I had enough for that. I didn't intend on cheating any man.

The one thing I didn't have worrying me still was selling the forty. John Lawes, the man Luke Sawyer had told me was inter-ested in the forty, had taken a look at it and had liked what he saw. He had agreed to nine dollars an acre, not the ten I had asked, but I had received no money when we made the deal, for I did not yet have title to the land. I would have to wait until my bargain with Filmore Granger was fulfilled for that. There was relief in knowing that I would have the money soon, but that wasn't easing my mind about the next months. I needed money now.

In the time since I had last seen Luke Sawyer, I had given much thought about working with him again full time. If I did work with him, at least I could get the money I needed for the monthly payments. But I had held back from that because I didn't want to leave the responsibility of the place to Caroline. If I left, she would have to make sure the timber was cut and the fields were tended. I knew that she would take it on, but I couldn't put that responsibility on her, not with her health and Mitchell's child at stake. In addition, if I were to leave, that would mean having to ask more work time of Tom Bee and Horace Avery. As things stood, I wasn't even sure how much longer I could keep them on. I certainly couldn't ask them to trust me for their money until I got the monthly payments out of the way, finished my obligations to Filmore Granger, and sold the forty. They had their folks to think of too. I wanted to tell Caroline all these things, but I couldn't.

"Paul-Edward, I want you to know somethin'," Caroline said

when I had given her no answer. "I know you been worried 'bout a lotta things, and that's includin' me and this baby. But I want you to know I ain't worried. Mitchell, he put his faith in you and I do too." Her eyes studied me. "So what is it? You worried 'bout gettin' these trees cut in time to meet Filmore Granger's deadline? If you worried 'bout that, then don't be. What with Mister Tom Bee and Horace Avery, Nathan, you, and me, we'll get 'em down in time."

I smiled at her reassurance. "You really think so?"

"Course. Don't worry 'bout it."

Caroline's words, as so often, were spoken as fact, and I took consolation from them. Still, though, I did worry, and I gave further thought of going to Luke Sawyer. I knew that if I did go, I would have to tell Caroline why. I put that off and as the days toward meeting the next note to J. T. Hollenbeck dwindled to within a few, I decided upon selling two of the mules and the wagon instead. Somehow we'd make do without the wagon and just the one team.

"Where you goin' with them mules?" Caroline asked the dawn I hitched the mules to the wagon.

"I've got to go to Strawberry," I said.

"You takin' them mules there, you gonna bring them back again?"

I looked at her. "What do you mean by that?"

Caroline glanced out at the rising sun, then back at me. "Where your tools?"

"What?"

"Your tools. You ain't used 'em in a spell."

"Haven't had time."

"Sent Nathan out to get your hammer other day. He done said he ain't seen yo' toolbox."

"Well, Nathan knows he's not supposed to use tools in that box for anything but woodworking."

"Maybe so, but he still ain't seen yo' toolbox."

I shrugged. "Maybe he overlooked it."

"S'pose he did, seein' it ain't there."

"What do you mean by that?"

She didn't answer my question as she went on with her own. "Where's yo' watch?"

"My watch?"

"Ain't seen ya lookin' at it here lately."

"Don't have time to check it."

Caroline grunted. "Then where's it at?"

"In safe keeping."

"You sold it, ain't ya?"

I gazed at her, stupefied.

"You sold it, ain't ya, Paul-Edward? Your tools too."

"Caroline—"

"What else ya sell?"

I tried to gather myself. "Whatever I sold, it's my business," I said finally. "Nobody else's."

"'Ceptin' mine," she retorted.

"Not yours either. You're not my wife," I reminded her.

"Yeah, but half of this here forty, it's mine," she returned. "And if you sellin' things, then that means you got a mighty need for money, and the only reason I can figure you t' need money is for that Hollenbeck note and to pay these men choppin' these trees. You don't finish choppin' these here trees in time, we lose this place. We lose this place, then you can't get that Hollenbeck land, so you sellin' even what's most precious t' ya to keep that from happenin'. That's all I can figure."

I stood there in front of her, holding the reins to the mules and not knowing what else to say to her. I wouldn't lie, I couldn't lie to Caroline, and there were no other words but the truth, which I couldn't speak.

Caroline saved me from that. She dug into her apron pocket,

then pulled out her hand, clutched into a ball. With her other hand she took my hand and placed her balled fist into it. "Here," she said. "You take this." She opened her hand and placed two bills in my palm.

I stared at the money, then at Caroline.

"You ain't the only one got things t' sell," she said.

"Caroline . . . I can't take this."

"You keep forgettin', Paul-Edward Logan, this here's my land too, and whatever worry you got 'bout it, they my worries too."

"What did you sell?"

"The hogs. They was mine, and I done chose t' sell 'em. Got a good price too. Don't forget I learned bargainin' from my daddy. And don't ya go tellin' me t' go get my hogs back, 'cause I done already made my bargain. Anyway, they probably sides of bacon and ham hangin' from a smokehouse by now. Rest of that money is what I brung with me from my daddy's house. It's all the money I got, but if I need to, I'll sell that cow too. But you can't go sellin' the mules, Paul-Edward. We need 'em too much."

I didn't have further words to say. I took Caroline's money and paid J. T. Hollenbeck. I vowed to pay her back.

"Nathan!" exclaimed Caroline on an evening a few days later. "Why don't you break out that harmonica of yours? Know you been itchin' t' play it." It was after supper, and Caroline was washing the dishes outside the cabin door. We hadn't yet burned the brush.

Nathan looked a bit apprehensive. "Ya sure, Caroline?"

"Yes, suh, I'm sure. Right sure. Been hearin' ya playin' it afar off, down by the creek. And don't be playin' no sad music. I wants something happy round here!"

Nathan grinned, sat down upon the stoop, and pulled out his harmonica from a shirt pocket. He lit into a lively tune. Caroline laughed and soon began to sing along. I watched, feeling the love and family they shared, then picked up the buckets and headed for the creek. Tom Bee and Horace Avery had gone to their own homes, and we still had the brush to burn. We needed water to dampen the ground around the brush, and even though hauling water was mostly Nathan's chore, I let him play. I was enjoying the music too.

When I came back, Caroline had finished the dishes and was seated upon the stump, where she always sat at the outdoor fire. She had a tin cup in one hand and a bowl in the other. "Put them buckets down, Paul-Edward," she ordered, "and come on have some of my tea and blueberry cobbler 'fore we get started with the brush."

I nodded and took the buckets over to the pile of brush. It was Caroline's custom to serve her dessert about an hour after her supper, once all the household chores were done. On the nights we burned the brush, she always had something for us to drink afterward. It seemed her way of bringing in peace for the night.

"Nathan, you put that harmonica down now and come on too. Got yo' favorite."

"In a minute," said Nathan, and went on playing by the stoop.

I took my seat opposite Caroline. She handed me the cup and bowl, and I took a sip of the tea, then set the cup on the ground. I spooned up the cobbler. As always, it was perfect to my taste, and I told her so.

"I'm glad," she said. "It was Mitchell's favorite."

"I know."

"Course now, sweet-potato cobbler wasn't too far behind."

I laughed. "Know that too."

She breathed deep of the night air. "This feels good," she said. "Sitting here talkin' easy on an evening, like we do."

I nodded, knowing exactly what she meant.

"Always figured this here'd be how Mitchell and me would spend our evenings." Suddenly she laughed. "Course, Mitchell wasn't never one for talkin' low and readin' and such, like you do. Still, he had hisself a way . . . yeah, he had hisself a way."

"I know you're missing him."

"Know you is too."

She was silent, her eyes lowered; then she looked at me and I saw her eyes against the fire glow. "Ya know, Paul-Edward, I'm so sorry I ain't married Mitchell right away when he asked me. My papa, my mama too, they wanted me t' wait t' marry, but I regret I ain't followed my own mind and gone on and married Mitchell when he wanted. We wasted so much time."

I had never seen one tear well up in Caroline's eyes, not even when Mitchell died. Whatever crying she'd done, she had done to herself or with her family. But now I saw the sparkle of tears, and I took my time before I said anything further to her. I finished off my cobbler, then set the bowl down. I looked at Caroline and spoke quietly. "You want to know what I think?"

"What's that?"

"Your folks were right. Mitchell, he needed that year. He always got every woman he wanted. He needed to wait on you."

Caroline frowned. "You think he was glad he done that?"

"I know he was. Things come easy in this life aren't very much appreciated, and Mitchell certainly appreciated you. He cherished you. You're worth waiting for."

The tears fell without sobs or sound of any kind, and Caroline did not wipe them away. Nathan joined us, and Caroline handed him his bowl of cobbler. Then she said to me, "You know, Mitchell done thought the world of you, Paul-Edward. He said he done figured you his family."

"Figured him the same," I said.

"Y'all was good friends."

"No," I said. "Not just friends. Brothers."

Caroline nodded to that, and we smiled at each other across the fire.

❧

Later, Nathan played and Caroline sang, then we rose and tended to the brush. I lit the fire myself. As the fire burned, we threw on more branches. Nathan brought more water. We kept the fire in check with long poles whenever branches fell too close to the edge of the circle. There was a bit of wind rising, but we didn't worry about it. The fire was well within the circle. On most nights it took us a couple of hours to burn all the branches we'd cut during the day. This night seemed no different. As the branches became ash and the fire lowered, Nathan ran off to the outhouse. "Boy, we need more water!" Caroline called after him.

"Gotta go!" he cried.

"Boy—"

"I'll get it," I said, and took up the buckets.

Caroline shook her head, as if at the ways of men, then she laughed good-naturedly. "Well, go on," she said.

Once again I headed for the creek. As I filled the buckets, I heard Caroline scream. I looked back up toward the brush and saw the flames rising, just as Nathan came running from the outhouse. Then I saw Caroline.

She sprang from the other side of the circle, running toward the creek. Her skirts were on fire. I leaped from the bank and raced toward her. I reached her before she was midway to the water. I pulled her to the ground and rolled her fast over the dirt, smothering out the flames. Then I tore off the long skirt she wore and the cotton petticoat beneath, so that her legs were bare. I picked her up and carried her quick to the creek, with Nathan hurrying behind. I immersed Caroline in the water, and she moaned with pain.

"Nathan," I said in a steady voice, "go get Ma Jones."

"But Caroline—" mumbled Nathan.

"Now!"

Nathan ran off. For several minutes I kept Caroline in the water, then took her back to the cabin, and carefully laid her on the bed. She continued to moan, and when I called her name, she could only look at me. The pain in her eyes frightened me more than I could have imagined. I couldn't lose her. "I think the baby's all right," I said softly, trying to comfort her. "We got the fire out before it got above your knees. Your baby wasn't touched."

Somehow I think my words must have reached Caroline, for her hands went to her stomach and she stroked it before she closed her eyes again. I got some of the salve Caroline had made for our many cuts and scrapes when she first had come to the forty, and rubbed it over her legs. Caroline cringed, but I managed to cover her legs with the salve. Then I waited.

When Ma Jones arrived with Nathan, first thing she did was put her hand on Caroline's stomach. She waited, and Nathan and I did too. Ma Jones nodded. "Good. Baby still kickin'." She asked me what I had done for Caroline. I told her. She nodded, then she ordered Nathan and me to leave the cabin. "I'll take care of her now," she said.

Outside, Nathan and I sat on the stumps. Fortunately for us, the wind had died and the fire from the brush had burned itself out. "What ya think, Paul?" Nathan asked fearfully. "Caroline, she gonna be all right?"

I looked at him and tried to reassure him. "She's strong," I said. "She'll be fine. She's got to be."

Ma Jones stayed on in that cabin day after day as Caroline fought back her pain, and all Nathan and I could do was keep on working and pray we didn't lose Caroline as well as her baby. Tom Bee came, and Horace Avery, and we kept on cutting trees and praying. I saw Caroline each day before I set out to work at the dawn. I checked on her when I came from chopping, and each night before I went to the shed I looked in on her once more. But each time I did, she looked at me with glazed-over eyes without recognition. Each night when I settled upon my straw cot, I said a prayer for Caroline and her child, and she stayed on my mind until I fell asleep, then filled my dreams. Finally, one day, Ma Jones called me to the cabin and she said to me, "Look like she comin' outa it."

I went in, and Caroline turned her head to me. I went closer and knelt beside her bed. "Maybe you'll listen to me now," I said softly. "Told you a long time ago, Caroline Perry Thomas, to stop doing all this hard work. I won't have you dying on me. I can't hardly carry on for both you and Mitchell."

Caroline's eyes smiled at my chiding, and her lips did the same. Then she put out her hand and took mine.

It was more than a month before Caroline was up again. Her baby was expected in less than five weeks, but once she was able to walk, she insisted on being up and doing, even though we could tell she was still in pain. Ma Jones had sent her granddaughter to stay with Caroline during her healing time, and once Caroline decided she was able to do for herself, she sent the girl home along with several bushels of corn and other vegetables from the garden, as well as two of our chickens. She didn't ask my permission about sending any of the vegetables with the girl; she did ask, however, about the chickens. She'd planted and worked most of the garden herself, so I guess she figured the vegetables were hers to give; the chickens she must have figured belonged in part to me, since hers had bred with the ones I had bought. I was happy to give the girl the chickens. Fact, if Caroline had asked for them, I would have given the girl all the chickens.

September had come, and with Caroline doing better and the

baby soon due, I looked forward to receiving my ownership papers on the forty from Filmore Granger, for all the trees I had agreed to cut had been run down the creek. As soon as I had title to the forty, I could get my money from John Lawes and seal my deal with J. T. Hollenbeck. In the meantime, Nathan and I had begun to pick the cotton. We had started picking in August, and I had sold a bale of the cotton along with the plow to pay the last monthly note. I intended to sell the rest as soon as I could. Whatever cotton was left unpicked, John Lawes had agreed to purchase. He had also agreed to purchase two of my mules, and I had found another buyer for the third mule I intended to sell. Soon I figured to have all the money I needed to own the land. We were within two weeks of seeing all our hard work pay off when Filmore Granger came to see me. I figured he had brought the papers to the forty.

I found out differently.

"Paul," Filmore Granger said when he had dismounted, "I hear you trying to buy land J. T. Hollenbeck's selling."

I wasn't sure where this was leading. "We have a contract," I replied cautiously.

"J. T. Hollenbeck bought that land from my daddy, land my daddy had to sell for taxes after the war. Now you're trying to buy it?"

I didn't say anything. I just waited for him to get on with what was on his mind.

He looked around. "You've got yourself a lot of land cleared here. Sizeable amount of cotton planted."

"As we agreed," I said, taking note of Caroline, who had come from the garden and stopped near the cabin with a basket loaded with vegetables. "Any land I cleared, I could plant."

Filmore Granger ignored my words, looked back at me, and went on. "Heard you planning to sell these forty acres of mine to help pay for that land Hollenbeck's selling. That right?"

Now, I didn't figure that was any of Filmore Granger's business, what I was doing with land that was now rightfully mine, but I couldn't say that to him outright. I knew I had to watch my words. "Well, you know, Mister Granger, our agreement was that after I'd cut all the trees for you, the land became mine. That means I can sell it, if I choose."

"Ah, naw! Not as you choose!" he thundered, the soft words now gone. "This here is not your land yet! Now, I told you the first day you come riding up here that I wasn't going to stand for any pilfering of my trees, but I see you been helping yourself to them anyway! You've been helping yourself to plenty of my good trees not on this forty acres!"

I stared at Filmore Granger, then I glanced over at Caroline, watching, and I tried to hold on to my temper, to do what was best for her. I didn't want to let my words spew out like I felt like doing. I thought on my daddy. "Mister Granger," I said, meeting his eyes, "I was very careful about the tree line we marked. All the cutting was done on the forty. We never stepped a foot off it."

Filmore Granger's temper grew even more fiery. "You calling me a liar?"

"I'm not calling you anything," I said, knowing my words were too loose in talking to a white man, but my temper was up too. "I'm just telling you we never cut off the forty. I know just where Mitchell and I chopped and where that boy Nathan and I chopped, know where the other men chopped too. We never chopped outside the forty."

Filmore Granger stared at me. I stared him back. "Maybe it was all a mistake," he said in a voice that mocked at me. "Maybe y'all done some cutting by mistake."

"We never set foot off the forty."

He glared angrily at me, then turned and walked back to his

horse. He didn't mount but faced me again. "I've decided to keep this land here."

"What—"

"You want land so bad from J. T. Hollenbeck, you go chopping trees don't belong to you to pay for it! Well, you don't go chopping down my trees trying to sell them—"

"I never did—"

"Now, you can stay on and sharecrop, if you want. I'm being as fair as I can be with you, considering what you gone and done. You don't want to sharecrop, then I want you and yours gone from here before the month's out."

"That's not what we agreed! Mitchell and I, we cut those trees for you, every one you said, and had them ready on time—"

"Cut yourselves some trees too—"

"Only what you told us—"

"You disputing with me?"

Those were dangerous words, mighty dangerous words, and I knew it. I let the silence settle and tried to catch hold of my temper again. Finally, in a steady voice, I said, "We have a paper."

Filmore Granger stepped back to me and faced me close. "You think I care about a paper signed with a nigger? Well, let me tell you something, boy. There was a time I owned hundreds of you people. I clothed you, fed you, tended you when you were sick, and I buried you. Then everything got changed all round, and here niggers got to thinking they're as good as white people, can talk the same as white people, live the same as white people, have the same kind of land. Ones like you think they as smart as white people too. Well, I'm here to tell you there hasn't been a nigger born can outsmart Filmore Granger. Not a one, no matter how white he looks." He pointed his finger in my face for emphasis, then turned and started for his horse. Once he was mounted, he looked down at me. "That crop in the ground, it's mine too. You try and harvest any of it without staying on, I'll have the sheriff after you. Same goes for any you already picked. I know you've sold one bale, but you try selling any more, you'll find yourself in jail." Then Filmore Granger spurred his horse and rode away, down the road I had cleared.

I walked over to Caroline at the side of the cabin. Her basket was filled with tomatoes, butter beans, cucumbers, and corn for dinner. She looked at me in silence.

"You hear?" I said.

"Heard enough." She slowly shook her head. "He can't do this thing."

"He's white," I said. "He can do what he wants."

"But you gots a paper—"

I repeated, "He can do what he wants."

She was silent a moment before she asked, "Well, what you gonna do?"

"I don't know." I looked out across the clearing to the field. "Only thing I know is, I'm not going to sharecrop my own land."

She nodded to that. "Well, one thing I know too. He ain't gettin' my garden."

All the rest of that day I walked the forty, thinking on what I should do. Most of the land was cleared, a field plowed, and a crop in. Filmore Granger had himself a real money property now, not to mention the money he'd already made from selling off the timber. It pained me more than I can say, all that work Mitchell and I had done, Caroline and Nathan too, all the nights with not enough sleep, all the sacrifices we had made, and for what? To end up with nothing. What pained me most, though, was that I had let Caroline down, and Mitchell.

I figured Filmore Granger had played me for the fool. I knew he hadn't just now heard about my intention to buy J. T. Hollenbeck's land. Too many people knew about it for him not to have heard before. He'd heard about it, all right, a good while back no doubt, but he'd kept his silence to keep his timber coming. He had kept his silence until now so he could take back his land, with all the timber he wanted cut, and a lie spread so I could buy no more land, land that once was his. I ended the day at Mitchell's grave and just sat there under the oak, talking to my friend, as if he could hear, and pondering what I should do. Night came and I did not even go in for supper when Caroline called.

The next morning, early, I set out for Strawberry, and Caroline with Nathan started gleaning the garden. Caroline figured to pick her garden clean and preserve every single vegetable that wouldn't keep. I figured to go see the banker in Strawberry, then continue on to Vicksburg to see B. R. Tillman again and the other bankers. Though I figured it was useless, I had to try. I didn't hold out much hope of getting a loan, but I couldn't think of much else to do. The banker in Strawberry turned me down flat, pretty much as I'd expected, and the bankers in Vicksburg did the same.

The last banker I saw was B. R. Tillman, who sat back in his big banker's chair and said to me: "Paul, I know about that deal you were trying to make to sell Mister Granger's forty acres. Also know what Mister Granger's been saying about you cutting down his trees. Know too you don't have the money to buy that forty acres of Mister Granger's and certainly not that two hundred from Mister Hollenbeck. Now, I told J. T. Hollenbeck he wasn't using good business sense in the first place to let you have it, but him being a Yankee, he agreed to sell it to you anyway. Now, here you come to me again trying to borrow money to pay him for it."

He took a pause. "I like you, Paul. I told you that before. You do good furniture work. My wife is still bragging on that chifforobe you made for her. But like I told you, that's what you need to be sticking to, working with your hands, not trying to handle business. You stay to working with your hands, then you'll do well by that. You didn't take my advice before, but you best take it now. You let this here Hollenbeck land go. Settle up your dispute with Mister Granger. I told him you was a good boy and that you'd just gotten in over your head and no doubt you didn't mean to chop his trees. You settle up your accounts with him, and if you still want to farm and raise a family, then you sign on with somebody and you sharecrop some land. You stick with what you know and don't be trying to do things you just not suited for. Now, that's the best advice I can give you, Paul."

I told B. R. Tillman, "Advice wasn't what I came here for."

After that I went straight to the telegraph office and did what I hadn't expected to do, and one of the hardest things too. I sent a telegram to Cassie and asked her, if she could spare it, to send me the money I needed. I told her that if she could spare me a loan, to send a bank draft to Strawberry within ten days. That's all the time I had. I didn't put much hope in Cassie's being able to help me, but I was desperate enough to ask. I left the telegraph office with a heavy heart and went to Luke Sawyer's store. There I bought several boxes of preserve jars for Caroline's vegetables.

"Got a lot of canning to do, I see," said Luke Sawyer as he figured my bill.

I just nodded.

Luke Sawyer eyed me over the spectacles. "How your crops doing?"

I looked away, then back to him. "I no longer have any crops. Filmore Granger's taking back the forty."

Luke Sawyer studied me with steady eyes. "I heard," he said. Neither he nor I spoke of the obvious, that Filmore Granger had reneged on our deal. "So what you going to do now?"

"Leave his land."

"What about Hollenbeck's land?"

I shrugged. "Way things stand right now, I won't be able to buy it."

"But you've already invested money in the place."

"Looks like I gambled and lost," I said.

"You just going to let that good money be thrown away, then?"

I didn't answer.

Luke Sawyer stared at me, then went back to figuring the bill. When he finished, he looked at me again. "What if I lend you the money you need?"

I stepped back from the counter, startled by his offer. I could feel my blood rushing, and I glanced away overwhelmed by what this could mean. My head began to pound with the possibility of saving the land. I could have a place of my own, a place to take Caroline. I could keep my promise to Mitchell.

"Well?" said Luke Sawyer. "What about it? I'd give you the same terms as the bank."

"No," I said, and it was hard. "No, sir. If things go wrong, I couldn't repay you."

"The land would stand as collateral."

I said no again. "I thank you, Mister Sawyer, but I couldn't be beholden to you."

"You could always work off your debt with me."

I smiled and declined once more. "I'd be an old man by then." I never wanted to be indebted to another white man, to have personal ties to another white man, but I could see in Luke Sawyer's eyes that he truly wanted to help me and I could feel in my heart his regret that I wouldn't let him. I thanked Luke

Sawyer again, paid for the preserve jars, and left the store. Luke Sawyer never knew how hard it was for me to say no to his offer and walk away. I wanted the land that bad.

✦

Upon my return to the forty the following evening, Caroline and I sat outside in front of the fire and spoke quietly once more while Nathan slept. I told Caroline about the bankers, about their refusing me the loan for J. T. Hollenbeck's land, but I didn't tell her about the wire. I knew Cassie would send me what she could, but she had her own family to worry about, and I doubted if she had the money to send. I now regretted putting that burden on my sister, and I didn't want to burden Caroline with a false hope. I didn't tell her about Luke Sawyer's offer either, because I didn't know how to explain to her how I could have turned him down.

"Then I s'pose nothin' for Nathan and me t' do but go on back home," Caroline said.

I nodded in agreement. I didn't want her to go, but I didn't tell her that. I had nothing to give her now. Still, I figured to watch out for Caroline—and her child—even if she wasn't my wife. I refused to break my promise to Mitchell.

"One thing, Paul-Edward," she said. "'Fore I leave this place, there's one thing."

"What's that?"

"I don't want Mitchell left here. I wants his grave where I can go to it, and once I leave from here, I ain't plannin' on steppin' foot on this place again. I don't want Mitchell buried where he ain't wanted."

I nodded. "I'll take care of it."

We were silent awhile thinking on our own thoughts. Then Caroline chuckled on a sudden and I glanced over. "Just was thinkin' 'bout what a lucky man that Filmore Granger is."

"How's that?"

"'Cause if Mitchell was here, Filmore Granger'd be in his grave!"

I smiled, knowing that was likely true. "Mitchell must be turning over in *his* about now."

"I reckon," Caroline agreed.

"Maybe I should go do what Mitchell would've done," I said. "I feel like it."

"And get yo'self hung? Paul-Edward, Mitchell ain't gone way he done, Filmore Granger'd be dead, all right, but so'd be Mitchell, jus' the same."

We were silent again. I knew Caroline felt my sorrow, and I felt hers, both about these acres we had lost and about Mitchell. "I'll take you home before the month's out," I told her.

She looked at me across the firelight and said softly, "I'd rather be goin' with you."

I met her eyes, then looked away. "I've got no place to go."

During those days while I waited to hear from Cassie, I helped Caroline in picking the garden and with the canning. I also made a crude trailer, and Nathan and I began to pack what few things we had. Now, it was in my mind, and Caroline agreed, that we should leave the day before Filmore Granger said we had to be gone. One thing we didn't need was for Filmore Granger to show up with a bunch of white men to put us off. Two days before our move, I rose early, long before the dawn, and rode into Strawberry. There was no bank draft waiting for me.

I didn't go back to the forty. Not right away. Instead, I went to the land. Now, I should've gone straight to J. T. Hollenbeck and told him that our deal was off, that I couldn't pay him his money. But I couldn't do that. I had two more days to think of this land as mine, and I wasn't ready to give it up, even if there was no hope in keeping it. I had thought of going to J. T. Hollenbeck, telling him my circumstances, and asking him for more time. But J. T. Hollenbeck had made it clear he wanted his money when it was due or the deal was off. All the money I'd already paid him would be forfeited. I had agreed to that with my signature. There was no changing it now.

I walked the land. I walked the meadow and the forest and finally rested by the coolness of the pond. I stayed there a long while, then went back to the slope and up to the rock where I'd first laid my head. I knelt down by that rock and I prayed. I prayed long and hard. Then I just sat looking out across the meadow and the forest until the sun set and the day darkened.

❧

When I got back to the forty, Caroline was standing by the bridge that crossed the creek. "There's a man waitin' for ya," she said. Her face was anxious. "A white man. He . . . he says he's your brother."

At first I just looked at Caroline, then I looked up the road. A buggy was stopped in front of the cabin, and a man stood beside it. Nathan sat on a stump nearby watching the man. I got down from the mule to walk with Caroline. "How long has he been here?" I asked.

"While," she answered, and we walked to the cabin without another word.

As we neared, I saw the man clear. It was Robert. I hadn't seen him in more than ten years, but I knew who he was. I would've known him anywhere.

"Paul," he said to me.

"Robert."

"Cassie sent me," he said, and shook my hand.

There was a fire burning in the outside pit. I motioned Robert toward the stumps, and he and I sat down. Caroline went into the cabin and she called Nathan in behind her.

Robert looked around as the door closed. "I heard about Mitchell. I'm sorry."

I nodded but said nothing.

"Cassie told me too about Mitchell's wife and the baby on the way . . . must be hard for her."

"She's managing," I said. I wanted to know why Robert had come. I didn't ask about our daddy or George or Hammond or anyone else; I wasn't interested in catch-up talk. "You said Cassie sent you?"

"Yes," said Robert, his voice changing as it took on a tone of business. He pulled out an envelope and handed it to me. Cassie's writing was upon it. I didn't open it. I looked at Robert with questions in my eyes. "Cassie came out to the house from Atlanta about a week ago," Robert said in answer. "She said she was getting ready to sell that plot of land belonged to your mama—"

"Land?" I questioned. "What land?"

"That ten acres your mama's house is on."

I was caught by surprise. "But . . . I thought that land was our daddy's—"

"So did I," said Robert. "For a long while. After you were gone, though—" Robert's eyes met mine at the mention of my running off, before he went on. "After you were gone, our daddy told us your mama had bought it from him. He said he'd told her he would just give her the land, but she said she didn't want that. She said she didn't want him to give her anything. She wanted to buy the land herself at the market price. But one thing she asked him to do. She asked him not to tell you, not sure why."

I looked at Robert, but I had no words to say.

"Anyway," Robert continued, "when Cassie came home, she said she wanted to sell that plot of land right away. Seeing that it was right at our doorstep, she wanted to know if our daddy was interested in buying it back. Our daddy asked her what she wanted for it, and she said she figured five hundred dollars was fair, seeing that it was right in the middle of our place. Our daddy didn't fight her on it, even though five hundred dollars is way more than that ten acres is worth. He bought it from her."

I turned the envelope over in my hands. "She say why she wanted to sell?"

"Just that the time was right."

"Then she asked you to bring this to me?"

Robert nodded.

"And our daddy didn't ask more?"

Robert shrugged. "It was hers to sell—and yours."

I looked at the envelope, then held it out to Robert. "I don't want money from my daddy."

Robert didn't move to take it. "It's not from him, Paul. It's from Cassie. She never told him a word about you." He studied me. "Look, like I said, it was yours and Cassie's to sell."

I turned the envelope over again and looked directly at Robert. "Cassie tell you why she wanted you to bring me this?"

"Just before she left, she asked me if I could make the trip for her here. You most likely know she's expecting again—"

"No, I didn't know."

"Anyway, she couldn't make the trip herself, and she couldn't send her husband, Howard, because of his business. She said it was important that you have this before tomorrow, and she didn't trust the banks to see that you got it. So she asked me to bring it to you. She didn't tell me anything else, but she'd told me enough. I took a train, hired a buggy, made inquiries how to get here, and here I am."

I was silent before I asked, "You tell our daddy what Cassie asked?"

Robert met my eyes. "No. That was between Cassie and me. She asked me not to tell him. All I told him was I had some business to take care of."

I looked again at the envelope.

"Aren't you going to open it?"

I slapped the envelope against the palm of my hand and gazed into the fire. Robert glanced at me, then got up, stretched, and without another word walked away toward the creek. For several minutes after he was gone, I stared at that envelope.

Finally, I opened it.

Inside was a bank draft for eleven hundred dollars, all the money I needed, plus some. Also inside were two letters. One was from Cassie. The other was from my mama. I opened Cassie's letter first.

Cassie wrote that she had sold our mama's land. She said she'd sold what few things our mama had left that she figured would bring some money too, all except for a broach with our mama's picture in it and her own, which she was sending along with Robert. She said the rest of the money came from her and Howard's savings and from what they could borrow against their business. She said she knew how important this land was to me, and she wasn't worried about getting her money back. She said anything she had done was what our mama would have wanted. She said our mama had told her to sell that bit of land of hers when the time was right and to give the money to me. She said she figured the time was right now.

My hands trembled as I opened my mama's letter. I tore open the envelope, and five bills fell out. They were all twenty-dollar bills. I picked them up in wonder, folded them, and put them back in the envelope. The letter itself was faded, and it was dated on Christmas Day the year Robert had betrayed me. I stared at my mama's letter, saw her words, so carefully and painstakingly written, but as I read, I heard her voice too, every sound of it. It was a letter that made me weep.

> *I aint wanted you to see this til you was full grown. Wanted you to know more of life than you do now. Right now, you feelin you know everythin there is to know, but you don't. You just know a spec of what life gonna bring. Now, I always done told you, I wanted you to have something of your own. That there's one reason I bought myself this bit of land from your daddy. Other reason was selfish. I wanted something of my own too.*
>
> *Reason I aint told you bout this land is cause right now you still thinking as a child. You love this here place and you love your daddy, no matter what the hardships are. That's all right, I suppose, but the way you thinking now, if you know bout this spec of land belonging to us, you won't probably never leave this place, and I wants you to leave. I wants you to leave this place and make yourself a new life, just like Cassie done.*
>
> *Paul-Edward, this here land is all I got of worth ceptin these few bills I'm going to leave you. I done put my watch in my box for you to have later on, but I decided with what done just happened between you and Robert and your daddy to go on and give it to you this Christmas Day. Now I'm giving you this land. Cassie got her start. Her daddy gave it to her when she got married and I gave her what I could. But this here land, son, it's yours. I always wanted it for your use—not for you to stay on it, mind you— just so you could use it to give yourself a new life. Cassie know all about it. I told her not to tell you*

nothing until the time was right. When that time comes, she'll let you know bout everything. What I got to leave you aint much, son, but least maybe it give you a start. Maybe you use it smart, you be able to get something of your own. Maybe you be happy.

Now, I can't express how I was feeling about then. There aren't words to say my feelings. When I finished the letter, I read it again. I heard Robert returning and I put the money and both letters in my pocket. I wanted to go into the cabin to tell Caroline the news Robert had brought, but I stayed myself from that. I wanted to have J. T. Hollenbeck's papers of ownership of the two hundred acres before I told Caroline anything.

"You know, Paul," said Robert as he settled on his stump again, "I was out around this area about a year and a half ago."

"I know. Mitchell brought back word from Vicksburg that you'd been there."

Robert's face showed his surprise. "Well, if I'd have only known you were here, I'd've looked you up then. Cassie never told us where you were, until now."

"I asked her not to," I said. "I thought that was best."

Robert nodded and looked at the fire. "Something you ought to know, Paul, something I've been wanting to tell you all these years. That day I told our daddy about you riding that horse, I wasn't trying to get you in trouble. I just didn't want to see you get hurt."

I stared at Robert, but left my thoughts unsaid. All these years he had worried about that, but he still had said nothing about turning his back on me. He went on, talking of other things and I listened to his words and no longer dwelled on his betrayal. We had long ago gone our separate ways.

Caroline came from the cabin and offered us supper. Robert accepted, and the two of us ate alone by the fire. After we ate,

Robert gave me my mama's broach. I opened it and gazed upon my mama's and Cassie's pictures. Robert watched me and was silent as I closed the broach again and slipped it into my shirt pocket, over my heart. Later I saw Caroline glance out the window, but as it drew late and Robert stayed on, I saw the light dim inside. Nathan came out and bedded down in the shed. Robert and I sat on by the fire and talked late into the night. Robert didn't ask about my business or why I needed the money Cassie had sent, and I didn't tell him. I told him nothing about the land or my dreams. Robert told me of our daddy and of George, who was still out west somewhere, and of Hammond and his family. He said that our daddy spoke of me often. He said too our daddy wanted to see me again, but that he wouldn't come looking for me. My daddy said I was the one who ran off, and I needed to be the one to come home and I had to do that on my own. Robert asked me about my running off, and I told him the truth of that. We spoke of the years since then. But neither of us spoke about what was really between us.

The night passed with our talk as when we were boys, but not as easily as then, and when the dawn came, Robert readied himself to go. He had had no sleep, but then neither had I. I gave him coffee, but he would take no breakfast except some corn bread from the night before. He got into his hired buggy and I said good-bye, not knowing if I would ever see him again. Then after he was gone, I mounted one of the mules and, without going in to see Caroline, rode off with my mama's and Cassie's letters and all they contained in my pocket to meet with J. T. Hollenbeck and take title to my land.

I put aside my pride about asking a white man for help. Before I made the turn up the Hollenbeck road, I went over to see Charles Jamison. I had decided that the world was as it was and I needed to put my trust in somebody. I wasn't going to play the fool again. "You once offered me your help," I said to Charles Jamison when I'd been ushered into his study. "I'd like to ask it of you now."

"And what's that?"

"I need a legal paper that'll hold up, no matter what color the parties happen to be."

Charles Jamison pulled on his ear. "This about that Hollenbeck land?" Underlying his question was the reason I needed such a paper. But he didn't ask it and I knew without asking him that he too had heard about Filmore Granger and the loss of the forty.

"Yes, sir, it is," I said. "I need to sign on it today, but I've got to know it'll hold."

Charles Jamison nodded and asked no questions as to how I'd come up with the money to conclude the deal with J. T. Hollenbeck. "Oh, it'll hold, all right. I'll go with you and we'll just make sure it'll hold."

He took some papers from his desk drawer, got his hat, and went right then with me to J. T. Hollenbeck's place. As it turned out, I made a good choice with Charles Jamison. He read all the legal papers, made changes in them, and before the transaction was done, pulled out his own agreements concerning the buying of Hollenbeck land and had me read them. In the end, the wording on his purchase and mine were the same, except for the acreage bought and the money owed. Then Charles Jamison himself signed as a witness to the transaction. In all, it took several hours before the deal was settled and I rode away with the ownership papers to my two hundred acres.

Finally, I had the land.

The sun was at midday by the time I returned to the forty. Caroline had dinner waiting, but I wasn't hungry. I wanted just to finish packing and leave. "You said we'd leave come dawn tomorrow," Caroline protested. "We leave now, no way we get t' Vicksburg 'fore dark. We be on the road at night."

"Doesn't matter," I said. "I just want to be away from here." I told her nothing else and she accepted my wanting to leave earlier than I'd said, I supposed, because she understood the pain I felt and the anger too at being on a land I had thought would be mine and was not. She didn't ask me anything about where I'd gone in the morning or about my visit with Robert. Maybe she thought it wasn't her right to ask. I don't know, but she didn't. She simply began to pack all those things that had been left unpacked, while Nathan and I went to the oak where Mitchell was buried and began to dig up his grave.

We brought the coffin and gently set it in the wagon. Then I took the window I had made, with the glass Mitchell had bought, and replaced it with wood. After that, Nathan and I broke down the beds and loaded them on the wagon, as well as the table and the chairs. We packed all the preserved goods, also the bushels of corn and peas and other vegetables, and placed them on the wagon trailer. The rooster and hens we put in crates, loaded them too, and tied the cow to the back of the trailer. We gathered everything that could be gathered, and loaded two years of living on the forty onto that wagon and trailer. Then I helped Caroline up to the seat of the wagon, and Nathan climbed on the back. I looked around once more at the cabin and the shed I'd built, at the road I'd cleared, at all the land open now because of Mitchell and me. I looked at the cotton crop blanketing the field, and I climbed onto the wagon and left it all. I didn't look back.

❧

I took Caroline to the land. I hadn't yet told her I had the deed to it, and as we rolled along, I'm sure she and Nathan too thought we were headed for Vicksburg. In the months since Caroline had come to the forty, she had not been again to Vicksburg and didn't know the roads that would have led us there. As for Nathan, soon after we were off the forty, he fell asleep for a while, and when he woke, he started whittling on a recorder he was making, and was paying no attention to the roads. We were in the woods, and one set of woods pretty much looked liked another to folks not knowing, so I didn't dispel the notion that we were on the road to Vicksburg. I just held my words, afraid of letting my happiness slip before we reached the land. Still, I smiled within myself and maybe that was why more than once I found Caroline watching me. We rode for some while, and when we came onto the land, Caroline looked around and smiled, not at me, but at what she saw. "This sure is pretty country," she said.

I smiled too and stopped the wagon. "It is pretty, isn't it?" I said.

Caroline took a deep breath of the fresh meadow air. "It's got a good smell."

I laughed. "You like it, then?"

"Course. Who wouldn't? Just look at all that green. Look at all them fine little hills yonder and that fine growth of trees round the place." She sighed. "It's a good place to rest."

"Glad you think so," I said, and got down. "We'll just stop here."

"You think that'll be all right?"

"I'm sure it will," I said, helping her down.

Nathan jumped from the back, and the three of us stood gazing out over the land. "Maybe we can spend the night here, huh?" suggested Nathan.

"I think that's a fine idea," I agreed. "There's only a couple hours of daylight left, and like Caroline said, it's a good place to rest."

Caroline frowned. "You don't think the folks own this place'll mind none?"

"I'm sure they won't." I smiled and took her hand. "Come on. I want to show you something. You too, Nathan." With Caroline's hand in mine, I led her up the slope. When we reached the top of it, I walked over to my praying rock. "I figure this here's a good place to bury Mitchell."

Caroline pulled away from me. *"Here?"* She turned, somewhat dazed, then gave me a look that questioned my sanity. "Why here?"

"Don't you like it?" I asked. "You don't like this spot, we can choose another. I just thought Mitchell would've liked it here. He could rest well."

Caroline hesitated. I'm sure she was uncertain as to what had taken hold of me. "I'd figured on burying Mitchell at Mount Elam."

"Well, you could do that," I said. "I just figured, though, maybe you'd like to bury Mitchell here, on our land."

"Our land?" Caroline stared out across the meadow with disbelief. *"Our land?"*

Nathan just stood silent, his mouth agape.

I smiled.

Caroline slowly shook her head, but she too was silent as her eyes took in the land.

"Well, what've you got to say?" I asked. I'd never seen Caroline speechless before.

She didn't answer me right away, but finally when she looked at me, she said, "This here J. T. Hollenbeck's land?"

"Not anymore. I took title to it this morning."

Nathan let out a wild holler, leaped into the air, then began to dance around.

"That why your brother come?" asked Caroline ever so softly. "He come 'bout the land?"

I nodded. "He brought the money I needed. My sister, Cassie, sent it to me, she and my mama."

Again Caroline was speechless.

"So . . . what do you think? You think we can bury Mitchell here?"

Caroline gave me the biggest smile, then she rushed into my arms.

We buried Mitchell before sunset. We said our thanks to the Lord, and all three of us spent the night on the slope beside the praying rock. The next morning I took Caroline's hand and led her through the woods to the pond. There I sat beside her on a fallen log and I said, "You know, Caroline, I loved Mitchell, and I always wanted to do right by what he asked of me. But what I'm saying to you now has nothing to do with Mitchell. I love you, Caroline, and I want you to be my wife."

Caroline didn't say anything as she looked upward to the trees where the rising sun splintered the branches with its light. I stood and stared up at the light as well before turning to her again. "So, pretty Caroline, how would you like to work this fine piece of earth with me? How would you like to be my wife so we can work this land together?"

Caroline remained quiet, looking up at the trees. When she finally spoke, she said, "Ya know, I always felt safe with Mitchell, just like I felt when I was with my daddy. Safe, like long as I was with them, nothing bad would ever happen I couldn't see through and I'd be happy." She turned to me now. "I feel the same with you." Then Caroline smiled her pretty smile at me and once more came into my arms. "I love you too, Paul-Edward," she murmured against my neck. "I love you too."

That same day Nathan and I put up a shelter for Caroline. Then I rode back toward the forty and gathered up the preacher and his wife, Ma Jones and her family, Tom Bee and his, the Horace Averys, and several others whom we held close, and led them to the land. Caroline and I were married before sunset. The following week Caroline gave birth to our first child, Mitchell's son.

"What we gonna call him?" Caroline asked from her bed.

I cradled the baby in my arms and gazed upon the face of my friend. "Mitchell," I said. "We'll call him Mitchell Thomas Logan." I then looked back at Caroline, waiting for her approval.

She was smiling.

LEGACY

(Epilogue)

Epilogue

Mitchell had been right. I have never regretted not one minute with Caroline. Caroline was and is a strong-willed woman who has always held her own with me. She is full of joy and giving and she fills my life. We have together worked this land and we've raised ourselves a family. We had ourselves four fine boys: Mitchell, of course; Kevin Edward, named for my daddy; and Luke Hammond and David George, named for Caroline's daddy and for my brothers. As things turned out, of our younger sons, Hammond, whom we call Hammer, is more like my brother George in temperament, and David so much like Hammond. We had ourselves two girls too, but they died in their infancy. Though we mourned our girls, we rejoiced in our boys. And we rejoiced in the land.

It was 1887 when I bought the land clear, but I mortgaged it some years later so that I could build Caroline a proper house and buy some livestock. I also bought Caroline a buggy of her own with that money, and I bought myself a couple of fine horses. I paid that money back in time and I had no more debt. I'd already repaid my sister. Now I've mortgaged the land again to buy that second two hundred acres I always wanted. Wade Jamison sold them to me.

Caroline through the years has been always telling me to write things down about myself, about the land, about my family and my history to pass on to the boys. Until now I've written down only one thing concerning those early days. I put down bold in a journal the date Digger Wallace was found floating facedown in the Creek Rosa Lee with a near-empty jug of moonshine floating along beside him. I put down that his meanness and the liquor had drowned him. But Caroline says she wasn't just talking about writing about Digger Wallace. She says she's talking about my life before the boys were born, about my struggle to get the land and about my family. She says it's important to pass these things on. I've told her that she passes enough stories on for the both of us, but she just laughs at that and says she'll keep doing it too. And she does. Whenever there's a quiet moment at the end of the day and we've gathered on the porch or around the fire with the boys, she'll ask me to tell again about my lumbering days or about the train ride when Mitchell and I left East Texas or about my life growing up on my daddy's land. I figured the boys would get tired of hearing about my life over and over, but they never have.

Fact, because of my stories, there came a time when the boys began to ask me about going to see our family in Georgia. They had already met Cassie, for in the years since we'd been on the land, Cassie had come twice to visit. The first time Howard had come too, along with their children. The second visit Cassie had come alone and I'd relished every moment with her. I wanted to see my sister again and I wanted my boys to know her as I did, but I put off the journey until Cassie wrote that our daddy was low sick. Cassie said it was time I came home. So when Hammer and David were still under ten and Mitchell and Kevin were in their teens, I took my boys on a segregated train back to Georgia. I wanted Caroline to go with me, but her own daddy was ailing at the time and she sent me on without her.

That first night in Georgia the boys and I stayed with Cassie and Howard and their family in Atlanta. The next morning I took my *boys to my daddy's land. Cassie went with us. When we arrived, we found Robert and Hammond there with their families. Robert was running the place now. Hammond lived in Atlanta. No one had heard from George in years.*

It was good to see my brothers again.

Hammond and Robert told me that our daddy had being lying without waking for three days now. They said they had kept talking to him through all that time and they had told him that I was coming home. That very morning of my arrival he had opened his eyes. He couldn't speak, but they knew he understood what they said. They figured he was waiting for me.

When I saw my daddy, he was sleeping and I didn't awaken him. I just sat beside his bed and thought of all the years that had slipped away. When he opened his eyes, he looked directly at me and he knew who I was. His eyes teared and he smiled. I had to cry too. That was my daddy lying there.

Throughout that afternoon I talked to my daddy and he listened. I held his hand and I told him all the things I figured he'd want to know about my life. I told him things I figured he already knew. I told him I loved him and the tears came again from both of us. I brought my boys to meet my daddy, and he smiled as I introduced them to him. Cassie then took the boys to stay with Miz Edna and Willie Thomas. I figured it was time Miz Edna and Willie Thomas met their grandson, but I stayed with my daddy. I didn't want to leave his side. Later Cassie, Hammond, and Robert joined my daddy and me, and my brothers, my sister, and I filled the room with stories. We filled the room with talk and laughter, and our daddy heard every word. He smiled often and I knew he was happy. Our daddy lay there smiling until he drifted off to sleep once again.

This time he didn't wake up.

Cassie, my boys, and I spent the night in my mama's house. The land was tilled, but no one stayed in the house now. It was just as it was when I had left. Our daddy, Cassie said, had kept the house for himself and only he had come there. Robert said he had come to the house to be alone. Cassie and I sat talking the night through, and the next morning at dawn we went back up to our daddy's house and ate breakfast. The wake began soon after, and people began to arrive. The wake went on all day and through the night. The following morning we buried our daddy next to Hammond, George, and Robert's mother. After the burial I walked the land with my boys, then went with them to my mama's grave. I had thought often of my daddy and my mama and what was between them. I can't speculate on what all their feelings were for each other outside of creating Cassie and me. What I know is that my daddy took care of my sister and me, and my mama stayed with him after her freedom came because she chose to stay with him. Now, some folks had looked down on them for being together, but I didn't live my daddy's and my mama's lives, and I've got no right to judge. I've reconciled myself to that.

Later that day I said good-bye to Robert and I haven't seen him since. I have seen Hammond. He opened up a considerable-size store in Jackson and he wrote asking me to come see him. I did visit Hammond, not at his home, but at his store, and I took Hammer and David with me. He told the boys to take a look around the store and to choose whatever they wanted. I protested, but Hammond said he wanted, he needed *to give them something. I conceded to him, but limited my boys to one gift apiece from their uncle. It was past store hours and I sat long with my brother that evening talking and remembering. After that Hammond came several times to visit on the land, and I went several times to visit him at his store, each of us without our families. But the visits haven't been regular. It's been difficult for both of us, living in separate worlds as we do.*

I won't deny that I miss the family of my youth. I loved my mama, and Cassie, of course. I loved my daddy, and I loved my brothers too. And I loved Mitchell. There are many times I miss them all. There are times I think of my daddy's land and my childhood there. I think on it, but I don't dwell on it, for I know that I have been blessed to have a family now of my own, and I have been blessed to have the land. I am, in fact, rich with "something of my own." My mama would have liked that. I believe my daddy would have liked that too.

Author's Note

In writing *The Land*, I have followed closely the stories told by my father and others about my great-grandparents. From as far back as I can remember, I had heard stories about my great-grandfather, who bought the family land in Mississippi. Born the children of an African-Indian woman and a white plantation owner during slavery, my great-grandfather and his sister were brought up by both their parents. Their father had three sons by a white wife, and he acknowledged all of his children. He taught his children of color to read and write and he ordered his white sons to share their school learning with them. All the children sat at their father's table for meals, and my great-grandfather often went with his father and his brothers on their trips around the community.

When my great-grandfather was fourteen, another phase of his life began. Having gone with his father to a horse fair, he was asked to ride another man's horse in a race. His father forbade him to ride because he thought the horse was too dangerous. He promised my great-grandfather that he would whip him severely if he disobeyed. My great-grandfather rode the horse anyway, and one of his brothers told their father. Fearing the whipping, my great-grandfather and his best friend ran away. They escaped onto a train and were hidden by several white women who allowed their skirts to act as curtains while the boys hid under the seats of the train.

Later, as a young man, my great-grandfather contracted for land. In return for clearing the land of trees for its white owner, he was to receive title to it. Instead, after he had cleared the land, the owner reneged on the contract. During this time, my great-grandfather's best friend married. The friend died soon afterward, but on his deathbed, he asked my great-grandfather to watch over his wife and take care of her and his unborn child. My great-grandfather promised his friend he would, and the woman he later married became my great-grandmother.

Just as I have included much of my great-grandfather's history in *The Land*, I have also woven much of my great-grandmother's history into it. Part of that history includes my great-great-grandmother's name being taken away during slavery because the slave master's wife wanted the name for her child, and that my great-grandmother was injured when her skirts caught fire while she was burning the brush. In addition, I have included my great-grandmother's dedication to family history, for it was my great-grandmother who passed on many of the family stories to her grandchildren after my great-grandfather's death. She did not want their grandfather to be forgotten.

During the years that followed my great-grandparents' marriage, my great-grandfather returned to his father's house, taking his children with him. Two of his brothers eventually settled in Mississippi, one in Canton and one, who owned a store, in Jackson. The three brothers saw one another occasionally, but it was difficult because of the racist views and laws of the time. Those views, however, did not preclude my great-grandfather from passing on the names of his father and brothers in his children's names, names that remain in the family today.

It was clear from all the stories told that my great-grandfather loved his family, both the family of his youth and the family of his marriage. It was also clear that he loved his land. In his quest for land, my great-grandfather, it is said, accumulated some thousand acres. After his death, it is said that my great-grandmother, known for her generosity, gave away much of the land to people living on it. I do not know exactly how much land my great-grandfather owned or exactly how much land my great-grandmother gave away. I do know that both my great-grandparents have been an inspiration to me, not only in my writing, but also in my struggle for land.

Like my great-grandfather, for many years I attempted to obtain land that many said was unattainable, and I have woven many aspects of my struggle into Paul-Edward's story. Like Paul-Edward, who immediately fell in love with land in Mississippi, I immediately fell in love with a flowered meadow nestled in the Rocky Mountains. From the first time I saw that land, I firmly believed that God had led me to it, and it became my dream to own it. Although I later learned that the land was for sale, there seemed to be no way I could buy it. Banks refused to finance raw, undeveloped land, and the owner wanted cash. I didn't have the money. I had to let the dream go, but I didn't forget about the land.

A year later while driving in the mountains, I passed the land for the first time since I had given up the dream of having it. A FOR SALE sign was on the land. I tried once more to buy it, but I ran up against one of the same obstacles as before: Banks refused to finance undeveloped land. One major change from the previous year, however, was that the owner was willing to finance the land for a short period, after which all the money owed would become due. I was able to contract for one section of the land, though not the meadow, which I longed to have. Several years later the owner put the meadow section up for sale and I was able to contract for that as well. But in order to make both these deals I had to pay money on signing, which I agreed would be forfeited if I defaulted on the monthly notes or on the final balloon payment. They were harsh terms, but it was my only chance to have the land, and I refused to believe that my dream was impossible.

Over the years, to obtain and keep the land, I sacrificed and sold many treasured things, including my house, some of my furniture, and my few bits of jewelry. But more precious to me than any of those things was my typewriter, which I sold for two hundred and fifty dollars. I cried when I sold it, for it was the typewriter upon which I wrote *Roll of Thunder, Hear My Cry*. I used the money to help pay the monthly note on the land.

During those years of struggle I often had no money in my pocket, no money in the bank, no money expected, and bills past due. Still, I refused to give up. My friends thought I had been foolish to buy the land in the first place, and especially foolish to sacrifice to keep it. They advised me to give it up. My family never did. They understood about land. They had faith in me, and I had faith in my dream. Even when I was served with a foreclosure notice on the first section of land, I had faith.

I walked the land and went to what I called my praying rock. Then once again I went to the banks, and once again I was told that the banks did not finance raw, undeveloped land. Late on a Friday afternoon, when foreclosure would take place the following Monday, all hope seemed lost. I got down on my knees and I prayed long and hard. When I rose, the phone rang. It was a banker. He told me the bank committee had reconsidered; the bank would lend me the money. As far as I was concerned a miracle had just happened. Later, when the same bank refused to finance the second section of the land, my family saved it by lending a portion of the money that was needed, so once again the bank reconsidered, and granted a loan on the balance. A second miracle had occurred. The land was finally secured.

Today my family still owns part of the land bought by my great-grandfather more than a hundred years ago. My family also owns the mountain land, and we cherish both. Neither the preservation of the family land in Mississippi nor gaining the land in the Rocky Mountains would have been possible without the family values and teachings passed on from generation to generation. It was my great-grandparents who left my family this legacy, and my grandparents, my father, aunts and uncles, and other family members who passed it on to my generation. Now my generation is passing it on to the next, and they in turn will do the same. I am grateful to my great-grandparents for leaving such a legacy. I am grateful as well to all those who passed it on. I am especially grateful to my mother, who has always had faith in me and my dreams, and who gave so much to save the mountain land, thus furthering the legacy, and to my father, who more than anyone made me so aware of my heritage. As I have said many times before, without my father's words, my words would not have been. I consider myself blessed to be able to share my family's legacy with all who read my books.

BOOKS BY MILDRED D. TAYLOR

Song of the Trees
Roll of Thunder, Hear My Cry
Let the Circle Be Unbroken
The Gold Cadillac
The Friendship
The Road to Memphis
Mississippi Bridge
The Well
The Land